LEATHER
MAIDEN

LEATHER MAIDEN

JOE R. LANSDALE

Alfred A. Knopf   *New York*   2008

THIS IS A BORZOI BOOK
PUBLISHED BY ALFRED A. KNOPF

All rights reserved. Published in the United States by Alfred A. Knopf,
a division of Random House, Inc., New York, and in Canada by
Random House of Canada Limited, Toronto.
www.aaknopf.com

Knopf, Borzoi Books, and the colophon are registered trademarks of
Random House, Inc.

Library of Congress Cataloging-in-Publication Data
Lansdale, Joe R., [date]
Leather maiden / by Joe R. Lansdale. — 1st American ed.
p.   cm.
ISBN 978-0-375-41452-7
1. Journalists — Fiction.   2. Cold cases (Criminal investigation) —
Fiction.   3. Texas, East — Fiction.   4. Domestic fiction.   I. Title.
PS3562.A557L43 2008
813'.54 — dc22   2007051854

Manufactured in the United States of America
First Edition

For Keith, Scoop Dog

Life is full of holes. The trick is to try to live between them.

—Jerzy Fitzgerald

In Preparation

1

When you grow up in a place, especially if your childhood is a good one, you fail to notice a lot of the nasty things that creep beneath the surface and wriggle about like hungry worms in rotten flesh. But they're there. Sometimes you have to dig to discover them, or slant your head in just the right direction to see them. But they're there all right, and the things that wriggle can include blackmail, mutilation and murder. And I can vouch firsthand that this is true.

But the day I arrived back in town there was no evidence of anything wriggling under the surface or anywhere else, unless you count my head, which seemed to be wriggling a lot. I was coming off a lowball drunk and felt as if someone had borrowed my skull to bowl a few frames.

As I drove through Camp Rapture, over the railroad tracks and past the dog food factory, I told myself I would never drink again. But I had told myself that before.

It was a bright day, the sunlight like a burst egg yolk running all over the sidewalk and through the yards, almost snuffing out the grass with its heated glory, and causing everything to be warm and appear fresh, even the houses on the poor side of town from which ancient coats of basic white peeled like stripping sunburn.

I tooled along with my eyes squinted to keep out some of the summer light, eased by Gabby's veterinarian office and tried not to rubberneck too much, and passed on. I finally drove up to the *Camp Rapture Report*, got out and stood by my aging car and looked around and hoped maybe this time things were going to go better.

Night before, I had driven over from Houston after leaving Hootie Hoot, Oklahoma, and my crazy Iraq war buddy, Booger, but only got as far as a bar, and later a motel on the outskirts of town, where I drank myself into a stupor in front of the TV set, watching who knows what. For all I cared it could have been a program on tractor repair or how to give yourself a lobotomy.

Next morning, I awoke feeling like something had died in my mouth and something else had crawled up my ass. I showered and brushed the dead thing out of my mouth and decided to live with whatever was up my ass, and drove to my scheduled interview for a possible position on the *Camp Rapture Report*.

Standing there beside my car, sweating from the late summer heat like a great ape in an argyle sweater, I took in a big breath of hot air. I checked to make sure my zipper was up, then examined the bottoms of my shoes for dog crap, just in case. I went along the sidewalk, strolled past the bee-laden, flowered shrubbery, the smell of which made my stomach roil, and went inside.

The *Report* looked pretty old-fashioned. Like a place where male reporters ought to wear fedoras with press cards in the hatbands and the female reporters ought to chew gum and talk snappy dialogue through bright red lipstick.

At the front desk I was greeted by a cute blond lady. She smiled and showed me some braces. I think she was in her mid-twenties, possibly even a little older, closer to my age, but the braces and the hairdo, which was too short and not evenly cut, along with a scattering of freckles that decorated her flushed cheeks, made her look like a spunky 1950s schoolkid as seen under a huge magnifying glass.

"Mr. Statler," she said. "How are you?"

"You remember me?"

"We went to school together."

"We did?"

"Belinda Hickam. I was a year under you. You were in the journalism club and you wrote for the high school paper. I think you wrote about chess."

"Actually I only wrote one article about chess."

"I guess that was the one I read. You've been hired to do a column, right?"

"I haven't been hired yet."

"Well, I'm going to be optimistic about it. Mrs. Timpson is waiting to see you."

"Which way?" I said.

She pointed at a foyer where I could see a heap of stacked boxes, advised me to start in that direction and she would buzz Mrs. Timpson that I was on my way back.

"Any advice?" I asked.

"Keep your hands and feet on the visitor's side of the desk, don't make any sudden moves, and try not to make direct eye contact."

2

I weaved around some stacked boxes and a couple of chairs and into the dark end of a foyer where there was light coming from behind a frosted glass door that had the moniker MRS. MARGOT TIMPSON, EDITOR, stenciled on it in black letters.

I tapped gently on the door and a voice that was well practiced at yelling asked me to come in.

Mrs. Timpson was sitting behind her desk and she had pushed back from it in her office chair and was studying me carefully. She had hair too red on the sides and too pink in the thin spots. Her face was eroded with deep canals over which a cheap powder had been caked, like sand over the Sphinx. Her breasts rested comfortably in her lap; they seemed to have recently died and she just hadn't taken time to dispose of them. I took her age to be somewhere between eighty and around the time of the discovery of fire.

"Sit down," she said, and her dentures moved when she spoke, as if they might be looking for an escape route.

I took the only chair and looked as intelligent as you might when you're trying to shake Jim Beam and way too many cold beer chasers.

"You look like you've been drinking," she said.

"Last night. A party."

"I've heard you have a drinking problem."

"Where would you hear that?"

"From the owner of Fat Billy's Saloon. He's my husband. You know, the little shithole just outside of town?"

"I was drinking, but I'm not a drunk."

"I thought you said it was a party."

"A party of one. It's not a habit. I just tied one on a bit. You own a bar, so you know how it is. Now and then, you just drink more than you should."

"The husband owns the bar," she said, capturing her teeth with her upper lip as they moved a little too far forward. "He and I are separated. Have been for twenty years. We just never got around to divorcing. We get along all right, long as we don't live together, or see each other that often, or communicate in any way. But he called and told me about you. He knew you, of course, knew you were trying to get on here at the paper. He said you mentioned it quite a few times between drinks."

"Guess I was a little nervous."

"He said you used to play football, quarterback for the Bulldogs. I looked you up. You lost most of your games, didn't you?"

"But I threw some good passes. I think I have a high school record."

"No. It got beat two years ago by the Johnson boy. What's his name? Shit. Can't think of it. But he beat you. Colored fella."

I thought to myself: Colored? I hadn't heard that used in many a moon.

"You were in the service?"

"Signed up for Afghanistan after the towers went down. I was there, but I ended up in Iraq. I kind of felt snookered on that end of the deal."

"You're not messed up in the head from being over there, are you?"

"No," I said, "but the whole thing left me feeling like a cheap date that had been given cab fare and a slap on the ass on the way out the door."

Timpson twisted her lips, and lined me up with a watery eyeball. "That was humor, right?"

"Yes, ma'am."

"Just checking." She swiveled her chair and looked at me from another angle. "I hire you, you don't have to sit behind a desk all the time, but I like to think you're working. That your time is my time, and my time is my own. You know this job doesn't pay much?"

"It's a start. I can work my way up."

"Hell, you're almost at the ceiling now, boy. Thing is, you come from skyscraper material. You had that job in Houston, a Pulitzer nomination. What was it, something about some murder?"

"That's right. It was luck I was nominated."

"I was thinking it might have been. Still, you didn't last in Houston."

"I came back here for a while, then joined the military."

"Could there have been a reason you suddenly dropped that job in Houston? What was the problem there?"

"My boss and I didn't get along."

"Because you drank?"

"No, ma'am."

"You know I can call him and ask."

"You call him, I don't know he'll have much to say about the drinking, but whatever he says I doubt any of it will be good, even after several years. He doesn't like me."

"You can be straight with me. Nothing you say will embarrass or shock me."

"I was banging his wife. And his stepdaughter. The daughter, by the way, was thirty, the mother forty-eight."

"No teenagers in the mix?"

"No, ma'am."

"And I assume your indiscretions do not include the family dog."

"No, ma'am. I believe you have to draw a line somewhere."

"You think you're quite the player, don't you, boy?"

"I did then."

Mrs. Timpson pursed her lips. "Go on out there and have Beverly, that's the receptionist—"

"We met," I said. "And I believe it's Belinda."

"Have her show you your desk. Working for a newspaper is like riding a bicycle or having sex, I suppose. Once you've done it, you should be able to do it again. But you can fall off a goddamn bicycle and you can fail to pull out in time when you're doing the deed. So experience isn't every-thing. Use a little common sense."

"I will."

"I hope so. Won't be much in the way of Pulitzer Prize material to write about here, though. Last thing we had in the paper, outside of world news, that was anywhere near exciting was a rabid raccoon down at the

Wal-Mart garden center last week. He chased a stock boy around and they had to shoot him."

"The stock boy or the raccoon?"

"There's that sense of humor again."

"Yes, ma'am. And I promise, I'm all done now."

"Good. I'm putting you on a column. That's the job you wanted, wasn't it?"

"Yes, ma'am."

"Maybe it was a skunk."

"Beg your pardon?"

"The animal in Wal-Mart. Now that I think about it, it was a skunk, not a raccoon . . . Your column. It's for the Sunday features. Most of the time you'll be out of the office, but you got a desk. Still, you'll report to me regularly. Get a taste today. Leave when you want to. Tomorrow morning, nine sharp, we'll toss you into the fire."

I got up and smiled and stuck out my hand to shake. She gave me a dismissive wave of the hand.

I started for the door.

"Varnell Johnson," she said.

I turned. "Ma'am?"

"That was the colored boy's name—one that broke your passing record. He could throw like a catapult and run like a goddamn deer."

3

When I came out of Timpson's office one of the reporters at one of the few occupied desks, a twentyish black guy in a bright yellow shirt with the sleeves rolled up, waved me over. It was like the president summoning a lackey, but I started over there anyway, went to his desk as he stood up and pushed his chair aside. He was short and broad-shouldered, with his hair cropped close, a crisp part cut into it. I stuck out my hand and we shook. He had one of those determined handshakes, not so brisk, but really strong, like it was more of a contest than a greeting.

"Cason Statler," I said.

"I know who you are. I'm Oswald, like the guy that shot Kennedy."

"Glad to meet you, Oswald."

"How did it go in there?" he asked.

"I'm part of the team."

"Oh, there are no team players here. We're all pretty much out for ourselves. Trust me on that. Bend over and you'll feel an intrusion. Look, I know Timpson seems old and grumpy and pretty much out of date, but I want you to know, she doesn't just seem that way—she is that way."

"We had a particularly pithy exchange about the colored."

He grinned at me, and this time it seemed genuine. "Welcome to nineteen fifty-nine."

"Actually, I'm from here, and I'd put this place more about late nineteen seventy. So don't go putting it down."

"I'll take your word for it," Oswald said. "I didn't move here until last year."

"Why?"

"I'm asking myself that every day. But people are always telling me how it was wonderful in the old days. Probably not so wonderful for black folk, though."

"Oh, I don't know. Wouldn't you love to come home to a shack out back of a white man's plantation and sing some Negro spirituals after a hard day of picking cotton? Kind of kick back to let your whip lashes cool?"

That actually got a snicker out of him. "The only thing I've ever picked is my nose. I heard you were in the military."

"That's been a little while back. I had an accident and they had to let me leave."

"You look fine now." He said that like I had never been hurt.

"Accident was bad then, but I healed quicker than they expected. I haven't made a big point of telling the military that."

"I heard you got some medals," he said.

"They were passing them out that day," I said. "See you, Oswald."

I saw Belinda putting down the phone, and as I walked away from Oswald's desk, she rose from hers and intercepted me.

"That was Mrs. Timpson. She said I should show you your desk."

She led me over to it and I was chauvinistic enough to watch her walk and decide she really was more than cute. She was a major looker, a little out of style in the hair and makeup department, but she dressed all right and I liked the way her skirt fit; it was tight enough and right enough to make the world seem like a happy place for at least a few moments.

"This is it," she said.

It looked like everyone else's desk. There was a computer on it and there was a drawer in the center and drawers on the sides. I opened them. The ones on the sides were empty. The one in the center had pencils and pens and paper clips and half a pack of Winterfresh gum. I took a stick, peeled it and put it in my mouth. It was like trying to chew a Band-Aid.

Belinda showed me her braces. "Good, huh?"

I took the gum out of my mouth, wadded it up inside the wrapper, dropped it in the trash can. "Not so much."

"It's been in there since the creation of gum."

"I believe that."

"So, how did you like our fearless editor?" Belinda asked.

"Very colorful."

Belinda smiled her mouthful of braces at me. "That's not what the others here call her."

"No?"

"No." She looked over her shoulder at Oswald, who had returned to his seat behind his desk. "What about the assassin of John F. Kennedy?"

"I can't decide if he's just testy or an asshole."

She smiled. "Actually, Cason, he's a testy asshole."

I went around and met some of the reporters, folks in the advertising office, and was told a lot of them were out on assignments and I would meet them later. I made a few promises of lunch, went over to my desk and sat for a while and moved a pencil around.

It wasn't as good as the desk I had in Houston. It wasn't as good a newspaper. The pencil was even cheap. But here I was. I had screwed things up so I could arrive at just this spot. I was deep into having myself a pity party when Oswald, the testy asshole, came over. I had hoped me and him were through for the day. But no such luck.

"Timpson just called me," he said. "She wants me to help you get your feet wet."

"Go ahead, dampen me."

"Well, Francine, the previous columnist, had a bunch of ideas she was working on, and Timpson thought you might want to look over those, see if you could get a running start before you had to come up with your own. You're not obligated to use any of them, but she told me to tell you to take a look . . . You know, I thought I was going to get this job."

"I was beginning to suspect that," I said.

"But no, she wanted a certain cachet. She thought it would be nice PR having someone who had been nominated for the Pulitzer."

"If it's any consolation, a nomination eats your heart out."

"No. No consolation. I'm used to getting screwed."

"I hope you don't think this is some kind of racial thing, because if you do, I just want you to know, sincerely, and I say this pleasantly and from the bottom of my heart, you are full of shit."

Oswald sat on the edge of my desk. "I don't. I'm just one of those people born to be screwed and to be bitter about it, but with a slight and engaging sense of humor, of course."

"You really believe that?"

Oswald nodded. "I believe some of us are born with a target on our butt, and dead center of it is a slot with a sign above it that says: Insert dick here."

"Do you look both ways when you cross the street?"

"I see this coming," Oswald said.

"That's what you can say if you look both ways . . . Do you?"

"Of course."

"Then you believe your destiny is at least partly up to you, otherwise you wouldn't be worried about being a hood ornament. It would be preordained. So I suggest you remove the target from your ass." Oswald gave me an irritated look. I said, "Let's change the subject. What happened to Francine?"

"She was either fired, or she died. I don't quite remember. Does it matter?"

"Suppose not. Where do I find those ideas of Francine's?"

Oswald patted my computer. "In yon machine. Francine's codes and information are on a pad in the desk drawer. So now my duty is done, and I go back to work."

The testy asshole went back to his desk. For all his talk, I had a feeling Oswald really felt more entitled than ambitious. I figured, you got right down to it, his greatest ambition was teaching his dog to lick peanut butter off his balls.

I looked in the drawer and found the little notebook with the information I needed, went to work. Most of the stuff I found in Francine's computer notes was about as exciting as counting the hairs in an armpit. There were terse investigations into the ingredients for Snickers Bar Pie, the major ingredients being the Snickers themselves and lots of butter. I was surprised the recipe didn't come with a funeral plan. There were bits on flower arranging and how to get stains out of damn near anything. Nothing that really grabbed me by the lapels, but I persevered.

And then I came across it. A six-month-old mystery.

Caroline Allison. A university student. History major. Age twenty-three. She disappeared on a late-night run to a fast-food place, Taco Bell.

A week later her car was found just outside of town, near the old rail station, not far downhill from the Siegel home. It was a creepy place to disappear.

The Siegel home had been a kind of legend for years. It had belonged to two sisters. Story was they had been high-tone in the 1920s. They were in their teens at the time. Then came the Great Depression, and their family lost money when the stock market fell. As the sisters grew into their fifties, their parents died, and the ladies knew nothing about how to survive. Soon people saw them digging in trash cans, and since they wouldn't take charity, folks put food in the cans for them to find. Finally, the ladies sold their home place and moved into another house where they lived upstairs. That place caught on fire and the firemen put a ladder up to the window, but the women, in their sixties now, were in their nightgowns and wouldn't come out the window dressed that way. It was not what ladies did. What ladies did was burn up like cotton wicks; death by fire and modesty.

The house the sisters had originally lived in had been bought, but nothing was done with it. It stayed abandoned, sitting on top of a hill spotted with trees, the yard a wad of greenery maybe three feet deep. The house was almost consumed by the vines until the whole thing looked like a large clump of vegetation with a couple of rectangular glass eyes.

Jimmy and I had played there as kids and gone parking up there behind the house with girls many years ago.

Had Caroline been there, near the old house, with someone? Had things gotten out of hand?

Had someone driven her car there, left it, gone away on foot? Did the person have an accomplice?

I scrolled down Francine's notes. Caroline's fast-food order had been found in the car, untouched. So had her shoes. The old train station had been searched, along with the house. The vines had been mowed down to see if her body was under them. Nothing.

I scrolled down some more.

There was information on Caroline, on her past. She had been raised as a foster child. She was as bright as a blast of nuclear light, according to the information Francine had gathered. In fact, Francine had a lot of meticulous notes. Perhaps even she had bored of Snickers pie and flowers in a vase, thought she was on to something.

No one could think of a single reason why anyone would want to hurt Caroline. Her only brush with the law was an overdue library fine that she refused to pay for some reason. The book was by Jerzy Fitzgerald, called *And the Light Is Bright Glancing Off the Fangs of the Bear.*

Francine had found one girl who knew her pretty well, Ronnie Fisher. Ronnie said she had known Caroline back in their hometown, that they shared a foster parent and had moved to Camp Rapture about the same time.

I leaned back in my chair and thought, what if I did a series of articles for the paper about her disappearance? About the illusion of safety in a small town? Then I could write a more ambitious article based on my columns, but with material I had left out of the local newspaper. I could get some interviews with the people who knew her, maybe a few shots of the car and that Taco Bell sack from the files, a photo of the young lady, then send the piece to some place like *Texas Monthly.* I had a few contacts there. The Pulitzer nomination still had some clout. Like a guy who had played in the Super Bowl and missed a pass, but had still played. I could probably slide the article right in.

If I set it up right, made sure the right people saw it, it might be just the sort of thing that would boost me into the big time. I had it all together once, until I started letting the little head think for the big head. Why couldn't I pull it together again?

When I went out the bees were still at work and the flowers still smelled strong, and they still made my stomach churn. But now I had a job and I was pretty sure my shoes were still clear of dog shit and that the Caroline Allison story could be big, so life wasn't sucking quite so much.

I thought about Caroline Allison for a while, then got out my cell, called Mom and Dad, told them I got the job, which they seemed dutifully excited about. I wanted to call someone else, but didn't really know anyone. My brother and his wife, maybe. But Jimmy was at work, and I hadn't seen them in a while, and I was working up to the moment.

Then there was Booger. I don't know why I thought of him. I was trying to get rid of him, lose all the old connections from the war. But I knew he'd like to hear how I had turned out, even if he did think it was kind of a weird job for a grown man, writing for a newspaper. Booger thought man had been put on earth to find out if he was ruler or slave, and to eat meat, especially anything chicken-fried. He liked women too, but they came third in his business plan, and then there was nothing romantic about it to him. It was all just a service.

It was Gabby I really wanted to call. And not about the job, either. I just wanted to hear her voice. I drove by the veterinarian office. Her car was there. The same one she had owned when I left for Afghanistan. There were two other cars and a pickup. A big black mixed-breed dog was in a cage in the back of the truck, and a lady who looked as if she might wrestle alligators for a living was letting the dog out, placing a leash around its neck.

As I drove on, I looked back in the side mirror. The door to the office opened and the alligator wrestler and the dog started through it. I thought I got a glimpse of Gabby, but the truth of the matter is, it was so quick, and I was out of sight so soon, I couldn't be sure. It could have been a dancing bear or a nude man carrying a slide trombone. It could have been anyone.

4

I drove over to Mom and Dad's house, parked at the curb, sat in the car and looked at the place. There was a new, white wooden plank fence between their house and the next-door neighbor's house. It was straight and freshly painted, so I knew it was my dad who had put it up. The vines that ran up twine runners all along the fence I recognized as my mother's work. The sun-yellowed grass that was ankle-high in the next-door neighbor's yard was all the work of nature.

When I lived at home, there wasn't a house next door. Just an empty lot with a couple of big elms, one of which grew next to the fence and extended boughs into Mom and Dad's yard, splashing shadow onto the roof.

When I got out of the car with my suitcase, I locked the car doors and walked up in the yard. A small voice from over the fence and from the boughs of the elm called down to me.

"You don't live here."

I turned and looked up. There was a little platform tree house up there in the elm, hidden behind smaller limbs and lots of leaves, and on the platform was a little girl about nine or ten with blond pigtails, wearing a sloppy T-shirt and blue jean shorts and no shoes. She was cute in a rawboned sort of way, would probably grow up and fill out her features and be quite beautiful. She sat on the edge of the platform and let her feet dangle. She had a lot of tomboy bruises and scratches on her legs, a couple of scabs.

I smiled up at her, said, "I used to live here. Long ago when I was your age."

"Are you Mr. Statler's little boy?"

"I was once. I mean, I'm still his boy, but I'm not so little."

"You're big. Are you six foot tall?"

"Six-two if I have on good shoes and I hold my shoulders straight."

"Why do you wear your hair so long?"

"Because for a long time I had to wear it real short."

"Oh. Did you know your daddy beat my daddy up?"

I took a moment to regroup. "And why was that?"

"He wasn't really my daddy. I was just supposed to call him that. He drank. He hit my mama and run her out in the yard with the leg off a chair, and your daddy knocked the shit out of him."

"You shouldn't talk like that."

"That's what your daddy did. Daddy Greg, that's what I called my daddy your daddy beat up. Daddy Greg messed himself and me and Mama could smell it standing out in the yard. It run down one of his pants legs. Mama thought it was funny. You should have heard her laugh."

"Well, don't say that word, okay?"

"What word?"

"About what got knocked out of him."

"Oh. Okay."

"Your dad, what happened to him?"

"Oh, he run off for a while. But he comes back sometimes. Mama's got me a new daddy now. Daddy Bill. Daddy Bill isn't home a lot, and when he is, he and Mama stay in the bedroom most of the time. They don't fight as much as her and Daddy Greg. Daddy Bill is kind of funny-looking."

"My name is Cason. It was nice to meet you . . . What's your name?"

"Jasmine. People call me Jazzy."

"Glad to meet you, Jazzy."

"You too. Did you know there isn't any ladder? I climb the tree to get up here. Like a squirrel, Mama says. Daddy Greg used to say like a goddamn monkey. I liked Daddy Greg better than Daddy Bill, even though he was kind of mean, but don't say I said that."

"I'm sure you're a very good climber."

Jazzy jumped to a new topic.

"I used to stay at Mee-maw's before I stayed here."

"Is Mee-maw your grandma?"

"No. But she let me call her that. She lives in Houston. Do you want to go play dead?"

"Dead?"

"There's a graveyard out back, and me and Mama go out there and lie on the graves sometimes. We play like we're inside them, and we're dead."

"Not a very active game."

"We do it at night sometimes and look at the stars."

I thought, Swell. A Gothic mother.

"You be careful up there," I said.

"I will," she said.

Inside Mom hugged me and said all the good things moms say when you get a job and they think maybe things are finally on track and maybe you're not going to end up living in a cardboard box and cruising Dumpsters.

Mom looked good. Healthy and a little thicker and there was no doubt she dyed her hair, but she still moved the way she always did, quickly. I put my suitcase down, gave her a better hug and this time a kiss on the cheek. She said she'd make a sandwich.

"That sounds good," I said.

"Turkey on rye, your favorite."

"Good."

She patted my shoulder. "We're going to put you in your and Jimmy's old room."

"That's great."

She looked me over, and hated to say it, I could tell, but she couldn't help herself. "Don't drink so much, Cason."

"That's what Mrs. Timpson told me. It's that obvious?"

"All you need is a neon sign over your head that blinks I'VE BEEN ON A DRUNK to make it any more certain. You might want to button your shirt buttons even too. That may not be a sure giveaway, but the way your eyes look and your face red like that, it kind of puts the capper on things."

I looked down at my shirt. "Damn," I said.

"You went to the interview like that?"

"Afraid so," I said, buttoning up correctly. "But I did get the job. Glad I wasn't interviewing for a male model."

She smiled. "I'm glad you decided to stay with us."

"Not too long," I said. "Just long enough to find a place. You know, when I get settled into the job."

"It's going to work out fine, isn't it?"

"Certainly," I said. "Did the boxes I shipped arrive?"

"They did. They're in the storage room."

"Good. Otherwise I'm going to be wearing the same three pairs of pants and shirts a lot. Rotating between two pairs of underwear and a pair of socks. I got a few things in the car from Houston storage. I'll unload them later."

She hugged me again. "Take your time on finding a place. It's good to have you home."

"Where's Dad?"

"In the garage, of course."

I went out the back way, across the backyard, with the smell of fresh-mowed grass in my nostrils. At the back of the yard, Dad had a little garage he had built after retirement. That way, officially retired or not, he could still work on a few cars, mostly for friends and neighbors. What he called tinkering. It brought in a few extra bucks. He and Mom had been smart. They had saved and invested in some good stocks, they had Social Security, and she had her teacher's retirement.

In the garage there was a light blue car with the hood up, and Dad had his head under it and was poking around inside. The car was an older model, from when parts were fixed, not just replaced like they are now. Even though I was a mechanic's son, I had never been interested in cars, and I didn't know one from the other. I couldn't fix a wheelbarrow, but I was always proud of my dad. You could have dropped him off in the Sahara with a screwdriver and a hair tie, and he could have fixed most any kind of car, made it run.

Dad lifted his head out from under the hood, picked up a shop rag and went to wiping grease off his fingers. "They've taken care of it. Sixty-nine Plymouth Fury. Front seat is big as a living room, and it runs like a scalded pig."

He came over and shook my hand. It was a big hand, callused and dark from years of putting it in grease and oil and gasoline. He still had the same sturdy body, though he had gained a lot more belly since I saw him last. His hair, which used to be as black as the bottom of a hole to China, was now as white as cotton.

"Congratulations on your job," he said.

"Thanks. I guess it'll be okay."

"Got to think positive, boy. Can't let the gremlins take over . . . Damn, son. You look like death warmed over."

"You ought to be on this side of it."

"Lay off the booze a little, boy. That stuff will mess you up."

"Mom said the same thing. And so did Mrs. Timpson."

"Good advice gets around."

"Yes, sir. The little girl next door—"

"Jazzy?"

I nodded. "She said you beat up her Daddy Greg."

"Me and him had words."

"Words won't hit you so hard they make shit run down your leg."

"The words led to a whipping. His."

"That's what she said. How many times did you hit him?"

"Hit a guy hard enough he shits himself, you don't need a follow-up."

I laughed a little at that.

"World has changed," Dad said and tossed the rag in the direction of the Fury. "Seems like every other girl you meet these days had a kid when she was fifteen or sixteen and the boy run off and the girl's raising it alone. Someone needs to tell those gals babies are caused by screwing. Hasn't everyone heard of a goddamn rubber by now?"

"Well, from my talk with Jazzy, I take it her mother isn't so hot."

"Good deduction there if you're talking about her parenting skills, but from another viewpoint she is as hot as the proverbial firecracker. I haven't seen anything that hot since Joey Heatherton danced on *The Dean Martin Show*."

"Who?"

"Thanks for making me feel old. 'Course, I've only seen Jazzy's mother twice and one of those times she was being hit with a chair leg by Daddy Greg. But she's a pretty, dark-haired thing. . . . Goddamn Child Protective Services. We've called them half a dozen times, but nothing. The agency is in disarray. There have been three or four scandals, them losing children, that sort of thing. So no help there. Not yet."

"Jazzy told me she and her mom lie down on graves and look at the stars."

Dad nodded. "When they cleared some of the land out back, down by the creek, they found a graveyard. There's still a patch of trees back there and the graves are under those."

"Me and Jimmy played there for years. We didn't see any graves."

"It's from the eighteen eighties. Gravestones were knocked over, buried. People in the community paid to have the place cleaned up, the stones set in place. Boy Scouts go out there and pull weeds, keep it clean. I guess the place just got lost. But I figure I was a mother I could find some other way to entertain my daughter than to go out and lie down on graves and look at the stars . . . Hey, you hungry?"

"Mom's fixing me a sandwich."

"Good. I want one too. 'Course," he said, patting his belly, "I could probably skip one now and then."

He put his arm around me and walked me out of the garage, across the yard and into the house.

5

We ate our sandwiches and had some apple pie, talked until the sun went down, and then we watched TV. We found some boxing and watched that. Mom decided she had things to do in the kitchen, which turned out to be reading her newspaper.

Dad talked some about the new lake house they had bought on Lake o' the Pines with my brother and his wife, and about how they wanted to go there this summer, and I was welcome and all that. I explained my job would probably keep me where I was for a while.

Boxing finished, we watched a bit of news until Dad saw the war news was making me uncomfortable. We went out back and sat on the stoop of the back porch with a can of Diet Coke apiece and talked some more.

It was just simple chitchat at first. Finally Dad cleared his throat like a cat coughing up a hairball, looked away from me, toward the backyard fence and our neighbor's rooftop as if something in that direction held his attention, said, "You still buddies with that guy, what's his name, Snot?"

I laughed. "Booger."

"Yeah, him."

I had written Dad about Booger when I was in the sandlot over in Iraq. I was honest about the guy. I was guessing Dad was hoping me and Booger had parted company.

"I guess I am friends with him," I said. "But I don't want to see him that much. Fact is, I sort of think I just said goodbye to him for good. He's great at war, but back here at home, I'm not sure he's a fellow I ought to stir up. He's in Oklahoma. He runs a shooting range and a bar."

"Well, it's good to have contact with people who have a similar history. That can help. But your letters made him sound a little strange."

"He's not bothered by stuff that would get to you and me. So even though we've done some of the same things, we don't have the same history. History is in the eyes of the beholder, and Booger's eyes, they're a lot darker and flatter than mine."

"That's an interesting way of putting it."

"I meant it when I said he was good at war. He didn't care what the cause was or if there was a cause. He just wanted a weapon in his hand and an enemy in his sights. He's kind of scary, actually."

"Next question is why are you friends with him?"

I shook my head. "I don't know the answer to that. Here, he's like a shark out of water. Over there, I liked him by my side, in front of or behind me. He throws in with you, he's there all the way. He doesn't throw in with many people, and he's not a man of regrets. He once told me a good center shot and a trashy woman with dirty underpants were about it for him."

Dad nodded. "I've known some folks like him. . . . The job. It gonna be all right?"

"I don't know yet. I found something a little curious." I told him about Caroline.

Dad nodded. "I remember that. Never solved, least not so far."

"Still, after Houston, newspaper-wise, it seems pretty bland around here. The Caroline Allison thing may be the only interesting thing I'll ever write about. Even Timpson seemed the most excited about a skunk in Wal-Mart."

"Don't fool yourself, son. This isn't Houston, but it's got its own blood and grits. You'll find that out soon enough when you go to work for the paper. Trust me, there's plenty goes on, and Timpson knows it."

"Like what?"

Dad raised his eyebrows. "Black and white tensions."

"I thought we were past that."

"There's this black preacher and politician, Gerry Judence."

"I know who he is," I said. "Snappy dresser, quick-witted and full of shit. I've seen him all my life on televison."

"There was a time when he was a serious civil rights leader. Marched with King, did good things. But as the nature of civil rights changed, he had to find a new way to keep himself in the spotlight. Recently, members of the black community decided that a school should be built down in the black section of town.

"Idea was some of the rich black folks, some rich whites too, would try and raise the level of the kids in that area by building a school. Most of the black people in town, and people in the white community, were for it. Judence threw a monkey wrench in that. He's got antennae for that kind of thing. Some assholes down in the black community made it out to be some white man's plot to change them from being black to white, and Judence latched on to that. It got him back in the news.

"Some of the kids down there don't even have birth records. Drugs are an everyday thing. Lot of those kids have never been inside a school. They need a chance. Education isn't white. It belongs to anyone who'll reach out and take it."

"I hadn't heard about this."

"It's ramping up as it gets closer to the time when the school is supposed to be built. Judence is doing a lot of talking up in New York, where he's from. Getting lots of camera time. He'll come down here a week or two before the ground for the school is supposed to be broke, make a big speech, and it'll get people fired up. And to make matters worse, to make him seem more the hero, there have been death threats from racist groups saying Judence is an outside agitator, which, in fact, he is. But calling a black man an outside agitator is old racist language for 'uppity nigger.' "

"And that fires things up more."

"School was proposed to be built where the old black Baptist church stands, partially burned. Someone set it on fire a year or so back. Rumor was it was white racists. Those who support the school want to build it where the church stands as a kind of gesture of spirit. Judence is telling the community that whites are trying to segregate them again."

"Sounds like segregation to me, Dad."

"I don't want segregation, and the school wouldn't technically be segregated, but building it in that community shows there's a chance for students to be educated there, and with good teachers, mostly black, it could happen. It would be a special school, privately funded, better than our public schools, which are just warehouses for warm bodies."

"Could it be some of the investors hope to run for office of some kind?"

"There's that. But the whites who don't want the school are strangely enough on the side of the blacks who don't. The idea there might be a school in the black community with the potential to be better than the schools their children attend annoys them. They say, well, the black people don't want it, so don't give it to them. But there are a lot of local black leaders, lots of parents down there that do want it. Most, I'd say. It's the loudmouth few, black and white, who are kicking this bee's nest around.

"There's this white group that calls themselves the League for the Advancement of Christian Thought. Crackers that get upset to the bone if they see a black man shake hands with a white woman. Think homosexuals are some kind of abomination against God, that they're trying to wrestle straight white men to the floors of public restrooms to suck their dicks. They're not that crazy about Jews either, since they think they killed Jesus. Can't get it in their heads Jesus was a Jew too. And illegal immigrants, that makes them gnash their teeth. Liberals and Democrats and moderates don't float their boats either.

"The big mullah for all that stuff, the local agitator, the white racist bastard stirring his side of the pot, is a Baptist preacher right here in Camp Rapture. Reverend Dinkins. He's head of that organization. Spouts racist mess on TV like he's talking about something truly Christian. They prey on poor screwed-up white kids who are nothing more than angry rednecks without a pot to piss in. All they need is some preacher like Dinkins to tell them they're on God's side, or someone like Judence to come down hard on whitey, and BLAM! It all gets set off."

Dad paused and turned the soft-drink can around and around in his hand; he was really giving that aluminum a workout. He said: "Judence will come here and give a speech and have a rally at the university so he can go home with a few copies of his appearance on DVD. He can lie around at night and watch it and jack off, claim he kept the whitey school out of the black section of town. Dinkins and the League can brag they kept things status quo. The blacks who didn't want change can feel like they've saved the world from white domination, and the blacks that did want change will throw up their hands in frustration and give up. Everyone loses but the rats and the cockroaches and humankind continues its slow march to oblivion, but with a wide variety of ice-cream flavors and television shows to choose from . . . What would really straighten the human race out is a good plague."

"I suppose that would clean things up," I said.

"By the way, did you drive by where Gabby works? I was wondering because she called me and said she saw a car that looked like your old wreck go by there a couple of times real slow, and the guy driving it, she thought he looked a lot like you."

"The road runs by there, Dad."

"But the speed limit there is forty-five, not a crawl. Not trying to pin you or make you feel bad. You've always been somewhat obsessive. Do you remember when you counted your steps?"

"I counted ceiling tiles too. I counted and arranged my comic books incessantly. I did a lot of things."

"You moved those obsessions to Gabby. Add the war, what you saw there, how it affected you—"

"I' m all right," I said.

"What's the doctor say?"

"I said I was all right."

Dad nodded. "Good. Have you seen your brother?"

"Not yet."

Jimmy was a university professor. His wife taught grade school. They were pretty close to being the perfect couple.

Dad crushed the Diet Coke can, said, "I'm going to bed." He stood up and paused on the steps and put his hand on my shoulder. "Good to have you home."

"Good night, Dad."

I sat on the back steps for a while and finished my Diet Coke. The night air was nice and cool and soft as velvet. I heard a frog bleat. The smell of mowed grass was like a perfume.

I leaned back and looked up at the stars. They were shiny and bright, and there was something right about the heavens that made me want to live forever. I had had that feeling before. It never lasted.

6

Each morning I awoke with the fresh point of view that things were going to change and that Gabby and I would get back together. I could sit down and think this over and realize just how stupid it was, but the thought wouldn't go away, and I clung to it like a fading movie star thinking just one more film would bring it all back.

I took off my clothes and went to bed just wearing my underwear. The bedroom was the one Jimmy and I had shared growing up. All the things we had loved as kids were still there. It was like stepping back through time, entering the past. The only major difference in the room between now and then was that the bunk beds were gone and there was just the one bed for guests.

After lying in the dark for some time, eyes wide open, I began to see the room more clearly, the outlines of things. I looked up at Jimmy's model airplanes hanging from the ceiling on wires, looked over at his desk where the frogs and mice he had practiced taxidermy on had started to lean against one another. The stands on which they rested, some kind of glued wood, had begun to come apart and the creatures had fallen together into a gruesome pyramid of arrested decay. I could see the outline of his Eagle Scout sash hanging on the wall. There was a long couple shelves of books, and I could make out a lot of the titles more from memory than from sight.

I got up, turned on the light and sat at my old desk. It was smaller than I remembered, the chair was uncomfortable. I opened one of the desk drawers. All my comic books were still there; at least my favorites were. I took out one and read it. I got up and walked around the room, turned out the light and went to the window and peeled back the curtain and looked out at the street. It was starting to rain, a slow, sweet summer rain. The pavement glistened in the streetlights, and then Jazzy appeared, wearing only a T-shirt and underwear, walking down the street in bare feet, the rain washing over her.

I watched her for a while. She walked until she came to the end of the street, where it met the highway, then she turned around and started back. I pulled my chair over and sat at the window and watched her through the crack in the curtain. I thought about calling Child Protective Services, and then remembered Dad had done that.

I thought I might call anyway. I watched her walk back up the street, lifting her head to the heavens, spreading her arms, enjoying the rain like some kind of nature nymph. She stepped onto our lawn and crossed to hers.

I couldn't see her after that, but I had an idea she might be climbing the elm, making her way to her platform in the boughs while her mother and her new daddy did whatever it was they were doing in the bedroom. Being uncharitable, my guess was they were passed out drunk. I started to go out and talk to Jazzy, to tell her to go to bed, that trees draw lightning. Or perhaps I just wanted to have her keep me company. But I didn't do it. I didn't do anything but watch the rain until it wasn't raining anymore.

Finally I stood up and went over and looked at the shadow shapes of the taxidermy frogs and rats my brother had fixed up, and remembered how it had all smelled out in the garage when he was preserving them. Even then, as a kid, I thought it was a shitty hobby. I reached out with a finger and gently pushed at the heaped-together dead things. They tumbled over and one of the rats fell and went behind the desk. I didn't bother to pick it up. Way it had been pumped full of chemicals, way the skin had been treated, it could lie there without odor for a century.

I looked up at his sash again. I had made Life Scout, not Eagle. I had gotten in a fight with the scoutmaster's son and kicked him in the teeth, knocking a couple out, making myself persona non grata at the Scout hut.

My swift kick didn't affect Jimmy's scouting at all. He was the kind of guy who could have shit in the middle of the Scout hut, set the crap on fire and burned the place down, and before anyone would say anything bad about him, it would have been blamed on arsonist rodents. He had the knack, Jimmy did.

I went to bed and thought about some of the things Dad and I had talked about, closed my eyes and went to sleep and dreamed immediately, saw all the dead I had seen in the war. Americans and Iraqis were lying in the middle of a blood-soaked street. There were so goddamn many.

As I watched, all of them crawled together into a bloody and mangled heap, made themselves into a zombie-style pyramid of writhing bodies, many of them missing limbs, dripping blood the color of oil. They wrapped their arms and legs around one another to hook up and form a moving mass, wide at the bottom, narrow at the top, with a headless baby at the peak; a pyramid of bloody, rotting flesh, acting as one, stalking toward me.

I awoke, sat up in bed, sweating. I got up, turned off the alarm, went into the bathroom with my suitcase, showered and shaved and brushed my teeth taking my sweet time.

I put on a loose blue shirt and some new blue jeans that I had to pull the tags off of. I went back to my room and put on my socks and shoes and sat at my desk and looked at my watch frequently and watched it grow lighter through the curtained window.

It had rained some more in the night and because of it the morning broke off cool. I went outside and enjoyed the cool as the sun came up and began to pour color into everything. Then the sun climbed up higher and it got hot and the wetness on the road in front of the house began to evaporate and rise up in a warm damp mist. There was a balmy, lethargic wind that came with it, and in a short time it blew the mist away. Then there was nothing but the heat, a kind of slow broil that turned everything sticky as the crack of a fat man's ass.

I drove to work, made it there at a quarter to nine.

7

Belinda had done something different with her hair. It was evenly cut and short and she had dyed it honey blond. Something about that light blond hair and those freckles made her look like strawberries and cream.

We exchanged pleasantries, and I went to my desk.

I immediately turned on the computer and tapped into the file on Caroline Allison. It was the same thing I had already read, of course, and it wasn't much, but it whet my appetite again. Francine's intent had most likely been to write a breezy little column about the missing girl and how horrible it was, and move on to how to make tuna casserole with olives the next week. Article-wise, I had something similar—but a little more intense—in mind, though I didn't intend to follow it with tuna casserole.

I hated to do it, but I got up and went over to Oswald's desk.

When I told him what I wanted, he pointed, said, "The morgue. I'll call down and introduce you."

The newspaper morgue was tucked around a corner and down a few steps, in a kind of basement with lighting that might have been bright during the ice age on a starless night, but for modern times it was a little dim.

Like Timpson's office, unless someone told you where to look, you might never know the place was there.

It was a small room with a low ceiling and file cabinets and computers and little clear plastic boxes full of computer discs. There were old out-dated machines that allowed you to flick through ancient newspaper text. There was dust in the air and the smell of slightly mildewed newspapers. I could imagine dust mites making their way up my nostrils the minute I entered, bringing in furniture, checking out the backyard.

There was a series of tables and desks, all of them covered in newspaper debris. There were several trash cans overflowing with refuse, a lot of it fast-food wrappers. Secret sauce on the wrappers had turned a little rank and the odor from it was muscling its way around in the air. There were printouts taped to file cabinets and pinned to boards. I leaned forward and looked at one. It was on some kind of weird cow mutilation in Kansas. I looked at the others. They all had to do with oddball events: strange murders, kidnappings, cats run up flagpoles. That last had taken place right here in Camp Rapture.

I looked up and saw a man coming around the file cabinets toward me. We introduced ourselves. His name was Jack Mercury. No joke.

Mercury was maybe thirty-five or thirty-eight, healthy-appearing, looked as if he might be able to bend a fireplace poker over his knee and on a good day bite the end off of it, but he wasn't big on sunlight. He had blond hair and sharp blue eyes that seemed even bluer in his pale face. His clothes were rumpled, looked like he might have gone three rounds with a bear while wearing them.

He said, "Welcome to hell. I'm transferring all our old information from the files, from the microfiche, et cetera, to the computer and disc. It's tedious, therefore, it's hellish. As for you, well, you're just visiting hell. It's not a bad place to visit, but you wouldn't want to work here."

"Can I buy a souvenir?"

"Sorry. No concessions stand in hell. But you can take back our worst wishes. This place gets to some people. The tightness. Cut a fart, and you start a paper blizzard. Turn too quick, the edge of a table will castrate you."

"All these things taped to the cabinets . . . This your personal interest?" I asked.

"Everyone thinks I'm nuts. Conspiracy nut they call me, paranoid.

That's why I'm down here by myself. I see connections where others don't. All you got to do is pause and look and consider."

"I'll keep that in mind," I said.

"Ah, you're humoring me. I do so hate that. What is it you want, fellow scribe?"

"I'm doing some research, and I was told you were the man to see . . . Mercury. That's an unusual name."

"I think it used to be something different, but my dad changed his last name, officially, to Mercury. Old hippie guy. I think he liked the band Queen. The lead singer was named Freddie Mercury. Now I'm a Mercury. Even though I'm not related to Freddie."

"Just a wild guess, but I bet Freddie's last name wasn't Mercury either. Least not at birth."

"Probably a good guess. What can I do for you? It's Cason, isn't it?"

I nodded, said, "Caroline Allison."

His eyes narrowed. "Ah, yes." But then he paused. "You're originally from Camp Rapture, aren't you?"

"Interesting everyone knows who I am."

"That Pulitzer nod. Hometown boy. Everyone knows about that. You ran some football, didn't you?"

"I did."

"Never cared for football myself. What's the point?"

"To get the ball to the other end of the field," I said.

"Again, what's the point?"

"I'm afraid that's it. If you played well, you might get in a cheerleader's pants later in the evening."

"Now I'm starting to understand football," Mercury said. "Come into my lair."

He led me through a maze of file cabinets and tables adorned with newspapers, books and folders. We came to a table that held only a computer, a pen and a pad. The computer screen gave off more light than the overhead bulbs. There were two chairs. He took one, I took the other.

"So what's up with you and the Allison case?" he asked.

"Francine was planning an article on it, and I came across her notes."

"Francine, writing about murder? That would have been a departure. She once did a series on common insects in the garden. An article a week in the Sunday paper, for, let me see, about twenty years is how it felt."

"So the insect world was not that mysterious to you?"

"Not the way Francine wrote about it," he said. "Under her firm and generic hand . . . well, trust me, a bug a week wasn't that interesting. And, of course, there was her famous article on cat hair and why it keeps cats warm. I couldn't wait to get up on Sunday morning and unfurl the paper to get to that one."

"About Caroline," I said. "No one knows for sure what happened, do they? There was never any body."

"True, but hell, what do you think?" Mercury said.

"That she's dead and her body has been lying rotting in some ditch somewhere collecting ants and worms, and the simple thing is no one has come across it, and someone she knew did it."

"When you put it that way, it isn't a lot more mysterious than the bugs or the cat fur."

"You believe so much in mystery and adventure, what are you doing down here?" I asked.

He looked a little wounded by that. "Again, I'm down here because I don't play well with others and am considered a loon. I believe in flying saucers, lake monsters and the rare twenty-year-old virgin. I believe our government has listening devices everywhere, and in some cases buried under our skin."

I didn't know how to respond to that, so I went right to business. "Francine left quite a bit of stuff on Caroline in her files, but I was wondering if there was more. Wondering if there had been a follow-up to the case. If there were any suspects, that sort of thing."

"There's always more to everything, but we don't always know what the more is. That's how it is with Allison. She went to a fast-food place and didn't come back. They found her car on the other side of town, near the railroad tracks, by the old train station. Police searched all over. Bulletins were put up. Dogs were used. People from out of town came to help search. It was all the news for weeks."

"Nothing else?" I asked.

"To do with Caroline?"

"That's what I'm asking about."

"I thought you might be interested in some other stuff for columns. Might as well get them lined up. This town, you wouldn't believe it, but there's all manner of things that goes on."

"My dad said as much."

"He's right. Cat's body run up the flagpole."

"I saw that taped to one of your file cabinets."

"And there's more. Someone put a bomb under the ass of the Virgin Mary statue in the Catholic church and blew the holy cunt right out from under her. There's all this garbage going on with the blacks and the whites over a school some folks want to build."

"I heard about that too," I said.

"It's all come down in the last six months," Mercury said.

"It couldn't just be coincidence?"

"Of course it could," Mercury said. "You see cop shows all the time where someone says they don't believe in coincidence, and let me tell you, those people are idiots. Coincidence is rife all over, my friend. But even though I believe in coincidence, I also believe in patterns and design. You have to pay attention and see the simple pattern under the chaos, beneath and between the coincidence."

I stood silent for a moment, trying to sort out what Mercury had just said.

Mercury grinned at me. "Profound, don't you think?"

"It's something," I said. "I don't know I'm trying to link anything. I thought maybe with Caroline being gone so long, and no closure, that an article on her would be appropriate. To show she's not forgotten. The other stuff, maybe I could get a grab-bag column out of it, mention in the last six months there's been all of this weirdness in town. Like a bad moon is rising over Camp Rapture kind of thing."

"To be frank," Mercury said, "and possibly to get punched in the nose, I don't think you are all that interested in remembering Caroline. I think you smell a good news story. Something you think the hicks in town have not followed up on. Am I right? And that you will be able to nose it out because you used to be a real reporter. No emphasis, mind you, on the used to be."

"Guilty," I said.

"Of course you are," he said.

Mercury turned to his computer, tapped the keyboard, brought up some information about Caroline Allison. There was a lot of it. It was much more than I had. I said, "Can you print this out for me?"

"Sure."

He scanned through some of it, came to her photograph. A head shot. Her hair was as yellow as sunlight, her eyes so blue they broke your heart, her skin looked soft and warm as a spring day. And her mouth. Men would have ideas about that mouth, and so would a lot of women.

"Jesus," I said.

"Looks like a movie star or a model, doesn't she?"

"She is stunning."

"Can you believe she was a history major?"

"Saw that in Francine's note," I said.

"Girl like that doesn't strike me as someone that would spend her time in the library behind the stacks. A face like that, there had to be some party girl inside. There's some devil in those eyes, don't you think?"

"I suppose."

Of course, from the moment I realized she was a history major, I had thought of my brother, Jimmy. She had been in his department, and most likely he had taught her, or knew her. And, of course, he would have known about her coming up missing, about her never being found. It was another lead-in, another angle. I filed that in the back of my mind.

Mercury reached in his shirt pocket, pulled out some greasy glasses, put them on, tapped at the keyboard some more, scanned through more files.

"Girl like that, in high school, you'd think she'd be more popular than a free back rub, but guess what, there's hardly anything about her in her high school annual."

"You have it?"

"I have it scanned in. I've looked through it. I think she was a member of the history club, and that's it. No Most Beautiful. No Most Likely to Succeed. No Most Popular. And except for the history club, where there's just the one picture of her and some other students, there's little to nothing. She wasn't too popular. Way she looked, that's peculiar."

"Peculiar, but not incredible," I said. "Sometimes people are afraid to approach the good-looking girls, maybe even give them the ass end of things because they're jealous. Print it out for me, if you don't mind. All of it."

"I'll have it by the end of the day."

"Perfect," I said.

"You need any more information, drop in anytime. I'm here late at night, sometimes midnight, two in the morning. I don't sleep that good, so I work."

That afternoon, the file Mercury had made me was on the corner of my desk. I picked it up and went through it.

Good. He hadn't added information about flying saucers and lake monsters. It was just the straight goods on Caroline.

Sweet.

8

I took off at four-forty-five. From Gabby's ads in the Yellow Pages, I knew she was open until five. I drove by there and saw that hers was the only car parked out front.

I parked, took a deep breath and went inside.

When I came in I could smell some kind of strong disinfectant and the pungent smell of wet dog coming from somewhere, and then she came walking through a door that led to the back, rolling her sleeves up, ready to go home. She was whip-lean and her hair was still long and dark brown and time had done nothing to her, except make her look better. I felt a little nauseous and my throat grew tight. I stood by the door and didn't move, and soon as she saw me her body twitched, then deflated a little.

"Cason, you shouldn't be here."

"I just wanted to say hi."

She shook her head, looked at the floor. Somewhere from the back of the place a dog began to bark. Gabby finally lifted her head, looked right at me. Her eyes narrowed, like a sniper about to sight down a rifle.

"How clear can I make it?"

Several dogs started barking. Maybe they knew it was closing time.

Perhaps they got treats before she locked up. Somehow, I was messing up their schedule.

"Cason, I don't know how to tell you this any better. I wrote you the letter. When you got back, I talked to you on the phone. I read all the notes you sent me. They don't change a thing. I tossed them. It's not about finding someone else. It's not about any of those things. It's about the fact I don't love you. Maybe I never did."

"Don't say that."

"There's an old saying: When the dog is down and dying, you shoot it in the head. Sometimes, love is down and dying."

"Is that a folksy veterinarian saying?" I said, and stepped forward.

"Stay where you are," Gabby said, and she held out one hand like a traffic cop.

"For Christ sakes, you don't think I'd hurt you, do you?"

"I don't know what I think, the notes, the calls . . . But it's done, Cason."

I shook my head.

"You were over there alone, scared, I'm sure. I was your anchor. It was a way for you to hang on to something. I represented home. Escape from fear, and you blew it all up in your mind, how we felt about one another. It was never that big a deal."

"That's not what you said, not how you talked when we were together. You telling me you were lying to me all along?"

I hadn't meant for it to happen, but my words came out a little loud.

"I'm telling you, Cason, I was caught up in the moment. I was in love with the idea of being in love, not with you. I didn't know it until you were gone . . . Cason, I didn't miss you. I felt sorry for you, and was worried about you, like I would be for any soldier over there in harm's way."

"Any soldier?"

I was starting to feel as if I needed to sit down. The dogs were really barking now.

"I can't tell you how sorry I am," she said.

I stood there for a moment. No words would come. I took my hands out of my pockets and put them back.

"I really need you to go, Cason. I see you again, I'm going to get a restraining order. I want you to stay away from me. No more notes. No phone calls. And if you have to drive by my office, drive by, don't coast by, rubbernecking. Six months from now, we pass on the street, I see you, we can wave, say hi, like old acquaintances, and that's it. Please go. While I at least don't hate you."

I went outside and got in my car and drove away, not even considering which direction I was driving.

9

There were all those months in Iraq, the earth the color of a dried-up tor-
tilla, the sky a bright blaze of hot blue forever, and always the sounds of
explosions and the smells of death, and me counting down the moments,
knowing to the hour, almost to the minute, when my time was supposed
to be up, expecting to have my stay extended, certain of it, feeling as if it
would all never end. It was as if I had been dropped down onto another
planet where the people and the world bore no relation to me.

There was the loss of my buddies and seeing innocent Iraqi people, as
well as those who were not so innocent, lying dead and bloated and full of
the stink of the bloody departed.

All those months, those days, those hours, those minutes, riding
around in half-assed vehicles with hillbilly armor, stuff we made for ourselves out of whatever we could find and tack on to our rides. So there we
were, cruising, expecting a blast to blow right through it all, knock shrap-
nel up our asses, then, to top it off, came Gabby's letter and nothing much
mattered anymore, except maybe dying, and then there was the big fight
in the Baghdad street, and I caught some business, and some buddies of
mine caught it too, killing two of them. I was injured, but saved.

Booger, he just got blown skyward, like some kind of goddamn circus act, and he did a few rolls and came up wearing smoking clothes, still had his piece in his hand, and baby, he let it rock. Rocked and rolled all over that street. I don't know if he shot anyone, had anything to do with anything, but he rocked it and bopped it and bullets tore this way and that, and when it was over there was meat all over the place, pieces of cloth, disconnected Iraqi souls colliding together into a rising smudge of thick, dark smoke.

I was saved. Booger did it. And saved for what, if not to go home to Gabby, to make a life with her? I could imagine her with her long brown hair brushed until it was so lustrous it glowed like wet chocolate, and I could see her in one of the outfits she wore, a blue suit jacket with wide lapels and white pinstripes, and a skirt to match, and I could remember the way her high heels made her legs look, long and muscular in dark stockings, the way her eyes flashed and the way she smiled, her teeth perfect. And in my imaginings we would come together and kiss. I would be the conquering hero. We would go to her place, and I would slowly take her out of that suit and pull her boots off and gently guide her stockings off her legs, and we would make love, slowly and happily, like we had always done, but this time, it would be even more wonderful, because it would be a new beginning, and soon we would marry, and the sunlight would always be warm and the moonlight would always be romantic, and our days would be full of fine moments and even the rain would be gentle and sweet to the nose and rhythmic to the ears as it splashed to the ground.

Such are dreams.

It was a hard pill to swallow, even now, and to make it go down good, I drove out to a little bar that didn't belong to my boss's husband. When I got inside it was cool and dark as if it were hours later. The place had that peculiar smell bars have that is a mixture of spilt liquor and cigarette smoke, sweat and shit-filled dreams.

There was a pretty good-looking woman on one of the bar stools wearing a dark blouse and a short blue jean skirt and some oversized white shoes. I could tell from the way she sat there, smoking her cigarette, her legs crossed, one foot bobbing a shoe, the near empty glass on the counter in front of her, that she was as regular here as the rising and the setting of the sun.

I sat on the stool next to her and looked at her and showed her the smile my mother always said was electric. I said, "Can I buy you a drink?"

"Actually," she said, "I'd rather just have the money."

"That's funny," I said, but from the way she looked at me, I suspected that my electric smile was short of wattage today.

I reached in my pocket and got out five dollars and put it on the bar, and said, "Okay. There's your money."

She turned her head without moving her body, said, "Francis, this fuck is bothering me."

A guy about the size of three guys came out of the back: The bartender. The bouncer. The owner.

He said, "You giving some trouble?"

"I don't think so," I said. "I just offered to buy the lady a drink."

"And I don't want it," she said.

"She don't want it," he said.

"Okay," I said, and picked up my five and went out. I went to a liquor store and bought a lot of beer and some Wild Turkey, drove around thinking about all sorts of things and none of them good.

I had a licensed conceal-carry pistol in the glove box of my car, and I remembered when I was in Iraq a soldier friend told me he thought about his piece all the time. Said he had read where Hemingway had called death a gift. I told him, if it is, you won't have time to open that little present, it'll happen so fast. But there I was driving around thinking of the pistol in the glove box and what that soldier had told me not so long ago about Hemingway's gift.

I drove out past the old abandoned sawmills. There were still a couple where the center of Camp Rapture had once been, back when it was a timber town, back when my great-grandmother Sunset Jones had been the first woman constable in the history of East Texas, and until recent times, only one of two.

Driving out there, I felt lonely and strange, like when you hear the sound of a distant train whistle, the cry of a bird as night falls down, or see a sad face on a passing bus.

Maybe I just needed to get drunk.

I drove back along the edge of town. I could see the clock tower on the campus, standing tall and majestic. The lights were bright behind the great glass that showed not only the face of the clock, but the stylized gear work inside. And there were other lights, little quarter-moon windows full of gold that ran all the way down the face of the tower. I turned and put the clock tower in the rearview mirror.

I drove out to where the last of the motels were, scattered about like cracker boxes blown into place by a wild tornado. I parked at a motel that had a jumping frog on a neon sign; it leaped forward and back as I watched. I got a room that was a slot in the wall. It was hot even as the air conditioner struggled loud as a car wreck to cool it.

It was a room full of flies and mosquitoes that had slipped in through a cracked window that was frozen that way by a lousy paint job that had dried it tight and incapable of shutting. I sat in a chair in my underwear and watched TV and drank, and then I made my way to the bed and drank some more. When I awoke the TV was still on and I was lying on top of the sheets, having pissed myself. The room smelled of urine and alcohol and it seemed as if I had been lathered in Wild Turkey; basted was more like it. It was furnace-hot in there and I was baking in my juices and the flies and mosquitoes were loving me for a landing pad.

It took me half a day to get out of bed. I was followed by flies into the shower. I let the water run hot and long while I sat in the tub and it rained down on me. I would have been in there longer, but the hot water ran out and turned cold. I took that for a few seconds, got out and dried off with shaky hands.

I threw the pissy underwear in the waste can, got dressed and left. I felt as prideless and empty of heart as a Thanksgiving turkey.

I parked at the curb and saw another car parked in the drive behind Mom and Dad's blue PT Cruiser. A black Hummer. Not new, but damn nice. I knew that would be my brother. Great. Mr. Successful, and now me, Mr. Drunk, soon to be under the same roof.

For a moment I thought about driving off, but there was really nowhere to go. I had some mints in my glove box. I got them out and put a few in my mouth and chewed them up and swallowed them, then popped another and sucked on it.

Just before I got out of the car, I realized that lying on the seat, where I had left it, was the mass of material Mercury had put together for me, all of it tucked into a kind of accordion file. I took a deep breath, picked up the file and got out of the car.

As I walked up the drive toward the front door, Jazzy called out.

"Hi."

I looked up in the tree at her. She was wearing blue jeans and a T-shirt today, still no shoes. Her hair looked matted. "I didn't notice you up there," I said.

"I fool you all the time," she said.

"Trust me," I said, "you're not the only one."

"I'm pretty sneaky. My mama says it's not bad to be sneaky. That part of life is being sneaky."

Jazzy was certainly getting a special education.

"You don't look so good," Jazzy said.

"I don't feel so good."

"Did you get beat up?"

"Nothing like that. Unless you count life as the thug."

"Do what?"

"I was attacked by a wild turkey and a big part of Milwaukee."

"What?"

"I'm joking. I'm just tired."

"You're not funny."

"I get that a lot too."

"If you got beat up, you can tell me," she said. "I been beat up."

That's all I needed to hear to top off a perfect day, something to charge on into the weekend with. Knowing the little girl that lived next door to us had had beatings. And my guess is she didn't mean spankings, but exactly what she said. Beatings.

"Who beat you up?" I asked.

"I'm not supposed to tell."

I understood exactly why my dad had knocked the shit out of Daddy Greg.

"You got bumps on your face," she said. "Do you have pimples?"

"I have mosquito bites . . . Have you eaten, Jazzy?"

"I had a banana this morning."

"You must be hungry."

"We don't have nothing but cornflakes and some beer. There's not any milk to put on the cornflakes. Mama puts beer on hers, but I'm too young for that, she says."

Thank goodness for small favors.

"She don't cook much, but she can do a Rubik's Cube. She's real smart."

"Are you going to school?"

"It's summer, silly."

"Did you go before summer?"

"Some. Mama slept late a lot and I didn't always get a ride. She had places to go a lot of the time. Mostly I wasn't here. I went all the time when I lived in Houston with Mee-maw. She died."

I got it then. Foster care. And now with Mee-maw out of the picture, the mother had once again ended up with the child.

"Why don't you come in with me, see if my mom can fix you something?" I said. I looked at my watch. It was after five. My folks ate dinner early. It was perfect timing.

"Your mama is nice. So's your daddy."

"They are at that. Come on. It's all right when you've been invited."

10

Jazzy climbed down and reached out and took my hand. I hoped that wasn't something she did with any stranger. She smiled at me and I smiled back. Jazzy smelled a little like the elm, a pleasant smell that comes from broken leaves.

I walked her through the open garage and to the side door that led into the kitchen. I wanted to make sure she got a meal, and I thought if she was with me, Mom and Dad might be less inclined to ask me where I was the night before. At least it would help me avoid a thorough investigation: fingerprints, a urine specimen, a cavity search and a DNA swab.

Inside, the house was a little warm, the kitchen full of the smell of something cooking and the smell was a good smell and it made my stomach roll both from too much liquor and not having anything to eat for some time. Mom was at the stove with a long wooden spoon, turning something in a boiling pot. She looked at me, and though she smiled, her eyes told me she had been worried about me. Of course, she knew I had been drinking.

"Jazzy's come to visit," I said.

"Oh, good," Mom said, as if it was the best idea she had ever heard. "Come in, Jazzy. Why don't you go to the bathroom and wash your face and hands. Supper is almost on the table."

Jazzy darted for the bathroom. I went over and kissed Mom on the cheek.

"Hello, sweetie," Mom said. "When Jazzy gets out, brush your teeth. I think there's a hops farm in your mouth, maybe a nest of wild turkeys, if you know what I mean. And those mints you chewed, they just make your breath all the more nasty."

"You still have that super nose, don't you?"

"I do. And you might put some alcohol—the rubbing kind—on those bites. Did you sleep under a tree?"

"Just a place with open windows."

Mom studied me for a moment, then patted my arm. "Go in and see your brother and Trixie. I've got a chicken in the oven, and it'll be ready soon."

In the living room, Dad was on the couch next to Jimmy. He was laughing about something Jimmy was telling him. Jimmy was thin and looked as if he worked out. He had strips of white hair over his ears. It gave him an air of sophistication.

Trixie, looking fetching in blue jeans and a loose green jersey, a silver-white necklace lying against her dark brown skin, sat with her legs crossed, flip-flops on her feet. She smiled when I came in. Her hair was like a golden helmet and she seemed to have more teeth than a human should have, but they were good and bright and straight teeth. She was so good-looking if you stared at her for long you might need a trip to the ER for heat exhaustion.

I went over as she got up and gave her a big hug, making sure I kept my brewery breath behind her shoulder.

I shook hands with my brother, smiled at my dad, sat down on the end of the couch, laying my file folder on the coffee table.

"Abducted by aliens last night?" Dad said.

"Yeah," I said, "but they gave me back."

"The anal probe," Jimmy said. "They didn't like what they found."

Dad nodded at the file on the coffee table. "Homework?"

"Kind of," I said.

"You look like you been in a fire-ant hill," Trixie said, in that peculiar voice of hers. It was Southern as all get-out, and it sounded as if it came from a throat that had just swallowed broken glass and followed it with a hundred-proof whiskey chaser.

"Mosquitoes," I said. Then to Jimmy: "See you got a big ride out there, brother."

"Gas-guzzler," Dad said. "Just supporting the goddamn oil companies. Don't they make enough money without you helping them?"

"Now they're making more," Jimmy said, "and off of me. I got it slightly used. We don't run it all the time. Trixie has a smaller car. We use it most of the time. That make you feel better, Dad?"

"Just a fraction."

The conversation changed then. We talked about this and that. Jimmy and I laughed about some past events. Trixie, making sure Jazzy was with Mom, told a very off-color joke, which I loved. We did all this as sounds and smells from the kitchen filled the background.

I finally went and brushed my teeth, then messed them up again because we ate chicken and dressing, mashed potatoes and gravy, had gallons of ice tea to drink, pies for dessert, apple and pear.

When we finished eating we spent some time bragging properly on how good the meal was, then me and Jimmy slipped off and went to our old room. He looked at the planes hanging from the ceiling. "I used to lie on the top bunk and look at those planes, pretend I was in them, and that I was flying away," he said.

"Where were you going?"

"Everywhere. Anywhere. Sometimes I was flying through a hole at the South Pole, going into the center of the earth where there was a world full of dinosaurs and cavemen and beautiful women who couldn't live without my intense manly loving."

"*At the Earth's Core.*"

"We read the same books."

"And played the same games," I said.

"You played Tarzan," Jimmy said. "Remember that? I had to be the monkey, and you were Tarzan. I don't know how you worked that out, but that was the way it was. You remember."

"I do," I said. "I climbed up in that elm where Jazzy stays, in my underwear, and got the sunburn from hell."

"You kept giving the cry of the bull ape, demanding all apes come to your aid. But none of them would."

"The bastards."

"But that didn't stop you from calling. You called all day long, and Mom couldn't get you to come down, and she called Daddy at work, and he said, he gets ready to come down he will, but it didn't much look like you were gonna get ready. You called until your voice played out and you sounded less like a bull ape and more like a dying goose. And you had on those loose underwear and your balls hung out, and you got sunburned there. Remember?"

"How can I forget? I still have a scar from when the skin started peeling off. Wanna see?"

"No thanks. I'll take your word for it."

We moved around the room as we talked, kind of time traveling. Jimmy came to his frogs and rats, and a feeling of guilt ran through me. I had purposely pushed them over the other night, and I suppose if you were a Freudian, you could find some deeply disturbing reason for that.

"I ought to throw this crap away," he said. "It really looks rough."

He opened the drawers on his desk, looked at the contents. He shut the drawer, said, "It's good to have you back in town, Cason."

"Thanks."

"The newspaper job is probably just the thing," he said.

"To tell you the truth, my feelings are mixed about being back in town."

"Gabby?"

"Part of it."

"You know she called me about you. She said you keep sending her notes, calling. It upsets her."

"It's just that I find it hard to believe."

Jimmy turned and looked at me as if he had just realized I had two heads. "Do you remember when we were kids, and you found out there was no Santa Claus?"

"Yeah."

"Thing is, you wouldn't accept it. You went for months believing it anyway. Persistent. You had fights with kids at school that told you there wasn't any Santa Claus. Dad finally sat down and talked to you. So you know what you did?"

"I do, but you're going to tell me anyway."

"You thought you were being tested. That Dad had been told by Santa Claus to test your faith."

"I remember quite clearly. And I hope this isn't something you tell to the faculty at the university."

"You believed this so much, you just wouldn't accept there wasn't a Santa Claus. You fixated on it. For you, January on until the next December, it was going to be all about Santa Claus and how you knew he existed and were going to prove it, and you could meet the challenge. No matter how many times you were told it wasn't true, that there was no such thing, you would not fold. You hung in there, thinking, in the end, you would be especially rewarded for keeping the faith. And you know what? One day, about mid-June, you came in here, and you had all this stuff on Santa Claus, books, comics, I don't remember. But all manner of stuff. And you put it all in a box and had Mom put it up in the attic for you. Remember?"

"I remember. I didn't make it until December."

"You were stubborn, you were obsessed with the idea that the truth was being thwarted, that Santa was testing you. You hung on to that past any time any reasonable person might. And then one day, you got it. You knew the truth. It wasn't about hearing it. It wasn't even about understanding it. It was about believing it."

"I get the point."

"Look at me, Cason. She doesn't love you. I'm sorry. It's sad. I like Gabby, and I love you, but she doesn't. It's time you took all the Gabby stuff, the memories, put it in a box and put it in the attic, so to speak. You have to put it out of your mind."

"You make it sound easy."

"I know it isn't. The doctor, what did he say?"

"That I'm obsessed. That I have problems from the war. That and a buck fifty might get me a ride on the horsey out front of the Wal-Mart."

"Knowing and believing is the way you solve it."

"Sounds like a bumper sticker."

"I suppose it does."

Jimmy got up and went to the window and I sat down at my desk. We stayed like that for a long time. Finally, I said, "Thing I'm looking into at work, it sort of crosses with your life."

He turned from the window, leaned against the wall. "How's that?"

"A missing-person story. Probably a murder."

"Oh."

"Caroline Allison. She was a history major."

Jimmy moved away from the wall and went to his old desk and sat down in his chair and picked up a pencil and used it to poke at his stuffed frogs and mice.

"What brought that up?" he said.

"The job," I said. "Looking for a place to get started. Columns to write. The lady who was there before me picked it out. I looked it over, liked the idea of it. All she had were some notes. I've been looking up a few things. You must have known her, right?"

"Everyone in the department was very aware of her. She was quite beautiful."

"I've seen her photographs. She was more than beautiful. She looks, or should I say looked, sort of otherworldly."

"She did. Yes." He pushed at the frog with the pencil until it fell over. I didn't feel quite as bad for messing with his keepsakes.

"Maybe you know something I could put in the article. Something about her."

"All I can tell you was she was gorgeous. Everyone in the department liked her. The guys anyway. I mean, you know how it is, good-looking girl and all. She was smart, and she was going to be a crack historian."

"You said everyone in the department, the guys anyway, liked her. What about outside the department?"

"Her personal life?"

"What do you know of it?"

"Nothing really. She didn't talk much about her life."

"If the guys liked her, how did the women feel?"

"Jealous. They knew she was a force of nature though. If you're getting at someone in the history department hating her enough to kidnap or kill her because she was a fox, I don't think so."

"A woman looked that way could drive someone crazy, even if she didn't know them. Might make them do things they might not normally do."

"So it's her fault?" Jimmy said.

"I don't mean it that way. Of course, whoever did what they did to her, they made the choice. Just saying, if there was someone out there two ounces short a pound, a woman like that, it could be the thing to set them off . . . Is this bothering you, Jimmy?"

He nodded. "She was a good kid. Just disappearing like that, it was painful. She'd been in a couple classes I taught. She had a great future. I was quite sick about it."

"Sorry."

"No biggie. It's what it is. No point in wishing things were different. She's gone . . . You know what? I think I'd like a cup of coffee. How about you?"

It wasn't a clever change of subject, but it was successful enough. Jimmy was already up and moving out of the room when I said, "Dying for one."

When we passed through the living room on the way to the kitchen, we saw that Jazzy was asleep on the couch. Someone, Mom probably, had covered her with a blanket.

Coming into the kitchen, Jimmy said, "Jazzy is out for the count."

Mom and Dad and Trixie were sitting at the table, already enjoying coffee. Mom said, "Keep it down. She's exhausted. I bet she slept in that tree last night. Sometimes they lock her out."

"Why won't someone do something?" Jimmy asked.

"That's what we'd like to know," Dad said. "We haven't even seen her mother or her latest shitass come out of the house in a couple days."

"Pete, don't talk like that," Mom said.

Dad ignored her as usual. "Her mother stays inside most of the time, like she's afraid of the light. I don't think she works, unless it's over the telephone. The new daddy, he has a van with something about upholstery work written on the side, so maybe he does upholstery at home. But my guess is he isn't a working fool. And then there's the former Daddy Greg, who I guess is just Greg now. He comes around now and then. No telling what Jazzy sees. That girl needs a better home life."

"Bless her heart," Mom said. "Jazzy is a smart little thing. She can learn anything."

"She's being wasted," Dad said.

Mom patted Dad's hand. "I know, but all we can do is stay on Protective Services."

Jimmy and I went over to the cabinet for some coffee cups, got coffee from the coffeemaker and sat down at the table.

"She'll spend the night here," Mom said. "And I bet her mother and her newest daddy won't even miss her."

"Drunk bastards," Dad said. "Or maybe it's something else they're hopped up on. Or maybe they aren't hopped up on anything, it's just the way they act. Hard to tell."

"Hopped up?" Jimmy said. "People still say that?"

"I do," said Dad.

"How about twenty-three skidoo?" Jimmy said.

"Or Oh you, kid," I said.

"Or the bee's knees," Trixie said.

Dad grinned at us. "You're asking for it, busters. And you too, young lady."

That night, after my brother and his wife left and everyone had gone to bed, I sat at my old desk and glanced through the file Mercury had put together for me. I found myself looking at Caroline's picture over and over. I read through all the notes and filled my head with all the facts that were available. It was like planting seeds in my gray matter, trying to get them to take root and break through and bloom.

I looked for clues as if I might find them: Colonel Mustard in the study with the wrench. That sort of thing. I thought of how terrible and surprising it might have been for her, attacked by someone she trusted most likely, since that's the way it usually worked out.

It wasn't a pleasant thing to think about before bedtime, but I stayed with it, tried to figure a little of this and a little of that. There were no parents to talk to. No relatives she was really connected to. There was just the girl who said she hadn't paid her movie rental bill, her library fine. The girl's name was Ronnie Fisher and there was an address for her, but I didn't see much in that. Still, I made a note to contact her. I finally went to bed. This time I didn't dream.

11

A month went by, and for some reason, though it interested me the most, I couldn't get up enough of a head of steam to write about Caroline Allison. I knew how I wanted to write about her, but for whatever reason I didn't have enough gas in the tank. I think the business with Gabby had evaporated my fuel.

There were people I ought to interview so I could get a larger picture of who she was and what might have happened to her, but I wasn't up to it. I was having a hard enough time just learning to be me again, not waking up and thinking I was still in Iraq and that pretty soon I'd be on the streets with my rifle and my asshole clenched, hoping today wouldn't be the day I got my head blown off.

In the meantime I wrote columns on stem cell research, people who took the Bible literally, and even wrote one on gardening gleaned from Francine's old notes. It was an easy thing to do, to use those notes, and I took advantage of it and got my column written quickly that week. It gave me more time to read through the research I had on Caroline, though what I had I had read a half-dozen times.

Then, one morning, all the notes, all my thoughts came together and I wrote a kind of lest-we-forget piece with the best photo of her and a shot of her shoes and that sad sack of food lying on her car seat. I wrote reminding the community that she had lived here, was well known at the university, was thought to have tremendous promise, that she had disappeared, and all these months later, no one knew any more than the day she disappeared. It was also about the fact that not only was there no information on her disappearance, when you got right down to it there wasn't much information on her before her disappearance. I thought it might be a two-part or three-part piece, the other two parts a little more investigative. It depended on the feedback I got.

Anyway, the column got done, and I was at my desk on a Tuesday morning, two days after it appeared, having managed not to get drunk and to think of Gabby only a few hundred times since I got up, showered, shaved and had my coffee. I brought some more coffee to work from the coffee shop and was still drinking it when Mrs. Timpson came out of her office, stopped at my desk and shifted her ample ass onto the corner of it, then shifted the teeth in her mouth.

"Cason, you kind of got things stirring."

"The column on Caroline Allison?"

"No. The one you did on Noah's ark."

"Oh."

"Christians are all fired up."

"Aren't they always? What did I do, misspell Noah?"

"You suggested that it didn't really happen."

"And you think it did?"

"Do I look like an ignorant yahoo? No one in their right mind thinks some fella put, what was it you said, 'thousands of species, times two' on a goddamn boat and sailed it around for forty days and forty nights. But for some Christians, it's like the best sex in the world to them. They can't let it go. They like getting banged in the ass by the Noah story."

"Actually," I said, "I understand that. Personally, I'm still mad about there not being any Santa Claus."

Timpson adjusted her teeth with her tongue. "Some of the people who put advertising in the paper are big Charlie Churches. We have to kiss their ass a little, right around the pucker hole."

"You're telling me not to write about that sort of thing anymore?"

"I'm not going to say that. But you followed it with stem cell research, and how we need it. Don't put two ass kickers back to back. Space them out a bit. It's all right to stir them up, but let's don't keep them stirred. Kick Jesus in the balls one week, then do some fluff piece or a profile, then come back for another kick. Give them time to heal. They get stirred enough, they'll get deep-fried and sanctified all over our asses. I'm going to let Reverend Dinkins address your article in his Sunday column. He'll take the fundamentalist view. It'll be stupid, but it'll make the church people happy."

"Isn't he the one trying to keep them from building a school down in the old black section of town?"

"He is at that, and so is Reverend Judence. Funny thing is, they both want the same thing, but not for the same reason, so they're mad at each other."

"Dad told me about it."

"I know your dad. He's not a bad-looking old man."

"I'm sure he'll be glad to hear it."

"Judence and Dinkins. They're real pieces of work, those two, but they've been good for news, and when Judence comes to make his speech, that'll be a hot news day for this little town."

"Wouldn't it be a better idea to get some other preacher for the rebuttal? Someone screwed down a little tighter."

"Dinkins is the celebrity, kid," she said. "That's who we'll go with. It'll spike paper sales and show we aren't godless heathens. Except for you."

"All right," I said. "Let him go at it."

"I was going to. Oh, that column on the missing girl. Not bad."

"Thanks," I said.

"A little fluffy, so I figure you're holding the good stuff back for a later column, or for a shot at a bigger article somewhere else."

I didn't say anything to contradict her remark. She might be an asshole, but she was damn savvy.

"Well, keep your powder dry," she said.

Mrs. Timpson got off my desk and went over to Oswald's desk, most likely to discuss his writing of the sports, or perhaps to offer her insights into the running and football-tossing abilities of the colored.

Belinda came over with a handful of mail. I knew some of it would be letters about my column. There might even be something nice in one of them. Mixed in with the mail was a FedEx envelope. There wasn't any address on it. Not the newspaper's address, not the sender's. It just had my name written on it.

I said, "How'd you get this?".

"It was in front of the door when they opened up this morning."

"It didn't really come from FedEx," I said, and showed her the envelope.

"I guess it's a hand-delivered fan letter," she said.

"It didn't quite make it to my hand, though, or anyone else's. So I figure, since it's a drop-off, it's not all that positive."

"Maybe they were just shy."

"I hope so," I said. "I could use a fan letter."

She patted the letters and the package she had put on my desk. "All this for you, and me I'm lucky if I get anything other than a water bill. Of course, that might be because I'm not a reporter."

"You'll get your shot."

"That's what they all say."

Belinda turned to go.

"Belinda?"

She stopped and looked back at me. "Maybe," I said, "someday soon, we could go get a cup of coffee after work. If we're feeling rowdy, a Diet Coke?"

She gave me a slow, braces-shiny smile. "I'll think it over," she said.

"Just a little conversation. Nothing serious."

"I guess we can swing that."

"Soon then?"

She smiled at me again. I was beginning to really like that smile, grill-work and all. "I'd love that," she said.

"Great. Then we'll call it a future plan."

"Certainly," she said.

When she was back to her place, I felt a little self-satisfied. That was good, Cason, old boy, I thought. You're moving on. Or at least you're trying.

I started in on the mail by opening the FedEx package. There was a DVD inside, enclosed in a plastic case. There was also a note written on cardboard with a black marker. It read: "YOU WILL WANT TO SEE THIS."

I studied the package again, but didn't come up with any new results.

Anyone could get a FedEx envelope, just had to drive by one of the boxes where they kept the supplies. I read the note again, but it didn't say anything different.

I sat and tried to work for a while, but the DVD was bothering me, lying there on my desk unseen, calling to me like a siren. My guess was it was some Christian propaganda sent to me because of my column on Noah's ark or stem cell research. I finally picked it up and left.

12

I had recently bought myself a police scanner for the car and had rented a little apartment not far from where Mom and Dad lived.

I was on the bottom floor of a duplex. Nothing cute, nothing fancy. Just cheap rent. I pushed against the moisture-swollen door and made my way inside. It smelled as if a rat had died in the walls; it had held that smell for the entire week I had lived there. In the morning it was at its weakest, but as the day wore on and it became hot, Mr. Dead Rat, or so I assumed it was, heated up in the walls and gave off an odor that could grab you by the collar and toss you out the door. I remembered a story I had read by Mark Twain about a cheese that had stunk so bad that he gave it military promotions. It was the same with my dead rat. He was a private in the morning, but by the afternoon I had promoted him to general. It was almost that strong now, but not quite. He was at about a captain's level.

I put the DVD in the player and turned on my little TV and sat down in a comfortable chair with only a bit of the stuffing leaking out. At first I thought the DVD was blank, but suddenly it sputtered to life. And then my heart was in my mouth. There were two people in it. Nude. One of them, the woman, was immediately recognizable to me. It was Caroline

Allison. On a bed. She looked like a movie star. A porn star. Her long brown legs moved sensuously over the man's back, her heels rubbing his buttocks. The man's face was turned away from me. He lifted up, supported himself above her on his hands so that he could thrust, and I could see the side of his face then, and that's all I needed to see.

I stood up from my chair without meaning to. The dead rat smell filled my nostrils. I felt dizzy. My stomach clenched like a fist. I walked around my chair, glanced at the television, watched as the man gently shifted and guided the woman into another position.

I could see more than the side of his face now. A lot more than I wanted to see. And there was no mistake.

I felt as if I couldn't swallow. As if I couldn't breathe.

The man making love to Caroline Allison was my brother, Jimmy.

I started to turn off the DVD, but couldn't. I walked around my chair and watched the TV with glances. When the DVD finished and went black, I stood there with my hands on the back of my chair, leaning forward, looking at the dark screen, as if waiting for some sort of revelation.

I went around and sat in my chair for a while. Finally I had enough strength to get up and turn off the set, eject the DVD. I robotically put the DVD back in its container, took it and slid it between two books in my bookcase, *All the President's Men* and *State of Denial.* I went into the kitchen and got a bottled coffee out of the fridge and drank it. It could have been nectar of the gods or lye from under the sink, and I wouldn't have noticed.

I took the FedEx package and put it in the trash. I took the note and read it again and put it between the two books with the DVD.

I got my cell phone out of my pocket and called Jimmy's cell. He didn't answer. He would most likely be in class, or having office hours. I took a deep breath and went downstairs and got in my car and drove around town, and finally out to the spot where the town almost ended, headed to where the old Siegel house sat and parked down the hill from it. The hill was specked with gangly pines and all around it the grass was the color of sandpaper, but in front of the house, and on the right and left sides, was a thick carpet of crawling kudzu that wound its way up in twists and twirls and eventually became a huge emerald wad at the top. The wad would be the Siegel house, consumed by vines, lying gray and silent in the belly of the green.

I drove around to the old clay road that led behind the houses. It was narrower than I remembered. Perhaps the grass had grown up closer on either side of the road. Maybe it was that old problem about being away for so long you remembered all things as bigger and wider and deeper and greater. Like lost love.

Driving up the road, I bumped into some big holes where it had washed out, tooled to the top of the hill and parked behind the vine-covered house on a gravel rise where the kudzu had been unable to make purchase. But at the back of the house were the vines. They grew along the outside walls of the house, covering some of the back door and all the windows except for a rare wink of glass.

I sat there for a long time and thought about Jimmy and Trixie. I had thought they had the perfect life. I wondered what in the world Jimmy had been thinking. Well, hell, I knew what he had been thinking. But why had he let it get the better of him? It was like me to let it get the better of me. I was the one who did stupid things, but not Jimmy. No wonder he was nervous the night I spoke to him about Caroline. No wonder he wanted to change the subject.

My God, I thought. He couldn't have had anything to do with her missing. He just couldn't have. Jimmy wasn't like that. He didn't have it in him. But where had the DVD come from? Why had it been sent to me? And by whom? And had Jimmy known he was being filmed?

A ton of questions fell down on top of me, but I didn't receive so much as an ounce of answers.

I sat up there on the hill with my window rolled down and the hot air not stirring even a little bit. I started the engine and rolled up the window and turned the air conditioner on full blast and sat there for a while longer. Then I put the car in gear and coasted back down the hill and out to the road. I drove slowly by the old railway station below, as if I thought Caroline's car might still be parked there and the law had overlooked the fact she had just gone out for a walk, was about to show up again, eat her fast-food dinner, put on her shoes and drive away.

I drifted back into town and got a parking pass at the campus police station, drove over to a lot behind the history department. I locked up and walked over to the building that housed the department, turned and looked at the clock tower. I could see the big, ragged gears through the face of the clock; they were silver now, not gold, because the light was different. The dark hands of the clock lay flat against the outside of the glass. I looked at my watch. I was either five minutes fast or the clock was five minutes slow.

Entering the building, I rode the elevator up to the third floor. When I got off the halls were silent except for a janitor pushing a squeaky trash cart. Summer classes aren't as busy as spring or fall, so there's not much excitement that time of the year. The janitor squeaked on by.

I had no idea if Jimmy was teaching or in his office. Maybe he had another coed locked in there and he was doing with her what he had done with Caroline. Maybe he was filming it?

There were a couple of hallways and there were offices on either side of the hallways, and I walked along looking at the name plaques beside the office doors, trying to find the one that belonged to Jimmy.

A man with a nose like a pink cucumber, a beard and about four strands of reluctant hair pasted down across the top of his head was sitting in an office with his door open. Behind him, through the window, I could see the university plaza, and beyond that, the parking garage.

I introduced myself and Cucumber Nose told me his name was Thomas Burke. I asked him about Jimmy, and he told me where to find him. I went there. It was an office two doors down from Burke's place. The door was locked. There was a schedule on the wall by the door, but I was so nervous I couldn't make heads or tails out of it. I might as well have been reading Sanskrit, the way my mind was working.

"Cason," a voice called.

I turned. It was Jimmy. He had a stack of books under his arm and was walking toward me, smiling. When he saw the expression on my face, he quit smiling, said, "Mom and Dad okay?"

I nodded.

"Trixie?"

I nodded again. "Brother," I said. "We have to talk."

Jimmy unlocked his office door and went inside and put his stack of books on his desk, turned and looked at me.

"You look like your dog just committed suicide," he said.

"Actually, I think my brother just fucked himself."

He gave me a puzzled look. I couldn't hold his gaze. I turned and looked out his window and took in a new vantage point on the plaza and the parking garage, the clock. I walked over to the window for a better view. It was an old-style window that cranked open. It was part of the original building, constructed back in the 1930s. Back when it was an all-women's teacher's college. I felt like I wanted to crank it open and get a taste of the warm fresh air. Anything to clear my head.

"The clock," Jimmy said. "All that money for it, and it doesn't keep good time . . . What exactly do you want to talk about?"

"There might be a better place to discuss it than here."

13

Jimmy's last class for the day was over, so we walked out to my car together. I drove us out of there, on out Highway 7, and then off of it and down a long winding road that had once, many moons ago, been a major highway. The sun was falling into the trees and it looked like a peeled red plum coming apart. A flock of black birds was moving from one tree to the other as my car startled them. They moved so well in tight formation they appeared to be a wind blown cloud of crude oil. Finally they had had enough and broke over the trees and flew into the face of the dying sun, black freckles on a bright red face. Jimmy sat silent, his head turned a little toward me. I could tell he was nervous, and I wanted to relieve him of it, but I hadn't found a way to say what I needed to say, and a part of me, pissed, wanted to make him squirm. "Jimmy," I finally said, "what about Caroline Allison?"

"What?"

"I can tell by the expression on your face that you know damn well what I'm talking about."

"No. No, I don't. What is wrong with you, Cason?"

I found myself pushing on the gas a little heavy. I let off.

"I got something in the mail today," I said. "It was curious. It was a DVD."

"Oh."

I glanced at Jimmy. His face had fallen and gone white, and in that one moment, he looked sixty, not thirty.

"You know then?" I said.

There was a slight hesitation. "I got one yesterday."

"And you've seen it?"

Jimmy nodded.

I came to a rest stop, and without really thinking about it, pulled in there and parked the car under the shade of some trees, rolled down the windows with the electric switches and killed the engine.

"Can we cut the crap now?" I said.

Jimmy nodded. "Yeah."

"Why?" I said.

"Why what?"

"Why you and her?"

He sucked in some air and let it out heavily. "You saw her. She was a goddess."

"That's it? She was good-looking? You'd throw away everything you've accomplished, your marriage, your wife, for someone who was good-looking? It's not like Trixie is a fishwife. And there's always someone better-looking somewhere. I mean, for Christ sakes, that's your reasoning? Trixie is smart as a whip and loyal and everything a woman ought to be."

"You think?"

"Fuck you, Jimmy. You know she is."

"Don't be so sanctimonious. You had some business with a married woman. Not to mention her daughter. That's pretty goddamn weird, don't you think?"

"I'm the idiot in the family. You aren't. I'm the one that screws things up, and you're the one that does things right, and that's how it's always been, and that's how it still ought to be. You're messing up my view of the universe, and I don't like it one goddamn bit."

Jimmy nodded. "I seem to be vying for the title of screw-up now."

"Oh, you've taken the belt, brother. You definitely have the championship now."

Jimmy sat there for a while, blowing out his breath, shaking his head, trying to collect himself.

"Does Trixie know?" I asked.

"Of course not. She did, you'd be talking to a mound of dirt and a gravestone."

"Anyone else know?"

"Obviously. But I don't know who."

"Does anyone you know have any idea that you and Caroline had a thing?"

"I don't think so. Of course, whoever sent the DVD may have told others. You got this stirred up, you know. You and that column. If you had just left it alone—"

"Jimmy. Are you nuts? Someone has known this for a long time. The column may have stirred them, but I get the impression they've been waiting on purpose."

"This long?"

"All right. Maybe they haven't been waiting. Maybe he, she, they, whoever, came across the DVD by accident? I don't know. Maybe it was the column that stirred the blackmailer, or blackmailers, up. But in time, something would have got them on this track. Something like that has a pretty damn good shelf life, Jimmy. Shit, for all we know it's on the Internet."

"Christ," Jimmy said.

"Did you know you were being filmed?"

"No."

"How does that happen?"

"Hidden camera, I guess. We made love at her apartment many times, so it didn't occur to me she was filming it. Or maybe someone else set up a camera. I don't know. It seemed innocent enough then. I was just . . . enjoying. When I was with Caroline I felt special. It was nice. She had a kind of power over me."

"Don't give me that. Power? She had a power over you? What kind of bull is that?"

"It's true. I'd do anything she wanted. She was experimental and I liked that."

"Don't tell me she did things you couldn't get Trixie to do."

Jimmy reddened. "It was the way she did it . . . I guess she really had me going."

"I think you had a little to do with it, brother."

"Sure I did. Back then, few weeks before Caroline went missing, I was thinking about leaving Trixie. We were having a few problems. Nothing big. Just that part where the relationship is moving from romance to something more solid. I missed the romance. I wasn't mature enough to understand what was going on."

"You've gotten more mature in a few months?"

"I don't know. Maybe I just had the hots for Caroline and that's the long and the short of it. I got the romance with her."

"What you got was some humping, so don't insult Trixie by pretending you were getting romance. Jesus, Jimmy."

"When I was home with Trixie, well, it really wasn't so bad, but it wasn't . . . exciting. Still, I couldn't imagine being without her."

"But you couldn't let go of Caroline?"

"I couldn't. And you know what? I'm going to backtrack. It wasn't just the hots. It wasn't purely sexual. I was in love with two women. They gave me different things."

"That's pretty clichéd, Jimmy. That's nothing more than the old bull-shit about having your cake and eating it too."

"I know. But it's true."

I leaned forward and put my forearms on the steering wheel. It seemed as if I were in a dream.

"Jesus, Jimmy."

"I didn't mean for me and her to happen. Everyone in the department, all the guys, probably half the women, had a crush on Caroline, even the women who were jealous of her. She was in a couple of my classes. Used to stop by the office, we had talks about history, then the talks went to other things. I couldn't help myself. That skin of hers, it just needed touching. Cason, she had the softest, warmest, smoothest skin I have ever touched. I was a train going down a steep grade. I could see the tracks were out and the bridge was gone, but I couldn't stop."

"Did you get a note with the DVD?" I asked.

"Yes."

"Did it say something like, 'You will want to see this'?"

"No. It said, 'If you don't want anyone to see this, await instructions.' "

"Blackmail," I said.

"Why would you get a note too?"

"Wanted you to know there were more copies than one. That you had to watch yourself. Figured your brother would most likely help you out, help you come up with the money, otherwise it gets posted on the Internet. All done with the tap of a finger."

"You got to help me, Cason."

"I'm not sure what to do. Aren't you the smart one?"

"You've got connections. You're a reporter. You can talk to people I can't. I start talking, pretty quick it's going to get back I was having an affair with Caroline. That happens, the job is over, and so is the marriage. I might deserve it, but I don't want it to happen."

I let go of the wheel and shifted in my seat. Through the windshield I could see a red bird bouncing about in a tree. The way the light was falling over it, the bird looked as if it were turning dark, transforming into a totally different kind of bird.

"I got to ask you something, Jimmy, and you got to be straight with me. Not even an inch of the bullshit."

"Shoot."

"I don't want to ask this, but I got to. You didn't . . . You don't know what happened to Caroline, do you?"

"You mean did I kill her? Jesus, man. You know me better than that. No, of course not. Are you crazy?"

"I had to ask. I been around enough to know shit can happen."

"No. A hundred times no. How can you ask me that?"

"Okay. It's asked. It's done. Do you have any idea what happened to her?"

He shook his head. "We were supposed to meet that night. Out near the Siegel house, at the old abandoned train station. She was doing a paper on the history of the house. About the sisters, you know? She thought she could get something good she could write about for class, modify later, maybe sell somewhere. She was the kind of person that thought ahead. A very clockwork kind of mind. When you assigned reading she could tell you verbatim what the author of the book said. She was a little less good at presenting her own opinion."

"But the two of you weren't meeting out there to discuss her article, were you?"

"No. At least I don't think so. I went out there and found her car and she wasn't there. She had picked up some food for the two of us. Taco Bell or some hamburger joint. I don't remember."

"Seems like a bad place for a sexual rendezvous."

"We were going to talk. I hoped it would become sexual after a while, as usual. But she said she had something she wanted to tell me. When I got there she was gone. I looked all over for her, even drove up behind the Siegel house, got out and looked around. I couldn't find her. Got afraid that if I called anyone on my cell they'd know we were more than student and teacher. I had some idea if I did call, and she turned up, me and her could make a story about her doing a paper on the house, and she asked me to come out and see it, as a teacher, of course. But that seemed too risky, not likely to be believed. So I left. I didn't think anything had happened to her at first. It was curious. And I was a little worried. But it's hard to think something like that might really happen to someone you know. I panicked. I drove around a bit. I came back, and she still wasn't there. Then I got afraid. I still didn't want to use my cell, but I decided I had to call, so I stopped at a phone booth, called the cops, said there was a car parked where it wasn't supposed to be and that it had been there for a while. Nothing else. I went home. The cops went out, and next day I learned she was really missing."

"And you never said a word?"

Jimmy shook his head. "No. I took the coward's way out. I hoped she would turn up, of course. But by then I had come to realize what a fool I'd been. Told myself, she turned up, that was okay, but I was going to break it off. I didn't want to ruin my life. As time went on, I thought I was safe. I figured something horrible had happened to Caroline, but that it wouldn't help any for me to let on that we had been having an affair. All that could do was hurt me. In my marriage, which was starting to work again, and in my career, which was going very well. And it's not like I had anything to do with her disappearance."

"Do you have any idea, any kind of idea, what might have happened to her?"

"You asked that."

"And I'm asking again. Think."

Jimmy gave it some thought, shook his head. "No. The next day I went over to her apartment. I had a key. I used gloves, so as not to leave any fingerprints. I went over to see if she was there. This was before I learned later that day that she was considered to be missing. She wasn't there, of course. The place was a mess. It had been tossed. I thought it was the police. But I don't know for sure. Nothing was mentioned in the paper about her apartment being tossed."

"That could be bad reporting," I said, "or it could be something the police didn't mention. Maybe on purpose. Did anyone see you there?"

"I was careful. I don't think so."

"Could you tell if anything was missing?"

"No. But a lot could have been missing and I wouldn't have known it. Stuff was spread all over the place."

"I presume by now everything in it has been taken out."

"Sure. It's rented. Don't think I haven't driven by there, maybe thinking she was gonna show. I don't know."

"What happened to her stuff?"

"I don't know. Not really."

"She had a friend, Ronnie. Did you know about her?"

"Just that they had lived together for a while, and then Caroline decided she wanted her own apartment."

"What then?"

"I went home. Got rid of her number. Anything I had written down that had to do with her. I kept thinking she'd show up. But days rolled into weeks, into months. I was sorry for her. But I was beginning to think I was home free. Then you mentioned her the other night. And then you wrote the article. And now the DVD arrives. You stirred up the shit, Cason. Whoever sent us the DVDs must be the killer, or know who the killer is."

I sat gripping the steering wheel for a moment, just to have something to hang on to. I said, "For now just be quiet about your relationship with Caroline. But I got to tell you, Jimmy, there may come a time when you have to tell the truth, let the chips fall as they may. All this time, all this water under the bridge, that DVD, it makes you look bad, man."

"Hell, I know that."

"Do you still have the DVD?"

"I've got it hid."

"Do one better than that. Destroy it. We don't know who else has a copy. Let's not help things out by leaving another one lying around. Trixie might come across it."

"If the cops find out I had it, won't that be destroying evidence?"

"Let's hope they don't find out. I'll hang on to my copy for a while in case that comes up."

"All right, I'll get rid of it."

"I want you to go home and give some thought to the things you've already answered. Something that may have seemed unimportant at the time. Remember something, let me know. In the meantime, I guess you wait for the blackmailer. Did the DVD come by mail?"

"No. It was in a package, stuck in my mailbox at work."

"Then it wasn't stamped?"

"No. We can get stamped mail there, but this wasn't stamped."

"Mine either," I said. "It was waiting for me at the newspaper office. Can anyone walk into the history department?"

"It's easy. You did it today. All you have to do is ride the elevator up. So many people come in and out it could have been dropped off at any time. Could have been put in with the mail batch, then delivered by someone in the office. The office secretary is the one who does that."

"Did she know Caroline?"

"She's new. About fifty. Has three kids and a husband and shows us pictures of them and a little brown dog. I can assure you, she's not involved with a months-old disappearance."

I started up the car and drove out of the rest stop, headed back toward town. As I arrived at the university, Jimmy said, "Thanks, Cason."

"I'll do the best I can, Jimmy. But I'm going to add this: I told you to destroy the DVD. But you might want to just go on and tell the police, give it to them. There's a good chance it'll all come out anyway. Blackmailing starts, there's no guarantee it'll stop, even if you pay the money."

Jimmy sat with his hand on the door handle. "I can't do it, Cason. I can't disappoint Trixie. I wouldn't want to lose her. Think about Gabby. How you feel about losing her."

"You're hitting low, bubba."

"I don't mean to play on your sympathies here."

"The hell you don't," I said.

He opened the door and stepped out, but before he closed it, he stuck his head inside, said, "You with me, bro? We okay?"

I looked at Jimmy. He was really scared.

"You're a shithead, but I'm with you," I said.

14

I went back to the newspaper the next morning and sat at my desk and tried to think about what to do. I had thought about it all night and nothing seemed like a good idea. The sun doesn't shine on the same dog's balls every day, but I sure felt as if I were long overdue for a little sunlight.

Then I thought about what Jimmy had said, and he was right. I could talk to people he couldn't. As a reporter, even a small-town reporter, I had access to people and places other folks didn't.

A follow-up article on Caroline. That was the deal. I'd need to do research, talk to a few people. I had the Allison file in my desk, and information on my computer, so it was all at my fingertips. No reason for anyone to suspect I was doing anything more than my job.

I got the accordion file out of the drawer and read through it for the umpteenth time, and made a list of names and ideas on a yellow pad, then I looked through the computer file and did the same.

It was a short list.

On it was the police chief and the girl, Ronnie Fisher. I thought the police chief might be the best place to start.

I called and he was in, so I drove over there.

. . .

His name was Lanagan and I was let in to see him. He was a big man with gray hair and a young face and a complexion that appeared to be pumped full of strawberry Kool-Aid. I introduced myself and he stated the obvious. "So, you're a reporter for the paper?"

I agreed that I was. He ran a hand through that thick gray hair and motioned me to a chair, checked his watch to show me how busy he was, then sat down behind his desk.

"Listen, I can't give you much time. I'm supposed to do a little talk for the Rotary Club today."

"I understand," I said. "I'm doing a kind of follow-up to an article I wrote about Caroline Allison."

"That was you? I read that. Good article."

"Thanks. I was wondering if there was anything special you could tell me about the case. Something I could do to expand on the article. DNA testing, anything like that?"

I was looking for some way to get a connection, any kind of connection that might tell me if there were ties to Jimmy.

Lanagan leaned back in his chair, cupped his hands behind his head and gazed upward, thoughtful.

"I wasn't here then. It was another chief. Moved here from Michigan. Did a little law work up there, was a constable. Applied for the job, got it. Chief then was James Kramer. He died. Cancer. I took over. As for DNA, I'm going to be real honest with you . . . What was your name again?"

I gave it to him.

"Thing is, Jason—"

"Cason."

"Cason. Thing is, you watch TV, you'd think everyone is doing DNA tests and cracking cases with all kinds of high-tech equipment, and in no more time than an hour TV show. Like everyone has a handwriting analyst that can tell if someone wrote a ransom note left-handed or with their toes. Sound equipment that can separate a car backfire from a dog fart. Ain't true, bucko. Our special-material budget, and that would include DNA and that nifty yellow crime scene tape we stretch around crime sites, is two thousand dollars a year. That's it. What we got here in Camp Rapture is some good hardworking cops, a drug dog so old he needs a live-in nurse and a leak in the department bathroom that slicks up the floor and makes it a death threat every time you go to the crapper."

"So, I guess I can mark DNA testing off the list."

"You can mark off DNA, ballistics, most everything. Drug dog dies, way they cost, I'll be out there sniffing tires and asses in his place."

"I see," I said.

"I'm angry every day I get up on account of it," the chief said.

"That you might have to sniff asses and tires?"

He smiled, but it didn't look particularly heartfelt.

"This girl, this Caroline Allison, don't think I haven't read her file and wondered," he said. "I've looked at her picture dozens of times. A face like that could make a priest quit fucking choirboys."

"So nothing was found at the scene?"

"All that was left was a sack of stale Taco Bell, some shoes. She just disappeared, like morning dew by mid-afternoon. If you quote me, that by the way could be a good quote."

I made a note on my pad. "Like morning dew by mid-afternoon," I said. "I'll use it. So, if you had the money for DNA you could do DNA testing, but you have nothing to test, so it doesn't really matter if you can or cannot do DNA testing."

"On the nosey. I'm going to lay that lack of evidence in the lap of my poor dead predecessor. No DNA was collected. Of course, that doesn't mean there was any to collect. But if there was, I wasn't responsible. I want it known that any incompetence was not my doing. Did you know speeding tickets have doubled on North Street because of a larger presence of officers?"

"I didn't know that."

"Well, it's doubled. That's my doing. Fines for unleashed dogs are up too."

"Are there fines for cats as well?" I asked.

The chief furrowed his brow. "You know, I don't think so. But we could make it that way. That's an idea, and I might steal it."

"It's yours. What happened to Caroline's car? Do you know?"

"From what I remember from the files, no one claimed it. No relatives. It eventually was sold at an auction. I might have made another choice, but—" He spread his hands in a "Whatcha gonna do?" motion.

"Fingerprints?"

"Car was dusted, but nothing was found."

"That means someone wiped it down, right?"

"It means no fingerprints were found. That's all it means. Oh, there were prints on the steering wheel, but they were all the same prints and didn't pop up in any systems, so we got to figure they were hers."

"So, nothing," I said.

The chief nodded and looked at his watch. "That's what I'm saying . . . Well, got that Rotary thing."

"What about her apartment?"

"Way I remember is it was searched."

"What happened to the things she owned?"

"My guess, auction and/or Goodwill. Really, I got to go."

"Thanks," I said, then: "Just for the record, what do you think happened to her?"

"Well, she's not living in Argentina with Hitler. My guess is what's left of her is under some mud somewhere, and the guy did it to her graduated or left town and is murdering folks somewhere other than here, which makes it a hell of a lot easier on us."

"You think she was the victim of a serial killer?"

"I don't know. Could be. Maybe she just had a date with the wrong fellow. Jealous guy. Kinky sex. It could have been anything. I figure it was the guy called in about her car. That's my take."

That would have been Jimmy. I said, "Oh?"

"Yeah, some turkey called in that her car was up there and it had been sitting there awhile, and he thought it was odd, but I think that's just the way the killer got the ball rolling. Wanted to see the circus come to town. He probably had her in the trunk of his car and was already thinking about maybe cutting her up and fertilizing the river bottoms with her. Got his jollies calling it in. Or maybe he had some real remorse and wanted to tell someone before he dumped her. No way to know."

"Could have just been a concerned citizen," I said.

"There's that," he said.

15

I shook hands with him and left out of there. At least there wasn't anything to tie Jimmy to the disappearance. Any DNA that might be tested, provided it could be afforded, had never been collected. Jimmy might have leaned against the car and left a print, but if the cops were as sloppy as I thought they were, and with the car gone now and no one to match the prints to, it probably wouldn't have mattered if he had, wouldn't have mattered if he had bled all over the seat, shit in the glove compartment and jacked off on the package shelf. I figured he was probably home free in the DNA department.

Next person I had to find was Ronnie Fisher. But right then, I needed to get back to the paper and do some work.

As I was driving back, my cell rang. I flipped it open as I drove, saw the number. Oklahoma prefix. Booger. I started not to answer. I didn't want to answer. But I couldn't help myself.

"My man," Booger said.

"Hello, Booger. How's things?"

"Well, I had an early morning at the range, and a very fine constitutional shit that caused me to strain enough to temporarily cross into another dimension, drank six beers, and right now I'm lying here in bed with one hand on the cell phone and the other lying between Conchita's legs."

"Too much information, buddy."

"I like to be thorough. That Gabby girl. You porkin' her again?"

"No. Me and Gabby. We're done."

"Well, all right then, come on back to Oklahoma. I told you I'd put you to work."

"I got a job."

"That newspaper thing."

"That's the one."

"You know what, Cason old buddy?"

"What?"

"You sound like you got some woes to live on."

"How do you mean?"

"Your voice. There's an imp down in it."

I tried to be very calm. Booger was like that. Some people thought because he was raw he was stupid. That would be far from the truth. And he had an instinct about things, could see the slightest disruption in the force. Not that he usually gave a damn how anyone felt, but he had keen radar. And in my case, he probably did care.

"I'm just tired, Booger."

"Do I need to come down there?"

"I can't imagine what for."

Booger laughed. "I know I make you nervous, bro, but you ain't got no worries. We done thrown in together. We been through hell's ass and out the other side. We're devils together."

"I guess we are."

"Sure we are. Now, listen up. You get to needing old Booger, you just flip the phone and hit the number. You'd do that, right?"

"Sure," I said.

"I don't want my little darling here to grow cold, so I'm going to hang up and mount up."

"Enjoy the ride, and go light on the spurs."

"Hell, Baby Man, I'm a professional."

When he hung up, oddly enough, I felt lonely.

· · ·

Before arriving in Camp Rapture I had made a detour to get my handful of things from Houston where I had them in storage, and then I had made a detour to visit Booger.

I call Booger a friend, but I'm not really sure I mean it. He may be more of an attachment, like a growth of some sort. It was like I told Dad. I want to get rid of him, cut him out, but there are complications and attachments.

Booger makes me nervous. He makes everyone nervous.

Booger has a real first and last name, but he doesn't go by them and doesn't like either mentioned in polite society. He isn't the kind of guy you take to a fancy tea. You tell him not to handle all the sandwiches, open them up to see what was inside, he might shove your head in the punch bowl and hold you there till you drowned, then piss on the carpet on his way out.

He lacks patience.

He's not tall, but he's thick and vigorous, and has a shiny shaved head the color of a penny. Racially, he's marooned somewhere between black guy and honky, with a slightly Asian cast to his eyes. In Iraq, the handful who liked him called him the Copper Cat.

He's the kind of guy who's not averse to scratching his privates in public or beating a smartass near to death with a car antenna, which he nearly did once. No one remembers the source of the disagreement that led to the beating, not even Booger, though he has a faint memory about an argument over a game of horseshoes. And though two witnesses saw him give the beating, they had a sudden loss of sight and memory when it came time for them to give information to the law.

They get free beer for life at Booger's bar now, or at least it's offered. According to Booger, they don't actually come around and hang out, not after what they saw in the parking lot. The guy Booger got onto, they found him out near the town dump with his pants pulled down and the antenna pretty far up his ass, minus lubricant, and he was running a low-grade fever and hallucinating. He lived, but he developed a solid case of memory loss himself, told some insane story about being attacked and raped by a roving band of belligerent homosexual Bible salesmen. He drives a car that won't get radio; missing an antenna.

Around his little town of Hootie Hoot, Oklahoma, the cops make a point of leaving Booger alone. To them, he's like the big bad ghost that lives on the hill, in the back of his bar.

Before I had come to Camp Rapture, I had been hanging out with Booger at his gun range, and then his bar. And though me and him are on good terms, it's always a little precarious when we're in the process of bonding. A certain shift of light, a fart blow in his direction, and he could go off the beam faster than a Baptist preacher in Las Vegas with a pack of ribbed condoms and the church funds in his pocket.

Booger had never gone off on me, but I had seen his eyes narrow and his mouth twitch from time to time, and I made a habit to watch for any telltale signs when we were together, minded my Ps and Qs around him and wondered why I bothered at all; that bother is something I keep coming back to, investigating and arriving nowhere.

I suppose it's our Iraq connection. That kind of thing, making war together, gives us a link; sometimes, for me, that link is like a ball and chain. Booger, in many ways, has yet to quit fighting the war. Originally, he moved his inborn hatred of just about everybody from Oklahoma to Iraq, and now that he was home again, shooting squirrels and deer didn't do it anymore. He kept hoping they'd call him back to Iraq. He liked the smell of blood, the charred odor of burning corpses. He liked being shot at. He told me so. He was that soldier who gave the rest of us a bad name.

It's possible he could go to Iraq again. They're taking anyone who can fog up a mirror these days. But last word from the military was they hated to see him go, but sort of had to let him, which gives you some idea of where Booger is on the reenlistment charter. They were beginning to suspect he might have killed some of our soldiers, ones he deemed weak, pussies not driven to take enough lives and enjoy the pleasure. They called it friendly fire, and he was suspected, but if it was Booger, one thing I can assure you, it wasn't friendly. I hoped it was just a rumor. I had to believe it was.

For some reason Booger forgave my not being gung ho about killing. I did what I had to do. When I killed, I felt as if I had collected the souls of the dead, and they were heavy, a weight I didn't want to carry. Booger knew how I felt, but in me he didn't see it as a weakness. Coming from me, somehow, it was novel, a point of interest that intrigued him, like watching a dog leap through a ring of fire in the circus. In others, thoughts of compassion for the enemy or civilians, doubts of purpose and feelings of guilt would have been suspect and common. I was Booger's soft spot, his Achilles' heel. He had saved my life more than once in Iraq. Maybe he thought of me as a pet.

When I had seen him last, we had gone to his gun range. Guns are a passion of his. Shooting things with big guns so he can see them blow up, shooting them until they grow smaller and smaller and finally become one with the universe, that's a big part of his life. He even has old cars out there and he has the big guns with the big bullets, as I have heard him say, and he likes to shoot those cars with the big bullets and see how things jump to pieces. The flying sparkle of those pieces in the sunlight is like a religious experience for Booger. In their quick bright bursts, it's as if he sees the face of, and hears the voice of, the god of war.

After the gun range, the bar was Booger's little slice of heaven. It's no more than a mile from his range. And it's where he offered me a job. But like everything else with Booger, even had I been interested, it came with complications.

Way I got the offer was we shot stuff up with the big guns and then went into the bar. When we came in, sitting on a stool was a very fine-looking Hispanic woman wearing a pair of shorts so small and tight, way she was sitting, at first I thought she wasn't wearing any pants, just a tight white blouse and some flip-flops. It was a thrilling moment, until she shifted and I saw the blue jean shorts, cut so thin and so far up her butt that the denim had to be tickling the back of her tongue.

"How you doin'?" Booger said to the woman. He grinned at her and patted her on the back. "You still ballin' for money?"

"I ain't won no lottery yet," she said. "You lookin' to clean your pipes, Booger?"

"Maybe later, or if not me, Cason, my buddy."

"No thanks," I said.

"He's kind of shy, ain't he?" the woman said.

"Naw, he's just polite, Conchita."

Booger picked us a table, got us both a cold beer and brought them back and put them down in front of us. He sat down and grinned and said, "You sure you want to go back to Texas?"

"Why wouldn't I?"

"What about that hot little Mexican meal over there? Ain't that got no enticement? You could stay, shack up for a few days. I'll pay. She'll turn you every way but loose, that I can guarantee you. She's finished with you, you won't know which end your asshole's on."

"Booger, I don't know how to turn down such an appetizing and aptly phrased offer, but I'm going to pass."

Conchita had the ears of a fox. She said, "What? You don't like some pussy?"

"It's very nice actually," I said, "and I'm a big fan, but I'm going to have to pass. Thank you."

"It's a racial thing," she said.

"No," I said.

"Hey," Booger said. "Don't diss my boy with that. He hangs with me, don't he? Ain't nobody knows what I am, not even me. The only color pussy comes in is pink, honey."

"There you have it," I said to Conchita.

Booger turned back to me, looked perplexed. "You haven't gotten a taste the red eye, have you? Something go on in the showers in Iraq I don't know about?"

"No. But I'd rather go home."

"Man, anyone would rather drive to Texas than fuck in Oklahoma, that do be on the confusing side, partner."

"That's kind of homo," Conchita said.

"Naw, he ain't no homo," Booger said, feeling it necessary to leap to my defense. Then he turned back to me and shook his head. "Texas. Man, why? It looks like right where you are now. Texas is just the ass end of Oklahoma."

"East Texas. Lots of big trees and plenty of water. It's better to me."

"So it looks like here with trees and a fucking lake. Stick here with me."

"I got a job interview."

"That newspaper shit?"

"That's the stuff."

"It's really that Gabby gal, ain't it?"

"I think that's over."

"No you don't. And I'll tell you now, bubba, you ought to drop her like a hot rock. I mean, hell, she dropped you. Come on, man. Stick."

"I'm going to pass, buddy."

Booger ran his slightly damp hand over his scalp. "I could make you a partner in the range," Booger said. "You could run it when I'm not there."

"You're always there. Only reason you're not there now is it's dark, and if the moon was full, you'd be there."

"I'd be there if it was half full."

I knew this was true. Booger was the kind of guy that always had a weapon on him, and he carried a duffel bag in his car that had weapons in it, including a rifle you could put together with nothing more than the edge of a coin and a determined attitude. Even had a silencer, and of course plenty of ammunition. I don't know why he needed the rig or what he used it for, and I didn't want to know.

"So, what you say, you gonna stay?"

"Thanks, Booger. But no."

"The bar, you could run the bar."

"You have Runt to run the bar."

"I could fire Runt."

Runt was about six-five with a shock of blond hair, a chest like a fifty-five-gallon drum, and two and a half teeth—the latter being snaggled from taking a tire iron in the mouth. I didn't get the details, but the guy who hit him was a traveling salesman for industrial vacuums from Arkansas. Booger said Runt just grinned some ragged teeth at the guy and told him he should have brought a Tootsie Roll instead of a tire iron, because they were a lot easier to eat.

I was glad I wasn't there. I wouldn't have wanted to see it or know about it, at least not firsthand. It all happened in the parking lot, same place where Booger had inserted the antenna. Bottom line is, somewhere in Arkansas, a vacuum cleaner company is missing a salesman.

"I don't think I'd want to be the one that told Runt I was taking his place."

"Oh, hell," Booger said. "I'll tell him."

"No. That's all right."

"How about another beer?"

"I've had all I want of this one. I'm about to get behind the wheel."

"Hell, you could drink three or four of those before you needed to worry."

"No thanks."

Booger looked at me in that way that made me hope I hadn't somehow offended his hospitality; it was that little shift I saw in his eye that made me decide, right then and there, I had had enough of Booger.

I got up and smiled and stuck out my hand.

Booger stood up. He shook my hand like he was pumping water, then slapped me on the back.

"Damn, boy," he said. "We had us some time over there, didn't we?"

"We did," I said, remembering it a whole lot less fondly.

"I miss getting up every day and looking forward to blowing some Man Dress out of his knickers."

"Well, got to go," I said.

"You missing out," Conchita said. "I got some business, baby. I can shoot Ping-Pong balls out of it. I had some, I'd show you."

"As enticing as that is," I said, "I'm going to leave." I turned to Booger. "Okay, man. I'm out of here."

Booger grabbed me and hugged me, shifting one of my ribs a little. "You need anything, call me."

"I will," I said.

"Good."

As I started out, Runt yelled, "See you, Cason."

"So long, Runt."

"Hey," Conchita said.

I turned. "Yeah."

"You don't say bye to me?"

"Bye."

She shifted on the stool, smiled, said, "You ever want some stinky on your dinky, you know where to show. And maybe you bring some Ping-Pong balls, I can show you that trick, man."

"I'll certainly give it some thought."

I went away then, hoping, praying, I'd never see any of them again.

Well, maybe Conchita.

But now that I had heard Booger's voice on the phone, I felt a strange kind of yearning to see the crazy bastard. And the fact that I wanted to bothered me.

Back at the paper, I forced myself to write a column that had nothing to do with Caroline Allison. I wrote a moderately humorous piece on how much I had loved Tarzan when I was young. Jimmy had got me thinking on this. I told about being up in the tree in my underwear and getting sunburned, but I left the part out about my cooked testicles. A mention of that would have had Baptists on the paper's doorstep, all of them carrying pitchforks and yelling Bible verses.

When I typed my last line and glanced up, there was Belinda. She looked good, and I got the distinct impression that she had just finished dabbing on fresh makeup. She had a way of wearing it light, so that it didn't hide her freckles. I liked that. I liked those freckles.

"Is that offer of a coffee after work still good?" she said.

"Absolutely," I said.

"Could we make it drinks instead of coffee?"

"Absolutely."

16

I went to see Mom and Dad and drank some coffee with them in their kitchen and told them about my new job, and tried to dress my life up as much as I could without making everything seem like one big, obvious damn lie. I mentioned that I was seeing someone, or at least I was about to, and I think that pleased them. Nobody said the Gabby word, and I tried to make sure they knew, without saying it, that I had moved on and that she was a thing of the past.

I hadn't moved on, of course, but I wanted them to think I had, and while I was telling that whopper, I wanted to believe it myself.

I finished the coffee and Dad and I talked a little about baseball, then Mom and I talked about Belinda. I told her just enough to satisfy her, and not enough to get her worked up into thinking we were about to elope and start making grandchildren, then I left.

As I came to the curb, was about to reach for my car door, instinctively I looked up in the elm. Jazzy was up there on her little platform.

"Hi, Jazzy," I said.

Jazzy swung out on a limb and twisted and hung upside down and clung there like a sloth, dangling her head backward and looking down at me.

"Hi Mr. Statler's little boy," she said. "I was hiding from you."

I grinned at her. "You going to stay up in that tree?"

"I like it up here," she said. "You don't live here no more?"

"I've moved."

"I wish I could move."

"Do you?"

"Can I come stay with you?" Jazzy asked, swinging back around until she was stretched out across the limb like a long lizard.

I slowly shook my head. "Sorry, Jazzy. You can't."

"Why not?"

"The law, for one thing. They won't let you. It's complicated, kid."

"I see." She didn't, of course. "You going to come back?"

"Soon. Right now I have to go."

"What you going to do?"

"I have a date."

"With a girl?"

"Yep. With a girl."

"Some guys date guys. I seen it once on television. They aren't supposed to."

"Can't say as I care one way or another."

"Guess I'll see you when you come back."

"Sure will. And kid, you need anything, you go see my mom and dad. They'll help you out."

"You're my best friend, Cason."

I found it hard to say anything for a long moment. "Okay," I said. "We'll be good friends."

"I like you," she said.

"Friends should like one another. You play safely, okay?"

She nodded and I got in my car and drove away from there.

I fought against it, but I wheeled by Gabby's clinic. Her car was gone and the place was locked up tight, but something about driving by gave me a boost, then a few minutes later the boost went away and I felt my stomach go as sour as if I had eaten something rotten.

I went home and had another cup of coffee. I was beginning to get a little tight on caffeine, felt as if my hair was going to detach from my head and weave itself into a potholder. I decided after drinking yet another cup, then half of another, that I ought to quit. I poured my last bit of coffee in the sink and rinsed out the cup and put it in the dishwasher.

After showering and brushing my teeth, I got dressed and made ready to meet Belinda. She called and said she was back at the paper, doing something or other, and would I come by there and follow her home and could we go in my car.

I went to the paper and followed her home and she parked her car and I drove us to a hotel bar, which she suggested. She had a fruity drink of some sort. I had a beer, which helped mellow out my caffeine, and we talked.

"I like your hair, long like that," she said.

"And I like yours too."

"It's not longer."

"But I like it. You've done something different with it."

"I had it recut. A few extensions added. Last time, my hairdresser tried something that didn't work and I tried to fix it myself, and that really messed things up. I looked like someone had cut it with a Weed Eater. But I went to someone new and they did a better job."

"You added extensions but it's shorter?"

"Don't try and figure the mysteries of women's hairdressing, it'll just give you a headache. Basically, to fix it, I had to cut it short, add extensions that helped it look better than it did, but they are shorter than my hair was before I cut it."

"I like it," I said. "That's all I'll say."

"That's the safe thing to say. It was expensive, I can tell you that. On my pay, too expensive. It cost me an arm and a leg, and once a day I have to go see the hairdresser and wipe her ass."

I grinned at her. "Well, it still looks good."

Unconsciously, she moved her hair a little with her hand. "You don't look like a happy man, Cason."

"I just try and look that way so I'll seem mysterious."

"You have that part down," she said. "You're mysterious, all right. What I wonder is, when you got back from Iraq, why didn't you go back to Houston and work there? What in the world could a little rag like the *Report* hold for you?"

"There's Mrs. Timpson. She's a peach. And Oswald. I guess it's the friendship that I find most rewarding."

"You got the job because everything Oswald writes is as dry as Mrs. Timpson's cunt."

"Do I sense some bitterness?" I asked.

"Oswald got the reporter job I should have gotten."

"Ah ha. You aren't just a nice pretty girl with a good heart."

"Damn right, I'm not. Hey, you know what? You managed to change the subject."

"From?"

"Why you came to work here instead of a larger paper."

"How about the weather? I like the weather here. That could be the reason. How about this? Houston smells bad and there's all that traffic."

"I can understand that being a reason. But I can't understand it being THE REASON."

"My parents are here. My brother and his wife. That's a lot to do with it."

"But not all?"

"All right," I said. Straight shot. "I got fired from the paper in Houston."

"Ouch. I heard you almost won a Pulitzer. That ought to have been a pretty strong recommendation for keeping you on."

"I don't know about almost won. I got a nomination. The firing had nothing to do with my writing, my performance at the paper." I hesitated only a moment, came out with it. "Thing is, my editor, I had a thing with his wife."

"That'll do it."

"It will. And when you have a thing with his stepdaughter, that does it even more. I got it from both ends. The wife and him. No one was happy with me. And that includes me. But I do want to add that neither wife nor daughter were innocents in all this, and the daughter was a grown woman."

She picked a cherry out of her drink and ate it in such a way as not to get it in her braces. "Are you wiser now?"

"I don't know."

"Are you looking to bang me?"

"I believe this is where I say 'I beg your pardon?' "

"Is that why you took me out?"

"No . . . well, of course it crossed my mind."

"If it hadn't crossed your mind," she said, "I would have been disappointed. I thought I might let you. But that's all hypothetical, of course."

"Of course."

"Would it be stupid of me to ask you to take me to dinner?"

"I like a woman who knows her mind."

· · ·

We went to a place that was a kind of cross between a club and a honky-tonk. There was a hipster country band up front with a pretty female singer at the microphone, and there were a few people dancing. It wasn't a big place, but they had some good steaks.

We ate and drank, and pretty soon we danced. I pulled in close to Belinda and we swayed to the music. Her breath was on my neck. It was sweet and warm. When the song finished, we took each other's hands and headed for the door.

It was odd, but we didn't go to her place and we didn't go to mine. Which was probably a good thing. I doubt the aroma of rotting rat in the wall would have been conducive to romance.

I drove us back to the hotel where we had had our drink, and without trying to hide anything, I rented us a room and we took the elevator up. The door to our room wasn't closed good before we were at one another, practically tearing our clothes off.

Belinda and I fell onto the bed, went together hard and quick. When that was done, we went at it slow, taking our time, enjoying ourselves, prolonging it. Belinda had to ask me to kiss softer, because her braces were cutting her. She said I was bleeding on my upper lip. I kissed softer. Finally it all ended, and I felt as if I had washed up on some distant shore beneath cool moonlight and the sound of the ocean, but it was the light through our window, from the patio below, where a jazz band was playing softly. We lay in each other's arms, kissing gently from time to time. Then at some point we closed our eyes and slept.

We awoke late morning, and though I really didn't have to do it, I called on my cell into work, said I wouldn't be coming in today, that I wasn't feeling up to snuff. Then Belinda called on her cell, saying she was sick. "They're going to put two and two together," she said.

"Let them. They don't know for sure, and they can't fire us for what they don't know. Hell, anyone can get sick."

"Are you sick?" she asked.

"Lovesick."

"Really?"

"Well, there are signs."

"I'm just afraid that seeing me now, in the daylight, naked, you'll feel like those guys who wake up and realize it was closing time that made a woman look good, and that they've discovered they've gone home with the college mascot, a goat."

"You look better in the morning light. And I wasn't drunk. But you know what would be nice?"

"What?" she asked.

"If you could make goat noises."

Belinda laughed, reached out and touched my lip gently with her finger. "Your lip is swollen some, from the kissing."

"It was worth it."

"I get this wire out of my mouth in a couple weeks, maybe three. I'll be less dangerous then."

"And you won't be picking up radio stations anymore."

She gave a thin grin. "Do you know how many times I've heard that?"

"Bunches?"

"Bunches on bunches with bunches thrown in."

We ordered up some breakfast. Belinda stayed in bed, and I put on my pants and took the tray at the door. I balanced the tray in bed and we ate. When we finished we put the tray aside and found each other again. We went at it that way, off and on, fueling up for another run until it was nearly time to check out of the hotel.

"I'm going to go in half a day," Belinda said. "Unlike you, the big-shot columnist, I don't really get sick leave. Not paid anyway. And I have a set time to be there."

"Damn. I didn't think about that. Sorry to make you miss."

"Don't be. I liked what I was getting last night and today just fine. But I want you to know, and believe me, I don't just jump in bed with people, not on the first date, and sometimes not after several dates. It's not that I'm against sex, as you can confirm, but I don't want you to think I'm flopping for anyone with a pulse. You were special."

"I never thought anything of the sort," I said. "You sure you're going to work?"

"I am."

"You're a doll and a real trouper," I said. "But me, I have sick leave without time gained, and it is oh so sweet."

She whacked me with a pillow. "Dirty devil," she said, and giggled like a little kid.

I grabbed her and pulled her to me and we kissed, gently. When I let her go, I said, "Give my regards to Oswald."

Back at my place I began to think I would have been better off going to work. Sitting there, I started thinking about Jimmy and his blackmail problem. I looked toward my bookshelf where the DVD was hidden, and had a strange urge to pop it into the player and look at it again, but didn't. The idea of seeing Caroline was okay, but to see my brother mounting her was disconcerting.

The activity of the night before finally caught up with me. I leaned back in my La-Z-Boy and cranked up the footrest and closed my eyes. I replayed in my head all Belinda and I had done, fore and aft. I felt my feelings shifting toward her and they felt the same way as when they had shifted toward Gabby. It gave me pause. It scared me. I didn't feel trustful of anyone or anything anymore. Especially myself. I drifted off to sleep, and then my cell phone rang. By the time I got myself awake and found my cell it had quit ringing.

I looked at the number to see who called. It was Jimmy. I called him back. It rang once and he answered.

"I just got instructions," he said. "They want ten thousand dollars."

"Ten thousand dollars. That's it?"

"Yep. That's it. And believe me, that's enough."

"When?" I asked.

"Tonight. Look, I'm standing in my office. I'd rather talk later, face-to-face. My last class is at three today. Can I come by your place?"

"You've never been here."

"But I know where it is."

"Okay," I said. "Bring the note."

17

Jimmy and I sat in my little living room and sipped on crummy instant coffee and didn't quite look at one another. He was ashamed and I was ashamed for him.

I was looking at the blackmail note. It was lying on the glass coffee table and I was bent over it, reading what I had already read many times since he brought it over, perhaps expecting to find some code there, and then crack it, but I didn't have any success.

Like the previous note, it had been written with a black marker. But this time the letters were smaller. It read:

TONIGHT. MIDNIGHT. SIEGEL HOUSE. COME IN THE BACK WAY.
BRING TEN THOUSAND DOLLARS OR WE MAIL COPIES OF THE DVD
TO EVERYONE. COME ALONE. DON'T FUCK WITH US. WE MEAN
BUSINESS.

Jimmy sniffed at the air. "What is that smell?"

"Dead rat," I said.

"That must be me," Jimmy said, "because I'm starting to feel like that's what I am. A dead rat."

"Perhaps," I said, tapping the note. "But now we know we're dealing with more than one."

"That's what we usually means," Jimmy said. "I'm going to tell you something, bro. I haven't got ten thousand. I mean, it's in the bank, but I can't get it. It's under both our names, me and Trixie. I could go up there and pull it out, but Trixie would know pretty damn soon. She does, I might as well have just let them show the video. Hell, hire out a movie theater and serve popcorn, then lay my balls on a chopping block and give Trixie an axe and draw a line on my nuts with a marker."

"Something about this whole thing doesn't add up."

"What do you mean?" Jimmy asked. "It adds up to about ten thousand dollars. That's what it adds up to. And they are trying to show they know the connection by having me meet them where Caroline disappeared. Oh, it adds up all right."

"Whoever took Caroline probably murdered her," I said. "That adds up. But why now? This DVD is months old. Why has it taken so long for them to want money?"

"Everyone wants money. Now or later."

"Thing is, though, they've gotten away with the crime and no one has a lead, so why surface now? What's the gain?"

"Again, the money. You said it yourself. It's perfect. They got away with the crime, and now I look good for it, and on top of that, they can pick up some cash. Sounds reasonable to me."

"But still, why wait so long?"

"Could have been in prison for some other crime. Or the loony house. Who knows? Thing is, they got the DVD somehow, and they want the money."

"So there's no money?"

Jimmy shook his head. "I thought about selling some things. I've got stuff I could get rid of. Motorcycles, a couple of old cars, things like that. But I couldn't manage to sell it before midnight."

"That would probably just be the beginning anyway. It's never enough money, and you can't be certain you'll get all the copies of the DVD back."

"Yep," Jimmy said. "That's what I been thinking."

"The police are starting to sound like the better deal, Jimmy. It would be rough for you, but it would be the right thing to do."

"These blackmailing assholes. They shouldn't be able to do that, kill people. And they shouldn't be able to ruin my life, even if I did make a mistake. They ought to be stopped. And there's a way."

I looked at him. There was a sudden gnawing in my stomach that wasn't hunger. "What way is that?"

"You know."

"No. I don't know. You got something, let's hear it."

"If something happened to them—"

"Wait a minute, brother mine. That don't work for me. No, sir. Not at all. Not even a little bit."

"You've killed before."

"In the service of our country. And by accident when I was trying to serve our country."

"Accident?"

"I'd rather not go into it. Let me just say you get a little trigger-happy. Something moves when you're expecting something to move, or even when you aren't, you tend to shoot before asking questions. Good guy, bad guy. The results are still the same. Someone gets handed their ass."

"I hear you, Cason. I'm not saying this lightly. I actually gave it some thought."

"Sounds like it."

"The law, they catch a killer, what are they gonna do?"

"Try them."

"That's right. And if they find them guilty, what they're gonna do is put a needle up their arm, after costing the taxpayers a lot of money to house and feed and clothe them until they do."

"You're worried about the legal system wasting money, suddenly? Some guy on death row is taking food out of your mouth?"

"I'm just saying. That's the way it would work. Hell, they might even get off. Get some slick lawyer and they might not get put to death. Might even pull an O.J., get turned loose, or just end up in prison."

"What you're worried about is Trixie and everyone else knowing you were riding Caroline like a bicycle, so don't come off all pious."

"I admit it. But it wouldn't be any loss if these killers bit the big one."

I looked at him. He looked earnest and eager.

"I asked you the other day if you had anything to do with Caroline missing, and I didn't like asking it, but it was just a technical question. I was sure I knew the answer, and the answer was no. That was what you said."

"And it's true."

"But now you're talking about killing the blackmailers easy as if you were talking about making an omelet."

"It's not the same kind of thing, and you know it."

"Close enough for government work," I said. "And I've done government work. Here are some problems. That's vigilantism. It's against the law. We get caught, we go to jail. Maybe we get the needle. Maybe we don't have the smart lawyer who can get us off. And here's another thing. You've never killed anyone."

"I've killed deer. I've killed moose, and even a bear. I go hunting all the time, all over the country. Mounted them myself. Their heads are on my wall at the house."

"They weren't human. And they couldn't fight back. At least you didn't give them a chance to fight back. Hunting doesn't impress me. Maybe you ought to give the little forest animals a rest. A killer, he, she, it, them, they may fight back in a way you don't expect. And I have killed humans. It isn't the pleasant and wonderful thing you think it is. Even if you think the ones you killed deserve it. It comes back on you. Blowback. I think about the people I killed every day. And that was for my country. That's what I was paid to do. That's what I was asked to do. And worse yet, I was good at it."

"Isn't this for a purpose? Doing these jerks?"

"To not embarrass you? To make sure you keep your marriage and your job? Stay respectable? Hard for me to get worked up enough to think killing for that is a good idea. The answer is no."

"I was just thinking out loud."

"Too loud."

"I was thinking about Mom and Dad finding out."

"That's something all right, but it was mostly yourself you were thinking about."

He looked angry, but it didn't hold. After a few moments, he said: "What do we do then?"

"In all that junk you got you could sell, do the motorcycles work?"

"Yeah."

"I know you prefer to shoot animals with guns, but do you have anything that takes pictures of them at night?"

"What?"

"Something that can take a night picture, a good picture without light?"

Jimmy shook his head. "No. But I got a friend, a fellow at work, and he believes in Bigfoot."

"Bigfoot?"

"Yeah. You know."

"Yeah, I know. What's that got to do with anything?"

"He has night cameras. He's always trying to get a snap of Bigfoot taking a dump in the woods, or some such thing. He sets the cameras in places where he thinks it comes. He ends up with pictures of deer and mice and raccoons, but he's sure Bigfoot is out there, even if he hasn't shown up yet."

"Can you borrow a camera?"

"I think so. And he's got some recording equipment too. Stuff you can put in one spot and hear what's going on some distance away, get it recorded. He's got everything. But I'll have to make up a story for him."

"Well, make up one. Even if you have to tell him you're hunting Bigfoot."

"I say that, he'll want to go."

"Here. Here's the story. Tell him you think your neighbor's dog is digging under your fence, digging in your flower beds."

"We don't have flower beds."

"He knows that, make it something else. Tell him the dog is shitting in your yard. But tell him you want to set the camera up to prove to your next-door neighbor that it's his dog, not an armadillo, as he says."

"I got you."

"So you get the camera, and we set it up tonight, and then we get pictures of them. We have photos of them, and they know we can connect them back to the blackmail scheme and the murder, they may be hesitant. We reverse it on them."

"Yeah, man. That's a good idea."

"We'd need the equipment soon, as in quick soon. And the motorcycles, gassed up and ready to go. Time-wise we'd have to be way ahead of the blackmailers."

"How would we know if we're ahead of them? They could be there right now, waiting until midnight."

"If they are, they're likely to be seen. They probably wouldn't want to take that chance. They'll wait at least until it's dark."

"What about us? Now we'll be more likely to be seen."

"That's a chance we'll have to take."

Jimmy had to tell some lies to Trixie to do what we wanted to do, but I figured the lies he told her now were no worse than the lies he told her before. The lie was we were going camping. A brother gig. Hanging. Chatting about old times. It was the middle of the week, but Jimmy arranged for the next day off, gave his class a free day. And me, I could go in late.

Jimmy borrowed the night camera, got a few other things we needed from his friend. While he did that I figured on a plan I thought might work, but I can't say as I felt real confident. It wasn't that good a plan, but it was some kind of plan, and that mattered.

Whatever might come, we were as ready as we were ever going to be.

In Motion

18

We got there late afternoon and went into the woods above the house at the summit of the hill. The woods were thick, but there wasn't much of it. It was hot and we had to sit down to rest because the trees held the heat and it was hard to breathe. There were hordes of mosquitoes and flies.

We had come on a couple of Jimmy's motorcycles. We had our camping equipment and the surveillance equipment strapped over the backs of the bikes. We broke out the pup tent and set it up and pulled the mosquito net down and secured the bar at the bottom of the tent against the ground. The way we placed the tent, we had a view through the net and through a little clearing in the pines, a straight-shot look down the hill. It was close in the tent with the two of us, and the trees were tight around us, and that made it warmer, but it really wasn't too uncomfortable. We had a pair of binoculars, and from time to time Jimmy put them to his eyes and glanced down at the Siegel house.

"What are you, General Patton?" I said. "Give those things a rest."

"I don't think they're there," he said.

"You said that already. Maybe ten times."

"Well, I just want to make sure."

"You know what I think? I think these guys are amateurs, and I think they see a way to make some bucks, that's what I think. And I don't think they're going to show early. They figure they got you by the balls, and they do. So they're going to wait until time and then they'll show, and you will show, and I will have the camera, and I will get them on film."

"By the way," Jimmy said, "did I mention we too are amateurs?"

"No. You didn't. But you're right. Still, I think we have the edge. They did something to Caroline, got away with it, it was most likely an accident. Now they've gotten greedy, and that could be their downfall."

"That's why you think they're amateurs?"

"That's why."

Jimmy scratched his chin, gave me a hard look. "And what happens when I don't have the money?"

"That part is tricky," I said.

"Since it will be my ass on the line, perhaps you could lay out the plan a little more clearly."

"I told you already."

"I got it down, but I don't like it. I keep hoping for more. Way it is now: They ask for the money. I say go fuck yourself, I haven't got any money. My brother is on the hill with a camera that has a telescopic lens and he's filming you. And if you don't believe us, we can swap a DVD with you tomorrow for the one you got. How am I doing?"

"Swell."

"Now, here comes my question. Why would they care? They got the good DVD, and all we'll have is a film of me and them standing around down there by the Siegel house. For all anyone can tell, me and them are going to sit down and have a circle jerk, see who can shoot it the farthest."

"That's why you will have the wire and I will have the recorder, and that's why you will say they do anything to you, it's on film and recorded, and I've got both."

"What if they don't believe me?"

"Talk your talk, and then point up the hill. I'll flash my flashlight at them in confirmation. You just have to talk some good doo-doo, brother."

"I still think we ought to do what needs to be done."

"Don't go there again, Jimmy. I'm not up for it. Not even a little bit. I'm here to help you, I got to believe you're not going to give me grief. We don't try and do anything to hurt them."

"What if they just decide to shoot me, then come up the hill after you?"

"I will run like the wind."

"I will still be dead."

"That is true, but I will tell heroic tales of your death for as long as I live."

We lay there in the pup tent, passing the binoculars back and forth, watching the house and all around the hill, as if Jimmy's blackmailers might come crawling up through the vines. The sun moved overhead and fell westward. The mosquitoes buzzed against the net, and a blackfly about the size of a pterodactyl lit at the center of the net and lay there as if waiting for us to make a move.

I thumped the fly and it flew off. I showed him. He wasn't so scary.

The falling sun had begun to cause a big shadow to stand out to the side of the house and it made the vines there dark as a pit. The sun melted bright red on the west side of the woods, and some of the rays from it came through and lay over us and made everything appear as if we were seeing it all through a red cellophane lens.

Then the redness sank down and the dark rose up. I checked my glow-in-the-dark watch. It was eight p.m.

"Only four hours to go," I said.

"Shit," Jimmy said. "That's like an eternity."

An hour or so later we had a false start when a car parked down at the bottom of the hill near a tall pine and a guy got out on the passenger side, stood in the darkness of the tree. From the way he stood, and from what little the moonlight showed us, we could tell it was just some guy stopping to pee. When he finished, he got back in the car, and his buddy at the wheel drove them away.

It was kind of like a signal. We got out of the tent and found a place for us to do the same. When we finished, we got back in the tent, behind the skeeter net, which was a good thing. The mosquitoes were really thick now and I had a dozen bites on me, all of them acquired during the time I was taking a leak. The crickets were very busy and there were so many of them, it sounded like someone sawing wood. Inside the tent, listening to them, protected from the mosquitoes, it was almost soothing.

We talked for a while, and when that played out, we took turns nodding off. About ten-thirty we heard a noise behind us, and it occurred to me that our blackmailers would probably come up on the house the way we did, from the top of the hill, or to be more precise from the opposite side of the hill and through the woods. They weren't on motorcycles, though, and they weren't coming up the trail alongside the woods the way we had come. They were walking along a trail on the opposite side. We could hear them whispering, and we could hear limbs being pushed aside not too carefully, and then someone, a woman, cursed, and Jimmy and I looked at each other in the dark.

We pushed the mosquito net up and eased out of the pup tent. We sat in front of it and were quiet.

The two people were not quiet. They were louder, now, and we could see them as two human-shaped shadows walking between a crooked row of trees and scraggly brush. If they had looked to their left, and had they really been watching for us, they would have seen us.

They fought the limbs some more, and I realized then that they hadn't really scoped things out before coming out here. I was even more certain, now that I could see their shapes and hear their voices, that they were young. Not kids, but young.

Finishing off the trail, coming out of the woods, they started down the hill, two shapes with the moon fully outlining them and the house below, the vines looking like some kind of strange dark ocean, the waves frozen, the house being the biggest, darkest frozen wave of all.

They walked down to the gravel behind the house and stopped there for a moment. They were wearing light coats. It was way too hot for coats. The guy leaned over and kissed the girl on the cheek, then they slid in close and held each other for a while.

After a moment, they broke apart and went on down to the house. They worked at the vine-covered door for a long time, and then it came open and they slipped inside.

"I don't know," Jimmy said. "I don't know what to do."

"It isn't midnight yet. Just wait. Could just be a couple grabbing a quickie."

We lay there in the tent behind the skeeter net until about eleven-thirty. No one else had shown.

"I can't believe it," Jimmy said. "That has got to be them."

I looked at my watch. "Still half an hour. Someone else could show. In the meantime, I think we ought to wire you up."

We got out of the tent, and while we fought mosquitoes, we put the receiver on his belt and pulled his shirt down over it. The way it was set was like a baby monitor. Whatever Jimmy heard, I'd be able to hear up here with a little piece that went in my ear, like one of those walking phones. And I could record it.

When I had him fixed up, he turned on the receiver and said a few words, and I could hear them in my earpiece. I said, "It seems all right. I don't know how it'll work when you're down the hill apiece, but it ought to be fine."

Jimmy went over to his motorcycle. There were saddlebags on it, like a horse. He reached in one of them and took out a pair of gloves and a little snubnosed revolver in a holster that was mostly just a strap with a little belt.

"I thought we went over the gun business," I said.

He came over with another pair of gloves and tossed them at me. "We might end up leaving some print somewhere down there, and we don't want to do that."

At the time, I thought Jimmy was being a little excessive, but later I was glad for the gloves. I pulled them on. When I was finished, I gave him a hard look.

"I still don't like the gun. You can keep ignoring me, but I'm going to keep saying it. The gun, it's not a good idea."

"Don't panic. I'm going to strap it to my ankle. It might be them that loses their cool. They do, I'd like to have a fighting chance."

"They're a couple of kids."

"And maybe," Jimmy said, "they're the couple of kids who killed Caroline, as well as the ones blackmailing me."

"I don't like the gun business."

"Don't worry. I'm not going in blazing. But I don't have any money either. They might take that personally."

"Thing is, you got to get them to come outside," I said. "I can hear you in the house, but I can't see you and I can't film. I need to get their faces on the film. Tell them you left the money outside, hid it up the hill. Anything to get them out of the house. What I'm saying as plain as I can say it is don't go in the house. Don't get out of my sight."

"I'll do what I can."

We climbed back in the tent and waited. Just after midnight, Jimmy and I got out of the tent and I got the camera and made sure my earpiece was in good, and we tested the equipment again. I adjusted the telescopic viewer on the camera and looked down the hill. The infrared view reminded me of the tools I had used in Iraq. Something about that made my skin crawl. I took a deep breath, looked at Jimmy.

"Everything okay?" he said.

"I think so. About that gun."

"I'm cool," Jimmy said. He reached in his back pocket and pulled out a short cylindrical pipe, or at least it looked like a pipe. He flicked his wrist and a narrower, longer piece popped out. It was an asp, an expanding baton. "I also got this."

"Why don't you pull a goddamn cannon down there with you," I said.

"Believe me, I thought about it."

Jimmy looked at the house below, took a deep breath, started walking.

19

I eased over to one of the pines and leaned against it, thinking I would look pretty much like part of it if the blackmailers glanced up the hill. Mosquitoes poked at me and flies attracted to the sweat on my face kept dive-bombing me. I felt like King Kong attacked by aircraft.

I held the camera up and used it to watch Jimmy walk down. He got to the gravel behind the house and stopped. His voice came to me softly, filled my earpiece.

"I'm going to call them out," he said.

I didn't say anything back. It only worked one way. A moment later I heard him call.

"Anyone in the house?"

No answer. Time crawled by like it was dragging a cross up the hill.

"Anyone in the house? Come on out."

I aimed the camera on the back door of the house and waited. After a while it budged open and someone stepped out. It was the guy. He had pulled a ski mask over his face. He walked a few steps toward Jimmy.

"I got backup," the blackmailer said. "I got someone in the house with a gun."

"What you got is a girl and yourself," Jimmy said.

I thought, Don't play it too heavy, brother. Take it easy. A girl can shoot your ass dead good as anybody.

"You got the money?" the male asked.

"Not right on me."

"That's not the deal."

"You got the DVD?" Jimmy asked.

"I got it."

"How do I know it's the only copy?"

"You don't. But I can tell you this much. You don't give us the money, this is going to be sent to people you don't want to see it. Like your wife. The dean at the university. The police department. Everybody. You'll see this sucker on the Internet, YouTube. I promise. We only want the ten thousand. We get that, we'll go away."

"I got to take your word for it?"

"That's the size of it," the blackmailer said. "Now where is the money?"

"You talk tough," Jimmy said, "but you don't look so tough to me."

"We're tough enough. Now, once again, where's the money?"

"I must have left it in my other pants."

"I'm telling you, don't fuck with me."

"Tell your partner to come outside," Jimmy said.

The man hesitated. "You got here early, didn't you?"

Jimmy snorted. "Earlier than you."

"Come out," Ski Mask said. "Come on out. It's all right."

The girl came out. She had on a ski mask too. She moved tentatively up the hill until she was close to her partner.

"You guys don't look like heavyweight blackmailers," Jimmy said. "What you look like are a couple of idiots about to rob their first filling station."

"That doesn't change things," the male voice said. "We got the goods, and we want the money."

"You sound familiar," Jimmy said. "You're disguising your voice, but I know it."

"You just think," the male said, but he didn't sound all that confident.

"No. I know that voice."

"You don't know shit, history teacher."

"How'd you get that DVD?"

"That's our business."

"Caroline. What happened to Caroline?"

"That's not the business we're working right now," the male voice said. Jimmy was right. He was trying to talk brusque. He sounded silly. The whole thing was silly. There didn't seem to be much here that smacked of professionalism. They probably just needed a good spanking.

"Show me the DVD," Jimmy said.

The male reached in his coat pocket and pulled out the DVD. He held it up.

"Quit fucking around," the male said. "Give us the money."

"Let me put this so you'll understand it," Jimmy said. "Give me the DVD, or I'm going to walk over to you and kick your ass up so high, when you need to shit you'll have to move your teeth."

The girl came up the hill a little then. She had pulled a gun from her pocket when I wasn't looking.

"Give him the money, Mr. Statler," she said.

"I got a guy up the hill," Jimmy said.

"Ha!" said the guy in the ski mask.

I pulled my little flashlight out of my pocket and poked it at them and turned it on, blinked it a couple of times.

"He's got a night-vision camera and a recorder taking in all of this," Jimmy said. "He's got a rifle too, and it's trained on you. So girlie, I suggest you put that pistol down."

"Your brother?" said the guy. "He's the one up the hill?"

"That's right. You know a lot about me."

The guy said, "I got this copy, but I got other copies."

"So now I know," Jimmy said.

"And we got a gun," the girl said.

"So you do," Jimmy said.

"We're going to take that money," the guy said.

"You might if I had it with me. But you move toward me, even if you shoot me, my brother up there is going to put a bullet in your heads so fast you'll never even hear the shot that gets you."

The two blackmailers stood their ground.

Jimmy said, "You put that gun down, girlie. Then the two of you stretch out on the ground, or I'm going to start feeling unpleasant. My brother up there, he's got an itchy finger. He'll blow your fucking heads off."

The guy turned toward the girl. He let out with a yell. "Run, baby. Run."

Problem was, they broke in opposite directions. The guy went left, the girl went right. Jimmy leaped toward the girl. His hand flashed out and she screamed. Her gun went sliding across the gravel and she did a somersault and rolled down toward the house and nestled up in the vines like a fly in a web. The guy turned and started running back toward her. He raised his hand above his head, like he was going to strike Jimmy with his fist. Jimmy stepped right into the middle of him and hit him quick with the asp. Hit him right between the legs. The guy went down, his knees folding under him, and then he lay back with his head on the gravel and I could hear him moaning all the way up the hill, and not just through the monitor. Jimmy hit him again, this time in the forehead.

I started down. Jimmy stood over the guy, raised the asp again. I could still hear him on the monitor. "You shit. You fucking shit. Give me the DVD or I'm going to crack your head wide open, then hers."

"Easy, Jimmy," I said, as I came nearer. "Just take it easy."

We made them go inside the Siegel house. It was dark in there, of course, and the only light was from my flashlight. It smelled musty inside and there were lots of spiders on lots of webs and the dust was thick and it came up from the floor when you moved. When I flashed the light around I could see the walls were the color of unchewed snuff. The girl was crying, lying on her side, holding her leg where Jimmy had whacked it with the asp. The guy was sitting with his back against the wall, his knees pulled up, his arms wrapped around them. We had pulled the ski masks off, and where the asp had hit the guy he was bleeding; blood was in his dark hair and running down his face. I tossed him his ski mask back, said, "Wipe your face with that."

The girl had begun to whimper less. I put the flashlight on her. She was pretty, with short blond hair, and thin as a rail.

Jimmy had her gun and he was pointing it at them. The gun business made me nervous. I had seen too many guns and I had seen what they could do, and I had seen how sometimes things happened that wouldn't have happened just because of them.

"Hold it by your side," I said.

Jimmy did that, but he walked back and forth, agitated.

"Where's the goddamn DVD?" he said. "All of them."

"I just got the one," the guy said, and worked it out of his coat pocket. He tossed it to me and I caught it and held it. The guy said, "Can I take off this jacket? It's hot."

"Why did you wear it?" I asked, knowing the answer.

"To keep the DVD and for a disguise," he said.

"You try and pull something besides your arm from out of that coat, and my brother here will put a hole in your head," I said, fearing he might do just that.

"You didn't have a rifle up there, did you?" the kid asked.

"No," I said. "But Jimmy's got your girl's gun now, and he's got one of his own. Don't push him."

"Girlie," Jimmy said, "why don't you take off that coat too, and be careful about it when you do."

She whimpered once, moved to a sitting position and worked the coat off. She was wearing a dark sports bra and she had dark tattoos on her stomach around her navel, all down her arms. I couldn't tell what they were, flowers maybe. She tossed the coat across the floor toward us. She said to Jimmy, "You hurt my leg with that thing. You hurt it bad."

"Forgive me if I don't give a shit," Jimmy said. "Put the light on that boy."

I did.

"Hold your face up," Jimmy said.

The kid did that. He had a red mark between his eyes where Jimmy had whacked him. It wouldn't leave a permanent mark, but it would bruise up.

"Hell, I knew I knew you," Jimmy said. "You're in the history department. I don't know your name, but I know you. You can fucking figure on failing now, 'cause I'll sure think of your name in time."

"I'm not in your classes," the boy said.

Jimmy let out with a laugh. "Well, that saves you, doesn't it?"

The girl bawled some more, paused to say: "I'm scared of spiders."

20

They had come by car, and it was on the other side of the hill. We all walked up the hill and through the woods, the same way they had come, then down the other side to a little dirt road where their car was parked. It wasn't much of a car and looked like the last time it had been washed someone had rubbed it down with sand and waxed it with a hammer.

We made them get in the front seat, the guy behind the wheel. Jimmy and I slid into the back seat and Jimmy waved the gun around a little too much.

"What are we doing?" the guy asked, and he was so scared his voice vibrated.

"Going for a ride," I said. "We want you to take us to your place, where you got the computer that copied the DVD."

"We made copies," the girl said, "but we found the DVD."

I tucked that bit of information away. I said, "What about Caroline Allison?"

"I knew her," the guy said. "She was in the history department with me. I knew her and that's how I came up with this idea."

"Stupid idea," the girl said. She had grown pouty, like a child whose birthday party had been ruined by bullies.

"It was stupid," Jimmy said.

"Yeah," the guy said. "Stupid. But Tabitha needed the money for school."

"Jesus," Jimmy said. "Whatever happened to a student loan?"

"I couldn't get one," she said. "I failed too many classes goofing off."

"Well, I'll be damned," I said. "You needed tuition money, so what better way to get it than to kill some girl and take her DVD of her and the kindly professor here doing the bop and blackmail him with it? That sure beats a student loan, or heaven forbid, working for the money."

"We didn't kill anyone," the guy said. "You know we didn't kill anyone."

He said that like he thought we really did know he didn't do it. And I was pretty sure they hadn't, even if I wasn't sure they were telling the total truth. In fact, I was more than certain they weren't.

"What's your name?" I asked the guy.

"Ernie Smith."

"And you, kid," I said to the girl. "You're Tabitha? Tabitha what?"

"Patrick," she said. "Tabitha Patrick. We're in big trouble, aren't we?"

"What do you think?" I said. "Start up the car and let's go."

Their place was near the hill where Jimmy and I were camped. It was a gray rental house by the railroad tracks with an outside light that didn't work. It was an ugly location and an ugly house. The neighboring houses were a little brighter and better looking, but there was nothing you could do about that location.

Inside, the place was long and narrow like a boxcar and smelled like cat piss, and when Ernie turned on the light, roaches darted for cover but no cats made an appearance. In the front room there was a couch that looked as if it had taken on a few land mines. It was partially draped over with a blanket that had more holes in it than a dartboard. There were a couple of folding chairs, a desk with a computer on it, and the only good chair in the place was the chair at the desk. Tabitha sat on the couch, and after a few minutes so did Ernie. We told Ernie we would be taking the computer.

"I got all my lessons on it," he said. "All my history work."

"You should have thought of that before blackmailing me," Jimmy said.

"You can't go to the police," Ernie said, "not with those DVDs around. That'll nail your ass."

"You're going to give them to us," I said.

"And if we don't?" Ernie said. "What then? There's nothing you can do to us."

"Except put a bullet in your heads," Jimmy said.

Ernie went quiet and put his hands between his legs.

Jimmy was starting to pull at the computer, like he was going to run off with it. I said to him, "Hold on. We're not going anywhere yet."

He stopped pulling, looked at me. I had taken one of the folding chairs and was sitting in it. Jimmy took one of the others and sat down. He still had the girl's revolver and he laid it on his knee.

"Don't hurt us," Tabitha said. "You can take the computer. We just thought it would be fun. And I needed the money. I didn't mean to hurt anyone."

"Sure," Jimmy said.

"How did you come by the DVD?" I asked. "You said you found it, but I'm thinking you didn't go out in the yard and it rained down on you like manna from heaven."

"We're urban explorers," Ernie said. "That's how we found it."

"You're what?" Jimmy asked.

"We like to prowl at night. Get into places that are locked up, preferably without anyone knowing we did it. We go in and take pictures. Used to be several of us. You learn locks, and you watch places to learn where all the ways of getting in are. It's a big game."

"What happened to the other explorers?" I asked.

"They graduated, moved off."

"The original ones," Tabitha said.

There was something in that, but I let it go for the moment.

"I see," I said. "Only thing throws me is, around here, we're sort of short on urban."

"Technically that's right," Ernie said. "But there are plenty of places you don't think about. That's how we came up with the DVD. All the DVDs. We found them."

"All the DVDs?" I said. "You just found them?"

Ernie nodded.

"Where?" Jimmy said.

Before Ernie could answer, Tabitha looked at Jimmy, said, "You killed her, didn't you?"

"What?" Jimmy said.

"Caroline. You killed her."

"Shut up," Ernie said.

"You're out of your mind," Jimmy said. "You killed her."

"No they didn't," I said.

Jimmy looked at me.

I said, "Trust me, they're too stupid to have killed her and set all this up. They're stumblers, and they stumbled on what they thought was good."

"That's right," Ernie said, liking the fact that I seemed to be taking his side; stupidity had its merits.

"If you didn't kill her," Tabitha said, looking at Jimmy as if truly surprised, "who did?"

"I don't know," Jimmy said. "I still like you two for it."

Tabitha became bold. "Well, I think you did it. I think you maybe planned it all along. Maybe you and your brother did it. You look like someone who would be mean to girls. You hit me with that stick."

"Asp," Jimmy said.

"It hurt."

"Hush, Tabitha," Ernie said.

Tabitha stopped talking. I said, "If we did do it, murdered Caroline, you'd be smarter not to let on you think we did. You consider that, Tabitha? You've been quiet most of this time, and now you're talking, and you're not thinking. You were smarter quiet. We were the murderers, you'd be next. You and him. We'd kill your asses right here. Do you really want to die on that filthy couch?"

I could see fear move across her face, and it made me feel small.

"We aren't the murderers," I said. "Listen up. We won't turn you in because that just brings up the DVD, and that hurts my brother. You're right about that part. But you'd be better off not to do anything either. We maybe got all the copies when we take this hard drive, but we don't, you'd be better off just letting us be. You don't want to stir us up."

"That's right," Jimmy said. "We're not for stirring."

I glanced at him out of the corner of my eye, thought: We're not for stirring. What kind of comment was that?

"We got you two on audiotape and film," I said. "Someone shows up with a copy we don't know about, it'll cost them. And when I say someone, I mean you two mental giants. Blackmail, that's no small crime. And, kids, it's going to look more like you did Caroline in than Jimmy. Jimmy here, he gets in the deep end for wetting his willie, but you two . . . I don't think you'd like how it turns out. You might be finishing out your education online in prison. They have that now. So you got that going for you."

Ernie and Tabitha looked at each other. "We didn't mean any harm," Ernie said.

"Sure you did," I said. "And you're not off the hook on Caroline's murder yet."

"We haven't really said anything that matters," Tabitha said. "There's nothing you taped that hurts us."

"Don't be silly," I said. "There's a device in my brother's pocket, and it's on, and I've got the receiver and everything you've said since we started dealing with you is recorded."

"Everything you've said too," Tabitha said.

"Yeah, but we're saying things to trick you. We say what we need to say. And besides, we get in trouble, so do you. It'll be a big cluster fuck."

"I don't know," Ernie said. "You keep saying it, but I don't know you have squat."

I took the recorder and the receiver out of my pocket and put it on my knee. I let him look at it. Jimmy took his part of it out of his pocket. "Surprise, motherfuckers," he said.

"By the way," I said, "I need to change cassettes."

Jimmy grinned at me.

I slipped another cassette in the recorder. I said, "And, we have you on film."

"We had on ski masks," Tabitha said.

"You sure did," I said. "But you weren't skiing. Won't help you a bit. We got too much on you."

I wasn't really sure about that, but I tried to sound confident. "Okay. How well did you know Caroline?"

"We didn't know her well at all," Ernie said.

"Bullshit," Jimmy said. "You already said you knew her."

"We saw her around," Ernie said.

"I'm going to call bullshit again," Jimmy said. "Bullshit."

Ernie looked at Tabitha. She nodded.

"That's better," I said.

I put the recorder on the floor by my chair. I said, "It's very sensitive, but it would still be nice if you didn't whisper. Tell us everything, and make it snappy. I'm starting to crave breakfast and a good cup of coffee."

21

There was a noise at one of the windows. I turned to look. Through a part in the curtains I could see a huge golden moth beating its wings against the pane, trying to work its way to the light. I sympathized.

I turned back to Tabitha and Ernie. I didn't say anything. Ernie just started talking.

"We've been doing the snooping thing something like a year now," he said. "There were several of us at first, all university students. We read about it, about snooping, urban exploring. We thought we'd give it a try. There aren't as many neat places here in Camp Rapture as, say, Houston, or Dallas, but there's more than you think. We scoped out places. We watched to see who had a night watchman, who didn't, what their weaknesses were. We even read about picking locks, which I've gotten pretty good at. We went all over. You'd be surprised the places we've been in."

"All I'm interested in," Jimmy said, "is where you were when you found this DVD, and what's your connection with Caroline."

"There wasn't just one DVD," Ernie said. "We got a bunch of them."

"Of me and Caroline?" Jimmy asked.

"No," Tabitha said. "Of a lot of men having sex with Caroline."

A moment of silence settled on the room. Jimmy looked stunned, as if he'd just discovered one of his legs belonged to someone else and they had asked for it back.

"You're lying," Jimmy said, standing up from his chair, pointing the gun at Ernie.

"Goddamnit, Jimmy," I said. "Put that thing away or I'm going to jam it up your ass. Sit."

Jimmy looked at me, saw I meant it. After a moment he dropped the gun to his side and sat back down in his chair, an angry man with bullets and no place to shoot them.

I said to Ernie, "So there are a bunch of DVDs?"

"Yep," Ernie said.

"Did you get them all?"

"What we could carry," Ernie said. "There were some left. You see, we didn't know what we were getting. Just trying to take a souvenir. We took a look at the DVDs, saw what we had. Figured we could make a little money. We've talked about going back for the others, but we didn't see any real reason. I mean, we weren't even sure the rest of the stuff was the same kind of thing, and besides, we didn't want to be greedy. We had enough here to work up a pretty good head of steam, you know, ten thousand or so a pop."

I studied Ernie's face, looking for any lies there. It was a pretty bland face. I said, "A man once told me he believed in coincidences. I feel the same way. I can accept a lot. But this? Just two college kids who happen to know Caroline find a bunch of DVDs of Caroline screwing people in a building where they are snooping? And even more precious is the fact you left some there, didn't go back to get them when you saw what kind of gold you had. Hell, Ernie. You're going to commit a crime, might as well go the whole hog."

"We didn't want to be greedy."

I let out a laugh. "Now that's choice. That's special. Did you know the others on the DVDs?" I asked.

"History professors. Prominent men about town. Some we didn't know, but we recognized a lot of them."

"Were you blackmailing them?"

Ernie nodded. "Most. We weren't blackmailing the girl, though. We knew her, and knew she didn't have any money."

"What girl?" Jimmy asked.

"Ronnie Fisher," Tabitha said.

"Wait a minute," Jimmy said. "Caroline was on some DVD with a girl?"

"That's right," Tabitha said.

"Making out?" Jimmy asked.

"If eating her snatch like it was a hot taco is making out," Ernie said, "then, yes, I would say they were making out. Also Caroline had one of those big rubber dongs—"

"Dildo," Tabitha said.

"Yeah," Ernie said. "Thanks, hon. One of them. With knots on it. They were putting that in a lot of places. So I guess they were making out, and then some."

"Oh, shit," Jimmy said, as if knowledge of the knots on the dildo was the final straw. "Who the hell is Ronnie Fisher?"

"I know who she is," I said. "I can fill you in later."

"You know?" Jimmy asked.

"Later," I said to him.

"I don't believe it," Jimmy said.

"The DVDs show it," Ernie said. "We've seen her on enough of them we can identify Caroline just by the birthmark on her ass. That ring any bells? A kind of strawberry-shaped birthmark. Almost purple in color. It's something that really shows up on her skin and that nice ass of hers."

"It's a little too big, I think," Tabitha said.

"The birthmark or her ass?" I asked.

"Both," Tabitha said.

"You could have just seen that on my DVD with her," Jimmy said.

"Could have," Ernie said, "but didn't. Trust me, the girl was a rodeo all by herself. She was the bull ride, the calf roping, and maybe even the rodeo clowns. She was a full evening of fun with a trip to the snow-cone stand afterward. She did it all."

"Shut up, punk," Jimmy said, and he looked as if he might be ready to pistol-whip Ernie.

"Cool your jets, Jimmy," I said. "We want the whole story. That's what we're here for."

"He doesn't have to be gleeful about it," Jimmy said. "He likes telling me this shit."

"Your brother asked," Ernie said, pointing at me.

"You're right," I said. "I did. Tell us about Caroline."

"We weren't close," Ernie said. "She was part of our crew, ones who did the exploring. We called ourselves the Subterraneans."

"How many of you were there?"

"Five, maybe six at first. Then Caroline, couple of others for a while. She added the later ones, two guys. Real odd guys, those two. We met her at school, talked a little, maybe too much, and I got to feeling a little too free with things—"

"He liked the way she looked," Tabitha said, and the words were as stiff as a classroom full of boys watching a cheerleader tryout.

"Anyway," Ernie said, "I talked about what we did. She wanted in. It all just seemed like fun then."

"I don't believe that," Jimmy said. "That doesn't sound like her at all. I would have known if she was involved in anything like that. You're making this up."

Ernie shook his head.

Tabitha said, "She could sound a lot of ways. She could fit anywhere she wanted to, or had to. Think about it. Was she with you all the time at night? Wasn't, was she? Slipped away with you at odd moments, am I right?"

Jimmy didn't say anything, but I could tell Tabitha had nailed it.

"Go on," I said to Ernie.

"We were just playing like we were flirting with death, sneaking around, taking pretty mild chances. I mean, if we got caught breaking into buildings we could have gotten in some bad doo-doo, but it wasn't life-threatening if you were careful. I did have a pretty nasty fall once, through the roof of an old rotten building. But I was okay. That was as close as it got. But with Caroline, I got the feeling she was dating death."

"How colorful," Jimmy said.

"You don't know the half of it," Ernie said. "She had this guy she brought around with her. He was right out of someplace just due south of hell."

"More colorful phrasing," Jimmy said. "Perhaps you should move from history to literature. You could make up these kinds of stories and get paid for them."

"He's not making up anything," Tabitha said. "We called him the Geek. She called him Stitch. He wasn't the only guy she brought around either. There was that other one."

I turned my attention to Tabitha. "Who else?"

"Some other guy, a kind of greasy drunk. Always showed up with a six-pack, stinking of liquor, and he had a flask with him. He'd finish off the beers then drink from that. Time it got late, he was feeling no pain."

"How did Caroline act?"

"Exploring for Caroline wasn't a big enough thrill," Tabitha said. "She was always trying to find out where the line was, then step over it. Got so we were, like, you know, taking big chances, not scoping things out like before, not preparing. We just started going right at it. We nearly got caught by a watchman over at the fertilizer plant. We started to have like minor accidents, wasn't as fun as before. We were letting her push us around. She could do it too. Not always directly, but one way or another you found yourself doing pretty much what she wanted."

Ernie nodded agreement, added, "The Geek found a dead cat on the road once. He ran it up the flagpole on campus. It was quite a chance he was taking, that we all were taking, because we were with him, in his van. He parked at the curb and just walked up big as you please and hooked the cat to the rising line, and jacked it up. I thought that was pretty weird. The Geek, he thought that was some funny business."

"How absolutely normal of you to be offended," Jimmy said.

"We weren't like them," Ernie said. "Not even a little bit. One time we slipped into the Catholic church. Us and Caroline, the Geek and the other guy, the drunk. But when we got inside, they had some explosives—"

"And inside the church you blew up the Virgin Mary's statue?"

"We didn't," Ernie said. "They did . . . You know about it?"

"It was in the news, Sherlock," I said. "I heard about the cat too. What about the drunk? Did he have a name?"

"Caroline and Stitch called him Glug."

"Glug?"

"Like the sound you make when you drink a beer. You know, glug, glug, glug. Least that's how Caroline explained it."

"How do you think she knew these guys?"

Ernie heaved his shoulders.

Tabitha said, "She may have picked them up at a bar, for all we know."

"I'm pretty sure they all had some kind of history," Ernie said. "Her and the Geek and Glug. It was obvious they all knew each other."

"Were they the same age as Caroline?" I asked.

Ernie shook his head. "Older. I guess the Geek was forty or so. The other guy, he maybe was in his mid-thirties. I got the impression they were military. The Geek said things now and then made me think he had fought in a war. Maybe not the Iraq war, but something else. Mercenary stuff. But it could have just been bullshit."

"They were creepy," Tabitha said, "way they looked at me, like I was a pork chop."

"Yeah." Ernie said. "Sex was on Caroline's mind all the time. And not just straight sex, or interesting sex. Caroline was always talking about how it would be fun to have a threesome, talking about me and Tabitha and her. Use all the holes, she said."

"Nasty bitch," Tabitha said. "She talked about getting pissed on. Golden shower stuff."

"I don't believe that," Jimmy said. "We never talked about doing anything like that."

"She knew who to play with and how to play with them," Tabitha said. "I told you that. Sometimes she played rough. I saw the Geek slap her once. She kept egging him on, jacking with him. I don't remember about what, but all of a sudden he was mad. He slapped her hard enough to drop her to one knee. Rest of the night, they acted like nothing had happened. She practically had her hand down his pants the whole time."

Jimmy made a noise like air going out of a tire.

"I think the Geek was daring me to get mad at him," Ernie said. "He would look at me funny. He was a big guy, had a kind of squint in one eye, like he was always winking. He'd do things that bothered me. Way he touched Tabitha. Always made it seem like there was nothing to it, just an accident as he lifted her through a window, got hold of her ass."

Tabitha continued. "He knew what he was doing, and he knew I knew, and he knew Ernie knew. I told Ernie to just let it go. I think that guy would have killed him."

"It made me mad," Ernie said, "and I did tell him not to do it. It took some real nut gathering to tell him, but I did. But I won't lie to you. I was afraid of him, and I knew Tabitha was right. He had a big clip-on knife and he'd take it out sometimes, flip it open and swing it around, grinning like some kind of idiot. Just slashing at the air. Warning us, I guess. He looked like he might have served some time."

"Why do you say that?" I asked.

"He had that look, way he carried himself, and all the tats."

"Tabitha called him the Geek," I said. "Why?"

"Reminded me of those old-time carnival geeks," Tabitha said. "Ones you put down in a hole and tossed a chicken, rat or something down there, and they'd catch them and bite their heads off, suck the blood out of the stumps of their necks. He looked like that. He had a lot of silver in his teeth."

A train went by and it was as if it were running right through the room. The house shook, the windows vibrated like cold teeth. The moth kept beating at the glass.

"Anything else you can tell us about Caroline, these guys?" I asked. "Anything else at all?"

"They talked about black magic and witchcraft and satanic stuff," Ernie said. "At first I thought it was kind of cool, but then I got the idea they meant it. Not that they believed it, but that they liked the idea of rituals and sacrifice."

Ernie paused for a moment, thinking. "Our group got whittled down to just us, Caroline and the Geek, sometimes Glug. The others didn't want anything to do with them . . . It got to be like a bad dream. One night we slipped inside this Mexican restaurant, the Hot Taco, the new place, and we decided wouldn't it be funny to go in there and fix us a big Mexican meal, eat it in the kitchen. Clean up after ourselves before we snuck out. Thought it would be funny when they went looking for something the next day and we had eaten up some of the supplies. That night it was me and Tabitha, Caroline and the Geek. That's all. We were slicing up some jalapeño peppers. In the back with the lights on, taking a chance, and the peppers were hot and it was causing my nose to run, and I saw Caroline's was running too, 'cause she was helping me while the Geek fried up ground meat and Tabitha did something or another."

"I was dipping taco shells in hot grease," Tabitha said, just so we'd know she wasn't a slacker.

"So I see some paper towels, and I get one for myself, one for Caroline.

She takes it and wipes her eyes. She says, 'The milk of human kindness. That's not hard, being kind. You know what's really hard?' And I said no. And she says, 'Killing someone that hasn't done anything to you, and maybe even someone you like or love a little. All the better if they love you.' She thought killing them, not on the spur of the moment, but planning it, was best. Making it a surprise. She thought that was a sign of strength, and she wanted to be that strong. I knew right then I wanted us to get away from her for good."

Jimmy's face had gone ashen and he was slumping in the chair. The gun was in his lap. He was no longer holding it.

"So after that, you cooled it with her?" I said.

"We'd see her at school," Tabitha said. "And there she was all prim and proper and shiny and acting like she was just perfect. Last time I spoke with her I tried to just be friendly, you know. No hard feelings we weren't doing the exploring anymore, and she just smiled and touched my cheek, and all that smooth personality stuff melted away, and that face of hers, it was like, you know, like it was from someplace dark and weird. She said, 'You're not forgotten.' "

"What did you think that meant?" I asked.

"How would you take that?" Tabitha said. "Especially after that little speech she gave Ernie."

"Anybody else you can think of she hung with?"

"The girl on the video," Tabitha said. "I saw them together at school. I don't know if they were any more than fuck buddies or not. I got the impression she was running a game on Ronnie, same way she did with your brother and everyone else."

"Can you describe the Geek?" I asked. "Maybe more about the tattoos?"

"He had a kind of slinky way of moving," Tabitha said. "Like maybe not all his bones were connected. He was big, but lean, and long-legged, and wore long sleeves no matter what the weather, and loose pants. Shaved his head. He had a squint, and all that silver in his teeth. Very pale skin; white as toilet paper. Usual jailhouse tattoos, done crude-like. The only one I really remember well was this blue one. Wasn't like the others, was professionally done, looked like fingers on the back of his neck. You know, like a dead hand was reaching up out of the collar of his shirt and grabbing him by the back of the neck."

"What about Glug?"

"He had a kind of bad eye," Ernie said. "I don't know it was dead or not, but it was discolored, milky blue. The other eye was brown."

I nodded. "Anything else about Caroline you can think of?" I said. "Anything at all?"

Tabitha shrugged. "She liked to read. And she liked puzzles."

"That's true," Jimmy said, almost causing me to jump. "She loved mysteries, true crime books and puzzles."

I thought: My hobbies are urban exploring, being peed on and hinting that I might be a murderous Satanist, reading mysteries and working puzzles in my spare time.

"She liked Edgar Allan Poe," Tabitha said. "And this obscure poet and writer Jerzy Fitzgerald. She quoted him sometimes. Another thing she did, and I suppose it's related to the puzzle and mystery stuff she liked: She was always taking a souvenir when we went out, which is something we did too, but she wanted to leave something that showed we had been there. Some subtle clue. We'd slip into an office, and she'd turn someone's name plate around. Put, like, you know, a paper clip in their chair. One time she put a ballpoint pen up herself."

"Ouch," I said.

"Not the sharp end," Tabitha said. "It was one of those fat pens, with a lid on it. She thought it was funny. I kept thinking, maybe even hoping, the cap would come off inside her. She put it back on the desk, placed the pen next to the guy's photograph of his wife and kids. She called it a statement."

"That's one way of looking at it," I said. "You think the Geek had anything to do with her going missing?"

Tabitha shrugged. "I wasn't surprised she disappeared, her and the Geek. I was relieved. That put them out of our hair."

"Was the Geek on the DVDs?"

"Not on any we looked at," Ernie said.

"Do you know where this Geek, Stitch, lived? Anything about them that you might not have told us?"

"No idea where they lived. But the Geek had a weird accent, like it was Southern and Northern both . . . I mean, he mixed words, phrases. Had a kind of eloquent way of speaking, mixed it with thug's talk. Always seemed to have some kind of plan going the rest of us didn't know about."

"That's an odd feeling to have," I said.

"Might not be anything to it," Ernie said. "But I felt that way."

"Can you tell me any more about Ronnie?" I said.

"Not really," Tabitha said. "We knew her through school. She seemed nice. Like we said, we think Caroline duped her too. She went home."

"Went home?"

"Dropped out, went home. Least I think she did. That's what I heard."

"All right," I said, "some of the coincidence is down. Let me ask this. You went and you got the DVDs, but you say you didn't know they were there. That sounds like too much."

"She mentioned she was making them," Ernie said. "So I knew there were DVDs."

"Why do you think she told you?" I asked.

"I think it was part of her chance taking," Ernie said. "The Geek, when she told us that, he said something like, 'You wouldn't want to mention that to anyone.' There's a part of me that thinks it was all some kind of game, like he was just wanting us to screw with those DVDs, or say something about them."

"Do you think Caroline was planning to blackmail all along?" I asked.

"She never said that," Ernie said. "She just said she had a way to make some people pay, so I think she might have had plans like that. It's where we got the idea."

"Where were the DVDs?"

"The big Baptist church," Ernie said. "It has a big gold dome on top. You probably know it."

"No shit?" Jimmy said. "North Baptist Church?"

"No shit," he said.

"What led you there?" I said.

"That's where Caroline went to church," he said.

"Church," Jimmy said. "She never went to church."

"That you knew of," Tabitha said. "That was part of her game, jacking everyone around. She went all right. And you want to know why?"

"Of course we do," I said.

Tabitha turned theatrical, gave us a long pause and leaned forward, said, "She fucked the preacher. Reverend Gus Dinkins."

Everything Dad had told me about Dinkins and his League popped into my head.

Ernie continued: "She saw him on TV. Has a Sunday show. He's not as big-time, rolling in the money as some of the God Squad, but for this town he's rich, and it's from milking people with his bullshit."

"Well," Tabitha said, and her voice took on a confessional tone, "he is good-looking, and he used to play football at the university. He quit because he didn't like the idea of showering in mixed showers."

"I never heard that," Jimmy said.

"And you never will . . . openly. But he told Caroline that. Pillow talk. She admired that about him. He was always talking about sin, and about how sinners who cheated on their wives, fornicated without the benefit of marriage, and those mixing races would go to hell."

"But he did all that, except for the mixing races part," Jimmy said.

"He thinks he's doing God's work," Tabitha said, "and because of that, it's okay that he does it. That's what he told her, or at least that's what she told me. I don't know why she confided in me, but she did. And in Ernie. Like we were saying, I think she liked playing it on the edge, liked to see where our loyalties were."

"And Caroline was all right with this guy?" Jimmy asked.

"She was a racist," Ernie said. "And big-time."

"I never heard her say anything like that," Jimmy said.

"Did you discuss race?" Tabitha asked.

Jimmy took a moment to collect his thoughts.

"No," Jimmy said. "It never came up."

"That's because something else came up," Ernie said.

I looked at Jimmy. He was blushing, but I didn't think it had anything to do with Ernie's comment. I think he was embarrassed about how he had been played.

"She probably would have lied had you discussed race, because she had a good idea where you stood," Tabitha said. "But, Caroline, she said the N word a lot. She called black people nappy-headed and burr-heads. Especially when she was with Stitch."

Jimmy shook his head.

"She told me she fucked him," Tabitha said. "I got the impression he might really mean something to her. Maybe not so much as a lover, but as a mentor. You should be glad she's gone."

"I don't know she cared for Dinkins at all," Ernie said. "That's how she played things. Made people think she cared. I think Dinkins was just another chump to her."

"Okay," I said, "but how did the DVDs end up in the church? Last time I ask, and then I let Jimmy pistol-whip the shit out of the both of you."

"We don't really know," Ernie said. "We aren't shitting you on that. We chose the church because Caroline talked about the Reverend. I guess we saw it as some kind of interloping against her, especially since she and Stitch were gone. We found the DVDs by accident. But it's not such a coincidence. We knew her, she knew Dinkins, and she talked about the church and we liked to urban explore. It all just came together."

Jimmy said, "How many history teachers were on the videos?"

Ernie looked at Jimmy. "All the men on the left side of the front office."

"The goddamn whore," Jimmy said.

"Is the preacher on any of the DVDs?" I asked.

"He's not," Ernie said. "Unless he's on one of those we didn't get."

"So you decided to blackmail?" I said.

"It was easy for us to sneak notes into the teachers' boxes," Ernie said. "We're up there all the time. They brought money. All of them. You were supposed to be the last. Though we been thinking about going back, getting the rest of the DVDs."

"And where is this money you got?" I asked.

"We have it hid," Ernie said.

"All of these guys, were they ten-thousand-dollar pops?" I asked.

"Mostly," Ernie said.

"That's a lot of college money," I said.

"I thought I could pay for college and get a good car and pay off some credit cards," Tabitha said. "It wasn't like we were stealing."

"No," I said. "It's exactly like stealing. You thought you were going to end up farting through silk. You ought to give it back some way or another. I'm not going to be the one to make you, but you ought to."

Neither Tabitha nor Ernie said anything to that.

"Where in the church were these DVDs?" I asked.

"The attic," Tabitha said. "Behind the Christmas ornaments."

I smiled at that. I said, "Tell me how you got in the church, what your method was."

"Who cares?" Jimmy said.

I ignored him, said, "Tell me."

"You can't go in from the front," Ernie said. "There are lots of lights.

The parking lot is well lit up, and so are the front and the sides of the church, bright as a floor show. There's a little stretch of trees behind it, and a creek. You got to come down the creek, go up from the rear. And you still got to be careful. There are lights back there, but no one is going to see you if you don't stand around, and they aren't as bright. That's where they ought to really be bright, but they aren't. There's an angle where you can be seen from the highway, but only if you stand around. You get to the back steps, there's a stone banister on either side, and all you got to do is duck down."

"How'd you go up the back way?" I asked Ernie.

"We left our car in the little park behind the fire station. You can walk down to the creek from there. There's a big culvert, and you can get inside of it and go along until it empties out on some gravel. There's a little run cut there so the excess water trails off into the woods. Some parts of the year, it wouldn't be a good trip. Water would be rushing through too high and too fast. You come out, you go to the back door of the church, change shoes, go in the back way."

"Change shoes?"

"Yeah," Ernie said. "The idea is for them to never know, or at least not be certain, anyone was ever there. No tracks. No clues. Except for the stuff like Caroline did, the paper clip, that kind of crazy bullshit, but nothing that will lead anyone to you. The back door church lock is pie. All you got to do is stick a credit card in between the door and lock, and that moves it, then you lift up and it'll open. They got this fancy, expensive church, and it has locks a blind, two-fingered retard could open."

"Describe where the DVDs were," I said. "In a little detail."

Ernie looked at me curiously, then slowly he began to explain.

"There's a stage up front. There's a big purple curtain and another stage behind that. It's elevated. I guess it's for the choir. You go back there behind the curtain, there's a little run of stairs and they go up to a landing. It has a rail on it and it looks down on the second stage, the one in the back. If you go along the landing, you find another stairway on the other side, and that one zigzags and makes the platform above. It goes around in a circle inside the dome, and there are three little rooms off the landing. Going up there I felt like that guy in that play, the *Phantom of the Opera*. It was the center room where we found the DVDs, back by the wall under a window, next to the Christmas decorations. There's a baby Jesus manger, a plastic lamb and a Christmas tree in a box, you know, an artificial one."

"I still find it hard to believe," Jimmy said, slowly shaking his head. "Caroline didn't seem anything like that."

"Oh," Tabitha said, looking right at Jimmy, "she was like that, all right. That's the kind of girl she was. She farted real hard, only thing that would blow out was shadow."

22

I took Ernie's backpack and poured his books and school papers out of it and he put the DVDs in it. Not just the ones they had of Jimmy, but the other ones too. I pulled the hard drive from their computer and packed it away, made Ernie and Tabitha drive us back to the hill above the Siegel house.

By the time we got to the hill and they let us out, the stars had been blanketed by cloud cover and a soft wind full of the smell of wet dirt was blowing.

We made our way up the hill. The wind picked up, and now there was dampness with it. Not full-blown rain, but a soft lick of moisture. We found our pup tent and pulled some things from the motorcycles inside and let down the mosquito netting again, though now we didn't need it. The mosquitoes and flies had fled before the oncoming rain. We unrolled our sleeping bags inside the tent.

From the vantage point we had made for ourselves on the hill, we could see lights in the town, and in the wet mist that was soon to be a full blowing rain, the lights seemed greasy, as if wiped over with Vaseline; they seemed farther away than they really were, as if they had taken the place of the stars and had become a galaxy of their own.

We took off our gloves, our socks and shoes.

Jimmy said, "I think we screwed up, bro. I don't like letting them go."

"What were we going to do with them? Keep them as pets?"

"I don't know, but I don't like it."

"We got them by the balls now."

"Just because we got some DVDs, the hard drive, doesn't mean they don't have others of me and Caroline. And besides, the Tabitha kid. She doesn't have balls."

"We in the intellectual trade call that speaking metaphorically."

"Is that what you call it? I call it bullshit. Cops come, find us with all this stuff, how's that gonna look?"

I had to admit, I hadn't thought about that.

"Jesus," Jimmy said. "I can't believe Caroline was like that. I thought we had something special."

"So did Trixie."

"Don't go there."

"Caroline may have been a bigger shit than you, Jimmy, but you don't come out of this shiny as a newly minted dime either."

"Still, don't drop it on me."

"You brought us to this place the minute you started lying and fucking around."

I stretched out on my sleeping bag and watched the rain, which was now coming down hard with a sound like someone standing above us flinging down ball bearings.

Jimmy shifted so that he was on his stomach with his hands holding up his chin, looking out the front of the tent.

"I hate this rain," he said. "It always depresses me."

"After all the dry I saw and lived with, all the dust I had to eat, anytime it rains I'm a happy man. I love the rain. I love to watch it, smell it, feel it."

"You believe what those two said, Cason? About Caroline? About what they did, how they came by the DVDs?"

"They probably prettied themselves up a little, but yeah, I think they're shooting straight for the most part."

"You don't think they killed Caroline, do you?"

"They're dopes, but they aren't killers."

Jimmy repositioned himself, turned his head toward me.

"You've found out a lot of stuff about me, Cason. I hate you had to."

"It's how it is."

"I want you to know I didn't do anything on purpose to hurt you."

"I know that. You think I don't know that? Come on, let's get some sleep."

I reached around the netting and pulled the zipper to the tent until it closed, and then I crawled inside the sleeping bag. For a little while I thought about Gabby, and then I thought of Iraq and all the sand and all the heat and all the emptiness I felt; the emptiness was for me a feeling like tumbling from an airplane without a chute. Finally I just closed my eyes and thought about a nice comfortable place in the woods and me all dry and at ease, listening to the rain, feeling the cool wind blow.

23

It was still dark when we broke camp. We had slept for a while, but during the night the comfort I had felt went away and the rain pounded against the tent so loud I couldn't sleep. And then, just as quickly, the rain was gone and the night was clear again and the lights were no longer greasy.

We got up and shook the tent off and rolled it up, Jimmy saying he would spread it out to dry when he got home. I took the shells out of the gun Jimmy had taken from the kids, and wiped them with a handkerchief and wiped the gun down and held it with the handkerchief, keeping my fingers off of it. I walked down to the kudzu, looked around and, when I felt no one was looking, tossed the gun and the shells into the greenery and went back up the hill to join Jimmy.

We packed up, me with the DVDs in the pack on my back, the rest of the stuff, including the hard drive, wrapped up in my sleeping bag, strapped across the back of the bike. We mounted up and pulled on helmets and kicked the bikes to life and rode down the slick hill without the tires sliding out from under us, went through the gravel spot behind the house and on out to the road that wound down to the highway below.

The rain had busted up the heat. Riding into town the air was cool and pleasant. When we got to Main we forked. Jimmy went left and I went right. I rode over to my place and parked the bike in front of the door. I unlocked the door and took the pack inside and dropped it on my couch. I got the sleeping bag with the hard drive in it and the rest of my goods, and shoved the bike inside the apartment and left it, muddy tires and all, just to the left of the door. I didn't know what else to do with it. I left it outside, it might be stolen. I got a towel and wiped the bike down, but didn't bother with the tires or the muddy mess it made on the floor.

I opened up the pack and prowled through the DVDs. They had numbers on them. The numbers didn't mean anything to me. I put the DVDs in the player, one after another, watching just enough to see if I recognized any faces. I did. Nearly all of them surprised me. One of them was the high school principal. One of them was the balding guy I had seen in the history department, the one who had told me where Jimmy's office was.

Caroline may have been smart as a whip in history, but her real gift was the con, and possibly commerce. And then, something had gone wrong, and the wrong of it seemed to be simply this: she had blackmailed the wrong person and they got their DVD back and put her down like a lab rat.

A suspect came to mind. Reverend Dinkins. Caroline might have decided he was the one to go after. He had a lot of money, and he had the most to lose. Showing his ass on a video, bucking with Caroline, wouldn't have been good for business. He could have killed her and taken his DVD, all the DVDs, stashed them in the church and destroyed just the one, his. But what would be the point in that? Destroying his, but stuffing the rest upstairs in the church. That was risky. 'Course, a guy like Dinkins, he could have been risky, and that's why he did what he did in the first place, messing with Caroline. And he could have had blackmail plans of his own.

I turned on my computer, got on the Internet and looked Dinkins up. It said all the things I already knew. It had pictures of him. He was a handsome guy who looked like he ought to be on the football team, or maybe the wrestling team. He had that kind of build, strong-looking, and he had a fierce look out of his eye.

For the hell of it, I looked up Judence. I knew a lot about him already, as he was worldwide famous, not just Camp Rapture famous. He didn't look all that different than he had always looked. A little grayer at the temples, but he still looked like the guy who had gone hand to hand with three racists thirty years ago and beaten all three, putting two of them in the hospital. It was a legendary event, and it might even have been true.

I looked at his eyes. His and Dinkins's, different colors, but they had the same sort of intensity. I wondered if either of them really believed in anything.

I turned off the computer and thought some more about Dinkins as Caroline's murderer. It was a theory, but I didn't like it a lot. I kept coming back to Stitch, the Geek. That fit better. It made more sense that something had gone wrong and he had lost it, and just did her in, tossed her out somewhere. But if so, he sounded like the kind of guy who would have taken over the blackmail business. Why hadn't he started blackmailing folks, and how and why had the DVDs ended up in the church?

And maybe the kids were lying to me. Maybe they weren't just a couple of stupids, but were a couple of stupid murderers.

I liked that theory least of all.

I put all the DVDs away in the backpack, went to my bedroom and got the footstool there, arranged it in the closet so that it was below the little trapdoor in the ceiling. I stood on the stool and moved the trap back and stuck the pack up there and got the hard drive and boosted it up there too. I slid the trap back in place and put the stool away. It wasn't exactly the world's best hiding place, but then again, as far as I knew, no one was looking for me to have a stash of DVDs and a hard drive with Caroline Allison screwing half the town.

I got a spare pair of old tennis shoes out of the closet, and some old socks. I got some gloves and a ski mask. I put on the tennis shoes and a windbreaker and fitted the gloves, tied my good shoes together with their shoestrings and threw them over my shoulder, stuck the socks in my pocket. I was carrying a lot, but at least it wasn't the battle rattle I had carried in Iraq. Compared to that gear, I was near naked.

I pushed the motorcycle back outside. When I locked up the apartment, I put on the ski mask for the wind, which had grown pretty chilly, then pulled on the helmet and looked at the sky. It was still dark, but the stars were less obvious, and a glance at my watch told me it wouldn't be dark long. Another two hours at the most.

I slung the good shoes over the back of the bike and rode over to the place where Ernie said they parked their car when they slipped into the church. I found a place down by the creek where I could push the motorcycle behind some brush, got the flashlight out of one of the saddlebags, threw the tied shoes over one shoulder and left the bike there. I walked down the narrow trail along the creek until I was under the big bridge that went over the highway. A wild run of water was pouring out of a huge culvert and emptying into the creek that ran beneath the bridge. The creek was churning along with a lionish roar. The rain had filled the creek and it was high, and when I flashed the light on it, the water was the color of dirty mustard. It was a lucky thing the creek bed was cut deep, or it would have been all over the park, maybe up in places that wouldn't have done some of the nearby buildings any good.

I remembered that Ernie or Tabitha, one of them, said when the water was running it was a rough place to be. The culvert was easily six feet high. I went to the mouth of it, saw that it was rusted badly around the edges, and when I looked inside it was dark, like the barrel of a gun. I poked the flashlight around inside, and the light didn't go far. Water rushed out and over my feet and I could already feel it seeping through my shoes and into my socks. The water was cold.

I stepped inside the culvert, stooping a bit, and began to move along. There was all manner of debris, and it stunk like a sewer pipe, and something sticky dripped off the sides and made me keep my hands close.

I kicked a plastic bottle of some kind out of my way, and then I saw something move in the water, and just a touch of the light let me know what it was. A snake. And not just any snake. A water moccasin. For a moment I froze. The snake didn't. He swam lethargically between my legs.

I turned and put the light on him and watched him move through the dark water, and then I couldn't see him anymore. I took a deep breath and was glad I didn't have to clean shit out of my pants. This time of year, it was almost too late for snakes. But almost, as they say, only counts in horseshoes and hand grenades.

I kept going. I finally came up against a barrier. The culvert ended. For a moment I was baffled, but then I saw a faint light to my right and realized the culvert turned slightly. It didn't go far before there was an opening and I could see out. There was a slight hill above it, and I could see the culvert had been designed to catch water running off the hill and to divert it into the creek.

When I was out of the culvert, I sucked in some fresher air and moved along the side of the bank. There was a little clay-and-gravel trail. I went up that and saw the back of the church was only a hundred feet away. So far, what Ernie and Tabitha had said checked out.

The light from the lot and from the back door of the church was strong enough to make a blind man put on shades. I moved quickly to the back steps of the church. I sat down on the bottom step and did what Ernie said they did. I took off my wet and muddy shoes, put on the socks and good shoes. That way I wouldn't leave any mud or any footprints. Maybe the chief of police was the kind of guy who could track a popcorn fart through a windstorm, but I doubted his sleuthing ability.

When I had the shoes on I put my other pair at the bottom of the stairs, stuck my wet socks down in them, set the shoes off to the side of the concrete banister. I went up the steps, put my little flashlight in my teeth, got a credit card out of my wallet, stuck it in the crack between door and lock and moved it around. Nothing happened at first. I was beginning to think the lock wasn't so easy, then it clicked a little and I felt the doorknob move slightly. I picked up on the knob, and when I did the thing moved again, and then it gave out with a soft snick and the door was open.

Slipping inside, I used the light to examine the door. It was a simple rig, and all I had to do for now was close it and flick the lock, then set the lock again and pull it shut when I went out. It would lock up fine until someone showed up with a key or a credit card. The gloves I was wearing would spare the fingerprints.

It was well air-conditioned inside, and that would be fine in a few hours, but right now it made me cold. Still, I pushed the ski mask up so that it was nothing but a hat on my head, flashed the light around. There were stained glass windows and there was faint illumination coming through from the outside lights. Dust floated up into the light and twisted about and the air was thick with it and it made me sneeze. It wasn't something you would see in common light, but the flashlight, there in the dark, picked it up like a particle beam detector.

I moved around until I discovered the stairs my pair of urban explorers had found. I climbed up. I followed the rest of their directions until I came to the door in the middle of the rooms up in the dome. The door was unlocked, and that made me wonder why anyone would hide something like the DVDs there unless they were looking to be found out, or were just high-risk, or had read Poe's "The Purloined Letter" one too many times.

Of course, Caroline had liked puzzles, and she had read Poe, and I had a sudden thought that maybe she had hid the DVDs here, without the preacher knowing. It could be that way. Hid them in plain sight until needed, and if they were found, it would be on the preacher's head. If it wasn't all so tragic, it would be funny.

I went inside the room. The place was full of boxes. I flashed the light around and looked in the open ones. I was in there for a while, poking around in boxes, weaving my way through stacks of this and that, and then I noticed the room was becoming lighter. The little round flying-saucer-style windows in the dome were taking in the morning light and throwing it around, and now in the apple-colored glow I could see cobwebs were stretched over some of the windows and the light coming through those appeared to be shining through cracked glass. I looked at my watch. My time was nearly up. Sunrise would soon be complete.

I moved around for another nervous fifteen minutes, and then at the back of the room I found a small, narrow box. It was under another box, a larger box. I found the little box because I knocked the bigger one over. It was full of Christmas decorations. I didn't bother picking them up. I picked up the little box and glanced inside. The DVDs looked the same as the ones I had. They were numbered and there were maybe a dozen of them. Good God. How did the girl find the time? I figured I had maybe twenty-eight DVDs, counting those hidden in my apartment.

I carried the box out of the room and down the stairs and went out the back way. When I got outside sunlight was falling ripe over the steps, and by the time I changed shoes and got down to the creek bed it was morning.

Just before I went over the lip of the creek bed, down toward the culvert, my box of DVDs in hand, I looked back at the dome on the church. It glowed bright gold in the morning light, and for a moment, looking at it, you could almost believe in something bigger than humanity, more thoughtful and kinder than the Big Bang.

For a moment.

24

I made my way through the culvert without seeing my friend the water moccasin, and put the DVDs in the saddlebag on the motorcycle, folded up the cardboard box with a bit of effort and crunched it small enough to go into one of the saddlebags. I changed shoes again, and pushed the bike up the hill, then cranked it and rode out of there. I stuck the ski mask in my windbreaker pocket as I rode. The cool wind was still there, but there was starting to be a few worms of heat in it.

I was excited about my find, and I drove by Jimmy's thinking of showing it to him, but I didn't stop. Wasn't any point. He would be asleep now, and if he wasn't, Trixie would be, so there was nothing to do there. I drove around town, keyed up about what we had learned and about the DVDs I had in my saddlebags. They were just more of the same, but it made what the kids told us true, and somehow I found that satisfying. I think I was feeling high on my exploration as well. Knew then what gave the kids their charge, sneaking around in forbidden places.

I drove by Gabby's office. It was way too early for her to be open, but I liked driving by anyway. Then I drove by her house because I couldn't help myself. In times of excitement, depression or just plain confusion, the urge hit me. Every time I thought I had let it go, the need would come back again, like some deep-buried coal under a load of wet leaves; the coal flamed up and the leaves became dry, and pretty soon there were flames.

When I went by her address, I saw her car in the carport, and I saw something unexpected.

Jimmy's motorcycle.

At first I thought it must be Gabby's bike, because I didn't want to think any other way, but I didn't remember her riding bikes. I had ridden with Jimmy back then, him and Trixie, and Gabby had never wanted to ride herself, not control the bike anyway. She would ride on the back, her face pushed up against my back, but she never seemed to like it and was always glad when we stopped.

Perhaps she had changed in the years since we had been together. Maybe it was just me she didn't want to ride with.

I stopped at the house down from Gabby's, parked my bike at the curb and walked back. It was Jimmy's bike all right. It still had the packed goods strung across the back of it. I tried to figure every reason in the world why it would be there, other than the reason that made the most sense. I took a deep breath, stepped back and kicked the bike so hard it fell over.

I went up her walk and pounded on her door. I pounded hard.

Time went by and I pounded again. The door was jerked open, and there was Gabby, her dark hair hanging over her shoulders, all fluffed as if she had just been jerked out of sleep, or something more dramatic. She wore blue pajama tops with blue bottoms with darker blue stripes. She had on blue fluffy house shoes, and when I saw her, my heart beat faster.

Jimmy came up behind her. He was still dressed in his camping clothes and he looked at me like I had been teleported there from Mars. I pushed past Gabby, and Jimmy said, "You don't get it, Cason. Don't, man."

But I had him by the shirt then, and when I yanked I heard the shirt rip, and then I pulled him through the doorway and sort of slung him out in the yard. He got up, pushed both hands out at me. I slapped his arms down and hit him with a right hook on the side of the face. It knocked him down. Gabby yelled at me, something I didn't quite hear, but nothing complimentary. She came running out then, squatted by Jimmy and lifted his head in her hands. When she spoke, she was so mad spittle flew.

"That's it, Cason. That's what I mean. That's all you know. Fight and bully."

"It's all right," Jimmy said. He moved as if to get up.

"You get up, I'll knock you down again, Jimmy."

"I've had it," Gabby said. "I'm going to put out a restraining order. I don't love you, Cason. I don't even like you. I wish you had been killed over there. There, I've said it, and worst of all, I mean it."

I couldn't move for a moment. I looked at Jimmy. He was wiping blood off of his mouth with the back of his wrist.

"You are a piece of work," I said to Jimmy.

"You're the one who's a piece a work," Gabby said. "You're crazy, Cason. Crazy."

"Cason," Jimmy started, but I was already walking away.

"Go on," Gabby said. "Go on, and keep going. Don't let me ever see you again. You'll be hearing from someone. My lawyer, the cops, some-goddamn-body."

I walked out to the street, and along it to where I had parked the motorcycle. I got on it, cranked it with a hard drop of the foot, then rolled out of there.

I pulled up outside Belinda's place on the bike and sat at the curb, thought about what I was doing. Belinda deserved better than a frustrated, angry, lovesick puppy who wanted nothing more at the moment than to get laid. I looked at my watch. Still way early. I pushed the bike off and stomped the starter to life, rolled back to my place.

I had been there about fifteen minutes when there was a pounding on the door. I went to the window beside the door, pulled back the curtain and took a look. It was Jimmy.

I went to the door, called through it. "Go away, Jimmy."

"Cason. You big asshole. You don't know a thing. It wasn't what you thought. I went over there for you."

"I'm gonna have to get the hip boots out."

"Come on, man. Do we have to keep talking through the door?"

"I don't want to talk at all."

"Come on. We're brothers."

"I hate you."

"No you don't. Come on. I'm your brother."

"You been playing that card awful heavy lately. And did I mention I hate you?"

"Come on, now. I mean it, Cason. Let me in."

"No."

"Yes."

"No."

"Pretty please?"

"Go on."

Jimmy paused, then: "Cherry on top?"

I leaned against the door for a moment. There must be some inbuilt genetic thing that allows you, even expects you, to take abuse from siblings, because I unlocked the door and opened it. He came in. The motorcycle was inside again, in the same spot. He had to thread his way around it, and when he did, when he was close to me, I hit him again. It was a hard lick, a straight right, and he staggered back. I slipped forward and landed a left uppercut in his belly and he went down on one knee and started sucking air.

I think he said something foul to me, but with him breathing the way he was, for all I knew it could have been something polite in Japanese.

After a moment he just sat back on his ass. He looked up at me, gulped like a guppy out of water.

"You want some more?" I said.

He shook his head. His breath had come back a little. "I didn't want any in the first place. It hurts."

"Good."

"Really, Cason. You hit too hard."

I got a chair from the table and put it down in front of Jimmy with the back of the chair toward him. I straddled it like a horse and put my arms on the chair back and looked at him.

"What the hell you doing?" Jimmy said.

"Watching you suffer."

"I might have a tooth loose."

"Good."

"You always could whip my ass."

"It was the one thing I could do better than you," I said. "You always had the grades. You were popular in school. And, of course, you could get the girls. Me, I could fight. I could always fight."

"Yeah. You could always fight, asshole. And you could outplay me in football, and you got nominated for the Pulitzer, so I think you could do a lot of things I couldn't do."

I hadn't really thought about that. I kept thinking of myself as his lesser. Shit, maybe he was right. I could do some things. Had in fact done some things. And I really could knock him down.

"If you had anything at all with Gabby, you fixed it this morning," Jimmy said, wincing as he spoke.

"You're the one had something going."

Jimmy started to get up.

I pointed a finger at him. "Stay right there."

Jimmy decided to sit back down. He said, "I went over there to talk to her about you, dumb shit. I went over to try and tell her to give you a second chance, and that maybe, just maybe, she was missing out."

"Don't give me that."

"It's the truth."

I sat for a moment studying him. He was a good liar. Always had been. I was looking for any sign of a tell. "Don't lie to me, Jimmy."

He held up one hand. "I swear, brother. I'm not lying. I went over there to tell her how you changed, and then you showed up and pounded on the door and pulled me outside and whipped my ass. That sort of threw a blanket over my heartfelt proclamations about your personality shifts."

"What's wrong with my personality?"

"She was under the impression that you were violent by nature."

"I was never violent with her."

"She just doesn't like the idea of it. For someone who doesn't want me to kill someone, you sure don't mind knocking my dick in the dirt."

"Was she listening?"

"What?"

"Was she listening?" I said. "Was she listening to what you said about me?"

"I ought to tell you she was, and that she was going to be okay with things until you did what you did. That would make me feel better. But no. She wasn't listening. She wasn't having any. I tried because of what you've been doing for me. And you're my brother."

"You telling me straight, Jimmy?"

"Would I lie to you?"

"I believe you would. Yes."

"I'm not, though. Not this time."

"Straight?"

"Straight as William Tell's arrow."

"Shit."

"Yeah. Shit. Help me up."

I got up and put out a hand, and watched to make sure he wasn't going to clip me one when he thought I wasn't looking. He figured that was what I was doing. He said, "I'm not crazy. You can take a punch. I can't. But I do want to note that you hit me when I wasn't looking."

"Best way."

"If I had been guilty of anything."

"I'm still not sure I believe you."

"I would say ask Gabby, but considering she wants to put out a restraining order and wishes you dead, probably you ought not to. And by the way: After you left, I think I talked her out of that restraining order business, and she told me to tell you that she really doesn't wish you dead, that she didn't wish you had been killed in Iraq. She was just angry. But she told me to tell you that she really does hate you, and she is going to stand by that statement. Come on, Cason. You know I'm telling the truth."

I studied his face for a while. It's hard to tell with a really good liar. "All right," I said. "I'm sorry."

"How sorry?"

"Pretty sorry."

"That's it?"

"Okay. Pretty damn sorry."

"Once more up the notch, baby brother."

"I'm real goddamn sorry."

"With a cherry on top?"

"A cherry on top."

That satisfied him. He wandered over to the fridge, got out a bottled coffee, went to the couch and sat down. He twisted off the lid and I went and sat in one of the big chairs across from him. I shifted my ass a little so that the loose spring in it didn't poke me too hard. I looked at Jimmy. His lip was swollen from where I had just hit him, there was a big bruise on the left side of his face, and he was rubbing his stomach.

"No need to try and make me feel bad," I said. "I feel bad as I'm gonna feel. You weren't messing with Gabby, you still had that coming just because you're you and all the bullshit you've caused."

He quit rubbing his stomach.

I said, "What you gonna tell Trixie, about the bruise?"

"I was thinking of telling her we got drunk and you hit me. But then she might not let us go out and play again. I'm going to tell her it was a motorcycle spill."

"All right. I can back that up. That's a lie I'm willing to tell, because it makes me look like less of a jerk. Damn, bro, you aren't working me, are you?"

"I was not banging your old girlfriend. I shouldn't have gone over there, not that early. But I was feeling kind of bonded. Like you and I had a moment akin to the old days, back when we camped and hung out. I haven't felt like that in a while. I decided to be stupid and wake her up and try to talk to her. Truth is, though, it wouldn't have gone well anytime. Morning. Noon. Night. It's over, Cason."

I let that settle, then said, "Listen. I went to the church where the kids got the DVDs. I found some more. All that were left, I think."

"You broke into the church?"

"Did it the way Tabitha and Ernie did it."

"Are they the same stuff?" Jimmy asked.

"Haven't looked at them yet, but my guess is yes."

"Well, I don't want to see them. I've seen all of that shit I want to see. I'm on any of them, destroy it. Destroy all of them."

"Will do," I said.

Jimmy pressed the cold bottled coffee to the side of his face before he finally sipped at it. He said, "Man, that was a hard punch."

"Just as hard as I could throw it."

"I don't doubt that," he said. "Listen. I've given it some thought. I think you're right. Those kids don't want any more shit from us. I don't have any real worries now."

"Now you're confident."

"I just want it to be over, Cason. Be done with."

I went and got a bottled coffee and sat back down in my chair. Jimmy said, "But you aren't going to let it go, are you? I know you. I can see it in your eyes."

"Aren't you the least bit curious? About her? Why, and all that? I mean, you got snookered by someone for no reason you can discern, and she did the same to a lot of others. So, don't you want to know?"

"I think I just got out of hot water, thanks to you, so why climb back into it? Sleep with the satisfaction that you saved your dear old brother some money and his marriage and his job, and I didn't shoot anyone. And you got to punch me for no good reason. Just let it pass. We're not the law."

"Man, you have made a turnaround," I said.

"I'm not as scared as before. I'm ready to let it go. You should be too."

"Can't. It's the reporter in me."

"It's the obsessive-compulsive in you. This isn't Santa Claus and this isn't trying to call up the bull ape. Whoever did this thing, took Caroline, I got a feeling he isn't like the kids. We don't want to fuck with whoever that is, now that we don't have to. He's most likely moved on, so why stir things up, man? Let's let this stuff be."

"You're probably right."

"I know I'm right." Jimmy put his empty bottle on the coffee table and got up. "I got to go home. I think I'm going to soak in a tub, try and treat Trixie right. Give her a foot rub, take her to lunch. Something nice."

I walked him to the door. I said, "I really am sorry about hitting you."

"I don't think you're that sorry."

"That was sort of for Trixie."

"Oh, it was, huh?"

"Sort of."

"Listen, man," Jimmy said. "We're done on this. Right?"

I nodded. "Sure."

I opened the door, and he reached back and slapped me on the shoulder, smiled and went away.

25

Exhausted and confused, I stretched out on the couch and was soon asleep. When I awoke the apartment was hot and full of the aroma of rotting rat. I got up and turned up the air conditioner and found something to eat in the fridge, compartmentalized my thinking about the rat to some deep section of my brain and tried to enjoy eating. I took a shower and put on some clean clothes and was happy that with the air conditioner going the rat was down to half level, demoted to corporal.

I didn't really have to check in, but I got my cell phone and dialed work and told Timpson I would be out today so I could work on a story at home. Then I dialed Belinda.

She answered immediately.

"Cason," she said.

"Wanted you to know I took off today, but I was wondering what you're doing tonight."

"I called in sick, not because I'm sick, but because I'm sick of the job."

"I lied and said I was working at home."

Belinda laughed. "What liars we are. I called this morning and went back to sleep, not wanting to get up, wondering if maybe you had already had your fill of me. I was thinking about what my mother used to say about giving out, and how when you did it was pretty much over."

"Mothers aren't right about everything," I said. "It's time you moved into the twenty-first century, though I've been living here for a few years now and don't think much of it . . . Look, I've just been a little wrapped up is all."

"Work?"

"You could say that."

"Is that what we'll say?"

"Yeah. Let's say that."

"Will I hear more?"

"Nothing really to hear."

"Okay, then. What are our plans?"

"It's as much about your choices as mine, kid . . . But I was just sitting here thinking we ought to go to dinner tonight and maybe a movie. After that, we could come to my place, but it smells like there's a dead rat in the wall, because there is."

She laughed. "Sounds like a plan. Maybe we can do the hotel again. I loved room service."

We worked out the details, and I lay down on the couch again and went right back to sleep. I woke up after a few hours of deep satisfying sleep, got into the boxes I had first shipped to my parents' house and brought over just a few days ago. I had yet to open them. What was in them was a new computer, the odds and ends that go with it. I spent some time setting it up and made myself a cup of hot coffee. I fiddled on the computer for a time, making sure it was working, no damage in shipping, just sort of cruising Web sites, looked to see if I could find a MySpace site for Caroline. I didn't.

I finally decided it wouldn't be a bad idea to work on a column, so I did. When I finished with a rough draft, I went back to playing online. While I killed time, I wondered about Belinda, thought maybe I ought not to have called, that it was just a way for me to soothe my banged-up heart and she deserved better. My penis argued with me for a while, and by the time I had to get up and brush my teeth and put on a better set of clothes, my penis had out-argued my brain and was trying to tell me that what we were doing was okay and that all that mattered was everyone had a good time and didn't get hurt. It was the greatest oration since Cicero.

I drove over to Belinda's place. We went to a nice steak house down-town, had some rib eyes and some drinks and a lot of conversation. We went to a bad movie, and then we went back to her place instead of the hotel. I don't know why we did it that way, instead of the hotel, which had been our plan, but that's how it came out.

Inside, the place was neat. It was about the size of my joint, but it was well furnished. Nothing fancy, but everything was nice and the colors were coordinated and there was no dead rat smell in the wall. That fact alone was enough to charm me.

We talked about having drinks, but we never got that far. Our hands found each other, and then we were kissing, and pretty soon she was leading me through a door and into her bedroom, which smelled of scented candles, which had a real leg up on my dead rat. She lit a fresh candle that was melted onto a saucer by her bed, and the smell that came off of it was banana nut bread. She started up her CD player, some soft jazz. She slowly took off her shirt and bra, smiled her shiny braces at me and shook her head, throwing her hair about. She began to move slowly to the music. It wasn't what I expected of her, but I stood there grinning like a fool, watching her move, watching her skin out of her pants and what little there was of her panties. She was someone who didn't overdo the shaving and had left a bit of womanly hair where it counts, and when she swayed the little guy in my pants swayed with her.

She danced over to me, took hold of my shirt and started to undo the buttons. I tried to help, but she pushed my hands away and did it herself, and pretty soon I was out of my clothes and we were in the bed. The smell of the banana nut bread from the candle was strong and I felt hungry. I took it out on her, and she didn't mind. The next thing I knew it was morning and the sun was shining through the thin white curtains, and we made love once more, just to make sure we remembered how, and then we went back to sleep and didn't awake until midday.

I woke up first and thought about trying to make breakfast in bed, but that time was long past, so I took a shower, and about five minutes into it, she joined me. That took some more time.

Dressed, we went to the kitchen. She got out some plates, the bread, peanut butter and jelly, and we made sandwiches and poured up glasses of milk and sat at her kitchen table and talked about silly things for a while, then she said, "You know, I knew her."

"What?"

"Caroline."

"You knew her?"

"Not well, but I knew her. I didn't say anything before, because I didn't know her that well, and I didn't want that to be the first thing between us, some work-related thing. What I've been thinking, though, is I'm not sure anyone really knew her. Not in any way that really told you anything about her."

"I've been thinking the same thing."

"When I was going to school, I took some night courses at the university, and I saw her one night. And you know what I remember about her?"

I shook my head.

"I'm standing in the hall, by the elevators, waiting to go up to the fourth floor, and I see her coming toward me. I looked at her, because you couldn't not look at her. She was stunning. She was coming toward me and her head was held down a little, but not so much I couldn't see her face, and I remember thinking, Wow, that is one beautiful but dead face."

"How do you mean?"

"When she saw me, she came out of wherever she had been visiting inside her head, and her face changed, lit up, and she smiled and said something friendly, and we rode up in the elevator together."

"People can look that way if they're thinking about something else. Dead-faced, I mean."

Belinda shook her head. "Not like that. I don't mean she wasn't carrying a lot of expression because her mind was elsewhere; she had these perfect features that didn't have any animation. It was like she was all made up for her coffin. It was like a book I read once about these things from outer space that were pods, and they were hid under beds and in closets while people slept, and the people didn't wake up. Their place was taken by the pods and the people ceased to exist. They looked the same and did the same things, but their expressions were gone, their voices lacked inflection. They didn't radiate emotion. They weren't human."

"*Invasion of the Body Snatchers,*" I said.

"That's it. That's the one. That's how Caroline struck me. I knew who she was because really anyone that went to classes in that building knew who she was. You were in that building, and you saw her, you never forgot her. But I tell you, that girl wasn't right. She was whatever you wanted her to be."

I had heard something similar from Ernie and Tabitha. But I said, "You can't know that."

"You're right. I can't. But we rode the elevator up together, and when we got to the top floor, she saw one of the professors unlocking his office door, and when she called his name, she changed. Her posture. Her face. It was as if something came from somewhere and filled her up with personality. She moved differently. She had something she hadn't had in the hall, or in the elevator, except for that little flash when she spoke to me."

"Maybe she knew how to handle men."

"No doubt she did. But it wasn't just that. There was something about her that was empty, and when she needed a personality, it was like she borrowed it."

"From who?"

"I don't know. From any source she might have seen or learned from. She was someone who imitated life. I know how dramatic that sounds. But riding up in that elevator, I had the coldest, saddest feeling, and I wouldn't turn my back on her. I pushed up in the corner so I could watch her."

"Did she watch you?"

"She did. She even smiled a couple of times, but it was like a beautiful tiger showing its teeth, not like someone happy to see you, or just being friendly. I know. I know it all sounds like some kind of creep show, and from the outside I must sound like the biggest creep of them all. She was gorgeous, and I won't lie to you, part of me was very jealous of her. I wanted to look like her, but I didn't want to be her. Not even in the littlest ways. I don't think she had feelings one way or another, except for the borrowed ones. I think had she not been so beautiful, she would have been found out sooner. People wouldn't have trusted her."

"You mean men, don't you?"

"I mean anyone, but men especially. She could charm when she wanted to make the effort. She borrowed charm from her memory banks, and she only needed so much, because men, they don't always have to have everything else just right if the woman looks good."

"That's a sad commentary on my sex," I said, "but what makes it even sadder is you're probably right. This professor you mentioned, way you said it, you're telling me something there, aren't you?"

"It was your brother. He was teaching a night class."

"And?"

"And the way they looked at one another, the way he touched her shoulder, even though it was nothing but friendly, there was something going on there. I think it was one way. I think she wanted to make him think it was two ways, but I think it was one way. I didn't even mean to get into this, and wouldn't have said anything at all, but we are getting closer, and I don't think a secret like that is good, even if it isn't much of a secret. I'm sorry to tell you something like that, and now that I think about it, I wish I had just shut up. And you know what, I could be full of it. It might have all been innocent."

"I know about it. And you're right. There was something there. Jimmy's married, you know?"

"I know. He and his wife have been in the news a few times. Stuff up at the college, even charity work. And he was in some kind of hunting club or something."

"I'd appreciate it if you didn't mention what you just told me. I don't want to make things worse for Jimmy. He knows he messed up, and now that it's over . . ."

"You've heard the last from me as far as their relationship is concerned."

"Do you know if anyone else knew they were having an affair?"

"I didn't really know much of anyone at the university. I knew your brother because of the newspaper, and I knew her because of how she looked, and some of the other students talked about her. I knew a few of the professors."

I thought about that a moment.

"I know what you're thinking," she said. "That my opinions about her may come from something someone else said. But no one said anything about her, other than the guys, and then it was just the usual stuff about how fine she looked and what they would like to do with her."

"Any of those boys ever sound weird about it? About what they'd like to do?"

"Not the way you're thinking. I don't have any better idea what happened to her than anyone else. You've been checking this out, haven't you? And not just because of the column you wrote. Because of your brother?"

It was hard to bullshit another reporter, or in this case, a would-be reporter.

"A little. I didn't really know about him and Caroline until I started checking things out. I think I'm through checking."

"I bet you're not."

"No?"

Belinda shook her head. "You're too much of a reporter, and you have something of an obsessive personality."

"You think?"

She grinned. "Yes, I do. I know about you and Gabby."

"That's old news."

"Not the way I hear it."

"You are a fountain of information, girl. How did you hear about it, and from whom?"

"Melanie Popper."

"Who?"

"She works at the vet's office. Gabby told her you came by and tried to patch things up, and Gabby asked you to leave. Or that's what Gabby told her anyway."

"Damn small town . . . Yes, that's true. I did try and patch it up, and if she walked through this door right now and said she'd take me back, I'd go. I wouldn't ask a question, and I wouldn't look back. I'd go."

There was a bit of silence, like a couple of respectful sailors watching a huge iceberg pass by.

"I can understand that," Belinda said.

"I don't think you can. Listen to me. I said I would go without one word, and I would. But she doesn't want me, and deep down, some place hidden behind the furnace, I don't want her and know she's wrong for me, and you're helping me understand that. I don't want it to sound like I see you as something to take her place until she comes back. I don't mean it that way, but I'm trying to be honest. I hope you believe that."

"I do."

"You know what I really fear?" I asked.

"That she won't want you back?"

"She won't. Believe me, we're through. What I fear is something different. I fear I might swap my obsession from her to you."

"That wouldn't be all bad."

"Obsession and passion are not the same thing," I said, "as has been recently explained to me by, how shall we say it, events on the ground. Straight up. I'm a mess. I've got war baggage. I've got Gabby baggage. I have drinking baggage, and some little side bags I'd rather not even discuss."

"Maybe I can help you carry that luggage, Cason. I'm small, but I am fierce."

"I believe it," I said.

Next day things cranked sideways and there were rips in the fabric of what I knew as hometown reality; it was the way I had felt in Iraq, realizing I was slipping through the cracks of reason and that I had my finger on the trigger of a rifle, beading down on a human being, about to cut him in half with a .50 caliber. In those clear moments, just before I sent the projectile hurtling, I could look through all the lies I had been told about nobility and the quest for democracy and know I was nothing more than a living pawn with a weapon and a dead-eye aim, and I was about to snuff out a human life that maybe didn't deserve to exist, but was it my right to take it?

All the Players in
Their Places

26

I got the surprising news Monday morning.

Mrs. Timpson came out of her office and placed her ample ass on my desk corner and looked at me with eyes that had probably seen the first star pop alive in the first night sky.

"Oswald isn't here today," she said.

"I noticed that. He isn't at his desk and has not been all morning. So, I deduced he was not here."

"Well, that's goddamn observant of you, Cason."

"I'm a highly trained and skilled reporter."

"And because you are so goddamn observant, and a little bit of a smartass, you can put your column on hold for today and do his job. My guess is you have a couple columns in reserve anyway. Am I right?"

"Well . . ."

"Yeah. I'm right. You still remember how to do a police report, I presume? You have done a police report, am I right?"

"I've done a few. Yes. For the Houston paper. It's a pretty big paper. They even have color funnies on Sunday and a crossword puzzle."

"That was my guess. Well, the police report is Oswald's job, and since he isn't here, today it's your job. It's also your job to take Oswald's job of running down a story off the police report, and there is a story to run down. You still with me?"

"Clinging to your every word like a sloth clinging to a limb."

I was pushing it, I knew, but I was tired and feeling irritable.

She gave me a hard look and shifted her false teeth in her mouth. "I glanced the report over, and what I want you to do is look at it, and follow up on this murder and kidnapping."

My ears perked up. I liked being a columnist, but the idea of some real raw news appealed to me.

"There's been a murder and kidnapping?" I asked.

"Well, I suppose the police who sent the e-mail could just be messing with us, but that's what the story they gave us says, and they're sticking to it."

"I'll get right on it," I said.

"There's two things I can smell quicker than anybody," she said. "One is shit, and the other is a good news story, and I'm pretty sure what I'm smelling now is a news story, and it wouldn't surprise me if it's related to that girl who went missing sometime back, one you wrote about."

"Caroline Allison."

"That's her. My take is this is related. Mark my words. The only reasoning I have behind that is my reporter's nose is twitching. I sense a connection. I could just need to pass gas, but I'm going to stand by the connection theory."

"Probably be more pleasant for all of us if you do," I said.

"Get on it."

"Yes, ma'am."

I was about to stand up from my desk chair when Timpson leaned forward and gave me the watery eyeball. "Cason, you've done a good job on that column. I don't give out compliments other than to tell the truth and because it seems to make people want to keep doing better, and that makes for a better paper, even if it makes my gums ache to say that crap. But you've done well. And you haven't come in drunk. Those are two things I wanted to congratulate you on."

"Thank you."

"But you do seem a little distracted."

"Nothing serious."

"I just want you to know that I'm not here for you. I want the paper run right. That's all I care about. If you got family problems, even if your mother is dying of some terminal cancer problem and it is eating her alive from the asshole out, you got to stay focused. She dies, you go to the funeral, and there's a hot news story, you better be taking notes with your pad pressed up against her coffin. Understand?"

I started to tell her to go to hell, but since my mother wasn't sick, I said, "I got you."

"Just wanted to remind you that you're always a worker here, and we're never friends."

"Wouldn't have it any other way," I said. "I mean, sometimes, I think, wouldn't it be great if you and me could just, you know, hang? Maybe shoot some pool. Take a bike ride. Moon some nuns together, just me and you. But mostly I think I'd rather not."

"As I've told you, I like a little comedy, Cason, but that's about as little as I like. Understand?"

I nodded.

"Get with it," she said, and walked away, back to her shadowed foyer in the back, disappeared behind the boxes there, possibly to kick a puppy or cut the head off a child's teddy bear.

The police reports had been e-mailed, and I read them over at Oswald's desk on his computer. One of them, the one the old bat had wanted me to look into, hit me like a truck. I felt weak in the knees and my stomach turned queasy.

Ernie was dead and his girlfriend, Tabitha, was missing.

It took me a minute to take in that information and believe it. I thought about calling the police department, asking some questions, but I decided to drive over to Ernie and Tabitha's place, get things a little more direct.

On my way out I passed Belinda and she looked a question at me, but I just nodded at her and went on.

I drove over to Ernie and Tabitha's house. The address had been listed on the police report, but of course I knew where it was.

When I got there the police were still working it. There were a lot of cop cars and unmarked cars along the curb. Uniformed cops were running about, and there were people wearing hospital footsies and plastic gloves and little masks pulled down under their chins. My first thought after seeing so many Houston crime scenes was simple. The Camp Rapture yahoos didn't have a clue what they were doing and if there were any clues in the yard, they were stomping them flat, contaminating the crime scene.

As expected, there were yellow strips across the front door of the house with POLICE, DO NOT CROSS written on them in big black letters. A couple of guys wearing the footsies and plastic gloves pulled their masks up and ducked under the tape and entered the house.

The chief was leaning against an unmarked car, glaring up at the sky, waiting for a revelation, or perhaps the Rapture.

He looked at me as I came up. "Reporter, how are you? I'm so goddamn glad to see you."

He sounded more than a little insincere.

"What's the scoop?" I said.

"It's ugly, Jason."

"Cason. How ugly?"

"Dead is pretty ugly," he said. "And the next-door neighbors, they tell us there was a girl, and she's missing. They don't think she could do such a thing, so maybe she got 'napped since we can't find her. That's what we're saying for now."

"But you're not so sure?"

"We got her name and we've notified her family, and we're going to notify the boy's family. Holding off on that for a little bit, wait until we can get him sacked up."

"Was the girl a student?" I knew she was, but if she was missing, it might give them a lead. An idea to start checking the school and who might have known her. Of course, that could lead them right to Jimmy, but it was better at the moment for me to fish a bit, find out what they knew.

"Yeah. She's a student. We've checked at school, class she's supposed to be in. Followed up a few leads we got from the neighbors. Doesn't look good. Damn. I need a drink."

I thought what he really meant was he needed another.

"No note?" I asked.

"Note?"

"From the kidnappers."

"Oh, no. Nothing like that. If there was a note, I'd know for a fact she got 'napped, now wouldn't I? I got that much savvy. I know how to pull my socks on one at a time, shit in the pot and not on the floor. I'm not totally useless. So, there was a note, I'd know if she was kidnapped, now wouldn't I, Jason?"

"Cason."

"You're not saying Jason?"

"No. Cason. With a C."

"I'll be damned. Could have sworn you were saying Jason."

"Nope."

"Huh."

"Doesn't matter," I said. "You're right. You would."

"Would what?"

"Know if she had been kidnapped . . . if there was a note."

"Oh, sure," he said. "Of course. They leave a note, you got their word, and who wouldn't believe the word of a murderer? I see you got a camera there. Nice little camera, small, easy to handle. Maybe you should have been sneakier."

"Why would I be sneaky?"

"There's nothing you're going to be photographing inside."

"I was gonna take some outside photos. You know, the POLICE, DO NOT CROSS strips. Maybe a shot of you looking very investigative."

"Again, you're not going inside. You did, you'd wish you hadn't. I did. I wish I hadn't."

"That bad?" I said.

"I'm always surprised at how much blood is in the human body. It's spread from one end of that shithole to the other. And it's pretty fresh, he's been dead, oh, I don't know, maybe today early, before light. Maybe yesterday late. Guy was naked and in bed. Well, a lot of him was. There was some more of him elsewhere, and, I'm sure you know this, being a crack reporter and all, but he shit all over the place too."

"How was he killed?"

"Machete or axe would be my guess. Sword if one was available. Might have been more than one person did it. It was one killer, it was a goddamn tiger. It was like someone held him down and ran a lawn mower over him. Meth heads is a good guess. They seem to always be hacking people or chopping heads off."

I tried to keep my face neutral, but what I was thinking was Jimmy and I had been in that house, our fingerprints might be in there. Then I remembered we had been wearing gloves and felt a shade better.

"So a tiger did it with a machete, or possibly a lawn mower?" I said.

"Find your own comparison. I'm not that poetic. Do I look like fuckin' Dylan Thomas?"

"No. But a lot of people will be surprised you know who he is, and a lot of them will wonder who it is you know about."

"I'm surprised you know who he is," the chief said.

"Touché."

"Literature major. That was me. Should have stuck with it. I'd be in a university somewhere, teaching kids that would hang on my every word. I could be looking up coeds' dresses watching beaver move inside underpants, and I could be talking. I like to talk. I'm good at it. Everything else for me sucks the big old donkey dong. I'm not cop material, you know? But don't tell the town council. I need the job. My wife and kids like to eat."

"So you don't know anything about the girl?"

"Officially, we haven't got a clue. Me, I'm thinking she might have done it, woke up in the night, worked the dirty deed."

He pushed away from the car to stand for a moment, took a deep breath. I decided he wasn't drunk after all. He hung his head and patted at his pocket like he might be looking for cigarettes, but nothing was there. I tagged him for an ex-smoker.

"Why would she do it?" I asked.

"He left the toilet lid up. I don't know. It could be anything. That's another thing to be answered, and guess who doesn't have the answers yet? Your one and only swinging dick of a chief of police, that's who, and that would be me, pardner. Shit, Jason—"

"Cason."

"Damn, I'm sorry. We just went through that. But I was going to say, I seen some car wrecks, shit like that, even a murder, a suicide, a guy jumped from an overpass and did a one-point on his noggin. He was all over the highway, like a dropped watermelon. Saw some things like that even before I was a cop. Had a job once where I cleaned apartments. Back in college. And this guy, he blew his brains out with a shotgun, and it was all over the place. And the company I worked with, we got hired to clean it up, and I thought that was bad, but now I got this, and let me tell you, this is bad, boy, bad. It looks like there was a tomato fight in the bedroom. Except it don't smell like tomatoes. It smells like what's in there, and there's some kind of cat piss smell too, only there isn't a cat. Let me just boil it down, and say it is some ugly goddamn business."

"I'm starting to get the picture," I said.

I remembered that cat piss smell from when Jimmy and I were in the house. It could have been from former renters; cat piss stays with a place better than fresh paint.

"Shit, boy. They chopped off his dick. Looked like a little sausage lying there on the floor. One of them, what do you call them, Vienna sausages, isn't that it? Isn't that the little ones?"

He was chattering on like a squirrel. He didn't wait for me to respond.

"I don't like this at all," he continued. "Not even one little bit. Today I have looked at the abyss, and let me tell you, it has looked back with both eyeballs and it is one hideous motherfucker."

"You should have finished college," I said. "Quoting philosophers and the like."

"I got too deep in debt. I only lack a year. Don't think I don't think about going back. As of today, I'm thinking about it a lot more. I got the job here because I thought it was even sleepier than the town I came from. Truth is, though, there's always something, and there isn't any such thing as a quiet town, unless maybe there are only two people in it and one of them is dead."

"So," I said, "you're thinking the girl gets up in the middle of the night and does a Lizzie Borden. That's not much of a theory."

"It isn't much of a theory," the chief said, "but I'm not much of a police chief either."

"Nothing else you can share?"

"Someone cut off the air conditioner," he said, "and I don't think it was to save on electricity. They did it so the body would get hot and stink. It worked. And there is a little thing we're holding back, so I won't tell you that. You can just say we're holding back some things that only the killer/kidnapper could know. That's good enough right now."

"Will you tell me in confidence what you're holding back?"

"No."

"Is it a good lead?"

"No. We're just a Podunk police department, did I tell you that?"

"You did."

A cop came out of the front door of the house then, and though we were a good distance away, out by the curb, an odor came out with him. The cop leaned over and threw up in the shrubbery.

"Close that goddamn door," the chief yelled. Another uniformed cop leaped out of the yard, padded up there in his paper pullover footsies, his gloves, grabbed the doorknob and closed it.

"Everybody here, get some goddamn masks on," the chief said. "Not just some of you, all of you. You're wearing one around your neck, get near that house, pull it up."

The cops scuttled about when he was finished yelling.

"I doubt murder is contagious," I said.

"These days, so much murder going around, you got to wonder. It's like some kind of disease. And you got the smell. A mask helps that . . . I know I don't sound like much of a cop, but I don't give a shit. I'm not much of a cop."

"You said that already."

"I'm just making sure the word gets out."

"At least you showed up. I heard the old chief didn't get out of the office much."

"He was smarter than me."

"What's okay for me to print? What facts are there?"

"Well, the guy is dead. That one is a fact. The girl is gone, and that's fact two. It's also bloody in there and the deed was done with something big and sharp. That's about it."

"Sign of forced entry?" I asked.

"Nope. Front door was unlocked. One of the neighbors remembers seeing a dark-colored van parked in the drive. It could have been black, green, blue, just about any color but white. Saw it late, before he went to bed. Didn't notice the time. Said he thought he had seen it before, some-time back. Few months back. But couldn't be sure. Looked out the win-dow for no other reason than he wanted to look. Saw the van and didn't think anything of it. No reason he should. People have visitors all the time. He didn't hear any yelling, but says his air conditioner runs loud and he had the TV on. None of the other neighbors saw or heard anything. Look, I'm going to go get a cup of coffee and worry about it later."

"I'd like to take those photos of the outside of the house, a shot or two of you."

"You do that, but you do it from the road. I don't want you on the lawn. A valuable clue that we probably won't find anyway might be there. As for me, I'm not up for pictures, and believe me, I like my picture taken, like it so much you bought some *National Geographic* footage you'd probably find me on it or in it. I'll jump in front of a camera, I get the chance. But not today. No fucking way. We catch whoever did this, it'll be an accident. Someone saw something and tells us, we might catch a break. Someone comes forward and admits it. Someone knows who did it because they bragged. My God, that bedroom was coated in blood. All over the bed, the walls. And there were bloody tracks, and there was that boy's shit smell. Jesus. A mess. A sickening mess."

"It's as bloody as you said, you ought to have some shoe prints."

"Oh, yeah. No one was trying to be careful, either because they were in a frenzy, didn't care or didn't expect to be caught. We got footprints, but it'll be a Cinderella job, going to everyone with that size shoe, matching it to their foot. I might as well just put an ad in the paper begging the killer to turn himself in."

"Cheaper than DNA."

"I told you about our budget. What DNA? Guy doing the fingerprints, sucker took a two-day fingerprint course. He might as well have got his training off the back of a gum wrapper."

"Was the place ransacked?"

"Torn apart, looked like the Tasmanian Devil had been in there. But that could have been a plan on the woman's part. Make it look like murder and robbery, and her taken by the killer. She could plan on showing up later, having escaped from her killers, so to speak. That would be clever."

He chattered on some more, finally got in his car and drove away. I walked around the outside of the house and took the photos, then I went back to the office and typed up a generic kind of report. When I finished typing it up, I filed it with Timpson, went to lunch, pulled up at the curb in front of the café. Before I went inside for a sandwich, I got out my cell phone and called Jimmy.

His cell went to voice mail, and I left a message: "Call me."

27

Went all day and didn't hear from Jimmy. I thought about going over to the university, but didn't. I didn't go to his house, because I didn't want to give Trixie anything to think about. She was a smart woman. I wasn't sure how well I could hide what was on my mind, pretend that nothing was wrong.

Belinda and I had dinner together at my parents' place. They loved her, and Mother fussed over her and made sure she had plenty to eat and asked her all manner of questions.

Belinda was a real hit.

When we went out, I saw Jazzy in her tree. She hadn't been there when we drove up, but now that it was growing dark, when she should have been inside, she was in the tree.

I looked up and said, "Hi, Jazzy."

She raised her hand and waved like she didn't really mean it.

"What's the matter?" I asked.

"Nothing," Jazzy said.

"This is my friend, Belinda."

"Hello, Jazzy," Belinda said.

"Are you still my friend?" Jazzy asked.

"Sure, honey," I said. "We're always friends."

"Okay," she said, but she didn't act like she meant it. She turned her back to us and sat on the other side of the little platform and looked toward her own house.

"Bye, Jazzy," I said.

"Glad to meet you, Jazzy," Belinda said.

Without turning, Jazzy lifted her hand in a goodbye wave.

We went out to the car. When we were inside, Belinda said, "That little girl has a crush on you."

"That's obscene."

"Nothing like that. She doesn't like seeing you with me. She thinks that's the end for her. In psych class I learned about that. She's not used to having friends, or they leave her. Trust issues."

"You can't know all that meeting her once," I said, starting the engine.

"No. But you've told me about her, and now I've met her. Didn't you say her mother is . . . well, a tramp?"

I eased the car out into the street. "That seems to be the case."

"We have to help her, Cason."

"I know. I've been a little preoccupied lately. Though that's not a good excuse. I get my head straight here in a few days, I'm going to push Child Protective Services hard. I may write a piece about their incompetence. They should have already done something. They've let Jazzy fall through the cracks."

"You're an all-right guy," Belinda said.

"And you're not so bad yourself," I said.

We didn't go to Belinda's place or mine. I told her I had some research to do, a column I was thinking about writing. She took it well enough, but I figured she was already thinking I was looking for a way to dump her; thinking maybe she had made a mistake with Jazzy, saying "we" had to do something, therefore making us a couple.

I couldn't let that worry me right then. I went home and sat in a chair and read a bit of a book, and then I paced awhile. I set the alarm and tried to take a two-hour nap, but I just lay there the whole time looking up, trying to make animals and insect shapes out of the water spots on the ceiling, then the alarm went off and I got up and walked around some more.

At about one a.m. I got a screwdriver out of my toolbox under the kitchen sink, got a container of Vicks VapoRub, put it in my coat pocket along with a neckerchief and the screwdriver. I added gloves and a flashlight to the pocket, pulled on the coat, which was a little too warm for the weather, wore my old tennis shoes, picked up an extra pair of shoes, walked out to my car and drove over to the murder site.

I drove past the place and glanced at it. I could see the yellow tape was still there. I wondered if the chief had stationed someone to wait and see if Tabitha came back, but truth was, I doubted he had thought of it. He was quite the mess, and the way he was handling things, it might end up with him hosing oil off a filling station driveway, maybe greeting people at the Wal-Mart.

I circled anyway, just to be sure. Second time I went by, I decided there was no one outside watching, not unless they were in a tree. To be safe, I checked those as much as the dark would allow.

There was one advantage: the house wasn't well lit from the streetlights. In fact, all the streetlights along that way had been knocked out; probably kids with BB guns or pellet rifles. Still, I didn't pull up in the driveway or park out front at the curb. I went around the block and found a place to stop under a tree in a little park. The park consisted of about a half acre, a dozen big trees and a picnic table. I locked the car and walked back to the house. As I went dogs barked, and one light went on in a house nearby, but no one came to the window and no one opened the door.

I walked faster, and pretty soon I was down at the corner of the block. The coat made me warm, but I liked the pockets. They held my tools.

I stood there for just a moment, then went back a few steps, slipped over a wooden fence without snagging my balls and went through a backyard that was dark. I went over the other side of the fence without getting attacked by a dog that turned out to be a stone yard ornament, and landed in the backyard of the house I wanted.

I got the gloves out of my coat and pulled them on. I took hold of the screwdriver. I went to the back window and tested it with my hands. I didn't need the screwdriver. It went right up. Maybe whoever had come in had come in this way. Or maybe the cops had unlocked it from the inside and left it that way. I could see it like that, in there with the stench and the body, and someone had to throw open the window, get some air.

When the window was up, a foul odor like the graveyard of all things long dead gusted out at me. I turned without considering and threw up in the unkempt shrubbery there. I got the Vicks jar out of my pocket, opened it up and dunked my finger in and rubbed it under my nose, and pushed some of it up each nostril. I pulled the neckerchief out and tied it around my face.

I stepped through the window and pulled myself inside, turned on the flashlight. The air conditioner was humming. One of the cops had turned it back on, to preserve the crime scene maybe. More likely because he couldn't take the heat and the stench. It didn't help much in the latter department, even with it on and my nose full of Vicks.

I took off the coat and draped it over the windowsill and took a look around.

First thing I saw was the bed. It was deeply stained with blood and feces; it drooped in the middle. There were hacks in the old-style mattress and the stuffing was poking out in spots, and the part of it that was not stained stood out prominently, white as ready-to-pick cotton.

The chief was right. It was hard to imagine there was that much blood in the human body. Because of the air conditioner, the blood was still drying and it had all gone dark as motor oil. The walls were splattered with it. The killer had moved around, striking from all angles; I knew that much from investigating crime scenes in Houston.

I took a deep breath of Vicks, flashed the light at my feet, and then spread the pool of yellow forward until it fell on the bloody shoe tracks the chief told me about. They were all around the bed. It looked as if someone had danced there. I eased over without stepping in the mess, and saw amongst the shoe prints bloody little bare footprints. I knew that would be Tabitha. The chief had either been playing coy with me or he was as stupid as he thought he was, because it was obvious she had been nabbed. And then I thought, maybe they fought alongside the bed, her with the machete, or the axe, and finally she had pushed him back on the bed and finished him off; that would explain some things.

But it wasn't an explanation I was buying.

I eased around the bed, had to tiptoe to keep from stepping on the prints and smears of prints that were everywhere. I could figure what had happened pretty easy. Whoever had hacked Ernie to death had then grabbed the girl and waltzed her through the bedroom and out the front door, into the van in the driveway. I went into the living room following her bloody prints; they went bloody to the door.

I went back to the bedroom and flashed the flashlight back on the wall. There was a spot where someone had put their finger in the blood and drawn little V-like shapes, like a series of shots of a blood-red bird rising. It went up from behind the bedstead to near the ceiling. There was writing there too, done in blood with a fingertip. It read: "And the birds of prey, having plucked the bones, had flown, leaving neither flesh nor soul."

The crude bird drawing and the verse must have been the bit the chief was holding back. Something he could use to nail the killer later, something only the killer and the police would know. I had a pad and pen in my pocket. As a reporter, I always carried them. I put the light in my teeth and wrote on the pad what I had read off the wall. I drew my impression of the V-winged birds too. I put the pad and pen away and stood there for a while with the flashlight back in my hand, moving it slowly around the room, just looking, unhurried and careful.

I came back to the birds and the verse. The way they were positioned meant someone had stood on the bed to do it, and that doing it meant something to them.

I thought about Tabitha again, and followed her tracks back through the door that went into the living room. There were a lot of bloody shoe prints, and I bent down and looked at them. There were two sets. I was sure of it. They were the same kind of shoes, same kind of treads. Tennis shoes most likely. But it was two pairs, no question. One large and one small.

I went to the front door, flipped the lock and cracked the door easily and looked out at the yellow tape across the door, and then I looked out into the driveway where the van would have been. From the door to the van was about ten feet. I could see faint bloody footprints on the driveway.

Nothing clever here. They had pulled up in the driveway and come inside and killed Ernie and hijacked Tabitha. Must have worked the door somehow and caught them sleeping, or maybe the couple knew them and let them in.

But who did it, and why?

Whatever the reason, I was pretty certain it had something to do with the DVDs, and maybe with me and Jimmy. Maybe it was as simple as them trying to blackmail someone who had the same idea Jimmy had, about killing them. Only it was more than an idea for this guy, and he had wanted to take it out on Ernie, big-time. But why kidnap Tabitha? Did he have other plans for her?

I locked the front door and watched my footing. I looked around with my flashlight. The computer was smashed and there were clothes thrown about and drawers were dumped and shattered dishes were on the floor. Maybe they wanted it to look like some kind of insane druggies committing a murder, or maybe they really were looking for something, like the computer discs and hard drive I had hidden in my closet ceiling. Maybe Ernie and Tabitha had hidden other copies, stuffed them under dinner plates, inside the couch, anywhere, and the searcher, or searchers, had found them. Or maybe what caused all the blood was that they didn't find them. No doubt in my mind Tabitha or Ernie would have told them about Jimmy and me, about us taking the DVDs. The thought of that made it feel as if someone had dropped an ice cube down my back.

I went through the bedroom and got my coat and went out the back window, and closed it. I put the neckerchief in my coat pocket, and went over the fence, across the yard and over the fence on the other side. I started walking back toward my car. I pulled off my gloves and put them in my pockets.

When I got to the car, I drove out toward San Augustine, a nearby town. I drove on out that way until the woods got thick. A few miles before I came to the town I came across a little red clay road and I took that. I parked alongside the road next to a slough of water, shining silver in the moonlight. I took off my tennis shoes and put on the leather shoes I had brought. I got out of the car and took the tennis shoes and tossed them out into the slough. If the police found my tracks back at the house, printed in some of the blood I might have accidentally stepped in, and if anything led them back to me, I didn't want to have the shoes in my closet for them to look at. When I got home, I had to remember to clean the gas and brake pedals with paper towels and flush them down the commode, in case any of the blood from my shoes had ended up there. It wasn't exactly a superhuman effort to elude the police, as I couldn't imagine them having anything that might lead them to me. But it was something to do, and it was all I knew to do, and it made me feel better to think about doing it.

I got back in my car, and when I put my hands on the wheel they were trembling. I drove down the road a ways because it was too narrow to turn around, drove with the window down, letting air blow on me, keeping me alert.

I imagined I could still smell that stink of death from the house. I even paused and pulled over to put some more Vicks up my nose. I drove until I found a narrow drive with a cattle guard. I pulled in there, backed out, got on the road and went back to the highway and drove into town.

I tried not to do it, but I drove by Gabby's. I didn't get the rush I usually got. Sometimes it was an angry rush, sometimes a nostalgic feeling. But tonight what I got was nothing short of a dead sensation, as if all my nerves had died and been hauled off for incineration.

When I got home, Jimmy's motorcycle was parked out front and he was sitting on my doorstep under the porch light.

28

I opened the car door and was getting out, but before I could, Jimmy was over by the car.

"While you were out screwing around," he said, "I been sitting here waiting on you. Do you know how late it is?"

"You sound like Mom."

"Have you seen the news?"

"Unless you're upset they're not going to be filling potholes on Lufkin Street anytime soon, I'm going to surmise you're here about the murdered kid and the kidnapping."

"Smartass."

"I left you a message, you know."

"You didn't say about what."

I shouldered past him and unlocked the door, and we went inside. I went straight to the refrigerator, got out a bottled coffee for both of us. I wanted whiskey straight, a beer chaser to tamp it down, but I knew better. Besides, I didn't have a drink in the house. I had purposely tried to make sure it wasn't handy.

I brought the coffee over and gave it to him. Jimmy twisted off the top. "Whoever got to those kids, what if they told them about us?"

"We don't know they did," I said.

"Got to figure, whoever did that to him, they didn't borrow Tabitha to take to the prom. They're asking her some questions. They could be coming for us right now."

"Chief of police thinks she killed Ernie and is on the lam."

"The chief is an idiot," Jimmy said.

"That's what he said . . . Isn't Trixie going to miss you this time of morning?"

"I have learned to be quite the liar."

"I don't doubt that."

"This thing, with Ernie and Tabitha. It's got me chilled to the bone, baby brother."

"You were wishing them dead before," I said, and sat down in my most comfortable chair, twisted the top off my cold coffee and drank.

"Yeah," Jimmy said. "I was wishing them dead. And I thought about doing it myself. But I didn't. They got hit by a truck, something like that, I don't know I'd feel real bad. They'd be out of the way. This is different. It's not that they're dead, it's that them being dead could somehow connect to us if they talked."

"For a minute there I thought you'd got Jesus, but no, you're still the asshole I thought you were."

"I know. I'm a shit. It's all about me."

"Agreed," I said. "As for what they might have talked about to whoever did this, my guess is there wasn't a lot of talking. Least not with Ernie. I visited with the chief of police today, and I went over there and had a look for myself tonight."

Jimmy raised his eyebrows. "You went in the murder house?"

I nodded. "I snuck in when it got dark. I don't know exactly why, but I did. I looked around, and what happened there was pretty damn brutal. I think Ernie was taken by surprise, in his sleep."

"And the cops think Tabitha did it?" Jimmy said.

"Chief likes her for it, but even he thinks he's got crummy detecting skills. Right now, a case this big, he's probably wishing he had a job jacking off sailors. Here's an oddity among many. In the house, on the wall, in blood, were crude paintings of birds. Or maybe it was supposed to be one bird, different views, rising up toward the ceiling, each one slightly off center of the other."

"Birds in blood?"

"Someone took time to stand on the bed, in the blood, near the hacked-up body, and draw those birds on the wall. It had to be important to them."

"Birds don't make any sense," Jimmy said.

"You got me there, but I'm sure that's what it was."

"You think it was a taunt of some kind?"

"I think whoever did it has some kind of agenda we can't begin to figure. And there were more than birds. There were words too, and they mentioned birds. The words were written in blood."

"What kind of words?"

I told him.

"You think it was one person?" Jimmy asked.

"No."

"How many do you think?"

"My guess is at least two. There were bloody prints and some drag marks. I think whoever did it had a stun gun of some kind. One person stunned the girl while the other hacked the boy. They dragged the girl out the front door. That's what the prints indicate anyway. Carried her out the front door and put her in a van parked in the drive and drove off."

"Surely someone saw the van."

"Next-door neighbor. Said it was a dark color and they didn't think anything about it when they saw it. I don't think the neighbor got the year or model, and I'm sure he didn't get a license plate."

"They were just lucky."

"I think playing poker online isn't near enough for these folks. They know exactly what they're doing, and they're not afraid to do it. They gamble big. They've maybe been doing this awhile, or something like it, and they're getting bolder."

Jimmy took in a deep breath of air. "Trixie has been wanting to try out that lake house we bought with Mom and Dad. And she's off for the summer. I'm finishing up the first summer session tomorrow. I just decided. Supposed to go two days beyond that, but I'm going to end the class early. Give everyone an A on the final, and then I can go."

"I want you to get Mom and Dad to go with you. They'll go easy. Dad has already mentioned it to me. Just don't tell them why."

"Of course not," Jimmy said. "Do you take me for an idiot . . . Don't answer that."

"Just take them," I said.

"I will," Jimmy said, "but I advise you to saddle up the old pony and go with us until this shit storm blows over."

"I'll join you in a few days," I said.

Jimmy lifted his eyebrows. "A few days? I'm thinking maybe I don't even need to teach one last class. I'd rather get a reprimand from the division chair, or the dean, than end up cut up like fish bait, and I'm telling you, you ought to go with us. That place is pretty isolated."

"I think it's best someone is on the ground here, paying attention. And I think I'm in a better position to do that than you."

"You'll get no argument from me," Jimmy said.

He stood up, said, "Look, there's phone service out there, isolated as it is. You need me, call. I can give you directions there."

"I'll do that," I said.

"You're crazy to stick around."

"Probably."

Jimmy gave me a hug. "Trixie calls, alibi me. Say you had me over to talk about Gabby or something. Sorry to bring it up. But, you know, I got to have some reason."

"And why not pick one that makes me feel really shitty, right?"

"It's something she would believe."

"Does everyone know how nuts I've been about Gabby?"

"Pretty much, yeah. Sometimes me and the grocer talk about it."

"That's funny, Jimmy."

"So, I got the alibi?"

"How and when did I ask you to come over?"

Jimmy took some time to consider, said, "You didn't ask. But today, talking to you, I was worried about you, got so worried I got out of bed and came over and we talked. Big brother trying to cheer you up, get you on the right course. Does that work?"

"Well enough."

Jimmy went out and I listened to his motorcycle roar away.

I went outside and cleaned my gas and brake pedals of blood, went back inside and sat down at my computer and tried to find the words that had been written on the wall in blood. I typed them in and clicked the mouse. The words came up. There was a site for Jerzy Fitzgerald. He had come up before in connection with Caroline. He was a poet and an occasional writer of prose. Mostly Internet poetry, and a lot of it, but he had done a couple of self-published books. He had a strong cult following. Some took him seriously; others looked at him as a kind of Ed Wood figure, bad but totally unaware of it. *This Bird Has Flown* was one of the books he had published, and one of the poems inside was of the same name, and part of it was what I had seen written on blood on the wall of Ernie and Tabitha's apartment.

I had a feeling that this whole thing was part of some bigger picture, and to borrow from one of Jerzy Fitzgerald's poems a terse fragment: "All of life is framed in fear."

29

At work the next day the office was abuzz, not only with the events of the day before, but with the way I had written my article on the murder and the kidnapping.

After plenty of compliments, reporters dropping by my desk, everyone but Timpson herself, Oswald came over. He stood by the edge of my desk with his hands in his pockets. He looked like he wanted to reach down my throat and turn me inside out.

"Nice article on the murder and kidnapping," he said.

"Thanks."

"I might have taken a slightly different approach."

"No doubt."

"Is that a smart remark, Cason?"

"What?"

"A smart remark. Like, I would have taken a different tack, but it wouldn't have been any good."

"I didn't say that."

"But you meant it."

"What I meant is no doubt you would have gone after it differently. It is not a smart remark."

"I do police reports here and the articles that come from them."

"Not this time. You weren't here, and Timpson assigned me to it."

"I had a cold. I would have come in for something like this."

"Talk to Timpson."

"You could have told her to call me."

"I suppose I could have, but that never occurred to me, and that's not my job description. Call Oswald when a good article pops up and he's sick. Nope, not on the list."

Oswald took his hands out of his pockets. "Watch it, buster."

I said, "You have highly overestimated your ability to intimidate, my friend."

He glared at me for a moment.

"Why don't you go sit down at your desk before I stand up and knock you down and we both lose our jobs," I said.

"You couldn't roll me over if I was dead, Cason."

"You don't want to get me stirred up, Oswald. I don't mean that to sound like a threat or like I'm trying to be a tough guy, but I kid you not, you fuck with me, and I will knock you out of your shoes."

Oswald considered the possibilities, decided he didn't care for them much. "Look," he said, "just call me next time."

"I work here just like you. Timpson wants me to do different, and she's not asking me to set my balls on fire or put a broken Coke bottle up my ass, I'll do what she asks. Same as you will. I didn't owe you a call. I don't need to send you an e-mail or a note tied to a pigeon's leg. No fucking flowers or a teddy bear wearing an I'M SORRY T-shirt. Got me?"

"That's no way to be," he said.

"Hey. Aren't you the one who said not to bend over here because I might find something in my ass?"

Oswald nodded. "I guess I did."

He went back to his desk and took his frustration out on a couple of ballpoint pens that he shoved around, a little notepad too. He twisted a couple of paper clips. That was showing me.

Belinda came over. When she spoke it was softly. "He's pretty mad."

"I seem to have that effect on people. I presume the rest of the office heard?"

"Hard not to. Both of you were speaking loudly. I was especially fond of the part about setting your balls on fire and shoving Coke bottles up your ass. Charming."

"Sorry."

"No apology necessary."

I turned around and looked at the other reporters. Most of them had their heads down, pretending they were on a hot deadline. One, a fellow I had actually spoken to only once, and whose name I couldn't remember, gave me a thumbs-up. I don't know if it was because he was on my side or thought Oswald was an asshole. I'd settle for either.

"I got two things," Belinda said. "First, the good news. I want to see you after work if possible. I have bought some very scanty panties and wanted to see if you are a real red-blooded male who will be overcome with passion when you see me in them."

"That one you can count on. You can just wear your socks, and you'll get the same results."

"You like socks?"

"Actually, you could show up naked or wrapped in wool or wearing a beanie propeller and you would get my attention. But, hey, I'm not dismissing new panties. I'm all up for that, as we say when we're having witty sexual repartee."

"Not that witty."

"What's number two? Usually that means a bowel movement, but I'm going to go out on a limb here and guess that's not what you mean."

"That's the bad news. Timpson wants you in her office."

"And me all out of dog treats."

"That was nice work you did, especially since it looks to me you wrote it without a whole lot of information," Timpson said. "Still, you found the good stuff."

I was seated in the office chair, as before, and Timpson was in the chair behind her desk. She shifted it so that she was facing me head-on.

"I want you to stay on this assignment. You've started it, and your article was better than the colored boy's would have been."

"Oswald," I said. "His name is Oswald. And unless he's changed either his first or last name to Colored, I believe the term is black or African American. I don't think he's a boy either. Maybe you could have him drop his pants and we could see if his testicles have descended. That's one way of telling. I am, however, sure he's old enough to go on ahead and start picking cotton."

Timpson watched me through watery eyes. "I ought to kick your ass out."

I hadn't meant to say that, but it had just popped out. I didn't even like Oswald.

Timpson gave me a grin that almost caused her to lose her false teeth. It wasn't a grin that said I like you, it was one that said, Okay, asshole, I'll let that one pass. "All right then, you take the African American man's place because his articles suck. How's that? And, if he wants to come in here and drop his drawers and show me his balls, I'm on board. Now, be honest. His articles. Think about it."

I sighed. "His articles do suck hind dry tit, and he seems to have graduated from the Winnie the Pooh School of Journalism. But I don't want to be a police reporter. I like being a columnist. I'm not saying it isn't fun, but I'm a columnist, and I don't want to take Oswald's job."

"Yeah, well, you will be for a while. Follow up this murder-kidnapping thing. Does that work for you, Mr. Pulitzer Prize nominee?"

"It does."

"Do what you need to do then. Get whatever help you need to get it done. Oswald if you have to. Talk to who you need to talk to. Go where you need to go. Write all the articles that pertain to this murder and kidnapping that you can. If nothing more is there, we'll move on. But, if you can find out about the couple, their lives, research it. Later, you can do a column on the murders. Something like this happens, like that missing girl, shit, boy— It's okay if I call you a boy, I suppose? Not that I want you to drop your pants."

"You said you'd let Oswald, so that doesn't seem fair."

"I've heard the colored are better hung." She scrunched up her mouth, and when she did, the bones in her face appeared to shift dramatically, like knobs and sticks under parchment. "If we're all out of being cute, let's get back to business. Bleed this crime for as many articles as you can. It's going to sell a lot of papers."

"Because of the murders, not the article."

"The way you wrote it helped."

"Is that a compliment?"

"Twice, already," she said. "One was slightly veiled, this one is direct, and two times, that's my quota. Or maybe it was three compliments. I can't remember a goddamn thing anymore. Anyway, I'm short on any more shit from you. Push it, and I'll write the goddamn columns and the articles myself and you can go home and pull your johnson while you read through the paper's help-wanted section."

"I hear you," I said.

"I'm thinking of another thing, of putting you on an article about those preachers and the shit that's going on between them. We've run a lot of stuff, but there's a big shindig coming up with the colored preacher doing a talk at the university, and there's all manner of bullshit coming down about a protest. I might want you to write that too. This thing has been going on for months, but with Judence's big talk and rally coming up, I think we can get a really good story out of it. If anything goes down there, protests, what-have-you, we can play it until it runs out of air, then we'll kick it around some more, see if it squeaks."

"I really think you should consider Oswald for that one. He'd do better than me in the black community, and that's who he'll need information from, the community. "

"Even if his writing sucks hind dry tit?"

"Even if," I said.

"You may have a point. People like to talk to their own kind."

"That's one way of seeing it," I said. "Maybe not the way I would have chosen to express it, but—"

"Like I give a damn," Timpson said.

I waited a moment. Nothing else was forthcoming. I stood up to go.

I went to the door, and she said, "Send the colored boy in, will you?"

30

After work I went over to Belinda's and we made love and lay in bed talking, sniffing a candle that this time smelled like fresh-baked bread. I had to get me some of those candles. Maybe they would cover up my dead rat odor. Most likely I would just sit around the house hungry. I wondered if they had a chili candle, an enchilada candle. French fries maybe.

"How did Oswald take it?" Belinda asked. Between thinking about candle possibilities, I had been telling her about my meeting with Timpson, the fact that the boss had put me on the murder and kidnapping case.

"Like I had planned it. He was pissed."

"How do you feel about it?"

"I like writing the columns, but this kind of stuff has its dark sort of charm."

"It's a big thing for our little paper."

"Yep."

"Cason. Something is bothering you. And even in my profound insecurity, I don't think it's me. Is it Gabby? Caroline? The stuff with her and your brother?"

"You know, funny thing is, I haven't thought about Gabby all day. That's the first time she's come to mind in a while, and only because you mentioned it."

"Me and my big mouth."

"No . . . No. I think I'm getting better. Far as she's concerned anyway. As for the rest of the stuff, yeah, I'm thinking about it. I have also started counting things again. There are eighteen thousand little black marks in your ceiling tile."

"I hope you weren't counting them while we were making love."

"Only when you were on top."

"Ha. Ha."

"No, you took a little nap after we finished, either because you were so deeply satisfied with my manly abilities, or because you were bored, and that's when I counted them. It's something that hits me now and again when I'm stressed: the urge to count, to know exact numbers. I can't explain it. But I want you to know, I did think about you a lot in between the dots."

Belinda shifted in bed so that her pelvis was touching me. I could feel her pubic hair on my leg. "Anything else on your mind?" she said. "Now that you've got the dots out of the way."

"World peace."

"You shit."

"Actually, something just came to mind when you moved like that, and in favor of honesty, I have to say it wasn't world peace. It was another kind of piece."

"You know what I mean," she said, slapping at me. "Is there anything you want to talk about?"

"And you know what I mean. But, yeah, there is something else. Belinda, I may be an idiot, but I do have something to talk about, and I know it's probably rude to say it, but I tell you this, you got to promise it stays between you and me. For now. Maybe forever. You know part of it, but I want to tell you the whole of it."

"Is this a big moment in our relationship?"

"I think it is."

"Then great," she said. "Sure. What is it?"

I told her all of it. About Ernie and Tabitha, the DVDs, how they tried to blackmail Jimmy, about us taking the DVDs away from them, the fact that I hid them. I told her about being in the murder house. I told her about Jimmy planning to take Trixie out of town, have my parents meet them at the lake house. The only thing I held back was where I put the

DVDs. For some reason, I thought that was something she ought not to know.

When I finished my story, I said, "I'm not even sure I should be seeing you, Belinda. Someone has my number, and anyone around me could be in trouble."

"I'm not scared . . . Well, not that scared. I'm not going to stop seeing you."

"Go slow," I said. "I'm trouble on the hoof, even when I don't mean to be."

"I'm here as long as you want me around. Tell me what we need to do, and I'll do it."

"Timpson may not like it."

"Timpson can go screw herself," Belinda said.

"My, aren't you rowdy. Come to think of it, she said I could use whatever resources I needed at the paper, suggested I take Oswald."

"I bet he doesn't have bread-scented candles."

"I bet you're right," I said. "I think Timpson will go for it. She can get someone else to work the front desk."

"When do you tell her?"

"Immediately." I shifted and pulled her to me. "Well, almost immediately."

31

I went into Timpson's office and asked if Belinda could be my assistant, a reporter in training. Timpson put both hands on her desk and leaned forward and gave me a severe look. She stayed that way for so long I thought for a moment she had died.

"She's gonna flop for you," Timpson said, "tell her to do that on her own time, will you?"

I tried to look somewhere between shocked and mildly surprised at her comment, but I'm certain the best expression I managed was somewhere between being caught with my pants down and extreme constipation. When I spoke, all I could come up with was, "That's not a nice thing to say."

"You're riding in her saddle, aren't you?"

I tried to look shocked. "Where did you get such an idea?"

"All the people who know me, who have seen you two around town together, they told me. And they've seen your car parked over at her house late at night. I suppose you could be helping her lay carpet, but my guess is you're laying something else."

I studied the old bat for a moment. "You're a little too smart and connected for your own good," I said. "But okay. That's on our own time.

Always has been." That was partly a lie, but it was close enough. "I like her. She likes me, but it won't affect our work."

"Relationships never affected mine."

I almost said I could believe that, but held back.

"It's not a problem," I said.

"Not for me it isn't. Do your job, and like I told you before, I don't care what you do as long as it doesn't cause the paper trouble. Same for Brenda."

"Belinda."

She and the chief needed to get together. They could rename the town population. Might as well, they were going to call people by whatever name they wanted anyway. Considering one was a policeman, the other an editor, you had to wonder why they couldn't remember names correctly.

"Very well, then," Timpson said. "Get on it, and take her with you. Besides, I've been thinking of moving her to reporter anyway."

"That's great," I said.

"Got to see how she performs while she works with you. That will make my determination. When I refer to performance, I'm talking about the reporter part."

I ignored that little jab, said, "She deserves the reporter job."

"Not really, but I'm thinking Oswald might quit, and that way I got a replacement. He seems kind of pissy around me lately."

I was thinking it might be all her nifty references to the colored, but I decided not to mention it.

First thing I did was go home and get the DVDs out of their hiding place; spent the morning going through them until I found Ronnie on disc with Caroline. They were a beautiful pair, and the way they went at it, it was like watching some very smooth porno film directed by a woman instead of a man. It was slow and sensuous, and I found myself getting aroused. I felt guilty about that, knowing there was a good chance Caroline was dead. I focused on that possibility, and became more clinical. I took in every aspect of Ronnie's face offered to me. She was almost as beautiful as Caroline. In fact, they looked somewhat alike, except Ronnie was dark-haired and Caroline was blond. There was also something about Ronnie that was different. She didn't quite have the unearthly beauty that Caroline had, but the way she moved, and smiled, she seemed warmer, sexier, more real.

I remembered what Belinda had said about Caroline borrowing personality and charm from her memory banks, and it occurred to me when you got past that incredible beauty of hers, the sexuality that was there because of her looks, there was in fact something missing. She moved her mouth in a passionate manner, but her eyes were as flat and uninteresting as the backside of a cardboard cutout.

I turned the DVD off. I had Ronnie's image in my mind. I knew who I was looking for. I put Ronnie's DVD with the others, packed up the ones I had looked through to find hers, took the one of Jimmy from between my books and put it with the others, then placed the box back in the closet hideaway.

I checked the notes I had on Ronnie, information that was in the stuff Mercury gave me. There was an address. I picked up Belinda and we drove over there. It was a duplex and Ronnie's address was on the top floor. I walked up and knocked. A woman answered. She wasn't Ronnie Fisher. She was good-looking, older than Ronnie would have been, said her name was Sharon Duran. I asked about Ronnie and she shook her head. Never heard of her.

I asked the name of her landlord, and got his number and called him. I asked him about Ronnie. His name was Leon Cripson, and when he talked, he sounded distracted, like he might be watching TV on mute, or perhaps checking his pubic hair for lice.

"Yeah, cute gal," the landlord said, "moved out a while back."

"How many months ago?" I said. I was sitting in the car with Belinda at the wheel. We were parked out front of Ronnie's former duplex.

"Hell, I don't know. You sure you're a reporter?"

I gave him my name and told him who my boss was. I could almost hear him considering things over the line. "Must have been, oh, seven, eight months ago," he said.

"Mr. Cripson, did you know Ronnie knew the girl who disappeared?"

"What?"

I gave him a brief explanation.

"Oh, yeah. I remember that. I remember because Ronnie was in the paper, saying something about it."

"About some fines the missing girl owed."

"That was it. I remember because the girl, what was her name again?" I told him.

"Yeah, she was so pretty, and I thought Ronnie was pretty too. I remember thinking it wasn't surprising they knew one another. Them good-lookers run in packs."

"Did you ever see Caroline with Ronnie?"

"No. I don't think so. I'd remember if I did, if that newspaper picture did her any credit."

"Did Ronnie leave your duplex around the time that the girl went missing? Could it have been then?"

There was a brief pause. "She did. She went owing me some rent. I don't know exactly when she got out of Dodge, but it was around then. All I know is she didn't pay me and didn't pay me and didn't pay me, and I went over and finally had to open the door and put all her stuff in storage. I called her cell number over and over, but nothing. I called up the college. They said she dropped out and went home."

"And left all her stuff?"

"Don't know she left it all, could have taken some things with her, but she left a lot of it behind."

"Do you remember where Ronnie's home was, the place she went back to?"

"No. I don't."

"So you have her stuff stored?"

"It's in a storage stall. I should have already gotten rid of it, and I'm going to, soon as I can get around to it. Have Goodwill come cart it off after I sell what I can sell. It's costing me more to store it than it's worth."

"Is there any way we could come look through it? We think she might know something about the missing girl, and there could be something that connects her to Caroline."

"Really?" he said.

"It's a thought," I said.

"You mean it might help with a murder investigation?"

"It's possible. Can we come look?"

"I guess so. But it has to be on these terms. You empty out the storage building. That's the deal."

"I can't afford to buy her stuff."

"Hell with that. I've decided to get rid of it all. Deal?"

"Deal," I said.

32

I rented a U-Haul truck and Belinda followed me in my car over to the address the landlord had given me. I called just before we got there and he gave me the gate code.

There were rows of storage buildings inside a fence, and there was a little outfit by the gate with buttons on it. I pushed the buttons Cripson had told me to push. The gate clicked open and swung back on its hinges.

In front of the building with the number Cripson had given me was the big black SUV he told me to look for.

Cripson got out of the SUV when we drove up. He was a short, fat, bald guy who wheezed when he walked, like a huge basketball leaking air. He was pulling a little tank on wheels and he had tubes hooked up to his nose that ran back into the tank.

I got out of the van and Belinda got out of the car and we moved through the summer heat like we were moving through gelatin; the heat rose up from the cement in wavy lines that made you feel dizzy.

I shook hands with Cripson. He didn't offer to shake hands with Belinda, but he gave her an up-and-down look that no one could really blame him for. She was wearing blue jeans today and a simple top, but those jeans fit her as close as baby oil.

"Here's the key," Cripson said. "You unlock it. This emphysema wears me out if I so much as vigorously wipe my ass."

I unlocked the storage shed and peeked inside. There were all manner of dusty boxes. The air was still and heavy and stunk of mildew and something spoiled. It was hot.

"What's that smell?" I said.

"Now and again, animals crawl up under the back, get in there and are too stupid to get out," Cripson said. "Possums, armadillos, rats. They die. Ain't nothing stinks worse than a dead rat."

"I can vouch for that," I said.

"Hence, the saying: I smell a rat," Belinda said.

"What's that?" Cripson said.

"Nothing," Belinda said. "I was entertaining myself."

"Well," Cripson said, "whatever. It's all yours. Dig in. Get it all. That's our deal. And when you leave, push the padlock in place. Give me the key now."

A moment later Cripson wheezed back into his SUV and was gone in a puff of dust, leaving Belinda and me inside the storage shed looking around.

"It's so hot I feel as if I'm going to swoon," Belinda said.

I felt the same way, so we went at it easy, a little at a time, took a break and hung the padlock in place without locking it, went back to Belinda's house to eat a sandwich, then returned to work before we got so comfortable we couldn't force ourselves back.

It took most of the morning and into the early afternoon, and the stink got worse as we went along. It was coming from somewhere amidst the garbage. We didn't find out what the stink was right then, but got everything loaded and over to Belinda's place, where we put it in her garage.

When we were finished, Belinda said, "I can tell you this much, Cason. Ronnie didn't just decide to skip out on her rent. She left in a real hurry, because she left her jewelry and her makeup, some awfully nice dresses and slacks, and a lot of shoes. I don't think she'd do that. I wouldn't do that, not unless I had to. Not unless I had to run quick."

"Maybe Ronnie knew more about Caroline than overdue library fines."

"And all those boxes," she said, "I don't know what's in them, but that's where the stink is coming from. My guess is Cripson hired someone to move all this stuff, and they unloaded her refrigerator and stuck the stuff in boxes and put it in the shed. The bottom is about to come out of a couple of them. Would she have gone off and left a whole refrigerator full of food?"

"Sometimes people do that."

"Okay. But what's her rush? And again, there's the makeup, jewelry and clothes."

"It's a little curious," I said.

We looked in the boxes, and sure enough, it was old rotten food that seemed to have mutated and become one with the boxes it was in. You couldn't tell what kind of food it had been, but it was certainly a lively creation. We bagged all of that up in plastic bags and stuffed it in trash cans.

We poked around in the other boxes, looking for what we in the newspaper business like to call a big ole goddamn clue. I was prowling through a box of books, mostly cookbooks, and one book on sexuality that had some nice pictures, which I examined closely, just in case it might contain information we might need. Like certain sexual positions that required peanut butter and jelly. I was looking this over when Belinda said, "Put that down, Cason."

I did.

"I got some letters here," she said. "They are kind of curious."

I went over and looked at them with her. They were letters from a Mrs. Soledad who lived in Cleveland, Texas.

"I don't know they mean anything," she said, "but it might not be a bad idea to look through them. It might give us some home information about Ronnie, where to find her. You can find anyone on the Internet these days."

"We can try that. Anything else curious?"

Belinda shook her head. "Not really, and that's pretty much all of it. We been through everything. Of course, if you need to examine that book a little more closely. . . ."

"Nope," I said. "Got it memorized."

"Perhaps you could show me some of the points of interest later."

"I can almost guarantee that," I said.

We bundled the letters together, and I drove the moving van back to the rental company, Belinda following in my car, then we went back to her place. We had the letters with us the whole trip, and as I drove us back, Belinda looked through them. When she was finished, she bundled them together again and we carried them into her place.

It was really cool inside, especially after we'd been out in the heat all day, and we put the letters on the coffee table and got something to drink. We sat and drank and didn't look at the letters. We soon found ourselves in the shower, where it was necessary to use the soap bar on each other so we could get to all those hard-to-reach spots. The water was warm but it wasn't warm like the outside air. It was pleasant and we spent a long time in there, then rinsed in cold water until we shook.

We toweled off and lay in the bed under the covers. I told Belinda some things about that sex book I had been looking at in the garage, but neither of us was particularly inspired; the heat had sapped us. Without meaning to, we fell asleep.

When I awoke the room was dark. Night had fallen. I got out of bed carefully, so as not to wake Belinda. Still nude, I padded into the living room and sat down on the couch and took the bundle of letters off the coffee table.

I looked through them. Caroline was mentioned in them. A lot. The letters were obviously Mrs. Soledad's response to letters written by Ronnie. Just being on the receiving end, not having Ronnie's letters, I wasn't exactly sure what some of it meant. But I could tell this: Ronnie was worried about Caroline and so was Mrs. Soledad, up to a point. I got the feeling maybe Mrs. Soledad didn't miss Caroline as much as Ronnie did.

I read through the letters a couple of times. A lot of them weren't about Caroline and were just hometown things. From the letters I understood that Soledad lived outside of Cleveland, Texas. That was about two hours from where we were.

I turned on Belinda's computer and looked up Cleveland, and I looked up Mrs. Soledad's address. It was there, easy as could be to find. There was even an aerial view of her house.

I was looking at the aerial view and thinking about some of the things in the letters when a hand clapped down on my shoulder and I jumped.

Belinda said, "Looking up porn sites."

I turned. She hadn't bothered with clothes either. I said, "Hey, I'm living one. Why look it up?"

She smiled at me. "What you got there?" she said.

"An address. Now all I need is a phone number."

33

It didn't take much research to find Mrs. Soledad's phone number. Next morning, I called her and told her I wanted to talk to her about Ronnie, asked if she knew where Ronnie was these days.

"No," she said. "But I don't talk about things like that over the telephone."

I gave her my background, told her I was running down a story about missing women, meaning Ronnie and Caroline, and from some letters I had come across, I knew she knew them well.

Mrs. Soledad was silent for a moment.

"Letters?" she asked.

I explained.

"Those were private," she said.

"Came across them by accident, and we're doing an investigation."

"We?"

"My assistant and I."

"I don't know I like you going through letters I've written."

"Sorry, Mrs. Soledad. We just sort of came across them."

"Did you have permission? Isn't there a law about that?"

"They had been confiscated by the landlord for back rent. He gave us permission to look through what was left."

No word from the other end.

"You know that Caroline went missing?" I said.

"Of course. Ronnie told me. We exchanged letters and phone calls. Mostly letters. I don't do that new thing everyone does."

"New thing?"

"Mailing off the computer."

"Oh. E-mail."

"That's right. We did it the old-fashioned way. Envelopes and stamps. But, yes, I knew Caroline. I knew her well."

"Can you tell me about her and Ronnie?"

"You come see me. I see you face-to-face, then maybe I'll want to talk."

"All right," I said.

"You get here, I'll be the one with a .357 in my lap."

"Oh."

"No. I mean it. Come on, but you better have good intentions."

"I use my powers only for good."

"Yeah, well, you better."

She gave me the directions I already had from the Internet. Belinda and I drove over to Cleveland in my junker. When we left, a dark cloud came in from the west and brought thunder and lightning with it. The noonday sky was dark as midnight. We drove with the headlights on. We saw a strand of lightning hit the ground out in a pasture, and when it hit, the world lit up brighter than a floor show in Las Vegas, made my vision go white for an instant. When we were a half hour out from Cleveland, the bottom of the cloud collapsed and down came rain. We had to turn the windshield wipers on high. One of my wiper blades was a wounded soldier. Part of it came loose, slapped frantically at the windshield.

It was still raining when we got into Cleveland. Mrs. Soledad lived in a little white house just off the highway with a covered porch with a swing on it and a couple of cloth foldout chairs. As we drove up in the yard, the wind picked up the chairs and slapped them across the porch and hung them up in the swing.

Belinda and I sat in the car for a moment. The driveway ended some twenty feet from the porch steps, in front of a closed-up garage. I said, "I'm thinking about the .357 she mentioned."

"She shoots you," Belinda said, "I'll go for help."

"Comforting."

About that time, a woman, who I surmised was Mrs. Soledad, came out on the porch. I didn't see the .357 in her hand. She waved us in.

"Here we go," I said, and I opened my door and slid out, and Belinda slid out behind me. We fought our way through the rain, and the moment we stepped up on the porch steps, the wind picked up again, jerked one of the cloth chairs out of its tangle against the swing, carried it away in a swirl, just missing us. I watched it fly off the porch, hit the yard twice, like a skipping rock, then go sailing into a stand of trees where it got hung up.

I gave a hand to Belinda and helped her onto the porch. I turned and looked at Mrs. Soledad. She was about five feet tall with black hair streaked with gray, and she had a little body and a pleasant face. She looked elderly, but spry, like an android version of a grandma. In spite of this, I kept the .357 she had mentioned in mind.

"Sorry about your chair," I said. "Rain slacks, I'll get it for you."

"Don't worry about the chairs," she said. She pushed the screen door wider. "Come on in. It's gotten chilly out here. Not to mention wet."

The other chair gave way then, came up and over the swing, banged against one of the chains that supported the swing, then darted off the open end of the porch and sailed out to join its cousin.

Inside it was a little cool, but nothing like outside. The place was dark and smelled of Lysol. After a moment my eyes adjusted, and I could see the place looked like the classic grandma home, with knickknacks here and there, and a big comfy couch with a Chihuahua lying on it like something stuffed. There was a small blackened fireplace and some really thick, comfy chairs nearby. Out a back window I could see a big fenced-in yard being rained on.

We stood there as she went away, and came back with towels.

"Dry off," she said, and we did. She took the towels, folded them up and placed them on an arm of the couch.

"Sit down," Mrs. Soledad said. "I'll make us some tea."

"Thanks," Belinda said. She and I chose the comfy chairs by the dead fireplace. Mrs. Soledad disappeared into the kitchen. A light came on in there and some of it fled into the room where we sat. I could hear pans clanging around in there.

About five minutes passed, Belinda and I not saying anything, just glancing at each other from time to time. Occasionally checking out the

Chihuahua, who had almost raised its head once, but had decided on a shrug and a soft sigh.

I looked around for the .357, but didn't see it.

Mrs. Soledad came out of the kitchen, came over and stood between us in our chairs. "Take about fifteen minutes for the water to be ready," she said. "I'll start us up a fire. Can you believe this?" she said, stopping to snap up some wood in a little metal bucket, and put it in the fire-place. "This time of year it ought to be hot. I had to turn off the air con-ditioner."

"Weird times," I said.

"Global warming," she said. "It makes the seasons all screwed up."

She built a fire in the fireplace, and I stood up and got some larger wood out of a bin on the other side of the mantel and gave it to her and she put it in the way she wanted. Pretty soon the fire was jumping and crackling and throwing shadows over the room.

Outside the rain came down hard on the roof. Mrs. Soledad sat on the couch beside the motionless Chihuahua.

"They usually yap, Chihuahuas," I said.

"He's too old for that," Ms. Soledad said. "He barks too hard, he might throw up a lung. He's twenty-one years old. I kid you not."

"Wow," Belinda said.

"About Ronnie," she said. "Do you know where she is?"

"We were hoping you might," I said. "She knew Caroline, and Caroline is also missing . . . possibly murdered, and it ties in with another inves-tigation our paper is doing."

Ms. Soledad shook her head. "No. I was hoping you knew where she is. I've tried shaking every tree you can imagine. I reported her missing, but nothing really came of it. They said she checked out of the university and left, just no one knows where."

"Wouldn't she just go home?" Belinda asked.

"This is home," Ms. Soledad said. "Home of a sorts. The one she knew best. I did home care. A foster parent."

"Ronnie was one of your foster kids?" I asked.

Ms. Soledad nodded. "And so was Caroline, for a while."

"Can you tell us about it?" I asked.

"Caroline and Ronnie came to me when they were preteens. They had been with an adoption agency, but no one adopted them. Ronnie would have been adopted, I suppose, but when she came to stay with me, she just never left. I pretty much became her mother, and she my daughter. I love her dearly, and I'm very concerned about her."

"Why didn't the police follow up?" I asked.

"I think they did. But there was nothing to follow. She checked out of school, left her apartment and just went away. There was no evidence of foul play, they said."

"Except she left everything she had in the apartment . . ." I said. "Oh, I didn't mean to worry you, Mrs. Soledad. It's just that I'm not that impressed with our police force in Camp Rapture, previous or present."

"Nor I," she said. "Fact is, I'm quite sure something has happened to Ronnie. She wouldn't have quit writing. She would have called me on Mother's Day. She always did, you know. I was worried because she was so close to Caroline, and that was like having a rattlesnake for a friend. In the end, it just doesn't work out."

"Can you tell us about Ronnie and Caroline?" Belinda asked. "Maybe we can help find them, if we knew more about them."

"Truth is, I hated Caroline," she said. "Isn't that an absolutely awful thing to say? I raised her to some degree, but, as they say in East Texas, that girl just wasn't right."

Belinda looked at me out of the corner of her eye, then back at Mrs. Soledad. "When she was a kid did you hate her?" Belinda asked.

Ms. Soledad nodded. "I never said such a thing to her. I tried in every way to like her and to get along with her, but she was . . . wrong. Don't misunderstand me. I don't think she was born wrong. Having helped raise many foster kids, I'm convinced that we humans make our own monsters. But sometimes, the monster gets made very early, and there's no rescue. The deed is done."

The teapot whistled and Mrs. Soledad walked into the kitchen and came back with a tray and three cups of tea. She gave one to Belinda, one to me. She sat down on the floor and fixed her tea, then got up without effort and went to the couch.

"Notice how I get around," she said, and it was easy to see she was proud of her agility.

"Yes," I said.

"Yoga. I swear by it."

I nodded. "I may have to take it up."

"Good for the back."

"I'm sure it is. You were saying about Caroline."

Mrs. Soledad sipped her tea. "Yes. She was a pathetic thing. Her parents, they had done a number on her. Her mother was thirteen when she had Caroline. Can you believe that, thirteen? I didn't even know about sex until I was fifteen or sixteen. Christ, are hormones really working at that age? I guess so, but it seems so amazing."

"Yes, ma'am," I said.

"Anyway, her mother had her at thirteen, and the old boy who was the father ran off and didn't come back, and when Caroline was two or so, her mother . . . what was her name . . . Jennifer something . . . Well, Jennifer took up with an older man. Some fellow twenty-five, worked as a pulpwood driver. This guy drank when he worked and drank when he was home, and he took to beating Jennifer like she was a dusty rug, and he didn't have a lot of patience with a baby either. I don't know what went on there exactly, but it wasn't good. I'm sure little Caroline took a few whippings herself. If not worse.

"Well, things looked like they were turning for the better when the old boy had a pile of pulpwood snap its chain and cover him up and kill him good . . . But Jennifer, therein lay another problem. She wasn't any smarter at sixteen than she was at thirteen, and the next thing you know she's pregnant again, some black fellow from over around Houston. Now, I know how some people feel. I don't give a damn about skin color. What I think's wrong here is that Jennifer was little more than a baby and this fellow was nearly thirty, and he wasn't any better than the husband she had before. Except he didn't drive a pulpwood truck. He kicked Jennifer one night while she was pregnant, and the baby died from the kick. The kicker, her old man, disappeared into the woodwork.

"Caroline was soon the stepdaughter or stepniece or pal to whoever came along and was shacking up with her mama, and that's all Caroline knew. She didn't know that these men weren't supposed to touch their daughters, or stepdaughters, and they sure weren't supposed to have sex with them. She started being molested early on, I figure, but certainly by the time she was eleven she was being taken full advantage of by her mother's boyfriends, or husbands, whatever Jennifer called them. And as Caroline got older, she turned into a real looker, and that brought all manner of boys around."

"How did you learn about all this?" I asked.

"Her social workers, people who knew her. Things she told me. Believe me, I did my research. I wanted to do whatever I could to help her. I had had abused children before, but this poor girl, she was the most worked over and manipulated I had ever seen. Her mother used her. It was a way for her to attract men to help take care of her and Caroline. She put her out there like bait on a line. And she didn't care if Caroline was servicing them like a show heifer. Long as it kept food on the table and she didn't have to bother with work or raising a kid. By this time my guess is the mother had pretty much worn out on sex, and she was just then old enough to really start having it.

"Sex isn't just an act. It's an emotional investment, though kids these days try to tell you different. They call it hooking up. At least they're making the choice to hook up. Caroline, she wasn't making the choice. Least not at first. But by the time she was fourteen she knew something about manipulation herself. Two men came to live with Caroline and her mother, and they both were there for Caroline. And somehow, Caroline worked them. Or that's my guess. And one of them killed the other, and the survivor ended up in jail. Caroline, she never went to see him or had anything else to do with him. She had played them. She was a hollow shell. All of her goodness, or any potential for goodness, had been sucked out and blown away dry. She took to hurting animals and setting fires, and finally she was taken away from her mother."

"And that's how you ended up with her?" Belinda said.

"That's right, sugar. That's how I ended up with her. Her mother swore she was going to clean up her act, but what she did was put a needle in her arm that was full of something that killed her. Caroline, when I told her about it, she said, 'Huh.' Just like that. Nothing else. She didn't go to the funeral. She didn't have any real connection to anyone, except maybe me a little, and Ronnie.

"But I don't know how to explain their relationship. I think Ronnie was someone she had feelings for, but I just don't think Caroline could have deep feelings. Wasn't in her. Ronnie was a way for her to travel with the normals, though Ronnie was a mess herself. She had had a bad family, but nothing like Caroline. Mostly just neglectful. She was damaged goods, but she wasn't ruined goods. More tea?"

"No thank you," I said. "So did they stay with you a long time, Ronnie and Caroline?"

"They stayed until they graduated. And here's the funny thing. Suddenly Caroline quit acting out. She did her homework, did well in school. She spent the rest of her time here in the back room playing games and writing stories."

"Do you still have the stories?" I asked.

Mrs. Soledad shook her head. "She took them with her."

"Did you ever read any of them?" Belinda asked.

"Once. They were mystery stories. They were stories where puzzle crimes were invented and the cops tried to figure it out, and the criminals got away with it."

"Not too unusual," I said.

"No. It wouldn't have been unusual, except that it was coming from Caroline. I lay down here at night, I locked my door. I didn't trust her, and finally I wasn't sure I could trust her with Ronnie. That was just instinct, nothing to validate it. Anyway, she graduated with high grades, and Ronnie got through on a hair and a prayer, and they got in the university, though Ronnie just barely managed it. I remember asking Caroline, trying to be mother-like, what she was going to major in. You know what she answered? 'Cleverness.' "

"What did you make of that?" I asked.

"I took her at her word. I think her life was about manipulation. She's returning the favor of what was done to her, by her mother and by a horde of men and lovers. I think she sees the world as just one big game to survive. She's just going through the motions, and she's going to try and make other people go through the motions she wants them to go through. Not because they have done something to her, but because they haven't. Because they are just innocents that she can hurt and make miserable. The way she was made miserable. Worst part is, she had her own child."

"A child?" I said.

Ms. Soledad nodded. "She had a child when she was thirteen, right before she came to be with me, by one of the men who raped her, or misled her . . . all the same. It's rape no matter how they had sex with her. I think this man was someone she really cared about, someone who had really done a number on her. From some things she said I got the feeling if there was anyone she might have trusted, it was this man."

"I assume that trust evaporated after she had the child and the man left?" I said.

"I don't know," Ms. Soledad said. "I think she always had something for this guy. Maybe she gave him all the love she had left and could never quite take it back. In a way, I hope not. That shows a side of her that's more truly human than most of what I saw. But her getting knocked up like that, it was just like her mother. History repeating itself."

"What happened to the child?" Belinda asked.

"A relative or a family friend ended up with the child. I don't really know any more than that. Maybe she put it up for adoption, but the story I heard was the one about the relative or family friend. I also heard they died. But it could have just been a story. I don't even know if the child is alive. I just know that she and Ronnie went to the university in Camp Rapture, and that I told Ronnie to watch herself, to make new friends. Ronnie began to write me, and she told me that she thought she was gay, and that she had fallen in love with Caroline. Thing is, I don't care who loves who, as long as it's healthy, and there wasn't anything healthy about Caroline."

"More gamesmanship?" I asked.

"Exactly. It's like Caroline was petting and grooming Ronnie for something mean. I think Caroline was always about something mean. And she was patient. She could wait a long time to do what she wanted to do, and the closer you were to her, the more likely you were to be a victim. My dog here, George, he had a companion, Albert. The day Caroline left I found Albert floating in a bucket of water out back of the house. It was a bucket I used to catch runoff from the roof. I put it on my flower beds. I had a hard time believing he climbed up there to get a drink and fell in. I think Caroline, as a kind of going-away present, dunked him in there and held him under until he drowned."

Outside thunder rumbled, like God falling down stairs.

"How did Ronnie take Caroline going missing?" I asked.

"Last letter I got from Ronnie she said she felt both sad and relieved. I think she had started to listen to me, or perhaps due to events there she had come to believe that Caroline was a real troubled little girl. I hate Caroline for what I think she became, but I feel awfully sorry for her too, but I'm glad she's gone and I'm glad she's dead."

"We don't know she is for a fact," I said.

"But that's how it usually is in these cases, isn't it?" Mrs. Soledad said.

"Yeah," I said. "That's how it is."

"You know what I think?" Mrs. Soledad said. "I think she tried to manipulate someone as bad as she was, maybe someone worse. And, like she did with my little dog, they killed her for the sport of it. It's sad and wrong of me, but I hope so. It's bad enough her killer is loose in the world, but it's a better place with her gone. And you want to know my guess? Whoever killed Caroline killed Ronnie, otherwise I would have heard from her by now. We were too close. That's why I agreed to talk with you. I want you to find whoever killed her and make them pay, even if they did kill that monster Caroline."

"We'll do our best to find out what happened," I said.

"One more thing. I have something of Caroline's, though I doubt it's of any importance."

Mrs. Soledad got up and went into a back room and came back with a little red book done up in leather. "I think this is something that one of her many daddies had. I think she kept it. Maybe she had some connection with the owner, or maybe she just liked the book. I read a little but couldn't get much out of it. It was behind the bed, hung up on the headboard at the back. Way it was back there, it was hard to see. I found it when I took the bed apart. I don't think she meant to leave it."

Mrs. Soledad gave me the book. The cover, like the rest of the book, was solid red, but in gold letters was written: *Leather Maiden,* Jerzy Fitzgerald. I opened it up. Inside was a handwritten inscription. "To the best girl in the world." I thanked Mrs. Soledad and slipped the book in my back pocket.

"She read that book all the time, and Edgar Allan Poe. She loved a story called 'The Premature Burial.' That was her favorite. She found an old movie of the story. She said it was different than the short story, but she liked it anyway. She watched it a lot."

"You think that was odd?" Belinda asked.

"I like Poe and I liked the movie. Lots of people do. But she was drawn to it for different reasons than you and I. She saw things with a different eye. Now, unless you want another cup of tea, that's about all I have."

"No, ma'am, we're good. We'll use your restroom if we may, and then move on."

She pointed to its location.

"One thing," I said. "Do you really have a .357?"

She reached under the couch cushions and pulled it out. "I decided I didn't really need it."

"That's good. You don't have kids here anymore, do you?"

"No," she said, replacing the gun. "I decided after Caroline, and what happened to poor Albert, and now sweet Ronnie, that I had had enough. There's only so much do-gooding a do-gooder can do."

34

The rain had slowed considerably and the wind was no longer blowing when we went out on the front porch. I captured Mrs. Soledad's chairs before we left, and she took them inside and then came back with something in her hand.

"I have a few of these, so you can have this one."

I took it. It was a photograph of Ronnie, for reference. I didn't mention that I had a DVD for reference. I thanked her, and Belinda and I went out to the car. Mrs. Soledad waved at us from her porch as we sat in the car, the motor running and the heater on.

We drove away from there, and after about fifteen minutes on the road, the sky turned clear. I shut off my wipers and we drove along until the sun came out and it turned hot. I turned off the heater. We stopped at a hamburger joint in a little town and ate lunch. Sitting there, eating our burgers and sipping sodas, I said, "What did you think about what Mrs. Soledad said?"

"I don't think she told us the half of it," Belinda said. "Caroline was probably worse than Mrs. Soledad could express. I actually think she was holding back."

"I got the same feeling," I said. "I think it was hard for her to come down on someone that way."

"Yeah, that's how I feel," Belinda said. "But what I can't figure is, where is Ronnie?"

"Think it could be like Ms. Soledad said—that whoever got Caroline may have gotten her too?"

"And what about the girl who's missing now, the one whose boyfriend was hacked up?"

"Tabitha. Yeah. I thought about her too. No doubt in my mind, it's all connected, and I think it may have to do with the Geek."

I had told Belinda all about the Geek, and she took a moment to consider. She said, "It's all like an ugly game. With puzzle pieces and clues, and blind alleys."

"And red herrings," I said. "Thing is, we don't know it's a game anyone's playing. In the long run we may not learn a damn thing more than we know now."

"That's true," Belinda said, "but we will have had an interesting road trip."

35

When we got back into Camp Rapture, I took Belinda home. We enjoyed each other's company, but I sensed that a little alone time for the two of us wouldn't be a bad idea. Too much togetherness had begun to tug at us.

I went by the newspaper, which was closed, and used my key to get in and sat down at my desk and banged out a column that my mind was halfway invested in. When I was finished I e-mailed it to Timpson's computer so that she'd have my column for next week.

When I went out to the car to go home, I thought I'd call Belinda, realized I had turned my phone off at some point and had not turned it back on. I brought it to life, and when I did, messages popped up.

One was from Jimmy.

I listened. He and Trixie were out of town, doing what he had told me he wanted to do. Mom and Dad had gone with them. They were going to be gone for several days. The message was simple and general and I assumed Trixie or Mom and Dad were nearby when he gave it.

The last message was from Booger. It just asked me to call.

I sat in the car for a moment, wondering if I should bother. I knew I shouldn't, but I couldn't help myself. I called.

"Hey," a voice said. I knew it wasn't Booger. He has a unique voice. But then again, so does Runt.

"Runt?" I said.

"Hey, punkin, how you doing down there in the wilds of East Texas?"

"Mixed report," I said. "Thought I was calling Booger's cell."

"You are calling Booger's cell. Well, one of them. I have another number for him, but he's not answering it. He left yesterday, and left this phone with me. He sold me the bar for a dollar."

"A dollar?"

"He does that now and again, so something happens to him, he says, it'll be in good hands. I got a contract and everything. When he comes back, we tear up the contract and he gives me the dollar back. He thinks every time he goes out for a while, it might be his last time."

"What if you didn't want to give the bar back?"

"I always want to give it back," Runt said. "He's my compadre."

"But if you didn't?"

"Fireworks."

I laughed. "I don't doubt that. Where is he?"

"When he gives me the contract and I give him the dollar, it means he could be anywhere. He's probably running whores in Oklahoma City, or Tulsa. That would be my guess. He might even be doing a cage match. He does that shit, you know?"

"No. I didn't know."

"Did do it, I mean. He got disqualified last time. Booger thought they really meant no rules. He poked a guy in the eyes and twisted the guy's nut sack and bit off part of the fellow's cheek. I think he got banned for life from cage matches, or some such shit. He said they had put him up in a hotel and given him a fruit basket, but after that little incident they locked him out of his room. He kicked the door down and got his clothes and the fruit basket. He's nuts about oranges. I think he owes some kind of fine, which, of course, he's unlikely to pay."

"Booger is a man of mystery, for damn sure."

"In your case, might be best you didn't find out some of that mystery."

"Well enough. You say you got another number for him?"

Runt gave me the number and I wrote it down.

"He misses you, boy," Runt said. "For him, you're the man."

"I'll buy him some flowers next time I see him, take him on a date."

"You know what he really likes?"

"What would that be? Slow walks in the rain, puppy dogs and kitties?"

"Malted eggs. He likes oranges, but malted eggs, that's his thing."

"Malted eggs?"

"Like they sell for Easter. He's like a nut for that stuff. One Easter weekend he put on five pounds eating that shit."

"And I thought I knew a lot about Booger."

"Nobody knows a lot about Booger," Runt said.

I drove on home. I sat in the car out front of my place and flipped open my phone and dialed the number Runt had given me for Booger, let it ring as I got out of the car and went to the door. I had no sooner put the key in the door and turned the lock than I heard a phone ringing inside my house.

It was ringing in conjunction with the number I dialed, same timing.

I listened to it ring another time or two, went back to my car and got the .38 out of the glove box and went back to the door. I turned off my phone. The ringing stopped.

I pushed the door open and eased around the motorcycle there.

Sitting on my couch in his underwear with the open phone lying on his knee, a beer in one hand, a .45 in the other, grinning like he had just found a fifty-dollar gold piece, sporting a chest tattoo that said TIGHT NOOKIE IS PROOF OF GOD, was Booger.

"I was hoping you were a burglar," Booger said. "That would have given me a reason to blow your head off."

"What in hell are you doing here?"

"Well, howdy to you too," Booger said.

"Again. What in hell are you doing here?" I said.

"Drinking a beer. Right before you came in I was scratching my nuts, and about an hour ago I was watching a cooking show with some hot lady on it cooking Italian food. I'd like to bend her over her pasta, I'm telling you right now. She had legs just like I like 'em. Feet on one end, poontang on the other. Come to think of it, I don't even give a shit if she has feet. Let's see, what else. I think before the cooking show I took a dump. By the way, your toilet has a slow flush. I think they got some Chinaman on the other side of the world using a hand pump."

"What are you doing here, Booger? Why did you pick my lock? And why in hell did you get that tattoo?"

"I couldn't get in. It was locked. So I had to pick it. It was easy, by the way. You ought to get some other kind of lock, something a little more serious than government work. The tat. I got that as a homage to what matters in life . . . Hey, how you doing, buddy?"

"Right now, I'm a little busy."

Booger looked hurt. "Man, you don't sound glad to see me."

Actually, in spite of myself, I was very glad to see him. "It's not that, Booger. I've been a little busy with something. How you doing, man? Glad to see you. How did you get here?"

"After a misunderstanding in Oklahoma, I drove here, and since I had my car's papers with me, I sold it to a gentleman down on a lot on the outskirts of town, and then I took a taxi to the store where I bought some provisions, and then I took the taxi here. Want a beer?"

"It's my house. I should be offering you something."

"Hey," he said, and held up the beer, "said I got provisions. Help yourself."

"I'm just going to have bottled coffee."

"Who the hell bottles coffee, Cason?"

"Starbucks."

"That's sissy shit. Whoever heard of drinking cold coffee out of a fucking bottle?"

"It's happening everywhere," I said, making my way to the fridge. "You should get out more. They even have soft drinks in cans now."

I opened the refrigerator. It was stocked thick with beer, two or three different kinds. I found the bottled coffee behind some tall green bottles and got one and went back to the living room, or that part of my apartment that passed for one, sat down in a chair and looked at Booger. My eyes had adjusted to the darkened room. He had a cut on his forehead and some bruises on his face.

"What happened to you?" I said. "You get caught up in machinery?"

"I got caught up in four guys in Tulsa," he said. "They wanted me to pay for some skank they managed who didn't know how to give a blow job. Way she worked, you'd have thought she was sucking a rock through a straw. Didn't do a man any good at all. I didn't want to pay. These gentlemen, her pimp and some bouncers, had different ideas."

"How did that work out?"

"I got cut across the head with a knife, and I got hit a lot because all of them, except the one with the knife, had blackjacks. But what I can report is that three of them are a little broken up, and one of them can now put his leg over his head with no real effort. He might even be able to remove it and swing it around. And I suppose, right now, a whore who can't blow a dick is looking for a new pimp to walk her around. And I have a new knife."

"How bad did you hurt the pimp?"

"He's not hurting now. So, after that, I needed a place to go and have a little R&R. But don't worry, they don't know who I am. I gave them Runt's name when I signed on there for business."

I smiled. "No you didn't."

"Of course not. I gave them yours."

"You are funny."

"Let's just say if they're looking for someone, his name is Delbert Littleball. I had it on one of my false licenses, so it's the one I showed them. These days, just to get your ashes carried, you got to have identification so they don't think some Arab has flown all the way over here to blow up some random whore with a bomb in a rubber."

"How long you been here?"

"Not real long. I got here it was raining like a cow pissing on a flat rock, so I let myself in. I slept a bit on the couch. By the way, I also played on your computer. Looked at porn, just the free stuff, and I found where you had a big old fat file on a chick named Caroline who was so good-looking I thought my left nut was going to go in orbit around my johnson."

"You looked at my personal stuff?"

"Hey, it wasn't coded or anything. All I had to do was turn it on and it came up on the menu, along with other stuff. I looked at everything there. Say, you get back with that Gabby girl?"

"No."

"Good. You don't need her. By the way, all those notes you got on Caroline, this business you got going, it's interesting."

"It is at that."

"Reporting is more fun than I thought. I thought you just mostly typed up shit, but you get into some action, don't you?"

"Booger, you ought not to have been in my business like that."

"I was bored, and after a while all the porno starts to look alike. I can't tell who's got the dick and who's got the tits. So, I got to playing. You got lots of notes, bro. I read them all. Those kids got killed, I read your article on that, all your articles in fact. I liked most of them. I even read about the town on the Internet. This little place is hopping. All that racial shit going on. Best way to keep yourself sane on matters like that is to hate everyone straight across the board, except your bros of course. Way I see it, humanity is like a hungry, parasitic dog without a home, crossing the highway, back and forth. Sooner or later to be hit by a car."

"What about your sisters?"

"Women I know aren't my sisters and I wouldn't trust them to hold five dollars for me while I went to the toilet. I'll tell you something, though: all this stuff going down, black preacher and white preacher, could be some action in the old town that night. Or is it midday?"

"Midday. Look, Booger—"

"Hey, man. Almost forgot something. In all that rain, a mailman showed up. Can you believe that? Rain and sleet and all that shit, and this guy meant it. Actually, though, he wasn't a government employee. He was FedEx or UPS or one of those things. Another kind of mailman. He had a package for you."

"A package?"

"What are you, a fucking parrot? Yeah, a package."

"I wasn't expecting anything."

"It's on the kitchen counter."

I went into the kitchen and got it. The handwriting on the front didn't look like any handwriting I had seen before. There was an address on the front, one that indicated who had mailed the package to me. I recognized it immediately. It was Jimmy's address.

I got out my pocketknife and slit the package open and eased out the contents. There was a letter and a photograph. I looked at the photograph and caught my breath.

"What is it, bro?" Booger said.

I turned back toward the living room and sat down in my chair again and looked at the photograph some more. It was of three women. I recognized one of them right off. It was Tabitha. She wasn't looking so good. She was stretched out on a board like those photos of Old West villains shot and displayed for the crowd and she didn't appear to have any insides, just a skull and a skin hanging off of that. Next to her, on another slab, was another woman. The face was withered and the eyes were gone and her body was in the same condition. Next to her was another withered body with long blond hair, and her lower body was partially covered by a blanket, or some kind of cloth. The only one I really recognized was Tabitha, and that was because she was the freshest. Above each of the women was a little cardboard sign. The signs read, left to right: TABITHA. RONNIE. CAROLINE.

At the foot of the photograph there was a longer cardboard sign that read BETRAYERS.

Booger said, "What, man?"

When I didn't answer, he came over and stood by my chair and looked down at what I was looking at. I put the photograph on the coffee table and Booger picked it up and looked at it while I opened the letter to read.

SO, YOU WANT TO KNOW WHAT GIVES? HERE'S WHAT GIVES. GO TO THESE ADDRESSES AND TAKE A LOOK. YOU'LL FIND WHAT YOU NEED TO FIND. ONE AND TWO. THREE SORT OF CAME APART AND IS NO MORE. THEY BETRAYED THE CAUSE AND THEY PAID. WHITE POWER WEARS MANY HATS. ADDRESS ONE, NOTICE THE PATH. ADDRESS TWO, SEEK THE TOWER. COME AFTER SIX TODAY. NO POLICE. POLICE COME, BAD THINGS COULD HAPPEN.

The addresses were listed, two of them. I knew generally where one of them was, and I had a town map in my car to find the other. What made me nervous was the package was supposed to have come from Jimmy's address. Probably mailed from a UPS store. They wanted me to know they knew all about him and where he lived. I was glad he was out of town. I looked at the date on the envelope. Today. I looked at my watch. Nearly six.

Booger said, "You know what? This photo ain't right."

I was up and moving. "No, it isn't. I'm going to check something."

I called Jimmy on my cell. It seemed like an hour before he answered, but he picked up on the third ring.

"Cason," he said. "What's going on?"

"Not much. You're out of town, right?"

"Oh yeah. Didn't you get my message?"

"Double-checking."

"We're out at the lake. Outside watching the sun start to dip. Trixie is lying in a lawn chair, looking good in a two-piece, reading a book, and I'm sitting here drinking a big old Pepsi-Cola and can't wait till bedtime so I can show Trixie all my manly tricks. Mom and Dad are in the house. Mom brought today's newspaper. Dad is reading a book."

"Don't say any more, and don't answer any calls that don't come from my number, and then be sure it's me before you start talking too much."

Jimmy was silent for a while. I got the idea he was moving to another location, away from Trixie. "Something coming down?"

"I don't think it's anything, really."

"You're lying to me, Cason. I'm the good liar, not you."

"It's anything, you'll be the first to know."

"I don't believe that either. You may not be safe. You ought to join us here."

"I got a friend with me."

"A woman?"

"An old war buddy. Nobody you know. I'm safe."

"I don't know what to say, Cason, except I don't want to come back there. I may never want to come back there."

"I don't want you to. At least not now. I'll keep you informed. Just wanted to check in."

"I feel like such a chickenshit."

"You're fine. Just stay there."

Jimmy had a few more things to say, but I was hardly listening. I hung up the phone and went to the closet and got the holster that went with the .38 and strapped it on my belt and put the .38 in it and pulled my shirt out and over it.

"Hey, man," Booger said, "hold your goddamn water till I get my pants on. Me and Mr. Lucky are going with you."

Mr. Lucky was Booger's .45. It was one of his small circle of friends.

36

The first address was a vacant lot in an area I knew, and behind the lot were some woods, and about two acres on either side of the lot were also woods, and beyond that, on both sides were houses. There was nothing to see that meant anything to me. I parked at the curb and Booger and I sat there and looked around. Night had fallen and the wind had picked up and there was a hint of more rain in the air.

Booger said, "You think you're being fucked with?"

"One way or another," I said. "Thing is, I wasn't supposed to bring you."

"It said no police. I'm not the police. Someone sends you a picture of dead women and says meet them in the dark, you ought to have someone friendly with you. This way, you got me and Mr. Lucky."

I got out of the car and Booger got out on the other side. I said, "I figure they want me to work for it. They said to look for the path."

"There it is," Booger said.

He was pointing at a little trail that rolled across the lot and down amongst the clutch of trees at the back. The moonlight made the path look like a twisty, silver ribbon.

"Could be an ambush," Booger said. "Like I was saying, you don't want to come here with nothing besides that .38 and a hopeful feeling.

Tell you what, bro. I'm going to kind of fade off to the side here, and come along on the right, and you go down the path. You got business you don't like, you get to cracking that peashooter, or yelling out, and me and Mr. Lucky will come running and barking and calling your name."

"Good enough," I said.

"I hope it is somebody," Booger said.

"Don't hope too hard. You might shoot someone hasn't got anything to do with anything."

"Everybody has something to do with something in my book," Booger said.

"I mean it, Booger."

Booger looked at me and smiled. That smile told me a lot. It told me he didn't really give a damn about what I had to say, but he would humor me. Up to a point.

The wind was blowing hard when I got on the path and started down it toward the wood line. I looked up to find Booger, but he was already gone. He was in his element. Stalk and destroy.

As I went along, the trail dipped down a hill and into the trees, and I could hear water running. The trees on either side of the trail were wind-whipped, and as they blew they tossed shadows along the trail. As I walked, the trail grew more narrow and the shadows grew longer and thicker. Pretty soon there was nothing but the dark. I had a flashlight in the car, but like an idiot I hadn't thought to bring it. Booger, he could see in the dark like a cat, so he wouldn't be bothered. Me, I wasn't that good.

I went on down and felt my way along with my feet, going slow, and then I heard something, movement in the bushes. I crouched and wondered if it was Booger. I almost called out his name, but held my breath instead. I felt as if at any moment the winged Oz monkeys would appear and grab me and flap me off into the night.

I made sure I had control of my breathing, waited and listened. I didn't hear anything. I stood up and started moving again, and as I went the trail opened and dropped down through the woods. I jumped over a narrow creek and kept walking until the woods split open and there was another clearing. I could see something in the clearing ahead. It was dead center of the clearing and it wasn't moving.

Then something did move. Something came out of the shadows up ahead and went across quick.

A shape. A man most likely, and not Booger. I'd know Booger's tank-broad shape anywhere. This was a leaner, lankier shape that moved like his bones were rubber. The moon had flashed on his shaved skull and I got a glimpse of what looked like a giant spider on the back of his neck—the hand tattoo the kids had told me about.

Stitch, the Geek.

I got the .38 out and eased onward, keeping an eye peeled on where I had seen the shape disappear into the woods. I went to where the shape had gone, moved as quickly as I could down a trail that was half my width. I took a few limb slaps in the face as I went. I heard something ahead of me, a cracking sound, and I went after it, moving pretty quick, and then I didn't hear anything. I stopped. I decided I didn't want to keep going. The brush was thick and it was dark and the shape was definitely in there. He could be anywhere, and all he had to do was be quiet and still and wait on me.

I took a deep breath, backed about twenty feet down the trail, then turned, and there he was. I just got a glimpse of that strange face, that mis-shapen, shaved skull. Before I could bring the .38 up, he hit me so hard I didn't remember falling to the ground, didn't even feel it at first. I tried to roll over, but he kicked me in the side. I tried to lift the .38, but realized I didn't have it anymore.

I heard Booger yell, and then I heard him crashing down the trail. There was a fleeting glimpse of pants legs, and then one more kick in the ribs, and then Stitch was gone.

I got on my knees and felt around and found the .38. I heard Booger calling again. I got up and staggered back down the trail and out to the larger path. I looked at the thing in the clearing again. I moved on down there, and didn't hear anything again, and didn't see anything, except for that thing in the clearing. As I grew closer, I saw that it was human-shaped and it seemed to be squatting, as if it had paused to take a bathroom break.

I had some idea what it was, but I went over there as quietly as I could, holding my side where Stitch had kicked me. My jaw was starting to ache from the punch.

The moonlight was spilling over the squatting thing. It was a woman and the woman was nude and her skin was leathery-looking, like there had been some kind of preservation attempted, taxidermy perhaps, or maybe she had just been stored in salt. The face was wrinkled and old-looking, but I knew the person wasn't old. I could recognize her even though I realized now her bones were gone and there was nothing but her skin and skull there. The skin was stretched over some kind of frame in the general shape of a human form squatting. The body was nude, and the woman's breasts had been stuffed with something that made them knotty-looking, and the squat was such that her ass was touching the ground; it too appeared to be stuffed with something. The hair on the woman's head was red but there were patches of it missing. She looked worse than she looked in the photos, except now the framework gave her shape. The tattoos on her skin just looked like scars.

There was a dark line on the forehead, and I found myself reaching out to touch it. It was a cut line, and it went all the way across. I got hold of her hair and gently lifted it and the top of the skull came right off, leaving a lower line of hair hanging around the bottom part of the skull. Inside, the skull was hollowed out and there was a fat envelope nestled at the bottom. I took a deep breath and took it out with my other hand, put the top of the skull back in place.

I heard a noise, turned, dropped the envelope, squatted, pointed the .38. It was Booger. He was walking toward me, the .45 down by his side.

He came over and looked at what I had been looking at. "Now there's something you don't see every day," he said. "You hear me calling, man?"

"Of course."

Booger wasn't paying attention anymore. He was looking at the squatting shape.

"I know her," I said. "Tabitha."

"Read about her in your notes. Saw her in the photo. She was the one supposed to be kidnapped."

"Guess she was at that," I said.

"What's that?" Booger said, pointing to the envelope on the ground.

"It was inside her skull," I said, picking it up.

Booger nodded. "There was someone out here with us, you know that? He got me confused in there. Cut back on his trail and I lost him. Got me going in the wrong direction for a while. I didn't think anyone could do that to me, trick me that easy. Hey, what's wrong with your side?"

"You know that someone out here with us? Me and him met."

"Shit, man. I'm sorry."

"Saw him cross the trail, went in after him a little ways, decided it wasn't such a smart idea after he punched and kicked me. If you hadn't yelled, he might have finished me. But what I really think is he doesn't want me dead. Not just yet. That would take the fun out of whatever it is he thinks he's doing. He wanted me to find what I've found. I bet he's got other plans for me. And now you."

"I see him again, me and him, we'll have a meeting of blood and bone . . . I guess the game is afoot, huh, bro?"

"Sherlock Holmes," I said.

"Damn skippy. Read him when I was in the orphanage."

That was the first I'd heard of the orphanage. Booger was slow to deal out facts about his life.

"We have another address to check," I said.

When we got in the car I opened the envelope. Inside were some religious tracts. About how Darwin wants the world to believe we came from monkeys and isn't that a crime. There were others that looked to have been printed about 1950, and they showed caricatures of blacks as monkey-like; one black man had his arm around a character that I assumed was Darwin. There were pamphlets of a more recent vintage that railed against the mixing of the races. There were also flyers about the speech that Reverend Judence would be making at the university. Outside of it all being hateful and stupid, I couldn't make heads or tails of it.

I handed it all to Booger, then studied the map from the glove box while he looked over the material I had given him. I put the map away and drove us to the next address quickly.

As I drove, I felt more and more uncomfortable. The location was near where Belinda lived, but when I finally turned on the street I needed and away from her place, I began to feel a little better.

We drove down into the black part of town, a very poor section about three blocks from where Belinda lived. There were no streetlights, and the homes nearby were dark. Right at the lip of that section there was a church, a big old white church that was charred on one side from fire and had a sign out front that said FIRST BAPTIST. It had a high tower that stood above it all and there was a window in the center of the tower that looked out at the night, and a big white cross at the peak. The fire appeared to have happened some time ago, and though it had smoked the building up good and burned it badly on one side, the other side seemed intact.

I parked at the curb and we walked across the moonlit, windblown grass on the front lawn. The grass had grown up high and was wet from the rain and sprouting some tall sticker burrs that we avoided.

"Man, we're just right out here in the open," Booger said.

"I know, but I'm not feeling all that sneaky."

We went to the front door of the church and pushed against it, but it was locked. We went around back and tried the door there, but it was locked too. I knew we could get in on the burned side without a lot of effort, as there were gaps in the wall there, but I wanted to stay out of the soot, which was damp from the recent rain and which would stick to us like ink to blotters. It seemed a funny thing to be concerned about right then, but it was in my thoughts nonetheless.

We found a window we could force up, and crawled inside.

There was a pile of pews. Half the place was charcoal. Across the way, it looked as if the fire had cut the wood in the shape of teeth rising up from the floor. You could see through those gaps and what you could see were a bunch of dark homes and a dark street that looked to have last been paved about the time pigs flew. A good wind and all of it on the burned side could topple like a smoldering fireplace log, and what made me nervous was we were having just such a wind. On the side that wasn't burned, the windows rattled in their frames like maracas, and the air still smelled of charcoal and soot.

"When did this place catch fire?" Booger said.

"I don't know exactly. Dad said it could have been arson."

I found a little narrow stairway that went up. I hesitated for a moment, but there was nothing else to see anywhere. I took out the .38 and looked back at Booger.

"I'm going up," I said.

"I'm not stopping you."

I went up. On the stairs, about halfway to the top, I could see where the skein of a spiderweb had been snapped and someone had gone through. I climbed into the room above. The smell of smoke was strong there. It had gathered into the lumber thick as the paint, even though there was only a slight bit of burn damage on the far right wall. The stench made my nose itch and my eyes water. Underneath it was an even more unpleasant odor.

I was still standing at the top of the landing, blinking through smoke-watered eyes, staring at something by the window, when Booger got there.

Booger looked too, said, "I feel like I'm in a Hardy Boys book."

I guess they had those in the orphanage as well.

We eased over to the chair that was in front of the window. The underlying stench became less underlying. In the chair was a human shape, but there was little human left of it. A telescope was mounted on a tripod in front of it, pointing out the tower window.

I moved around so I could see the thing in the chair. It was a woman, withered and near mummified like the other; another leather maiden, like the title of the Jerzy Fitzgerald book. The hair was mostly there, and it was long and black as a raven's wing. The upper teeth showed where the flesh had dried and drawn back, and I could tell that beneath the yellowed skin there was some kind of frame, like before, wire or wood. The breasts were stuffed and knotty and misshapen. The legs had nothing in them. They were just skin, dangling like empty stockings over the edge of the chair. It was Ronnie, pretty much as she had appeared in the photograph that had been sent to me. Her head, like Tabitha's, had a cut line.

I took a breath and took hold of her hair and lifted up her skull. There was another envelope inside.

Booger reached in and took it out and I set the skull cap back in place.

Booger opened the envelope. He looked inside. He made a grunting noise.

I took it from him and read it. It said:

DON'T BUMP THE TELESCOPE. LOOK THROUGH IT AND THINK ABOUT WHAT YOU SEE.

I got hold of the chair Ronnie's remains were in and moved it back so that I could get to the telescope. A corpse without its insides is very light.

When I finished moving her, Booger took out a handkerchief and wiped down the chair where I had touched it. He studied the corpse, said, "Looks like she's been frozen and stored in salt. There's still salt in her hair, and the rest of her looks and smells like freezer burn."

"What she smells like is dead," I said.

"I had some fish sticks went bad smelled like that."

I turned my attention to where the telescope was pointing. There was smoke and dust grimed over the other windows in the church, but this one had been cleaned, and I could even smell a bit of window cleaner in the air.

I didn't touch the telescope, just looked through it. It wasn't an expensive telescope, but it was powerful enough, and for a moment I wasn't sure what I was looking at. Then I realized exactly what I was seeing. A slow warm horror settled over me.

A few blocks over. Belinda's house. It was lined up dead center in the telescope.

37

We parked at the rear of Belinda's house, at the curb. It was dark behind the windows. When we got to the back door, Booger used his little lock pick and it opened easily. This time I had my flashlight, and I moved the beam around as we walked inside. The house was silent and there was a kind of emptiness about the place, like a funeral home. There was a faint smell of the bread candle in the air. I hesitated a moment, and then I couldn't help myself; I said, "Belinda?"

I turned to look for Booger, but he had already gone deep inside and was moving through the dark like, well, like a copper cat.

I turned on a light. Booger was standing in the open bedroom door-way, blocking it. He said, "All we needed was you banging some fucking cymbals and blowing a kazoo with your asshole. Man, don't lose your focus, woman or no woman. Come here."

I followed him through the doorway, into Belinda's bedroom. The bread smell was strong in there, and the door to the bathroom was open. Booger went over and leaned against the doorjamb. I peeked in. There was water in the tub, some soap scum on the water. There was a throw-away razor on the edge of the tub along with some kind of shaving gel. There were splashes of water all over the floor.

"She's in here getting a bath, shaving her legs, and they came in on her," Booger said. He went over and sat on the edge of the tub and dropped his hand in the water. "Water's still warm, she just ran it and had most likely got in. The floor's wet, so they pulled her out. Gals don't like to get out wet. They dry."

"Damn," I said, and I felt my knees get weak.

"No time for that shit," Booger said. "Let's check the place good."

We went into the kitchen. I saw there was a note propped up on the kitchen table. I had seen it earlier, but it hadn't really caught my eye, as I was looking for Belinda.

I eased over and took it and opened it. Unlike the others, it was written in a tight little script by someone who fancied themselves stylish.

It read:

WE KNOW A LOT ABOUT YOU AND A LOT ABOUT THE PEOPLE WHO KNOW YOU, AND WE HAVE BORROWED ONE OF THEM. WE WANT YOU TO KNOW WHAT YOU'RE UP AGAINST AND TO UNDERSTAND THAT WE ARE ABSOLUTELY RUTHLESS AND PROUD OF IT. SHE MIGHT BE OKAY AND SHE MIGHT NOT. WE ARE THINKING OF REMOVING HER BRACES WITH PLIERS AND EXTREME PREJUDICE. GO HOME. AWAIT INSTRUCTIONS. SHE RESTS IN THE TRUNK OF OUR CAR FOR NOW, BUT THAT IS NOT AS DARK AND AS TIGHT A PLACE AS SHE MAY END UP. SKIN COMES LOOSE EASY WITH THE RIGHT KNIFE AND PLENTY OF EXPERIENCE.

I sat down in a chair at the table. Booger came over and picked up the note and read it. "Look here," he said. "She's dead, she's dead. If she's alive, we got a chance to get her back. I don't know her and it's not anything to me, but it's something to you, so that makes it my business. Now get your shit together and let's go to your place and wait for instructions."

I nodded.

Booger clamped his hand down on my shoulder. "Come on," he said. "Just like when we was over in Sand World, you got to cinch up your drawers and get to cracking before you get a bullet in the head and your pants fill with shit. Got me?"

I nodded again and got up. Booger drove us back to my place.

. . .

When we opened the door and turned on the light, lying on the floor, near the motorcycle, was yet another note. It had been slipped under the door.

"These fuckers are quick," Booger said. "A little too quick."

"There's more than one," I said.

"Yep. And they stay in communication by cell phone. People sneaking around behind my back, it chaps my ass, partner."

I read the note. It said: "Call this number."

I studied the number, then called it.

There was an answer right away. A man's voice, almost singsong-like.

"Mr. Statler. You have been drawn in, and now that you are in, I should tell you that we have captured your queen."

"I don't get it," I said, although I did.

"It's a game, and your brother brought you in, and then you became a player in the game. But that's all you are, a player. A pawn. A knight maybe. There are others and you don't know their will, and you do not know our purpose."

"Belinda has nothing to do with this," I said. "Actually, neither do I."

"She is with you, and therefore, by extension, she is in the game because you are, and we have decided you have something to do with it, and that is good enough." ·

"A wink is as good as a nod to a blind horse, huh?"

"Exactly," the voice said.

"Let her go, and I'll take her place."

"Doesn't work that way. And another thing, you have brought another player into the game. The high yellow you got with you. Intriguing, isn't it, that we should know so much? We know a lot about you because we have been watching you. Acknowledge to him that we know he is there."

"He knows you know, and he doesn't give a damn," I said.

"Acknowledge."

I paused and said to Booger, loud as I could: "He says I should acknowledge that they know you are here, and that you are a high yellow."

"I think I'm more copper-colored," Booger said.

"Okay," I said back into the phone. "I told him, and I owe you one for the punch in the face and the kick in the ribs."

"You hear quite well. Perhaps you have good instincts. Perhaps it's your time in Iraq that has made you alert, paranoid maybe. But remember, just because you're paranoid doesn't mean they're not after you. Now, we will trade your brother for the girl. We consider him a more important piece in the game."

"Who's we?"

The voice on the phone laughed. "Now that would be telling, wouldn't it? That would ruin the game."

"This is no game, buddy," I said.

"Sure it is. Sooner you figure that out, the better, because all that matters is how you play the game. There is no purpose to life, Mr. Statler. There is only chaos from which you can create purpose, and a game is as purposeful as you can get. There is no real reason anyone feels for anyone other than the lie we tell ourselves. The lie where we make importance out of the simplicity of emptiness."

"You ought to put that last line in a fortune cookie," I said. "The rest of that shit, it would take a whole box of cookies to say it. And it would still be shit."

"Insults," the voice said. "I'd save them right now. I was saying how you failed to take no for an answer, when in the end a no is as good as a yes. Humans are fools. They try and jump-start the dead; dead people and dead ideas. We convince ourselves there is more to our life than there is, and truth is, we are nothing more than empty shells motivated by some kind of electrical current. To make it through the years, we create games. The success game. The marriage game. The war game. The life game. The race game. The religion game. That's okay. I play them all, to some extent. Or have played them. But the difference in you and me is that I know I'm playing."

"What do you really want?" I said. "Because if you want my brother, you won't get him. I couldn't give him to you if I wanted to. He went out of state and didn't tell me where, and I told him not to tell me."

I tried to tell the lie as convincingly as I could.

The voice on the other end didn't speak right away. I could hear him breathing, though.

Finally the voice said, "I'm going to accept that, because we only wanted him so we could have all the game pieces, but you, you have become one of the most important players in our game."

"I thought I was an insignificant pawn," I said.

"Not anymore. As for your brother, we will, at least for the moment, consider him removed from the board."

"Then what's the new plan?" I asked.

"We want you to wait. And this phone. It's a one-time shot, baby. When I hang up I destroy it. You can't find me by this phone, and if you want to stay in the game, you got to hang tight. Hang tight and wait for instructions. They will come soon. Don't call the cops. Keep the high yellow out of it. One false move, and this pretty girl of yours, who, by the way, is without clothes, only a bathrobe, will be a whole lot less pretty. So again, wait for instructions."

"I hope the instructions will be briefer than the line of shit I've been hearing."

"Have you ever seen a woman skinned?" the voice said. "It is quite a process. And the women, they are very noisy during the process."

I was about to respond when the connection was dropped.

"Sonofabitch," I said, and raised the phone to toss it, then thought better of it. I closed it and shoved it into my pocket.

"Well," Booger said, stretching out on the couch, "we got plenty of beer."

I was sitting in my one really comfortable chair, having just explained to him in a nutshell all that had been said to me.

"There's nothing funny about this, Booger."

"Am I smiling?"

"You are."

"You know me. I get curious, I smile. First thing I'd consider is how much this gal means to you. She's just like a good poke, well, they're making new pussy every few minutes."

"What in hell are you saying, Booger?"

"I'm saying, she don't mean that much to you, me and you can pack up your car and go back to my bar, or damn near anyplace you want to go until the money runs out, then we can make some more and go somewhere else."

"It's not like that for me," I said.

"I know it isn't. But I had to say it. Thing is, I understand what the guy told you. He makes sense. It's true."

"Sometimes, when I wake up in the middle of the night thinking about things, stuff he says makes sense," I said. "Rest of the time, not so much."

"All that matters is that he believes it."

"Or that they do," I said. "He keeps saying *we.*"

Booger studied me for a long moment, like maybe it was the first time he had ever looked at me. He said, "On your scale, do I rate somewhere?"

"You're on the scale, Booger."

"Where?"

"You're on it. That's as good as I can say. I've kind of got other things on my mind right now."

Booger took a swallow of his beer. "All right," he said, still not looking right at me. "That'll do. That Caroline girl, she's not dead."

"What?"

"The picture they sent of the three dead girls. The Caroline girl. Way I figure it, she's not dead. At least that's not her in the picture."

Booger got the photo, put it on the table. "I thought this looked wrong before, but we got caught up in other business. I been thinking on it again. It's Photoshopped, my friend. What you got here is the girl in the middle, twice. Ronnie it says. The one called Caroline, that's Ronnie again, but with a blond wig on. It's shot in the same place, and they've covered her up some so she'll look different, and it's a reverse image, but it's her. You see that little mole on Ronnie's cheek? I got a good look at it earlier. When we were in the church with her body. The mole is prominent, even with her skin rotting. The mole is on the other side of her cheek now, in the picture, and the blond wig makes her look a little different, but look at those empty eye sockets, the eyes are near closed up just the same as the girl in the middle, and there's a little wrinkle in the eyelid that's on both the body with the Caroline label and the one with the Ronnie label."

I grabbed the photograph and studied it.

"I look at a lot of photographs of dead bodies," Booger said, "so I'm observant about that kind of thing. I got all these books with that stuff in them. It calms me."

"Dead bodies?"

"Reminds me I'm not one of them. And another thing, there's a pattern."

"What pattern?" I said.

"Two girls were killed the same way, and that's a pattern, and it means it may have been done before. So there could be an even bigger pattern. There could be some kind of records somewhere of this kind of shit. It might show a connection to the killer, or killers."

"That's smart, Booger. It really is."

"It is, isn't it? Another thing, there were those flyers about the preacher, Judence. He's talking at ten in the morning on the campus. Why would they put the flyers in there? Call me a high yellow?"

"Because it means something to them," I said.

"They are telling you all the facts without stating them. They want to do it all like an onion skin, peeling a layer at a time. It's a game within a game, and there may be a game within that. Tabitha and . . . what was his name?"

"Ernie," I said.

"They got in the middle of a plan, and so they became part of the plan and didn't know it. Caroline has to be alive and in on all of this, otherwise none of it fits. Those two dumb kids messed up the Geek and Caroline's plans for the DVDs, and they got snapped."

"The blackmail scheme?"

"It's too complicated to be just about money," Booger said, scratching at his ass.

"Everything is about money or sex," I said.

"Even money and sex are part of something else, my man. Power. I know their kind better than you. I am their kind."

"I hope not."

Booger grinned at me. "Thing you got going is I like you. Them I don't like. And the fucker called me a high yellow because he wanted to insult me, so I don't like him."

I looked at Booger. His eyes were as cold-looking as the ice machine in my refrigerator.

"Wasn't for me," I said, "would you try to stop something like this, whatever it is?"

"I don't know, bro. Maybe just to be in the game myself. Actually, I kind of admire this whole wonderful mess they've created. Thing you got going is I'll help because this girl means something to you."

"I appreciate that, Booger. As for Caroline, I've suspected she was alive for a while. Just never could wrap my head around the idea completely. Not until you pointed out that's not her in that photograph."

"That's the difference in me and you," Booger said, and he got up and went to the refrigerator and pulled a beer out, still talking. "I listen to what I'm really thinking, not what I should be thinking. Want a beer?"

"No thanks."

Booger came back, screwing the cap off the beer as he sat. "Way I see it, they want to cause trouble with this Judence guy. One thing I got from your notes was that Caroline was involved with a preacher who had some, shall we say, negative views about the brothers. I don't think these folks really give a shit one way or another about race. There's a thrill in manipulation. Women do it all the time. They know how to use that good thing. Using it, they can get a man to do almost anything they want, including murder. There are some guys, the ones got the bullshit talk, the promises, that's their form of pussy, and they can talk so smooth everyone wants a piece of their ideas and their glory, even if they make less sense than a motorcycle jacket on a poodle. And religion, man, it's got heaven. There's people want to believe that so bad they can already taste the air there. Politicians, they promise a chicken in every pot, and they promise the poor a pot to put it in."

"You're losing me."

"I'm saying they like to see everyone else look silly so they look smart. And they like to kill because it is soothing and powerful and controlling." Booger took a swig of his beer. "I'm a goddamn sociopath, so I should know."

Beat the Clock

38

I let that settle in for a while. I sat back in my chair and thought. Booger drank his beer and let me think. I feared they would call at any moment, giving me instructions, and I feared they wouldn't. I thought about Belinda. I thought about the bodies, the leather maidens. I thought about all the notes and the flyers and I thought about Booger, who was like them, sitting in my rented duplex, drinking beer on my couch, thinking more clearly about my notes than I had.

I looked at my watch. It had grown very late.

I told Booger I was going to the paper, taking my phone with me in case of calls. I asked him and Mr. Lucky to hold down the fort. He said, "Now, if someone I don't know comes through that door, I may just terminate them. You understand that?"

"Don't let anyone hurt you," I said, "but don't kill anyone just for the hell of it. I want to find Belinda."

"I'll blow their kneecap off and stand on their leg until they tell me where she is."

"That I can live with," I said.

"Sure you don't want me to go with you?"

"Not this time. I need you here in case they decide to contact by arriving in person."

"You're just saying that because you know it makes me excited to think I might get to shoot someone."

"I am a tease."

I drove over to the paper and used my key to go inside. I went to the little basement where Mercury worked. The light was on and Mercury was there.

He said, "My God, Cason, it's past midnight, what are you doing here?"

"You said you worked late, so I took a chance."

"It's not all that chancy," he said. "I'm here a lot. Still putting old files into computers. I'm thinking, I get it finished I'll be able to sleep again. I was just about to leave and wash the paper dust out of my throat with about a gallon of malt liquor, then I got to download some pornography for my home computer. It damn sure won't get done if I leave it to the dog. Want to join me in a drink?"

"A nice offer, my friend, but I'm going to pass. I'm riding the wagon a little. Before you go, can you do a kind of cross-check for me? I'm doing some research on a series of murders, and I need an expert."

"You're flattering me."

"I'm trying."

"Would this still be about the Caroline Allison disappearance?"

"In a way," I said. "I want to do some across-the-board comparisons in different towns, for a variety of things, and I need someone who has the skill and the programs to do it."

Mercury grinned at me. "You have come to the warehouse, my friend. It'll be a nice break from what I'm doing."

I smiled, like it was all just work-related. I told him I wanted to check on murders where women were skinned, careful not to let him know I had seen just such a thing in our town this very night.

I could tell he was curious about what that might have to do with Caroline, but he didn't ask. He surfed from one place to another on the Internet, cackled to himself a few times, stretched several times, cracking his back and neck when he did, and then he began to print out bits and pieces here and there from the computer.

"Wow," he said. "I don't know where you came up with this business, but there have been a number of these skinning things. All women. They run all the way from Wisconsin to Texas."

"Can you check for any kind of similarity in those towns where the skinnings took place? Anything that appears in one town that appears in the others."

"That could be all kinds of things," Mercury said.

"I know. But give it a shot. Start with fairs and carnivals. I've got a hunch."

Mercury typed a bit, paused, said, "Fairs and carnivals and circuses and horse shows and local festivals. The festivals are connections only in that all these towns have some festival or another. Blueberry Festival, Crawfish Festival, Multicultural Fest. Every town has that kind of thing, so no real deal on that."

I thought for a moment. I thought about Stitch, and how he looked, and it was a long shot, probably a dud, typecasting from Ernie and Tabitha, but I said, "Put the festivals aside for a moment," I said. "Look at the carnivals."

"Again, all these towns will have carnivals. They pass through on a regular basis. That's how they make a living."

"Try to find a particular carnival in the towns where the murders took place, one where the dates of the murders and skinnings and the passing of the carnival are similar."

He did, and after a moment, he said: "You got certain carnivals and circuses that have been through all these towns, and you got a carnival that not only was in all these towns, but at the same times you asked about. It was going from Wisconsin to Texas, from Texas to Wisconsin. Fact is, the carnival was here in Camp Rapture, but there's no connection. No woman skinned."

I didn't correct him.

"That carnival was here?"

"Several months ago."

"Was it here when Caroline went missing?"

"No. It came before she went missing."

"What about the last murder and the last carnival?" I asked.

"The last murder was in Kansas, a skinning. That was two years ago. You want more specifics on that?"

"Not just yet. I don't guess there's any way to look at who worked in these carnivals?"

"Not that I know of. You might find the owners, but a lot of these carnival people are seasonal, or they know when to meet up, and they are paid cash under the table. So there's no list. I know, because my aunt worked in a carnival as a bearded lady. 'Course, her beard was glued on and she had also been Miss Carthage, Texas, when she was younger. She did the bearded lady thing for two, three years. She had a crush on the guy who worked the whirligig. They got married and he became an accountant and she sells Mary Kay products. Without the glued-on beard."

I tried to smile in a way that didn't let on that at this moment in time I didn't give a shit about the romance of false bearded ladies and whirligig operators.

"What I want to know then is if there is something else these towns have in common?"

Mercury pursed his lips and twisted them around and cocked his head toward the ceiling. I didn't mean to, but I looked up as well. The tile up there was black and white and in squares. I had a sudden urge to count them.

"All right," Mercury said, "let me try something else."

I sat down in a chair and tilted my head back on the headrest and started counting tiles. After a while, I shifted the chair and counted some more. I paused and took out my phone and looked at it to make sure the ringer was on and the battery had power. Yes and yes.

I went back to counting the checkerboard tiles. It soothed me and kept me from pushing Mercury, bad as I wanted to. It kept me from thinking about Belinda in the hands of those cold-blooded killers and that I had left a self-confessed sociopath killer waiting in my living room with a .45 named Mr. Lucky.

"Here's something interesting," Mercury said. "Well, there's a lot interesting. But let me start with the small stuff and move upstairs. Every one of these places had a series of slightly odd events during the times of the skinned women. It didn't all happen on the days the carnival was there, but a little before or after, and sometimes during. One of the women was found out in a field, made up like a scarecrow, on a post, wearing a hat, dressed in a black coat. Or rather what was left of her was on a post; she was skinned and stretched over a frame, then someone had put the coat and hat on her. All the others were skinned too, and found in different ways, different positions, and there were notes found at all the sites, inside the women's skulls, but at the same time all this was going on, lesser weird things were happening: cows were found dead in front of schools in a town in Wisconsin. Silly things like yard gnomes were stolen and later were found in prominent buildings: schools, courthouses, that sort of thing. In another town, in Oklahoma, during the night, someone took the back doors off an entire row of houses. That took some goobers, something like that. You know what you're doing, you can take a door off, but that requires some time and attention and maybe some noise. Man, you got something going here, but I got a feeling it's more than you've told me. You want to tell me?"

"Games," I said. "Someone is playing games, and it always ends badly. Whoever is doing it arrives with the carnival, then the games begin, and gradually become less gamelike."

"The skinnings?"

"That's right. Then they move on to the next carnival site. You notice it's not every town, and it's not every time the carnival arrives, so this is someone who works there part-time. Someone of a transient nature. Someone who knows how to hide out in large towns without giving himself away. A night person. A work-as-needed kind of guy, or guys. Someone experienced at this kind of work, who can pick up a carnival job as needed."

"And when he's with the carnival he plays his games," Mercury said.

"And sometimes when he's not. But the carnival is the original connection. Maybe he has money now, from somewhere, and this time is his own."

"There's something else," Mercury said. "There's this pattern of the games, the pranks, gnomes, dead cows, and then the murders, and finally there's one other connection in all these towns. You holding on to your ass?"

I assured Mercury that I was.

"Here's the biggie. And these events were in the news. I remember some of them, but they took place over a period of time, so there was nothing to link them. There were assassinations."

"There were what?"

"Assassinations. There's not a better name for it. In Wisconsin, at a rally for gay rights, the speaker was shot from a distance. A professional hit. It made all kinds of stink."

"Hell, I remember that," I said. "I was living in Houston then."

"And in Arkansas a team mascot wearing one of those outfits was killed."

"What kind of outfit?"

Mercury scrolled around on the screen. "Team called the Indians. A high school team. A kid got shot, seventeen years old. And get this, they figure someone positioned themselves under the stands, with a silencer, and shot the kid, right through the big Indian head he was wearing, and killed him. Here's an added corker: the kid was a real American Indian. At a Texas university, an animal mascot, a longhorn steer, was stolen, killed and found cooking on a barbecue grill in front of the post office. The first assassination, though, was of an armored car guard. This was Illinois. Guard would sit in the car and open the door and let the smoke out while his partner went inside, I guess to get more money. He wasn't supposed to do that, open the door that way. Someone shot him with a .22 rifle, proba- bly silenced. The money was taken before the other guard even knew about it, over three million dollars, and no one has got a clue to this day who took it. They just took the armored car and drove it off, and it seems that an accomplice followed in another vehicle. They dropped the car off in a church parking lot minus the money and a bunch of cashier's checks. All that was left were some wrapped coins. Later that day, the car and the guard's body were found. Few days later, the checks that were in the rip- off were mailed back with a thank-you note for all the money. It said: 'The money was nice, but we can't cash the checks easily enough, so we are returning those to show our appreciation.' "

"More games," I said.

"You have a pattern," Mercury said. "A real pattern. A real goddamn mystery. Murders. Skinning. Assassinations. And someone with stolen money."

I thought: Who was the little girl who loved mysteries, puzzles and games, and the darkness of Edgar Allan Poe, the bleakness of Jerzy Fitzgerald?

Answer: Caroline.

She couldn't have been in on all the assassination business, any of that stuff. It happened over too many years. She would have been a kid, and I had some idea where she was during that time.

But Stitch, he fit. He was the one behind it all. He had other accomplices then. But now he had added Caroline to his team. Why and how I didn't know, but I was sure of it. As sure as I was that if I ever caught up with Stitch or Caroline and they had harmed Belinda, they would never live to see another day.

39

Mercury and I looked through more records, trying to make comparisons, and then I had had enough. What I needed to know was, where was Belinda? And there was nothing more Mercury could tell me that would help answer that. But at least I was armed with some information about my adversaries, and the first rule of war is Know Your Enemy.

I left the newspaper office feeling as if my small corner of the world was ruled by something dark with tentacles that reached into all parts of my life; some monster from behind the veil of reason. Only someone like Booger could enjoy a world like that. I tried to remember what it was like before I knew of Caroline and before I knew of the war and Booger, and even before I had loved Gabby. What it was like when I was a child in my underwear playing Tarzan in what was now Jazzy's tree, calling out to all the apes to come and save me.

I drove on through the night, back toward my place and Booger. I glanced in the rearview mirror, saw there was a car behind me, the only one on the street, and I watched it in my mirror, then I turned off. I hadn't gone far when I realized the car had turned too.

It could be a coincidence.

I decided not to drive home. I drove over to the twenty-four-hour Wal-

Mart, went inside, but not before I saw the car pull into the lot. It was an old car and maybe it was green. It was hard to tell in the lights of the parking lot. I was beginning to think I had seen it before. I tried to think where, but all I could think of was that I had seen it; a spot here and there, a time now and then.

Maybe it was like a déjà vu thing, where you think you've seen something before, but your mind is playing tricks on you. Tired and stressed as I was, it could be that way.

I went inside and stopped at the magazine rack by one of the checkout counters and stared at stuff there. Out of the corner of my eye I saw a guy come in. He looked a little ragged in the clothes department, but he had a hard-looking body and close-cropped hair. I couldn't make out much else about him, not from that distance, but I figured he was the guy in the car.

I moved away from the magazines and down some aisles, but he didn't follow. There were more people in the store than you would expect that time of the morning, and they trailed along the aisles like zombies.

I found a large diet soda and went back toward the checkout counter. I didn't see my guy anywhere. When I got near the checkout, he was there. He suddenly came out of nowhere and pushed a case of beer onto the runner in front of me and the sleepy-looking kid behind the register checked him out while I studied the back of the guy's head. He took his beer and left.

I paid for my diet drink and left. I drove away, and behind me I saw the lights of a car come on, and pretty soon the car was behind me. It was a good distance behind me, but I could tell it was the same car from the way the headlights were set. It was hard for him to be sneaky this late at night when the streets were damn near empty.

I decided to ride out to the edge of town, where it was dark and the roads were narrow. The car followed. I went a little more swiftly, and then I took a curve and saw a road that he couldn't see, not yet, not until he made the curve behind me. I whipped onto that road as I cut the lights, looked back over my shoulder through the back window as he passed and went over the hill, on down to the other side.

I turned on the lights and backed down the road, back onto the highway, went the way he had gone, driving fast.

I came down the hill and saw his taillights, noticed he was slowing. He had just figured out he had been snookered. He pulled to the side of the road and sat, waiting for me to pass. Maybe he didn't know for sure I was on to him.

I went on down the hill like I was going to pass him, but I turned off the road toward him suddenly and gave my car a little gas. I could see his eyes in the headlights, big as saucers. I hit his car with the front of mine and knocked it, flipping it over a couple of times, and the front end of my car went off in a ditch and if my old wreck had had airbags they would have popped out. But all I had in my car was a seat belt and a hope for good luck.

I sat there and looked at his car through the windshield. It was resting on its roof, rocking a little from side to side. The lights were still on and I could see him hanging upside down in his seat belt. Some of the beers he bought had busted open and were spraying and foaming about. He didn't have air bags either. Good, I thought. I hope he busted his head on the steering wheel.

I didn't even know the guy, but I didn't like being followed, and I figured he had some connection to all the bullshit I was dealing with.

I put my car in reverse, and was surprised I got enough traction to back out of the ditch. I parked the car alongside the highway, turning it so that the front pointed the way I had come. I turned off the lights and pulled the key, pulled the .38, went over to his car and tugged at the upside-down door without success. I kicked at the glass in the window, but all it did was bulge. I bent down and looked at him. He had been stunned, but now he was starting to twist in the seat belt, trying to figure out how he had ended up the way he was. I hammered at the glass with the butt of the .38 and the glass popped, made a kind of gooey-looking star that spread from one end of the glass to the other. I hit it a few more times, finally got it busted out good. I reached through the window and grabbed the guy by the ear, turned his head toward me and hit him with the butt of the .38. I did that two or three times. Once or twice because he needed it, and once because I wanted to. He went out.

I had to work at it, but I got his seat belt unsnapped, and when it let him loose, I got hold of him and dragged him out of the car, cutting him on the broken window. I dropped him on the ground, still unconscious. I reached inside the car and turned off the lights, and then I killed the engine by twisting the key. I pulled the key out and threw it in the ditch.

When I turned around he was waking up. I said, "Pardner, I don't like being followed."

He was up on his hands and knees now. He lifted his head, said, "Go fuck yourself."

I kicked him pretty hard in the throat, and he rolled over holding his throat and making a noise like someone trying to swallow a couple of Ping-Pong balls.

I got him by the back of his belt and dragged him up the side of the ditch and over to my car while he continued to grab at his throat. I stood back and kicked him hard in the ass. "Get up," I said.

He got up. I watched in case he went for a gun. "I don't want to hurt you," I said.

He almost laughed, but his throat was too sore to give more than a kind of cough.

"I don't want to hurt you any more than I have, but I will," I said. "Put your hands on the trunk and spread your legs, and I'm going to put this .38 to the back of your skull with one hand and search you with the other. You make a move, you might get to see your brains jump out the front of your head before you die."

He was breathing better now. He stood up slowly, put his hands on the trunk and said in a voice that was raspy and tired, "I haven't got a gun. It's in the car."

I put the .38 to the back of his head and patted him down anyway. He didn't have a gun, like he said, not even a pocketknife. All he had was a pocket comb and a cell phone. I put the cell phone in my pocket and threw the comb away. I had him stand back, and I used my left hand to unlock the trunk.

"No man," he said. "I hate tight spaces."

"Bullshit. Get in the trunk or I'll leave you here beside the road and let the vultures pick the lead out of the back of your head."

He looked at me. Maybe trying to size me up, see if he could take me. He finally turned and got in the trunk and I closed it.

I went around and looked at the front of my car. The bumper was bent, but nothing else. Even the lights still worked.

I drove us back to my place.

. . .

When I got the guy in the house and made him sit down on the couch, I gave Booger a little rundown on what had happened.

"And so," Booger said, "you thought you might bring me a present, and it's not even Christmas yet."

"I'm not sure I'm going to give him to you," I said.

"Oh, please, please," Booger said. "I ain't had nothing to play with since my pet alligator died from strangulation."

This caused the guy on the couch to turn his head and look at Booger in an odd way.

Now that I had the guy inside, and I could look at him good, I saw he had a bad eye; it was the way Ernie had described it. He also had a bunch of bruise spots I had given him. They made him look a little like a speckled pup.

"Glug," I said, "good to meet you, you sonofabitch."

"I don't know you," he said.

"Yeah, but I know you, and I know you're following me so you can report to Stitch."

"You're gonna know your girlfriend's skin right off," Glug said. "Something happens to me, I don't report back, then that bitch is as good as dead. Dig?"

"Her name is Belinda," I said, "and any more disrespect concerning her, and you will be looking for your head. Dig?"

He nodded.

I got his cell phone out of my pocket. I tossed it to him, said, "Make that call, and tell him you're watching, and nothing is happening. You don't make the call right, I pop you right here."

He called and the call was short and sweet. He told Stitch, or whoever was on the other end, things were good and that I was at home. He said he was sitting down the street from my place, watching. When he finished the call I took the phone. I said, "That was all right. Now, there's some information we need to know."

"Stitch finds out I talked," Glug said, "you don't know what he'll do."

"That's right," I said. "We don't. But I know what we'll do if you don't."

"You know what," Booger said, "to do this right, you know, so we can have like some room to work, and a little privacy, we need someplace protected, some place where you can't hear a fellow scream."

40

I cut the electrical cords off some lamps and we used those to bind Glug's arms behind his back. We tied his legs together too, leaving enough room so he could move at a kind of shuffle. I put a pair of my dirty underwear in his mouth, something with some slick stains on it, and tied it in good with a rag I tore off an old sheet. Then we got a phone book that Booger wanted, and he got his duffel bag, and I got a lawn chair, and we put all of it, including Glug, in my car.

We did it quickly and carefully. I was pretty sure no one saw us.

Booger sat in the back with Glug. Booger had Mr. Lucky pointing toward Glug's lap, the barrel of the shooter against Glug's balls. Glug didn't struggle at all.

I drove us to the place where Ronnie's landlord had stored her goods, and I rolled down the window and touched the code, and it was still the same. The gate unlocked itself and folded in. I drove us past the gate and over to the storage shed where Ronnie's stuff had been.

Booger got out and went at the lock and opened it quick. I drove the car inside and Booger closed the doors. I cut the engine and left the headlights on, pulled the gagged and bound Glug out of the car. Booger sat the lawn chair in front of the car, center of the headlights. He grabbed Glug and pulled him over to the chair and pushed him into it. He said, "You sit there, and be pretty."

He went back to the car and got the phone book. I grabbed his wrist, said, "I don't know, Booger. Maybe we ought not."

"Depends on if you want that girl of yours skinned or not."

"How do we know if he's telling the truth?"

"Torture works, in spite of what people tell you. But the only way it works is the guy's got to know we don't care if he dies, and you know me, I don't care. He'll tell me the goddamn truth, you can count on that. But whatever you want, buddy. Have it your way."

I let go of his wrist.

Booger walked over to where Glug sat and hit him hard in the side of the head with the flat of the phone book, hit him so hard he fell out of the chair and sprawled out on the ground. He was trying to yell, but that underwear gag was holding.

Booger sat him up in the chair, gave him a pat on the head, then hauled off with the book and hit him again over the same ear, not quite knocking him out of the chair this time.

"I just want you to know," Booger said, "that I can do this all night, but you can't. I'm going to take out that gag, and when I do, you yell, it'll be all over for you except for us throwing your dead ass out somewhere beside the road. Got me?"

Glug nodded.

Booger punched straight down and hit Glug in the balls. Glug bent over, almost fell out of the chair, but Booger helped him up by kneeing him hard in the face. When he sat Glug back up in the chair, Glug was bleeding from his nose and it had taken on a new shape. His lips didn't look so good either. Blood had colored the underwear in his mouth.

I went around and stood behind the car and looked at the closed doorway of the building and tried to pretend I wasn't part of this. I heard Booger hit him a couple more times with either the phone book or his fists, and I got myself together and walked around front, and found a position between the headlights.

Booger untied the rag that held the gag, said, "How's the teeth?"

Glug nodded.

"Good," Booger said. "Can you talk?"

"Yeah," Glug said. His voice was small and seemed to be climbing up from his throat on broken legs.

"That's good, you can talk. You couldn't, wouldn't be any good to me or my man here. What we want is some information. In case your man Stitch calls. We want to be ready to do whatever we need to do. You're kind of like our little inside mole."

"He won't call," Glug said.

"No?" said Booger.

"No."

"And why is that?" Booger said. "That don't seem like good manners, saying you're gonna call, then not calling."

"Because he's playing his games."

"You're playing games too," Booger said. "And I got to tell you, me and Cason here, we ain't good sports. We don't play to lose, and we sure don't like to play when we don't know we're playing. But if we're in, hey, we're playing for keeps. Know what I'm saying?"

"They're nuts. I play for the money. But they're nuts."

"Tell us about the money," I said. "And tell us about who *they* are."

"You don't understand. It's the money to me, and they like money fine, but they like this game they play. I'm just a man for hire. For them, it's a whole different thing."

"Them being Stitch and the supposedly dead whore Caroline?" Booger said.

"Yeah," Glug said.

Booger looked at me. "Told you she was alive, bro. I am one smart motherfucker, give me that."

"I give you that."

"You didn't know that, did you, bro, that I'm a smart motherfucker?"

I told him the truth. "No. I knew you were smart, but not like this. I didn't know that."

"You're finding out all kinds of things about me, aren't you, Cason?"

"I am," I said.

Booger walked around behind Glug and touched his head a couple of times with the phone book, made Glug jump a little. "I'm thinking, without even asking a question, I might just swat you for the fun of it, pilgrim."

"I'll answer," Glug said. "You ask, and I'll answer."

Booger clapped his hand on Glug's shoulder, and Glug startled like a rabbit. "Oh, hell, I know that. I'm just talking about what I might do because I want to do it. There ain't no other reason behind it than an urge. You ever get an urge, my man?"

Glug didn't know how to answer that question, so he gave a statement. "Whatever you want, man. Whatever you want."

Booger looked at me. "He wants what I want, bro. Ain't he agreeable?"

"He is," I said.

"What we want," Booger said, "and I believe I can speak for my bro here, is some no-bullshit answers. No cleverness. No hesitation. You hesitate, and you meditate horizontally. So, what we want is to know where . . ." Booger turned to me. "What's her name again?"

"Belinda," I said.

"He wants to know where Belinda is. And if he wants to know, so do I. What me and him got going here is what they call one of them hive minds. He thinks it, I think it. That's how we're playing this. You understand?"

Glug nodded.

Booger turned to me, said, "Ask your question, bro."

"I want to know where she is," I said, "and I want to know what this is all about. I want to know everything, and I want it in a nutshell, and pretty damn quick. But mostly, I want to know where Belinda is."

"She's all right until the morning, ten a.m.," Glug said.

"What happens then?" I said.

"Stitch pops the nigger."

I thought about that a minute. "Judence?"

"That's him," Glug said.

"Why?" I said.

"He likes games, and there's the money he's getting."

"And what do you get?"

"Money, sometimes a little poontang, depending on how Caroline is feeling. Mostly she's just banging Stitch, but sometimes, she'll do me a favor. She can make you crazy, way she acts."

"Who's giving Stitch this money that you get a piece of?"

"That white preacher," Glug said. "The one on TV."

"Reverend Dinkins?" I said.

"Yeah, him."

"You got a real name other than Glug?" I asked.

"Gregore," he said.

"What kind of fucking name is that?" Booger said. "Don't hunchback assistants have that name?"

"That's my name."

"Well, it sucks," Booger said.

Coming from a man who preferred to be called Booger, I wasn't sure exactly how to take that.

Booger hauled off and hit Glug with the phone book in the back of the head, knocking him out of the chair, hitting him so hard he went smooth out.

"Goddamnit, Booger, what was that about?"

"Sorry," Booger said, "I just got bored."

41

When Booger slapped Gregore awake, the bastard began to chatter like a squirrel. There was no information he wanted to hold back; he was ready to tell us everything, including potty-training problems he'd had as a kid. I didn't blame him for being so informative. Besides the slapping, Booger had done some things with his pocketknife that had to hurt and had given Gregore's ears that look hunting hounds get after a number of vicious encounters with coons in the wild.

Even though he was open with his answers, Booger didn't think he was quick enough or giving us enough of the answers we needed, so he took about ten minutes to beat him savagely with the phone book.

I had to go stand behind the car again. When the beating was over, I went back and Booger put Gregore in the chair again and I asked the questions I needed answers to the most.

I got them: Stitch and Caroline were well into their game, and the end of it was the assassination of Judence by Stitch. Dinkins was paying for the assassination to take place.

Way they had it fixed was they blackmailed all of the history teachers to not be in their offices that day. It was not an unknown custom for the professors to watch events in the plaza from their offices above. They were to be out. That was the request. It was a simple request. Vacate your offices on that day and don't come back and we don't show the DVDs of you humping Caroline. In fact, you stay out of your offices and meet at the old sawmill grounds with a thousand each, the DVDs will be returned and it'll all be over.

It had a kind of poetry about it. Of course, I had the DVDs. Or at least some copies of them. There may have been more. I wanted to ask that, but Gregore, he was on a roll and I didn't want to interrupt him. In the meantime, while the history teachers were out, thinking they were going to be paying off and getting the DVDs back, Stitch would show up in the history department dressed as a janitor, pushing a trash cart. He knew what to wear, and how to look and act like a janitor.

In Stitch's trash cart would be a high-powered rifle. He would pick an office lock and go to the window and crank the old-fashioned thing open. He would point the gun and pick Judence out when he stood up to make his speech, and kill him. One shot, one kill.

Across the way was part two. I was going to be punished for meddling. Not by killing me, but by killing Belinda. The gears on the clock tower would do it. The minute the tower struck ten, Stitch would shoot, and Belinda would die. If there was some delay on the part of Judence, the plan would mutate.

"How will she die?" I said.

Gregore shook his head. When he did, blood and sweat flew off. His voice had turned raw. "I don't know. I don't have those details and don't want them. I just know she's supposed to die at ten. That way, when Judence is shot with a silenced gun, they'll be trying to figure what happened, and in the meantime Stitch will go down the stairs and out the back way, and the girl will be dead in the tower. And after all the Judence stuff calms down, someone will go inside the clock tower, for maintenance maybe, and there will be the girl. Something extra, Caroline called it."

"How do they get in the clock tower?" I said. "Won't there be guards around for Judence's speech?"

It was starting to be work for our boy. His voice sounded as if someone had used sandpaper on his vocal cords. "Some, but they won't be concentrating on the clock tower; this isn't a town with a real SWAT team or any kind of cops that matter. If there are guards there, Caroline, she's not afraid to do what she thinks needs to be done. If they have to, she and Stitch will change plans. They're versatile. They're proud of it."

"Shit, you're one of them," Booger said. "How proud are you?"

Gregore looked at Booger, fearing this was a trick question. "I'm not that proud," he said.

"That's good," Booger said, giving him a gentle pat. "Otherwise I'd have to knock some pride out of you."

"I'm just getting paid," Gregore said.

Booger grinned at him. That alone made Gregore wince.

"So what about the clock tower?" I asked.

It was obvious that he was starting to wear down, but the way Booger looked at him gave him strength. He said, "Caroline will be wearing what looks like a janitor's uniform. She will be pushing a trash cart, same as Stitch. But in her cart will be Belinda, drugged. She'll work the lock. She knows how. She'll go inside the tower with the cart. That's when she'll do whatever it is she plans to do to Belinda. Skin her most likely. They drugged the others and started in on them alive. Had rubber balls in their mouths, scarves tied over those for gags. I saw them do the Ronnie girl. It was really horrible. They eviscerated them so they wouldn't smell so bad and put them in the freezer and poured salt over them. They were alive when they went to work. Man. Ronnie, such a pretty girl. And even as the skin came off her skull, her eyes—they looked so big without the skin—there was still hope in them. And then Caroline pulled her eyes out with pliers, said she didn't want them looking at her."

"You sonofabitches," I said. "Don't tell me any more about it. Don't tell me one little thing more."

"I'm interested," Booger said.

"For Christ sakes, Booger," I said.

"All right, all right," Booger said. "Want me to hit him some more? Just for fun this time?"

"No. It's time to tell the cops, stop this whole thing."

"Well, you can do that, but that means we got some explaining to do," Booger said. "I'm not much wanting to get in the middle of this thing that way. I'll go to the wall for you, brother, but I don't want to go to jail. Torture, it's frowned on. It upsets some people's stomachs."

"Mine among them," I said.

"Hell," Gregore said. "You ought to be on this side of it."

"You get us in the middle of it," Booger said to me, "then your brother Jimmy has some explaining to do. I don't think it's the way to go. I believe a man ought to take care of his own problems. Do his own work."

"This isn't my work."

"Sure it is," Booger said. "You signed on a long time ago for this one. You're riding for the brand till this range war is over."

I looked Gregore over. He was pathetic. I almost felt sorry for him. I said, "Anything else we should know?"

"I can't think of anything," Gregore said.

Booger raised the phone book. "Oh, come on, Gregore, give us a little more. Anything as long as it isn't a lie."

Gregore gave a nod; his voice was hardly audible. "They're gonna pick up the money from Dinkins and leave town, but before they do, they're gonna fuck Dinkins up too."

"Kill him?" I asked.

"No," Gregore said. "When it's over, they're going to send a note with a DVD Caroline has been holding back. One of her and Dinkins doing the crawdad shuffle. That'll ruin him."

"Who's going to see it?" I asked.

"Whoever they want. Cops maybe. Dinkins gets picked up, he can tell them all the conspiracy theories he wants, but he'll have to implicate himself in the assassination plot. He'll have to prove Caroline's alive, and that she's some kind of co-mastermind with some guy who looks like something out of a horror movie. It's so complex and weird, it'll be better he just takes a fucking for doing the fucking."

"Why screw Dinkins?"

"You still don't get it," Gregore said. "The game, man. The game."

"Cops, they got to wonder where the DVD came from, don't they?" I said.

Gregore studied me. I could tell he was reluctant.

I said, "Tell the truth, and I won't have him hit you any more."

Booger raised the phone book. "Give me a reason not to believe you," he said.

"It'll be mailed from your brother," Gregore said, keeping an eye on Booger. "The note to the cops will be typed. She got your brother's signature off an old test paper, and she can copy it. She's a damn good forger. That way, he doesn't get off scot-free. Way Caroline sees it, your brother has got to get his too. She's mad about those two geeks stealing the DVDs, and she's mad you and Jimmy got them away from them. She likes throwing curveballs, but she don't like catching them. God, man. If I could just have a little water."

"You know," Booger said, "I'm a little thirsty myself. Working this phone book has dried me out. But, you know, I still got my swing."

42

We put Gregore in the car and drove on out toward the scenic overlook. As we went along, me at the wheel, Gregore weak and bloody beside me, Booger leaned over the seat and pressed the .45 against Gregore's head.

"Man," said Booger, "you're not looking so good."

"I'm not feeling so good," Gregore said. "You didn't have to hit me so much."

"Hell," said Booger, "I know that."

"I'm still thirsty," Gregore said.

"People in hell want ice water too," Booger said.

I thought about everything Gregore had said. I understood a lot of it now. Mostly I understood Stitch was playing Dinkins through Caroline, and he was playing the black and white communities like a finely tuned instrument.

He had done the same sort of thing in other towns, playing his games, all of them ending in an assassination that didn't seem connected to other events and oddities. It was all a happy game to Stitch.

As for Caroline, once upon a time Stitch had been her mother's lover, and then he had been hers. He had impregnated her, then gone away. Caroline had dumped their love child, and then, in time, Stitch came back. He was full of promises, rich with lies about love and how he wanted her and needed her back.

Caroline wanted to believe, and so she had. He was probably the only person in the world she would believe. I bet he was the one who had given her the Fitzgerald book when she was a child. Maybe he had read the Poe stories to her, including her favorite, "The Premature Burial."

The whole goddamn thing creeped me, big-time.

I remembered a line I had read from Jerzy Fitzgerald's book. He said life was full of holes and the trick was to live between them. Stitch was not living between them. He was living in them, and loving it.

We came to the top of the hill and I parked in front of a lightning-struck oak that had split down the middle almost to the ground. The tree was still alive and the split was wide and made a large V of darkness, and from that height the moon seemed wedged there in the fork. I turned off the lights and the motor. We got out of the car. Gregore could hardly stand up. He looked as if he had lost ten pounds and an inch in height.

Booger gave him a kick in the ass, said, "Go up there and stand by that tree, limp dick."

Gregore trudged up the hill like Jesus carrying the cross up Calvary. When Gregore got up there, he stood in the fork of the lightning-struck tree. He put one hand on half of the tree to right himself. The moon was at his back like a spotlight. He was a silhouette up there.

"You said you'd let me go," Gregore said. His voice sounded hollow, floated down from the top of the hill like a dead leaf falling from a tree.

"We're going to leave you here," I said. "I advise you not to come back to town. You stay out of this mess. Be done. You deserve worse than what we're giving you."

"Doesn't everybody?" he said.

"Not everybody," Booger said. "Some are just unlucky. They get nominated for the big ticket. Right now, I'm punching yours."

By the time I realized what Booger meant, the .45 went up and the sound of it going off was like a mortar shot. Gregore's head split and something jumped out of it and landed wetly in the grass and he went down, falling backward into the fork in the tree. He hung there for a moment and then his head went back and his body flipped after him. All that was left was his shoe hung up in the fork. I could hear him tumbling down the hill in the grass on the other side, and then I didn't hear anything but the ringing in my ear from the blast of the .45.

"Goddamn, Booger. Why, man?"

"Don't be silly," Booger said. "You think he was just going to hitchhike to Lufkin, catch a bus to Vegas? He'd have been back in the game in no time. He might have warned that other guy, Numb Nuts . . . whatever his name is."

"Jesus, Booger."

"No one heard that shot. Not out here. And like all my guns, it's a cold piece. You couldn't trace this gun if you were Sherlock Holmes. Any of my weapons. There's no record. Shit, I pretty much made some of them. Give me a pipe and a wrench and a cutting torch, I can make something that will shoot like a sniper rifle."

"It wasn't necessary."

"Sure it was. Someone finds him, even they know who he is, who's gonna miss him? Anybody that would deserves to be miserable. He was just as much a part of all of this as they were. You're gonna do this thing, you can't be fucking around and letting shits like him go and depend on them to be on the honor system. Once you wipe your ass on them, you flush them. And I got one other thing. He ain't gonna get up. Let's go on back to town and get that girl of yours before the mosquitoes eat me up. I done got a good bite on the back of my neck."

I drove us back. I sat silent. I had had my fill of death. That damn shoe hung up in the fork of that lightning-struck oak would be in my head forever.

Booger turned on the radio, began tapping his fingers to a song. I wondered what he was thinking about. I wondered if he was thinking about anything.

As I topped another hill and sailed around a curve, a fog settled on us and I had to go slow and lean forward to see. After a while the fog faded and the lights of Camp Rapture sprang up in front of us like Brigadoon rising from the mist. The tower on campus had a warm, gold light behind the face of the clock. All the little half-moon windows that ran up the front of the clock were lit up too, including the little half-moon above the face of the clock. The clock stood two stories above the building that housed the history department, and the windows there were dark. All around the tower there was darkness, and then there were lights way out from the tower, and they were the lights of the town. We came down from the heights of the hills and leveled out and cruised on into Camp Rapture. By then, the moon was a lost dream in the rearview mirror.

I wanted to go to the campus right away, but Booger didn't like that idea.

"You're so goddamn tired you're trembling," he said. "Me too. I wouldn't mind something to eat, a bathroom break."

"We're not on vacation," I said.

"No, but we're serious, and we got time if what Gregore told us is true. We need a little rest. We can't be off the beam."

"And what if Gregore is wrong?"

"He could have been wrong yesterday, bro. Know what I'm saying?"

I did. Belinda could already be dead. What Gregore told us could have been lies.

We drove to my place, and when we got there I took a shower and put on fresh clothes and got Ernie's backpack out of the hiding place in my closet. I took the DVDs out and put them back in the hole, and I took a couple of books from my shelf and put them in the pack; I might look a little old for a student, but they come in all ages, so I thought I could pull it off if someone stopped me.

Booger was on the couch and he had taken his duffel bag from the car and had it open. In it was a long black barrel, a wooden knob for a stock, a trigger and a long telescopic sight and a silencer, a few other odds and ends. He put this stuff together quickly, screwed the bolts down with the edge of a coin, had a rifle with a silencer and a scope within instants.

He said, "When this thing goes off, it'll sound softer than a mouse farting with a cork up its ass. Unless you're the one firing it, you won't hear a thing."

"You just go around with a rifle in a duffel bag?" I said.

"You know me, I got all manner of shit in here, and nearly all of it says Bang. A few things, they cut. I get away from guns and knives, I start to feel like I've lost my friends, 'cause this stuff, you and Runt, are about it in the friend department."

"This friend good for what we need to do?"

"He's the goddamn ticket, bro. Made this dude," he said, holding up the rifle. "Shoots one shot, .22 slug."

"One shot?" I said.

"You're me, you don't need but one. We get in that tower, those little windows, there's bound to be some way to get to them. They got to clean that shit somehow. I can position myself at one of them and aim across at the building where Stitch is gonna show to shoot. I give him one in the eye, he's done."

"What if you don't hit the eye?" I said.

"Hell, you're asking something you know the answer to. He's still dead. But you know me, I can shoot the tip off a mosquito's dick if you can point it out."

"What about the glass in the window?"

"Let me worry about that."

I took a deep breath and walked into the kitchen and stood at the window over the sink and watched the light of morning bleed into the darkness and melt it. I got a bottled coffee out of the fridge for me, a beer for Booger, his usual breakfast. When I got back to the living room area, he had already taken the gun apart and put it back in the duffel bag.

"It'll come together smooth," he said. He took a folding knife from the bag, held it up. "Take this. I got one."

"I don't want it," I said.

"Take it anyway." He tossed it to me and I slipped it into my front pocket.

"And put this in your pack," he said, bending over the bag like some kind of malignant Santa. He came up with a .38 automatic. He screwed a silencer on it. He tossed it to me. I caught it, made to toss it back at him.

"I got a gun," I said.

"Not a clean one. Get through with this one, wipe it down and toss it. It's a good shooter but it's expendable. Leave your .38 here."

I took the automatic and didn't put it in the bag. I thought if I got stopped, that bag and those books were a way of maybe convincing someone I was a student. The .38 might be a little hard to explain. I put it under my shirt, stuck it in my pants. It lay cool against the small of my back.

Booger took a shower and came back and drank another beer, crushed the can and dropped it on my coffee table. I gave him a look and he grinned at me and picked it up and took it into the kitchen and put it in the trash under the sink. When he came back he said, "Sorry, I was raised bad."

"Should we go?" I said.

Booger looked at his watch, shook his head. "On campus too early, we'll be suspicious. Campus cops might come down on us. We'll make our way to the tower and I'll do the lock magic. We'll be in before anyone knows it, before the speech starts."

"Cutting it close," I said.

"If we cut it early, we're more likely to get caught."

"They'll be watching for shit when Judence is there. They'll be expecting shit."

"We'll come up behind the clock tower. Like Dickweed said, the cops here are yokels."

I thought about the chief of police. I couldn't argue that.

"Still," I said, "they might post guards."

"They do, and they're any good, they'll catch Caroline before we do. They do, then we got no worries, bro."

Booger could see I wasn't taking this well. That I wanted to go. Now.

"We get seen too early by the cops," he said, "we're screwed, doo-dooed and tattooed, especially carrying heat. We get spotted too early by Stitch or Caroline, we're screwed. Everyone has to be busy. The cops and our dynamic duo. Stitch and the bitch, they got to be in their zone so they don't expect us."

"Makes sense," I said, but I didn't like it.

Booger, who had been standing, sipping beer, sat down on the couch and closed his eyes, and within minutes he was asleep.

All the Chickens Come Home to Roost

43

I went into the bedroom and set the alarm for a couple hours' sleep and stretched out on the bed. The clock tower was in my head. That and all the things Gregore had told me. I wanted to jump up and start running toward campus.

I thought about it over and over, trying to come up with some plan that solved everything, but nothing would come beyond what we already planned to do. At some point I felt myself drift into sleep, and it seemed that almost at the same moment the alarm went off.

We decided nine a.m. was about right for us to be there, because the campus was not too far away. We could park some fifteen minutes' walk from the tower, and start across campus on foot. I would look like a student on the way to class, and Booger, who wore a lot of khaki duds, might even look like a janitorial worker carrying a duffel bag. The duffel bag part was a little tricky, and the more I thought about it the less I liked it. Then I thought about him putting the broke-down rifle into a toolbox I had. We dumped the tools on the carpet and put the rifle parts in there, and when Booger picked it up and shook it a little, he said, "It's light."

About eight we drove to the far side of town and got breakfast and coffee in a filling station that had a few tables and some stuff you could buy from behind the counter. All of it was deep-fried. It didn't matter if you were having doughnuts, catfish or pigs in the blanket, it all tasted like greasy batter and crackled to the touch.

We sat inside the little place and ate and drank. It was all I could do to not get up and run out and jump in the car and drive over there without Booger. I no longer gave a damn about Judence, or Jimmy. All I cared about was Belinda. I was starting to think like Booger, about killing because it was an easy way to solve your problems, and the thought of that began to crawl up inside my gut and squirm around and make my stomach growl. I bought some chewable stomach tablets, took those and had another cup of bad coffee, and tried not to look at my watch every thirty seconds.

I thought some more about killing, and the idea of it bothered me, but mostly it bothered me because I was getting used to it. When I left Iraq, I thought that was over with, and now here I was, having not so long ago watched Booger not only torture but kill a man, and now we were planning on killing another, a woman too, and we were having breakfast and drinking coffee. If we only had a board and some checkers.

A girl in a tight T-shirt and white shorts came in, and Booger looked her over like he was inspecting her for the USDA. She paid for some gas and went out. I looked at my watch. Twenty minutes had gone by.

We sat and sipped coffee and then my stomach started to hurt, so I went to the bathroom. My bowels were loose from nerves. When I was through in there I washed my hands and looked at myself in the mirror.

I didn't look like a killer.

I went out and sat back down, said, "Man, I hate this."

"I love it," Booger said.

When it was a couple minutes until nine, we went out to the car and started over there, down the main highway, and just as we passed Wal-Mart, the car started acting funny, and then I realized what had happened. A flat. We had a goddamn flat.

I pulled over to the side of the road and got out and went around and looked. The back right tire was blown. I looked at my watch. Five after nine. I opened the trunk as Booger got out of the car, and pulled out the spare tire.

"Take it easy," Booger said. "We still got it made."

But we didn't have it made. I had a spare tire and a jack, but there wasn't anything to take the tire off with or to jack the jack up. I remembered I had the tires replaced a year or so back, and probably someone at the tire place had left the tire iron out. I didn't have a way to change the tire.

A man and his young daughter stopped and he asked if we needed help, but he didn't have the right tool to take the tire off. He was the only person who stopped, and he discovered to his surprise that he too was missing a tire iron. What were the odds?

I thanked him and he left and I walked over to Wal-Mart, leaving Booger with the car.

It was nine-fifteen when I went inside. I walked as fast as I could without running over to the automotive section and looked around. At first I thought there weren't any tire irons to be found, but then I stopped one of the workers and he located them for me. They came as part of a set with a jack. I wasn't sure the jack was right for my car, but I was pretty certain the tire iron would work as both handle and lug bolt remover; the directions said that was its purpose. I thought I might also be able to go faster if one of us worked the lug bolts loose and the other jacked. I took a flier and got two different kinds of jacks and went to the checkout counters.

All twelve registers had lines. I went over to the one that was supposed to be a dozen items or less, but there were two people in line with buggies full of groceries. I was the third in line.

I looked at my watch.

Nine-twenty-two.

I yelled up to the checker. "Hey, isn't this supposed to be twelve items or less?"

The checker, a lanky, greasy-haired white kid with acne, looked at me in desperation. I had opened a can of worms, something he hadn't had the courage to deal with. He turned to the fat man who was first in line and said, "It is supposed to be just twelve items."

"I don't give a shit," said the fat man. "I'm first in line. I'm a paying customer. It's no set rule, is it?"

"Well," the lanky kid said, "it's supposed to be twelve items."

"Just check me out," said the fat man.

"Hey," I said. "And this lady in front of me. She's got a buggyful too."

The lady had already turned to look at me, perhaps sensing she was my next target. "Well, I never," she said. She was a short lady with a nice face and an ass about the size of a travel trailer.

"Let me go first," I said. "I only got these jacks."

The fat man looked at me. "Maybe if you had been nicer."

"I certainly wouldn't let him go," said the woman to the fat man.

"How about this," I said, calling past the lady to the man. "How about I give you twenty dollars to let me go first. I got a car broke down on the side of the road, and not in a safe place."

"Then you should have moved it to a safer place," the fat man said.

"All right, then," I said, looking at my watch, seeing it was nine-thirty, "what would you say to moving your buggy before I kick that package of frozen peas so far up your ass you'll have to get a pair of salad tongs to pull them out of your throat?"

"Well, I never," the trailer-ass woman said again.

"I bet you haven't," I said.

"I think the customer with the fewer items should go first," said the checker.

"Fuck you, pimple face," the fat man said and gave his buggy a boost that sent it sliding past the counter and over into the wall next to the photo shop. It hit so hard a box of crackers and a can of chili hopped out of it and landed on the floor. The can of chili rolled along and out of sight, as if on a mission.

The trailer-ass woman left her buggy and went on past the counter, heading for the door. Maybe the two of them could commiserate in the parking lot.

I went up and paid for my jacks and went out, and there in the parking lot near the door were the fat man and the trailer-ass woman, doing exactly what I thought they might be doing, commiserating. She said, "You shouldn't talk like that," as I walked by.

"You're right," I said. "Sorry."

"He doesn't mean it," said the fat man, as I kept walking, talking louder so I could hear him. "He doesn't mean it at all. He's not the kind of person that cares about anything."

I didn't pay any more attention to them. I liked to think I had put a fat man and a trailer-ass woman together on the road to romance. I darted rapidly across the lot, which was no small stretch of real estate, and on out to the side of the road where the car was. The morning had already turned hot and I was red-faced, and sweating.

Booger said, "Give it here."

I dropped the jacks by the car and used my knife to cut them out of the packaging and gave one to him. He put it under the car and starting working it. "It doesn't fit exactly right. It'll scratch your car up some. It's not tapered enough on the end."

"I don't give a shit," I said. "Do I look like a man who gives a shit about scratching a car?"

I looked at my watch. It was twenty-six minutes until ten.

Booger went to work on the jack while I turned the lug bolts with my spare tire iron. I got them loose just before the tire was off the ground, and then I twisted them the rest of the way off with my fingers. I pulled the tire off and got the spare and slipped it on and twisted the lug bolts back as Booger lowered the car. I used the lug iron to tighten the bolts better when the tire was settled on the ground. I put the wrecked tire in the trunk and closed it and was behind the wheel again.

Booger got in and tossed the jacks and the tire irons in the back seat, because I had forgotten, and closed the trunk. I drove us out of there.

"Scratched the car some," Booger said.

"Fuck it," I said.

The traffic was pretty thick. By the time we got to the campus and I found a parking place, which might have been the only place left in the visitors' area, it was ten minutes till.

We went on across the campus, walking fast, but not so fast we looked like we were in a Charlie Chaplin movie. It should have taken fifteen minutes at a comfortable stroll, but we made it in about five. Booger had the toolbox, and I had forgotten the backpack.

I looked up at the clock tower. For a moment I thought I saw someone move across the face of the glass, but it could have been expectation. What I did notice, however, was that my watch was not in line with the clock's time. According to the tower clock, we had another five minutes; then I remembered it was slow.

We saw a crowd had formed between the tower and the building that housed the history department. We went around behind the tower. There was some tall shrubbery there, and I could see the narrow door that was at the back of the tower. There was no one there. We looked around carefully, and there were people to be seen, but they all had their backs to us, were already in position at the sides of the tower so they could hear Judence speak. A lot of the people we saw were black.

Without breaking stride we made our way to the tower door and Booger had his lock-beating tools in his hand before we got there. He put the toolbox by the door and put a little crooked tool in the lock, and worked it. The lock snicked. We went inside quietly, into the cool dark, and closed the door quietly.

Just inside, near the door, was a cloth trash buggy that I assumed Caroline had used to carry Belinda inside. I looked in the buggy. If she had been there, she wasn't now.

The inside of the tower was nearly all clock, and the clock had huge gears that were designed in a kind of German Gothic style; the big gears were turning slowly and meeting the teeth of other huge gears and causing them to move; the gears looked to be larger than ancient round Greek shields. You could hear the gears when they clicked and rolled. You could feel them moving the hand on the big clock because the tower vibrated. Way up you could see light coming through the face of the clock, and all along the little quarter-moon windows was more light, and there was dust floating up from the smooth wooden floor and it hung in the air like a tan mist. Near the gears, as if they were different levels of geological strata, were wooden platforms. There were stairs that wound up between the gears and up through trap openings in the platforms; the stairs zigged and zagged their way up. I could see something halfway up the stairs on one of the platforms. It was in shadow and it was odd and I couldn't make it out. I started up the stairs. I took out the .38 with the silencer Booger had given me. Booger was ahead of me, going up with the toolbox. He was going to find a place to take his shot. I wondered about the glass. How would he manage to take his shot? I wondered about it only briefly, because I was more worried about Belinda. Had Gregore lied to us? And what in hell was it I had seen on the platform? All of these thoughts charged through my brain like an electric shock.

According to my watch, it was just after ten o'clock. That meant it was right at ten, big-clock time.

When I reached the third platform, I could see one of the huge gears, and I realized, now that I was closer to it, that it was much larger than a Greek shield. It was turning and its teeth were causing a somewhat smaller gear above it to precisely catch its teeth in the bigger gear's fangs. They temporarily clicked together and the big gear moved the small gear. This was part of the complicated mechanism that moved the hands on the face of the clock. I could also see just behind the gear what I had seen before from below, but due to angle and shadow had not been able to make out.

It was Belinda. There was a cloth bag over her head, a pillowcase probably, but I knew her body and was certain it was her. She was wearing a white terry cloth bathrobe, her ankles pulled together and bound. There was a rope around her neck and it was stretched up into the darkness. Her feet were tied to one of the struts that came out of the platform and supported the huge jagged-tooth gear wheel that was next to me.

"It's her," I said.

"So it is," Booger said. "You get her. I'm going to be busy. She's got nice legs."

Booger was already moving up the stairs when he said that, leaving me behind.

I went out on the platform, and now I could see and understand what was happening. The rope was wound around a gear above me, and as the gear turned it wound the rope, and the rope was pulling at Belinda's neck. Her feet, bound the way they were, didn't allow the rope to hang her. Another instant, caught between the ropes and the pull, the rig would most likely jerk her head off.

I put the .38 back under my shirt, took out the clasp knife Booger gave me, and popped it open and tried to rush over to Belinda.

As I rushed forward something flashed and I caught it out of the corner of my eye, and I moved, but I was too slow. A long blade caught light from the quarter-moon window in front of the big face of the clock and winked at me. In that moment I saw Caroline's beautiful face twisted up in a knot of rage under a head of dyed black hair. The blade hit me, slicing down my back. But I turned quick enough that it went in shallowly, then it stuck my hip. I let out a yelp.

I slashed out with my knife and missed. Caroline moved away quickly, to the side of the gear, then she came at me, the knife moving like a lightning strike. I was cut on the arm before I felt it. I knew enough about knives and knife fighting to bring the backs of my arms up. You're going to get cut, that's the part you want cut. Soft sides of the arms, that's where the vital vessels are. You get cut deep there you can kiss your ass goodbye because you're going to bleed out fast. Caroline knew the knife, she knew what she was doing; someone had taught her.

I skipped back, tried to catch Belinda out of the corner of my eye. Her head was lifting as the rope pulled her. I did a somersault, rolled up to a squatting position in front of her. I used my knife to cut the rope at her feet. She went up on her tiptoes as the gear pulled. Now, instead of being pulled apart, she was only in jeopardy of being strangled slowly.

Caroline's blade struck as I rose to my feet, trying to cut the rope around Belinda's neck. Her blade went into my back and I saw a white light, almost fainted. I turned as she was stabbing again. I dodged, went low and hit her just above the shins with the side of my body. It made her bend in half over me and the downward thrust of her knife carried her forward and the tip of the knife stuck in the wooden platform.

I whirled to face her. She was trying to pull the knife out of the platform. I kicked her in the ribs as if I were trying to make a field goal from the fifty-yard line. She rolled almost to the edge of the platform.

Above me, in the darkness, amidst the clicks of well-oiled gears, the moving of the clock hands, I heard Booger say, "Peep-eye, motherfucker," then there was a sound like a tubercular octogenarian coughing up phlegm, followed by, "That knocked a turd out of him."

Caroline recovered. She jerked the knife free, came at me. The rope lifted Belinda off the ground. Her head twisted beneath the hood. She shook her head hard and the hood came off and fell. It landed on Caroline's back, caused her to jerk around and slash at the air.

I tackled her, drove her back. We almost went off the platform. She came down with the knife and it went into my shoulder. I let out with a grunt and my butt cheeks pinched together hard enough to crack a pecan. I caught her knife hand in my left hand, brought my knife down. As it descended, in a micro-moment I saw all those bodies in Iraq, saw Gregore's head jump apart, then that damn shoe in the fork of the tree. All of it rushed at me like a freight train balling the jack down a deep grade. The blade went into Caroline's throat and the force of it was so hard I could hear it stick in the platform as it came out of the back of her neck.

Her eyes flashed with surprise and then something moved there that almost appeared pleasurable. She dropped her knife and her fingers clutched at my shoulders, dug into me like talons. She let out a birdlike shriek and then blood was shooting up from her throat and hitting me in the face and her hands fell back and the backs of her knuckles slammed against the platform.

I stood up, leaving the knife in her. It was then that I remembered the .38 resting at the small of my back.

I looked at Belinda.

The gear had turned, raising her up. I grabbed Caroline's knife, ran toward Belinda, but the gear turned again and lifted her higher than I could grab.

She was wriggling and thrashing. I turned and raced up the stairway to the platform above. When I got there I couldn't reach the rope. Another moment she would be equal with me and there wouldn't be anything I could do but watch her pass. Climbing higher to another platform wouldn't change that. It would be the same thing all over again all the way up.

I leaped and grabbed at the rope, ended up clinging to it like a spider, just above Belinda. I cut the rope above my head and it dropped. As we fell there was light and shadow and then a sudden jolt and an explosion of lights. The lights went away and for a moment there was darkness; the floor felt like it was spinning. When the spinning stopped, I opened my eyes slowly. I was looking up at the ugly face of Booger.

"Belinda?" I said.

"You're lying on top of her, bro."

44

Belinda and I had landed on the platform where Caroline had died. It had been a pretty good fall, and it was the only platform in line with us. Had we been one platform higher when I cut the rope, we would have landed in the same spot, but a whole lot harder.

Belinda had a gag around her mouth, and when I took that off there was a blue rubber ball clenched between her teeth. I pulled that out and she coughed and gasped for air. I held her head up and she began to gulp the air and pull it in more naturally. Her throat was red with rope burn.

She grabbed me and hugged me, but she was as weak as a minute-old kitten.

I looked at Booger. "Is Stitch dead?"

"Only way he'll move again is if a ventriloquist sticks his arm up his ass. Got him right in the eye. His left."

I continued to hold Belinda, letting her get her strength back.

"You know how I made that shot?" Booger asked.

I didn't care, but I let him talk. He was as proud as if he had just discovered the cure for cancer.

"Used the rifle stock nub to crimp the glass at the corner of one of the windows. You hit it there it'll crack, but the whole glass won't come out. Doesn't make a lot of noise. I used my knife to pick the cracked glass out till there was a space for the rifle barrel. I'll tell you something cool. I put that rifle through the hole, maybe an inch of it sticking out, and I saw him at the window across the way, and it was one of those windows you can crank up, an old-style window—"

"I know," I said.

"And I put the bead on him. He was looking down at the crowd, picking out his target, you know, and then just as I was about to squeeze, he had that doe-in-the-forest moment, when he senses something. He turned his head slightly and looked at me. I could see the look on his face through the scope. Everything he ever was or thought he was drained out of his face like shit running out of a sick dog's ass. I pulled the trigger. It was choice."

"I heard the silencer cough."

"Well, no one else did. No one will know that sonofabitch is dead in that office until someone comes in to take out the trash. I see you put the bitch down."

I looked over at Caroline. Her arms were outstretched and her head was hanging off the platform and the knife was sticking up from her throat. There was a lot of blood.

"Yeah," I said.

"Damn," Booger said. "She's a looker. What a waste of good ass. Well, I'm going to get your knife, there's fingerprints all over that."

"My blood is all over the place too. Not to mention hers."

Belinda finally had it together enough that I could help her walk. She tried to talk, but nothing came out but a kind of squeak. I got her downstairs and set her on the floor with her back against the wall by the exit.

Booger and I got some cleaning stuff off the side of the janitorial buggy Caroline had used to bring Belinda in, spruced me up, stuffed some paper towels into my wounds. None of them were bad, but they hurt.

We found some rags in a closet, and some more janitorial supplies there, a mop and bucket, and Booger carried all of it up to the platform and went to work. I used the rags and helped him clean. Booger pulled the knife out of Caroline's neck and we wrapped her head and neck in rags and carried her downstairs and put her in the janitorial buggy, her knees under her chin. Then we cleaned the blood that had leaked down from the platform onto the floor below. Even though there was a lot of blood, altogether this only took us about thirty minutes.

The rope had wadded up in the gears, but the gears were strong and they had broken the rope and dropped pieces of it on the floor. I gathered those up and Booger climbed up the stairs and got the rope that had tied Belinda's feet, the hood, the rest of the stuff, and brought it down. We dumped it all in the trash buggy on top of Caroline's body. We dumped the rags in there and stuck the mop down beside her. We tore up some paper towels and wadded them and put those on top of the rags so the blood couldn't be seen. We rolled the buggy into the closet and closed the door.

By this time Belinda could stand, but she couldn't talk, and she seemed confused and not altogether with it. Booger took his rifle apart and put it in the toolbox, toted the box out the door, went out to the parking lot and got our car. He called on the cell phone when he was near.

We went out the door toward the circle drive, which was close by. The shrubs near the clock tower door gave a little protection, but we finally had to walk out from behind them. Belinda was in a dirty white bathrobe, and she walked as if she were drunk. All it took was one inquisitive eye and we could be done for. I wasn't up to shooting a student or a campus cop to make sure we got away. They caught us, they caught us. But fate worked for us. The crowd was involved in Judence's talk. I looked over my shoulder to check it out. The speech was still going on, and I heard some clapping, and a roar of agreement from some of the crowd. All I could see were the backs of listeners. I couldn't see Judence, but I could hear him over the microphone. He was talking about equal rights and how the school the white community wanted to build was a way to bring back segregation. Some people were saying "Amen" and "Right on, brother," and stuff like that.

I put my arm around Belinda and we reached the drive as Booger pulled the car around. We got in and he drove us out of there.

We were back at my place and Belinda was on the couch. She had gone right out, but I could hear her breathing, smooth and normal. Booger and I were sitting in chairs. He had a beer and I had nothing.

"Tonight, when things are settled down," Booger said, "I'll go back and get the buggy with Caroline in it and dump the body."

"What if someone finds her first?" I said.

"We'll hope they don't," Booger said. "She's been missing, so we'll keep her missing if we can. The other building, not so easy to move around in. We'll have to leave Stitch. I kind of like that. I think it's funny."

"And they get to see what a great shot you made," I said.

"That too."

Booger looked at Belinda, said, "You know, she gets that metal shit out of her mouth, she'll be one hell of a looker."

"She's one hell of a looker now," I said.

"What say I go get us something to eat, some burgers or something?"

"Sure, but bring some yogurt, or ice cream. Belinda may not be up to chewing."

"Got you, bro," and Booger was gone.

I went in the bathroom and took off my cut-up shirt and looked at my wounds. A couple of them were pretty bad rips, but nothing had caught too deep except for the back wound, and I had a lot of muscle across my shoulders, so I was going to be all right there. I did need some stitches, and I had the stuff to do that and Booger knew how. It would hurt like hell, but we could make it without seeing a doctor. Main thing was to keep out infection. I took a quick hot shower, and when I got out there was blood running down the drain.

I patted myself dry, threw the bloody towel away and did some awkward work with peroxide, alcohol and bandages. The one in the small of my back was hell. I couldn't get it just right. I finally managed to get a square bandage to stick back there. It quickly soaked up blood.

I took it off and started over, and this time there was less blood. I got an old dark shirt out of the closet and put it on. That way blood wouldn't show so bad, and in a way, it would help serve as a second bandage.

When I was dressed, I went back into the living room. All of a sudden Belinda sat up on the couch. She looked at me. Her eyes were big as headlights.

She said something that didn't sound like any word I knew.

I sat by her on the couch. I took her hand, said, "Take it easy. It's over with."

Belinda shook her head. She tapped her left hand with her right, her fingers set like they were holding a pen. I got her a pen and some paper.

She wrote: "Caroline had a little girl. I think she did something to her."

"I don't get it," I said. "I know she had a child. We both know that."

Belinda shook her head, wrote furiously: "A little girl. She was at the house with us. Caroline said to me you had to know how to destroy the things you love if you want to be strong."

"The child was with her?"

Belinda nodded. She tore a page off the pad and wrote anew: "They drugged the little girl. They drugged me. I woke up in the clock tower, the rope around my neck."

"Where is the little girl?"

She wrote in very large letters: "IT'S JAZZY, CASON."

Belinda pulled on one of my T-shirts and a baggy pair of my pants, wore some of my house shoes. I made sure I had the .38, and we took the motor-cycle, Belinda clinging tightly to me as I rode as fast as common sense and a fear of arrest for speeding allowed. As we rode it came together for me. Caroline had moved in right next to my parents. Probably saw the listing in the paper, and as everyone thought she was dead, she decided, wouldn't it be funny to rent a place next to Jimmy's parents. Hell, maybe it was just coincidence, but thinking about Caroline and Stitch, and their love for games, I doubted it.

Gregore, he was Daddy Greg. The one my dad had knocked the shit out of. And Stitch. He was the new daddy. Somehow, perhaps for no other reason than to bond with Jazzy for a while, before making that ultimate sacrifice Caroline thought made her strong, she took the little girl in, like fattening a calf for the slaughter.

When we got to Jazzy's house, we pulled into my parents' drive. I parked the bike in the carport. Belinda was getting along better now, and her voice, though metallic-sounding, was coming back. I climbed up in the tree first, but the platform was empty except for a cloth doll that had been faded by rain and sun.

Next we went to Jazzy's house and I touched the front door with my shoulder and it moved; it hadn't been locked or completely closed. I pulled the .38 and went inside, Belinda behind me.

The living room was void of furniture except for a couch, a foldout chair, and a television, a DVD player and a stack of DVDs. There were all manner of pizza cartons and papers lying about. There were stacks of books.

We went into the kitchen. The stove was six inches deep in grease and there were flies in the grease, some of them dead and stuck there. The sink was full of dishes and the place smelled. The trash can was overrun with paper plates and paper cups and boiling with roaches.

On the table was a manila envelope. I picked it up and looked inside. A DVD.

I didn't look at the note or touch the DVD. I was certain without looking and putting my fingerprints all over everything what it was. Caroline and Dinkins. Caroline figured after Belinda was done in, she'd come back here with Stitch and forge my brother's name to a note and mail it off to whoever she thought was a good idea, make sure my brother would be discovered as the source. That would give Dinkins his pig sticking and Jimmy his too.

I went out of there carrying the envelope.

The bathroom was a nightmare.

The place was empty. I was looking in a bedroom that had nothing but a mattress on the floor and a pile of sour-smelling clothes nearby when I heard Belinda try to yell to me. It was more of a squeak.

She was in another bedroom, a smaller one, and when I went in there I saw that there was a little blow-up mattress and a blanket on the floor, and there were a few toys, mostly junk from fast-food places. On the floor under a curtained window was a square line of dust where something like a trunk had sat.

"Oh, shit," Belinda said, her voice still a rasp. "Caroline kept me in here with Jazzy."

I had to lean close to understand her. She held her throat with her hand as she talked.

"They kept pills in me and Jazzy," she said. "Sometimes Caroline came in to talk. Gloating."

Belinda cleared her throat, strained out some more information. "She told me about all their plans. It was horrible, Cason. Just a game to them. She said it took courage to do things that hurt people you love. But she didn't love anyone, Cason, not really. Maybe Stitch."

Belinda swallowed, took a deep breath. "She said she had the strength to destroy anyone, even blood of her blood, bone of her bone . . . So, where is Jazzy?"

I shook my head. Belinda's little speech had almost taken her voice away again.

"When did you see her last?" I said.

"This morning. They came in and gave me pills, and they gave Jazzy something to drink. By the time they had me tied up and we left, Jazzy was asleep, here on the air mattress. A minute later and I was nearly out of it. I didn't come awake until we got to the clock tower and I was tied up. They wanted me awake. They knew their drugs."

I glanced at the square of dust, pointed at it. "Was something here?"

"A toy box," Belinda said. "But there was hardly anything in it. I think it came with the house. That little girl, they wouldn't let her leave the room after they grabbed me. Made her stay in here. She comforted me, Cason. She didn't know what was going on, not really, but she tried to make me feel better. Shit, my throat hurts."

"We have to go next door, right now. Get a shovel from the carport."

"What?" Belinda said.

"Come on," I said. "No time to explain."

From my parents' house we walked swiftly to the graveyard amongst the trees, by the creek. I was carrying a shovel, and Belinda had my mother's trowel. I had put the envelope in the car.

I said, "Poe's 'Premature Burial.' Caroline's favorite story. The box missing. Jazzy gone. And Jazzy told me she and her mom used to come here and lie down on the graves."

"Oh, no, Cason," Belinda said.

We came to a line of thick oaks and hickories, and just below them were the graves. Some of them had old markers, some markers had recently been replaced. A few graves were nothing more than rough spots on the ground. Along the creek there were some willow trees growing, and there were more graves closer to the creek. An explosion of thrushes broke from the willows and fluttered against the leaves of the nearby oaks and hickories and took to the sky.

I walked amongst the graves quickly.

"That would have been hours ago," Belinda said. "She couldn't last that long."

"Don't say that," I said.

"She wouldn't have air to breathe."

"Was the toy box deep?"

"Pretty deep."

"I know it was big from the dust lines," I said. "Half the size of a coffin. She's drugged, buried in that big box, she wouldn't be awake, frightened, sucking up air. She'd be breathing shallow, and—look there!"

It was a mound of fresh dirt, red clay heaped up between two old graves.

I stuck the shovel in the dirt and went to work quickly. Belinda tried to dig with the trowel, but I was going too fast and nearly took her head off with the edge of the shovel. She finally sat back and I dug.

The ground was soft and easy to dig and hadn't been packed down. It looked to have been a job done quickly, and as I dug, I couldn't help but wonder what would be going through Caroline's mind; a woman burying a child, her own child, for some kind of game that made her feel strong. I couldn't find any way to get inside the framework of that kind of thinking.

The shovel hit something. I got down on my hands and knees and started pushing dirt. It was an old gray wooden box. The toy box. I pushed the dirt aside with my hands until I had the lid completely uncovered, and then I took the trowel from Belinda and stuck the point of it under the lid and grunted and pushed and felt all my wounds start to gush, but I kept at it.

The lid creaked up part of the way, and then it hung, and I had to really get my shoulder behind it. That made the wound in my back tear. I could feel blood running down my spine and down the back of my pants.

I tore the lid off.

Lying in the bottom of the box, very still, covered in sweat, wearing only a T-shirt and shorts, was Jazzy. I lifted her out of the box and laid her out on the ground, and called her name up close to her face a couple of times.

"She's breathing," Belinda said.

And she was. Her little chest was rising and falling. I peeled back an eyelid, and when I did she stirred ever so slightly, and then she didn't move again. But she was breathing. She was just out from whatever Caroline had given her, probably in the drink she made her take.

I bent over Jazzy, and then it came out of me, gushed up like an oil reserve, and I started crying, bellowing. I lifted my head and yelled, and when I did I saw the sky had gone gray with storm clouds blowing across the heavens like tumbleweeds.

Jazzy opened her eyes, not wide, but enough she could see me. She almost smiled. Her hand came up and touched me. Her eyes closed again and she grew limp in my arms.

Belinda touched my arm. "She's going to be all right, Cason. She's going to be okay. Come on, baby. It's okay. She's breathing . . . She's just gone back to sleep. But you . . . you're bleeding all over the place."

I suddenly felt a lot better. I smiled at Belinda. I laughed. I said, "You sound like a frog."

We called Booger and he drove the car over, and I used my house key and we took Jazzy into Mom and Dad's place, put her on the couch. Booger had brought the fast food with him, and we ate it. I had to eat it, and so did Belinda. I was about to faint.

Finished, we put Jazzy back in Caroline's house, on the little mattress in her room. She was still sleeping. She looked so innocent.

We drove to a pay phone and I called the cops and gave them an anonymous tip. I told them there was a little girl staying by herself in a home where the adults had left, and I was just a concerned citizen, and then I hung up.

Back at my place we cleaned my wounds again, and Booger sewed me up with a needle and some strong thread. He did this while I bit down on a paperback book to keep from screaming. Booger talked and joked all the while he was sewing. He sewed deep and stitched tight. Belinda got so sick watching, she had to leave the room.

That night I took some pills I had left over from when I had a bad case of the flu, and I slept like the dead.

There's not much to tell now.

Booger stuck around a couple of days and Belinda moved in with me during that time, just to make sure my wounds were healing all right. We got Booger a big bag of malted eggs and took him to the rent-a-car place, and he rented one and drove it back to Hootie Hoot with his duffel bag in tow, back to his gun range and his bar and his friend Runt, and probably Conchita, to whom Booger could show his new tattoo.

He had been nice to have around, all things considered, and when he left I felt both lonely and damn glad. At the bottom of it all, I feared someday soon I'd hear from Booger again.

Next day I called Timpson and told her I was sick, and wanted her to know I wasn't chasing a story, not today. She said, "You sure get sick a lot."

Belinda went to work for a while. When she came home for lunch we got a new envelope, and wearing gloves, Belinda and I cut out an address using letters from magazines. It was addressed to Oswald at the newspaper. The idea was, when Belinda went back to work, she would deliver it to Oswald and say she found it leaning against the door when she came in. That way anyone could have put it there. We also wrote out a note and put it in the envelope with the DVD, and the note was about Dinkins hiring an assassin to kill Judence. In that note we told where the two leather maidens could be found. It said all of this was connected to the body found in the history office killed with a rifle. The office turned out to be Jimmy's office, but no one tried to make any connection there. Not then or later. The mysterious provider of the information was never detected.

Good thing.

As for Caroline, right before Booger left, he and I went over to the campus at night, got the janitorial buggy with Caroline's body in it. We were careful when we emptied her and the rags and the paper towels into the trunk of my car, lifting the bag off the buggy rack and dropping it in the trunk. I drove the car off campus and around the block while Booger pushed the buggy cart back and put it inside the clock tower and wiped it down and walked back to the drive just in time for me to come back and pick him up.

We were careful and we were smooth and we were very natural about everything. We drove out to the Siegel house, took Caroline out of the trunk and out of the bag and rolled her down the hill and into the kudzu, which wrapped around her like green ocean waves.

Maybe someone would smell her. Maybe not. If a year from now her remains were found, the police might think they had overlooked her the first time around. That she had been dead since the night she went missing.

I destroyed the rest of the DVDs.

Mom and Dad are trying to be foster parents to Jazzy, and maybe they have a shot. For the time being, she's with them.

Child Protective Services is having a hard time finding the mother who lived in the house with Jazzy. Her name turned out to be a fraud. I could help them on that matter, but I won't.

Jazzy didn't seem to remember me out at the grave. She got quizzed by cops and Child Protective Services workers and a psychiatrist. But that never came out. She either really didn't remember, or she's even smarter for her age than I thought.

Jimmy is back at the university teaching. He even has a story to tell about the time a would-be assassin was found dead in his office. The cops figured someone shot the would-be assassin from the tower. An accurate assessment, but they thought it was a Judence supporter; no one has any real ideas who did it or how to go about finding out.

Jimmy never asked me another question. He may have suspicions about what had gone on, but all he knows is what I told him. "It's safe. Everything is as it should be. Now go home."

Oswald wrote a really good piece based on what he knew about the leather maidens found in the church and at the back of the field. He wrote about Dinkins, the note and the DVD. Dinkins looks to be prisonbound. A month later, Oswald wrote an article about a rotting body found on the scenic overlook. Another anonymous tip led him to that. Oswald thinks he has fans amongst the underworld. It makes him feel important.

They ran a picture of Gregore's somewhat weathered shoe stuck in the fork of the old oak tree. Oswald took the picture.

Oswald and I talk now. I think it's because he feels more content. He didn't get nominated for a Pulitzer, but he did get a lot of attention, and Timpson doesn't call him "boy" anymore. But she does refer to him as colored.

The school in the black section of town didn't get built. I see Judence on TV from time to time, always looking to be the nation's moral barometer. The black racists and white racists have turned relatively silent for the time being.

The world still sucks.

I drove by Gabby's work the other day, just out of the blue. I saw her car there, and through the window I got a glimpse of her. I didn't feel a thing.

I drove by her house to see how that felt. It was just a house. After that, I drove home to meet up with Belinda. We like to have dinner together when our jobs permit. She got a job as a reporter in the town next door. She's real happy about that. I'm not writing hard news anymore, just the columns, and a lot of them have turned to fluff, but I like it that way.

Now and again I drive by the old Siegel house on my way out of town, or on some errand for the paper, and I wonder how Caroline's body is doing up there. She had once been just a kid who maybe had some possibilities. A smart kid who thought she might be a princess or some such thing, the way little girls do. She became a woman whose soul and heart had been turned to leather, just as surely as the bodies of those poor dead women she and that psycho Stitch had tortured and killed.

Caroline was the true leather maiden. She had been that way a long time. And, to this date, as far as anyone else knows, she's still missing.

ABOUT THE AUTHOR

Joe R. Lansdale has written more than a dozen novels in the suspense, horror and Western genres. He has also edited several anthologies. He has received the British Fantasy Award, the American Mystery Award, seven Bram Stoker Awards and the 2001 Edgar Award for best novel from the Mystery Writers of America. In 2007 he won the Grand Master Award at the World Horror Convention. He lives in Nacogdoches, Texas, with his family.

A NOTE ON THE TYPE

The text of this book was set in Electra, a typeface designed by W. A. Dwiggins (1880–1956). This face cannot be classified as either modern or old style. It is not based on any historical model, nor does it echo any particular period or style. It avoids the extreme contrasts between thick and thin elements that mark most modern faces, and it attempts to give a feeling of fluidity, power and speed.

Composed by Creative Graphics, Allentown, Pennsylvania
Printed and bound by Berryville Graphics, Berryville, Virginia
Designed by Virginia Tan